Also by Gordon Doherty:

LEGIONARY

The Roman Empire is crumbling, and a shadow looms in the east . . .

STRATEGOS: BORN IN THE BORDERLANDS

When the falcon has flown, the mountain lion will charge from the east, and all Byzantium will quake. Only one man can save the empire . . . the Haga!

GORDON DOHERTY

Mithras, God of the Midnight, here where the great bull dies,
Look on Thy children in darkness. Oh take our sacrifice!
Many roads Thou hast fashioned: all of them lead to the Light,
Mithras, also a soldier, teach us to die aright!

'A Song to Mithras,' Rudyard Kipling

High Command Structure of the Eastern Imperial Army

See glossary (at rear of book) for a description of terms

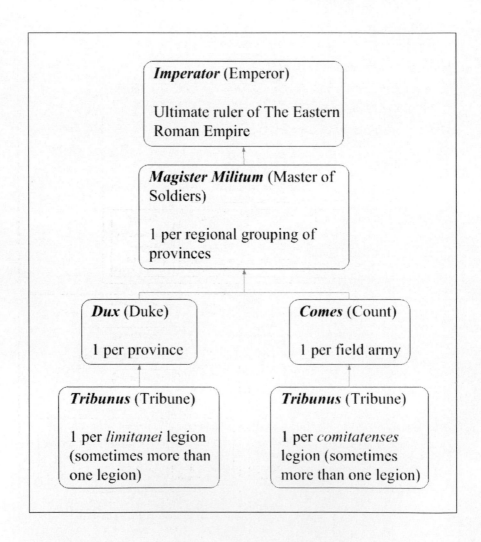

Imperator (Emperor)

Ultimate ruler of The Eastern Roman Empire

Magister Militum (Master of Soldiers)

1 per regional grouping of provinces

Dux (Duke)

1 per province

Comes (Count)

1 per field army

Tribunus (Tribune)

1 per *limitanei* legion (sometimes more than one legion)

Tribunus (Tribune)

1 per *comitatenses* legion (sometimes more than one legion)

Structure of Legio XI Claudia Pia Fidelis

See glossary (at rear of book) for a description of terms

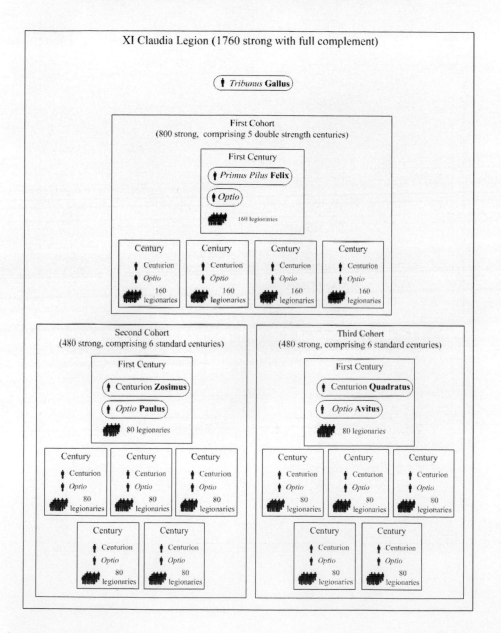

The Eastern Roman Empire circa 376 AD

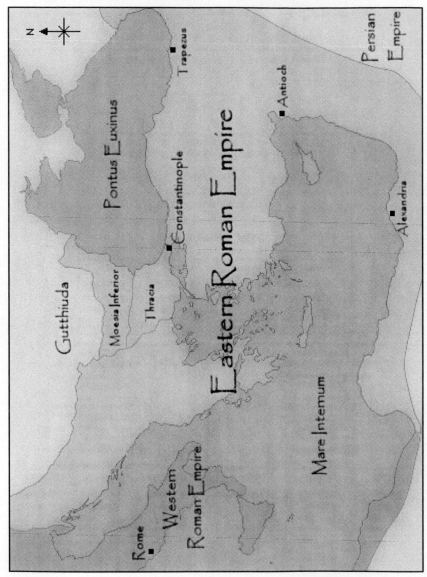

The Danubian *Limes* and Surrounding Lands circa 376 AD

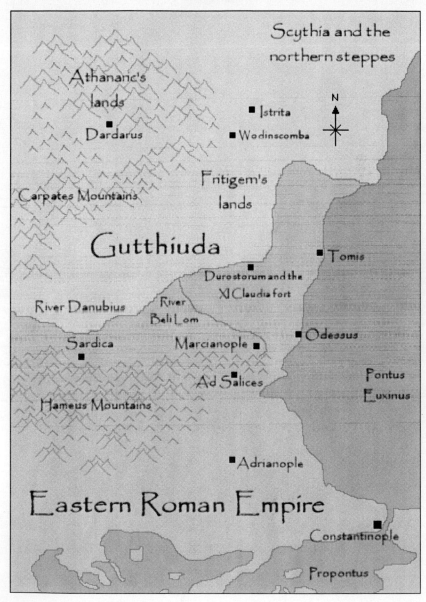

Prologue:
Constantinople, Summer 352 AD

On the northern lip of Constantinople, just a stone's throw east of the Prosphorion Harbour, the midday heat baked a secluded wharf. A small party of legionaries from the wall garrison stood there, gazing across the shimmering waters of the Golden Horn to the northern headland. Behind them, the sea walls hid them from the grandeur and bustle of the great city, with only an occasional muffled roar from the Hippodrome echoing onto the dock.

Optio Traianus shuffled in discomfort; sweat trickled down his back underneath his scale vest and the salty sea air did little to quash his nagging thirst. His hooked nose wrinkled and he shielded his eyes from the sun's glare as he scanned the waters once more. Only trade vessels and fishing boats dotted the placid surface while the galleys of the imperial fleet lay docked nearby and unaware of what was to take place on this wharf. He shuffled again, one foot tapping restlessly.

'He'll come,' Centurion Valgus muttered.

Traianus looked to his superior and frowned; the ageing, white-haired centurion's craggy face was curled into a baleful grin, and his hand seemed overeager to rest by his scabbard. He darted a glance around him to see that the other eight legionaries wore the same looks. Then he noticed something on the battlements of the sea walls; a gleaming conical helmet with the distinctive noseguard of a *sagittarius*. Then another, and another.

'Archers too, sir, to oversee an exchange of prisoners?' He asked Valgus. 'This may seem a little heavy-handed to our . . . visitor?'

'Then you do not know the true measure of the man who comes here today, Optio.' Valgus turned to him, his eyes sparkling. 'You know why they call him the Viper?'

Traianus rubbed his narrow jaw; *Iudex* Anzo of the Thervingi Goths, a ruthless warlord hailed by his followers as the Viper. As the number of previously disparate Gothic tribes pledging allegiance to the Viper's banner grew, so did the sense of unease within the senate and the upper echelons of the army. And today, the Viper was to come here, to the heart of the empire. 'I know of him; the Goths say he earned his name because he is a ferocious fighter and slayer of men. A man with the mind of a strategos. Cunning and lethal.'

Valgus shook his head. 'Aye, but ask the few Romans who have faced him and lived; they will tell you a different story. Sent whole legions to Hades, he has. Slaughtered just as many Roman citizens too. And he's slain any Goth who has stood in his way. A stone-hearted, murderous whoreson.' He turned back to the waters, sucked air through his teeth and squared his shoulders.

The gate clunked open and he turned to see a trio of legionaries leading a boy onto the wharf. This was Draga, Iudex Anzo's son. Draga had lived as a political prisoner in the capital for over a year. Barely ten by the look of it, he wore his fawn hair in the Gothic style, scraped into a topknot, revealing green eyes that were cold and spiteful. He wore a Roman-style frayed, red tunic. This exposed the skin around his shoulders and a blue-ink snake *stigma* that wrapped around his collarbone like a torc.

Suddenly, the boy flicked his gaze up and glared at Traianus. Traianus' jaw stiffened at first at the cold stare. But behind the coldness there was something else there. Perhaps a glimmer of hope at being reunited with his father. Traianus gave the boy a tentative nod.

'Don't look at him and see a boy,' Valgus whispered in his ear, 'look at him and know that his mind is filled with the same black thoughts as his father. Yes, they'll be reunited today, one way or another . . .'

Traianus' face fell as he noticed Valgus again touch a hand to his sword hilt as he said this. He had not reckoned on drawing his own *spatha*

12

today, but it seemed a certainty now. 'Sir, the *tribunus*, he briefed us only on an exchange of prisoners?'

'Aye, he did,' Valgus shot a furtive glance around to see who was within earshot, then looked to Traianus with his eyes narrowed, 'but the senate have paid for an alternative outcome.' He winked and patted a hand against his purse, which clunked with coins. 'I briefed the rest of the lads earlier. Don't worry, follow my lead and you'll get your share, and the tribunus need never know.'

Dread swelled in Traianus' gut as he glanced around him, then to the gate leading back into the city. Locked.

'A vessel approaches!' One of the archers called out from the walls.

All heads turned to the north. A medium-sized cog slipped from the headland and into full view. Its triangular sails were sun-bleached and at the tip of the mast a dark-green banner embroidered with a viper writhed gently in the breeze. It was a run-down ship with only a few mercenary crewmen dotted around the rigging and rows of crates were piled on the deck. They watched as the vessel drew in to dock; all was quiet apart from the creaking of dried-out timbers, the gentle lapping of water on the wharf side and the screeching of the gulls and terns that followed the vessel in hope of a meal. Traianus watched the birds swooping and darting. Despite his best efforts, he could not shake the thought of the carrion birds he had become so accustomed to seeing on the battlefield.

Two tall Gothic warriors, wearing their hair scooped up into topknots and armoured in red leather cuirasses, emerged from below deck. They roped the vessel to the wharf by leaning from the side of the ship. They then laid a gangplank from the ship's edge to the dockside and walked over it to stand either side. Silently, each erected a pole bearing a smaller dark-green viper banner. Then, from the far side of the deck, two more figures emerged and walked forward.

The first figure wore a dark-green cloak, hood raised, face in shadows, hands clasped. Despite the heat, Traianus could not suppress a shiver at the sight as the figure drifted forward. Then, ever so slowly, the figure reached up with knotted hands to lift the hood down, revealing sharp, cold features and a thick fawn moustache that hung over taut lips. The hood rested on his shoulders, revealing the fangs and licking tongue of a snake stigma on his collarbone, just like Draga's. This was Iudex Anzo. This was the Viper. His gaze felt like ice on Traianus' skin.

The hulking Goth who walked beside the Viper was draped in a fine scale vest and carried a longsword, an axe and a dagger in his belt. His sleek, dark hair was knotted back and his face was flat and broad, with an arrowhead of a nose between dark eyes and a neatly trimmed beard filling out an already bold jaw. From his left ear dangled three bronze hoops. Each of his forearms bore a snake stigma like that on the necks of Anzo and Draga. Most ominously, his hands dangled close to his weapons as he cast a look of barely disguised contempt across the waiting legionaries.

'Ivo is Anzo's sword, his trusted man,' Valgus whispered. 'Keep your eye on him.'

Traianus shuffled to stand straight as Ivo's gaze swept past him.

Then two more Gothic warriors emerged from below deck. They bundled before them a bedraggled, bald and ageing Roman in a filthy tunic. So this was the ambassador who was to be exchanged for Draga. Traianus winced at the sight of the torture wounds that pockmarked the man's skin and wondered when the poor wretch had last seen the light of day.

'Ave, Romans,' Iudex Anzo spoke in a rasping Gothic twang, his tone sour. He did not wait for a reply as his gaze quickly fell on Draga, held by two legionaries. 'My son, you are unharmed?'

The Gothic boy's face remained grave. 'That, we can discuss once we have set sail for our homeland, Father.'

'Aye, *Gutthiuda* awaits us,' Anzo replied, casting a glance northwards in the direction of the Thervingi homelands. Then he turned to Centurion Valgus, his face curling into a sneer of contempt. 'Now, the exchange?'

Valgus' eyes narrowed and he nodded to the legionaries. They relaxed their grip on Draga, while the Goths did likewise with the old ambassador.

14

Traianus watched, the breath hanging in his lungs as the prisoners stepped forward. Draga moved towards the Goths as the ambassador moved towards to the legionaries. Then he glanced to the Goths who watched on; each of them seemed as tense as the legionaries, their hands resting unnervingly close to their longswords. Then there was Iudex Anzo and Centurion Valgus; both wore the look of predators waiting to strike as the prisoners stepped carefully towards the middle ground. Then he noticed Ivo's eyes darting to the Gothic ship and the piled crates. Instinctively, Traianus touched a hand to his sword hilt too, sweat forming on his upper lip. But at last the prisoners passed each other in the centre and the tension eased from all watching on.

A sweet relief flowed through Traianus' veins momentarily.

Then, something caught his attention; Valgus' eyes were narrowed. The centurion gulped and moistened his lips, as if readying to give some order. Traianus' blood ran cold.

Then it ran like ice when he saw the tips of two masts emerging beyond the tapering headland. Dark-green banners rippled at the tips of the masts as they rounded the coast to enter the Golden Horn.

Gothic warships.

Traianus glanced to Valgus; the centurion's words seemed to catch in his throat at the sight. Then he glanced to Anzo, whose eyes smouldered like hot coals. The Viper lifted a hand, extended one finger, then swiped it down.

Suddenly, and in one fluid movement, Ivo ripped a dagger from his belt, then lunged forward to grab the Roman ambassador, tearing the blade across the old man's throat. Blood leapt from the gaping wound and the ambassador fell to his knees, clawing at his neck, heaving and retching a pink foam while his eyes bulged from their sockets. At the same time, the Viper leapt forward to pull Draga towards him. He shielded his son and threw off his cloak to reveal his lean, athletic frame, hugged by a scale vest and a swordbelt. Then he drew his longsword, pointed it at Valgus and backed away towards the Gothic cog, casting a wicked grin at the Romans.

15

'*Whoresons!*' Valgus roared, his eyes bulging as the four Gothic spearmen on the wharf levelled their blades and pushed up to flank Ivo. Holding up round wooden shields, they braced, forming a wall between the legionaries and Anzo, who ushered Draga back towards the cog. Valgus tore his spatha from his scabbard and roared the legionaries forward. 'Kill them, kill them all! Don't let the Viper escape!'

At this, the sagittarii shot up from behind the walls, nocking arrows to their bows. But Ivo roared out as they took aim. 'Chosen archers!'

In a heartbeat, the docked Gothic cog was transformed as a line of red-vested, blonde-locked master-archers appeared from behind the crates stacked on the deck. Thirty of them, bows stretched, targets already sighted. As one, they loosed their arrows at the walls before their Roman counterparts had even taken aim. With a hiss and then a punch of iron cutting through flesh, a score of the sagittarii toppled from the battlements, gurgling their last while those unscathed loosed their volley in reply.

When one Roman archer turned his bow on the Goths on the wharf, Ivo stretched out to wrap an arm around Valgus' neck, then twisted the centurion round to use him as a shield. The arrow aimed at Ivo smashed into Valgus' thigh. Then Ivo wrenched sharply. With a crack, Valgus' neck snapped and he fell limply to the ground, blood pouring from his lips and his eyes rolling in their sockets. The purse fell from Valgus' belt and the coins spilled across the wharf where they were quickly swamped by the centurion's blood.

As arrows flew overhead from both sides, Traianus instinctively joined shields with the other eight legionaries. Then he set his sights on Anzo, who was lifting his son onto the Gothic cog. At the same time, Ivo readied the Gothic warriors to cover the Viper's retreat, roaring them towards the legionaries with grand swipes of his longsword.

'At them!' Traianus roared, sensing the other legionaries' hesitation at having lost their centurion. The legionaries rushed forward and smashed against Ivo and his line, the screeching of iron upon iron filling the wharf. One of the legionaries was felled by Ivo's sword, white bone and pink lung glistening from a gaping wound in his chest. Then a Roman head was sliced

16

from its shoulders and the wharf was soon slick with blood. Traianus held up his spatha to parry the giant's next strike, but the force of the blow shook him to his bones and sent him staggering backwards. But he leapt back into the fray, seeing the Viper and his son were now onboard the cog.

But Draga was struggling, snarling. 'Let me fight!'

Then the boy shrugged free of his father's grasp, then pushed his way from the ship and into the melee, taking up a longsword from a slain Goth.

'Draga, no!' Anzo roared, 'Get onto the ship!'

But Draga plunged into the fray, heedless of his father's cries. He bore the weighty blade like a seasoned warrior, swiping and parrying with force and guile that belied his years. Then he ripped the blade across the chest of the legionary by Traianus' side.

Iudex Anzo lunged forward, slicing through the thigh of a legionary then thrusting an arm out to pull his son from the skirmish. But the Viper's step faltered as an arrow from the walls punched into his stomach, then another burst through his throat. Dark blood showered over Draga, who gawped in horror as his father toppled to the wharf side, his body shuddering in a pool of crimson.

A cheer rang out from the sagittarii on the walls as the corpse stilled. 'The Viper is dead!' They roared.

Traianus staggered back from a longsword blow and saw that Draga was crouched by the pool of his father's blood, a single tear dancing down his cheek at the sight as he touched a hand to the corpse. Then the boy lifted the dark-green cloak, soaked in gore. With that he stood and stared straight at Traianus, eyes shaded under a furrowed brow. Traianus shuddered; the glimmer of hope was snuffed out. There were no more tears. Only cold conviction.

Then he saw a wounded legionary, blood pumping from a mortal wound to his thigh, stagger up behind Draga, spatha raised. The legionary punched his spatha into the boy's shoulder, then ripped it clear, before toppling to the ground himself.

Traianus remained, frozen, watching as Draga swayed by the wharf's edge, blood washing from his wound, soaking the snake stigma coiled around his shoulders. The boy's brow wrinkled as he looked to the cloak in his arms, then to his wound and then up to Traianus. For a heartbeat his gaze grew murderous, eyes burning like hot coals. Then his legs trembled and he toppled towards the water.

'No!' Ivo cried, rushing to the wharfside to reach out a ham-like hand. But the boy's body toppled into the waters and Ivo swiped at thin air.

Ivo fell to his knees, his fingers outstretched to the ripples in the water before they curled into a shaking fist. Then he leapt up with an animal roar, spinning to swipe his longsword around him in a fury, slaying the last two legionaries in one blow.

Suddenly, Traianus realised he was alone on the wharf with the giant Goth, while the two bands of archers exchanged fire over their heads. Ivo glared through a mask of blood at Traianus, then he stalked forward.

Traianus' body tensed in fear at the creature that came for him, but he readied himself, raising his sword, setting his feet. He filled his lungs and let loose a roar, then surged forward to meet the challenge. Then there was a smash of iron and a spray of sparks as a Gothic arrow smacked against his blade, then ricocheted up and across Ivo's face. The big warrior roared, clutching his left eye, a soup of blood and eye-matter sputtering down his cheek.

At that moment the wall gate clunked open and a century of fresh legionaries spilled onto the wharf, clustering around Traianus. Only the covering fire of the Gothic chosen archers kept the legionaries at bay as Ivo stumbled back into the cog, scooping up the Viper's body on the way. With that, the Gothic warriors onboard untied the ropes and pushed the ship from the wharf side, then dipped one bank of oars in the water to pivot the vessel away from the city.

As the cog departed, the two Gothic warships slowed to flank it. The waters of the Golden Horn were otherwise dotted only with Roman merchant ships. The workmen repairing the Roman warships, docked and crewless nearby, could only cry out in futility. Thus, the three Gothic vessels retreated unopposed.

Regardless, the Roman sagittarii continued to loose arrows at the departing ship and the Gothic chosen archers onboard the cog replied in kind.

Traianus stood amid this deadly hail, transfixed on Ivo. The giant was poised at the stern, holding the Viper's corpse in his arms. Roman arrows thudded down onto the Gothic cog, some only inches from him. But Ivo did not flinch, his good eye remaining trained on the cluster of legionaries while his ruined eye seeped blood. Then his chest heaved and he roared, his words echoing over the city walls;

'This is only the beginning, you dogs. The day will come when the Viper will rise again. On that day, the tribes will be united. And on that day, Roman blood will flow like the Mother River!'

His words chilled Traianus' blood. Then a silence hung in the air. He felt his limbs tremble as the battle rage subsided, and a dull nausea swam in his gut.

'What in Hades happened here, soldier?' A voice spoke from beside him. It was the young centurion who led the fresh legionaries. His face was pale as he scanned the carpet of gore on the wharf side.

Traianus looked him in the eye and moved his lips to speak, but found no reply forthcoming.

Twenty Four Years Later

Deep winter, 376 AD

The Roman *Limes* of Moesia

GORDON DOHERTY

Chapter 1

Durostorum's winter morning market halted to watch as Legionary Numerius Vitellius Pavo of the XI Claudia stood to face the three troublemakers.

The slit-eyed drunk before Pavo roared and rushed forward, right hand balled into a fist, the left grasping a cup of foaming ale.

Pavo watched his assailant's footsteps. He fought the urge to draw his spatha, then dodged back out of the man's right hook, sticking out a foot. The man's roar tapered into a yelp as he tripped, the contents of the ale cup showering Pavo's face, cloak and mail vest. The man himself crashed to the frozen earth, face-first, shards of tooth spraying from his mouth.

The townsfolk watched with bated breath, eagerly eyeing Pavo and then the two sidekicks who had backed the drunk until only moments ago.

Pavo eyed the pair, stabbing a finger at the grounded drunk who moaned in agony. 'Now I could have let him hit me,' he panted, his breath clouding in the chill, 'and then he would have lost the skin from his back for it. So take your chance; walk away and sleep it off!'

The two couldn't hold Pavo's gaze, and backed away then melted into the crowd. Then, with a groan, the grounded man pushed himself up. He held up his hands in a gesture of submission, blood streaming from his shattered array of teeth.

'Look, there's barely enough food to go round,' he said, nodding to the town *horreum*.

Pavo kept his face stern, but the man was right; the grain store was running dangerously low and winter had yet to reach its depths.

'So if we can't eat our fill then we may as well drink what's left in the ale barrels,' the man continued, jabbing a thumb over his shoulder.

Pavo glanced over the man's shoulder to the squat stone inn, distinguished by the stirring pole and vine leaves resting by the doorway. *The Boar and Hollybush* was the favourite haunt for the men of his legion. But today, like every other market day, it was full of inebriated locals. Worse, when he had ventured inside earlier, there was no sign of her. *Felicia.* His mind flitted momentarily to the last night they had shared, her warm skin against his, her sweet scent, her locks whispering over his chest.

'Besides,' the man's grating tone snapped him back to the present, 'there are hardly enough of your lot over in the fort to keep this place in check,' the drunk slurred, then turned to trudge away.

Pavo made to fire some retort, but the drunk was right again. In the last few weeks, many Gothic settlements that had sworn loyalty to Fritigern, the dominant iudex of the Thervingi and a tentative Roman ally, had reported disturbances and rebel uprisings. Thus, numerous *vexillationes* had been summoned north, stripping the XI Claudia of their already understrength complement. Now, barely three hundred men including auxiliaries, recruits and Gothic *foederati* were housed in the fort.

As the crowd dissolved back into the daily bustle of market day, Pavo spat the traces of beer from his lips. He pulled his hands together across his face to the point of his beaky nose, then wiped them across his hazel eyes, thick brows and dark, stubbled scalp. He picked up his *intercisa* helmet from the ground where it had fallen, brushing the dirt from the iron fin. Then, realising his woollen trousers and the tunic he wore under his mail shirt were not quite so white anymore, he pulled his grey woollen cloak around his lean frame, wincing at the stench of the ale-soaked garment.

Footsteps rattled up beside him and his heart leapt. He spun, fists raised, then slumped in relief at the sight of his fellow legionary. 'Sura!' This blonde-mopped and cherub-faced lad had been Pavo's loyal friend since the first day of enlistment. 'Did you catch the rest of them?'

'I caught one and kicked his balls,' Sura gasped for breath, resting a hand on Pavo's shoulder. 'Nearly broke my bloody foot. The others . . .

24

they'll think twice about starting a ruckus when I'm around. Now do me a favour – let's head back to the fort.'

'Aye, this place is becoming bloody treacherous!' Pavo muttered. 'If things carry on like this I'll *have* to draw my sword on them one day.'

They walked through the flagstoned streets, past the timber arena, the domed Christian church and the squat tenements until they reached the town gates. Here, Pavo cast a foul glare at the two auxiliaries atop the thick stone gatehouse. The pair pretended not to notice, just as they had turned a blind eye to the drunk and his friends wreaking havoc at the market despite having a perfect view of the incident from the walls.

Outside the town, Pavo shivered, pulling his cloak tighter. The morning chill was stark and the air was spiced with woodsmoke. Winter had gripped the banks of the River Danubius and the cornfields lay brown and fallow, cloaked in a frost that was insensitive to the best efforts of the morning sun. To the east, about a half-mile from the south bank of the great river, the squat bulwark that was the fortress of the XI Claudia Legion stood like a titan's gravestone. Coated in moss, sparkling with frost and framed by the distant shimmering waters of the *Pontus Euxinus*, this place had been his home for nearly a year. The towers of the fort were crowned with the ruby-red bull banners of this legion and the battlements were punctuated with the distinctive iron fin-topped intercisa helmets of the precious few sentries. Meanwhile, the rest of the legion trained on the plain to the northwest of the fort, and the sight of them warmed Pavo's heart.

Then a distant moan of a Gothic war horn sounded to the north. Instinctively, he and Sura spun towards the noise. Then the pair slumped and Pavo chided himself, realising it was just another echo of the troubles going on deep in those foreign lands. They halted there for a moment, gazing north over the canopy of dark forest and the hazy outline of the distant Carpates Mountains. Gutthiuda; land of the Goths, and a cauldron of trouble for the imperial borders and the *limitanei* legions who manned them.

'Every time I hear it,' Sura said, 'I feel my sword arm itch, and my shield arm tense. I'll wager my savings that it's Athanaric behind these rebel uprisings; anything to agitate Fritigern and endanger his truce with Rome.'

'Aye, I have my doubts over this mooted peace parley with the man,' Pavo agreed, squinting into the winter sun at the outline of the Carpates. Deep in those mountains, the belligerent Gothic Iudex was holed up with his war-hungry followers. There had been talk for some time of a group of diplomats being sent to Athanaric's lands. The idea was that they could meet with the iudex and broker some truce, but the idea jarred with Pavo; at every turn, Athanaric had sought to bring trouble upon both the Roman borders and Fritigern's lands. It was a blessing indeed that Fritigern held stock in his truce with Rome. 'I just pray to *Mithras* that the vexillationes over there come back to us safe and well.'

Sura issued a gruff sigh beside him, pointing to the fort gates. 'And if it's not vexillationes heading north, its Emperor Valens draining man and sword to the east.'

Pavo turned and shook his head at the sight; a wagon laden with shimmering armour and arms rumbled from the fort gateway and across the walkway straddling the triple ditch. The driver whipped his horses into a canter towards the road that snaked east to the coast and the port town of Tomis. From there it would be shipped to Trapezus, then hauled overland to the eastern frontier and the war with Persia. This had become a common sight since last summer. First, a few of the *comitatenses* legions had been summoned east from the field army of Moesia, not enough to cause huge concern, as plenty more of the elite mobile legions remained. But then, as autumn arrived, more and more of them were plucked away, and just last month, the last two left. And then the entire field army of Thracia had followed.

Now, the limitanei were alone to man the borders while the populous lands to the south lay virtually unprotected, all the way to Constantinople. Inside the fort, the supply warehouse was an empty shell, and then there was the still and silent *fabrica*. The workshop had been out of use for some weeks now due to lack of wool, linen and iron with which to craft new garb, weapons and armour. War was pulling these lands apart from every direction, it seemed.

Pavo snorted and walked on; this was the calling of a legionary, just as it had been for his father, so it would be for him. Since joining the XI Claudia nearly a year ago, Pavo had grown into legionary life, developing a necessary callus over his heart. More importantly, the legions had saved him from a life of servitude. He suppressed a shudder as his mind flitted back to the death of his father and the descent into slavery that followed. All those years living in the stinking cellar of Senator Tarquitius' villa in Constantinople. Images of the beatings, the violation and the murder of fellow slaves he had witnessed there barged into his mind uninvited.

He closed his eyes to blot out the memories, then he carried out the ritual that had kept him strong through those dark years; under his cloak, he touched a hand to the battered bronze *phalera* that hung from the leather strap around his neck. The legionary medallion was his one possession that linked him to his father.

He was roused from his thoughts by a tap-tapping of wooden training swords, a rumbling of hooves and barked orders. He looked up to see that they had reached the training field. Some two hundred men – cavalry, archers and legionaries – went about their daily drills, breath clouding in the air as they were put through their paces. As the pair made to walk on past the field, a voice called out.

'Oi, you two! Over here!'

Pavo turned to see a silhouetted figure waving at them from the northern end of the field, where the recruits were being put through their paces. Even from this distance, Centurion Quadratus' hulking build distinguished him from any other on the field. The big Gaul was a true veteran, one of the precious few who had served and survived in the legion since before Pavo enlisted. Indeed, Pavo thought, life expectancy in the limitanei was so short that he and Sura were also considered veterans, both at the ripe old age of just twenty one.

'He'd better not be looking to use me as an example barbarian again,' Sura cocked an eyebrow, touching a hand to his ribs and then wincing. 'He made me look a right bloody idiot in front of those recruits.'

'Aye, but you helped,' Pavo smirked, then dodged a playful punch to the arm from his friend. 'Now come on, I find it's best not to keep him waiting.'

They cut across the training area, examining the goings-on around them. To the east of the field, a thock-thocking of iron splicing wood rang out from the newly constructed archery range. Here, the two *sagittarii* archers who had recently been sent to the fort stood dressed in scale-vests, ruby cloaks and conical helmets sporting nose-guards. They watched the legionaries' dubious attempts at hitting the centre of the timber targets. This was the latest edict from Emperor Valens; all legionaries were to be trained to competence with the bow. It was a meagre balance for stripping the land of its legions, Pavo mused as he watched. One legionary hit the centre of the target and made to punch the air in celebration, when one of the sagittarii stopped him, shaking his head, pointing out some minimal distance between his strike and dead centre.

Then they came to the cavalry training area. Here, ten of the *turma* of thirty *equites* stationed at the fort were being put through their paces by their *decurion*. The commanding officer yelled at his Roman cavalry as, dressed only in boots and tunics, they practiced vaulting onto the saddle and then off again, repeating the motion over and over.

'Come on, men, in time!' The decurion barked. 'If you can't do it in time now then you'll never manage it in full armour!'

Pavo sympathised, then he turned back to Centurion Quadratus. The big Gaul with the thick blonde moustache was berating a ragged group of some fifty young men in an even more ferocious manner. He grinned, reserving his sympathy for these lads instead, and made to stride forward.

'Careful!' Sura yelped, slapping a hand across Pavo's chest.

Pavo stopped dead as the other twenty equites thundered past in full kit; mail shirts, iron helmets and ruby cloaks, frost spraying up in their wake. They rode their mounts around the training field, leaping over a raised timber bar erected on the far side before coming back round on another circuit. This time, as they approached, the decurion turned to them and roared; 'Equites Sagittarii, loose!' With this, the rearmost ten pulled bows from their backs

28

and twisted in their saddles, still keeping pace with the foremost ten. Then they trained their sights on a battered post in the middle of the training field and, as one, loosed their arrows. Ten arrows hammered home, sending splinters of wood up into the air.

'Thirty of them,' Sura muttered, 'when we need hundreds.'

To the side of the field, a small clutch of Gothic foederati watched their Roman counterparts, chattering in their own tongue. On entering Roman lands and enlisting, these men swore loyalty to the empire; some served as legionaries, others – like these – retained their Gothic armour and appearance and served as cavalry scouts. Pavo had known some good-hearted warriors of their ilk in his time with the legions, but he had known at least as many black-blooded ones too. They seemed disinterested in the proceedings, and this irked him. Then again, he mused, this lot could train every day with the legion until they collapsed of exhaustion, but only the adversity of battle would reveal the true colour of their hearts.

Finally, they reached the recruit training area. Pavo stepped over the form of a prone and panting youngster who had crawled to the eastern edge of the training field to spit blood into the earth. He looked over the latest spluttering and red-faced intake; boys scraped from the border farms and undesirables drawn from the cities. 'Were we ever this poor?' He cocked an eyebrow.

'You were,' Sura fired back, then grinned. 'Ach, relax,' he continued, pointing to the hulking figure standing in the midst of the recruits, 'Centurion Quadratus will have this lot fighting like lions in no time!'

Right on cue, the Gaulish centurion smashed his wooden training sword on his shield boss and roared. 'Enough for today – I can't take any more of your pansy fighting! Fall into line, you pussies! Faster!' Then one rotund recruit went over on his ankle and crumpled to the earth with a high-pitched squeal. Quadratus shook his head and rubbed his eyes with his forefinger and thumb. 'In the name of Mithras! Fall out!'

Pavo could not help but crack a smile, remembering his own time as a recruit.

Finally, the recruits jostled back towards the fort in some semblance of order. Quadratus walked over to Pavo and Sura, still shaking his head.

'Even you two were less shit than that lot,' he mused absent-mindedly, his eyes hanging on the last of them as they entered the fort.

Sura frowned in indignation, but the big man continued.

'And I missed out on all these sorties over the river because apparently *I'm well placed to train the recruits.* I'll bloody well place my foot right up their ars . . . '

Pavo leaned forward and coughed, jolting Quadratus back to them.

'Mithras! Have you been swimming in ale?' Quadratus recoiled at the stale stench from Pavo.

'Trouble in town sir, I broke up a fight between drunks.'

'They don't have anything better to do than sup ale before noon?' Quadratus mused, then cocked an eyebrow, folded his bottom lip and tilted his head from side to side as if considering the logic.

'Er . . . sir, you wanted us for something?' Pavo asked.

Quadratus looked at them blankly for a moment, then clicked his fingers. 'Aye, I did,' he nodded up to the banks of the Danubius and grinned. 'You'll like this. Come on,' he beckoned them forward up the dirt path that wound over to the banks.

They headed towards a bobbing timber structure that straddled the river. The pontoon bridge had been pulled together from the remaining husk of the *Classis Moesica*, the rotting hulls of the triremes roped together and boarded over. At the near end of the bridge, a sturdy *castrum* had been erected, the timber construction serving as both a bridgehead and a fortlet. The bridge itself seemed impossibly long, the power of the river's current bending it into a gentle crescent. All this to provide a means of rapid Roman response to the trouble in Fritigern's lands. *The price of truce*, Pavo mused.

As if reading his thoughts, Quadratus nodded north-west, over the river. 'Let's hope Tribunus Gallus and the lads can nip these uprisings in the bud.'

30

Gallus. Pavo's heart warmed at the mention of the tribunus' name. True, the leader of the legion was cold and utterly resolute, and Pavo had feared and hated the man in equal measure in his early days as a recruit. But time had served to show him that the tribunus' iron heart was but a necessary veneer. And what a fine leader of the XI Claudia he was. Indeed, if there was any one soldier he would bet on to walk into Hades and better the demons that lay in wait there, it was Gallus. Over a week ago, the tribunus had headed north with a strong vexillatio, intent on tracking down the lead band of these Gothic rebels, leaving Quadratus in charge at the fort. Pavo's gaze grew distant as he issued a prayer that they would return safely.

Then he was shaken back to the present with a thick crack of rope, then a hissing followed by a stark series of thuds.

'Did I really just see that?' Sura frowned, elbowing Pavo.

Up ahead, by the castrum, a cluster of four legionaries were fussing over some contraption beside which sat an empty cart, lopsided with one wheel buckled. As they approached it, he frowned: it looked like a mutated *ballista* – it had the frame of a bolt-thrower but it was bristling with four missiles instead of just one. Three lengths of rope, each as thick as his forearm, were coiled at each edge of the device. The legionaries pulled at winches, stretching this rope taut along the slider. Then they slipped four massive iron-headed bolts in place between the ropes and the bow-shaped iron front-piece.

'Ah, ladies! Glad you could join us at last!' The short, bald *Optio* Avitus grinned as he spun round from the device.

'Ladies?' Quadratus cocked an eyebrow.

At this, Avitus' face fell and he quickly saluted. 'Ready for inspection, sir!'

Pavo suppressed a grin. Avitus had never quite adjusted from the days when he had shared a *contubernium* with Quadratus, Pavo and the other veterans. They had shared a tent, rations, reward and punishment together. And the banter . . . he cocked an eyebrow as some of the stories and pranks flitted through his mind . . . the banter had been brutal.

But then Quadratus' grimace melted into a grin. 'Ready for inspection? Aye, whatever. Let this pair of pussies see this beauty do her thing,' he tapped a finger on the front-piece of the device from which the four missile heads poked.

Avitus nodded and grinned at Pavo and Sura. 'Who needs comitatenses legions when you have one of these?' He lifted a hand and addressed the four who manned the device. 'Ready? Loose!'

Pavo flinched as the device jolted like an angered bull. Then, with a whoosh, all four of the ballista bolts ripped through the air in a low trajectory. They sped across the broad waters of the river before smashing into a felled spruce on the far side, frost and splinters spraying up as the missile heads burst from the other side of the trunk. The four bolts quivered as if pleading to be set free in flight again, and Pavo gawped at the dark crack that ran the length of the tree.

'Told you you'd like it,' Quadratus muttered smugly. 'Athanaric can line up his *mighty* cavalry over there for us. Yes . . . that'd do just nicely.'

Pavo walked around the device. He noted that it was set on the ground on thick stilts; the nearby cart had probably been used to haul the hefty piece of equipment from the fortress before collapsing on its axles.

'Static artillery,' Avitus said, reading his thoughts, 'I wouldn't fancy hauling one of those on a sortie! The smith and the carpenter at the fort reckon they might be able to develop an axle and wheel that'll carry this bugger more than a few hundred feet . . . but they've been saying that for weeks.'

'Shame. Still though, are there any more of them?'

Avitus lifted his helmet and scratched his bald head in mock bewilderment. 'Son, when was the last time you saw a new pair of boots issued, never mind a piece of artillery?'

Pavo glanced down at his boots; split at the shin and with soles worn to almost nothing. He shrugged. 'So where did this one come from?'

Avitus glanced at Quadratus, who nodded. 'Thrift and, er, swift thinking,' he replied.

Avitus continued; 'Aye, let's just say we, er, salvaged what we could before the vultures took everything we had east, with the comitatenses. This fine device you see is hand-crafted from timber hewn from the warehouse shelves and iron smelted from a set of mail vests that . . . went missing.'

Pavo grinned. 'Nice work . . . ' his words tailed off and the ground started to shake, he spun in the direction of the fortress. The decurion from the training field led his turma of thirty equites at a trot towards the bridge. The riders were carrying the ruby and gold shields of the XI Claudia, holding *hasta* spears vertical and wearing mail shirts and intercisa helmets, their ruby cloaks fluttering in their wake. Behind them marched a column of fifty legionaries.

'Really? *Another* vexillatio?' Sura moaned.

Pavo mouthed the same question. This was the sixth detachment that had been sent out in the last two days.

'Aye. Something's very wrong over there,' Avitus frowned, looking north. 'It's all very well keeping the peace with Fritigern, but we must be down to what, a few hundred men?'

The decurion at the head of the vexillatio issued a brisk salute to which Quadratus responded. Then, with a thunder of boots and hooves on timber, the party moved onto the bridge and on into Gutthiuda.

Quadratus sighed and shrugged almost apologetically. 'The order for that lot to be despatched came direct from Dux Vergilius, tucked up in the safety of a villa, miles to the south. What can we do when we are at the whims of a fool like him?'

Pavo frowned. He had never met in person the *Magister Militum Per Illyricum*, the man nominally in charge of the armies of all Moesia and the river fleet. However, he had witnessed the man's last visit to the fort: a grossly overweight, red-faced and constantly trembling individual, at ease only after he had emptied several goblets of wine.

33

'Hello?' Avitus chirped, shielding his eyes from the sun to look back to the fort. 'Seems we have reinforcements?'

Pavo and the rest of the group turned to look. There, approaching the fort gates from the southern highway, a column approached. A cluster of some fifteen finely armoured riders headed a column of two centuries of legionaries who filed up behind them, carrying freshly painted blue shields. The lead rider, distinguished by an old-style and somewhat exaggerated horsehair plume on his helmet, was calling up to the gatehouse. The sentry atop the walls was pointing north, right at the giant ballista. The leader nodded then barked to his infantry and all but ten of them split off to file inside the fort. Then, the remaining ten legionaries and the riders moved towards the ballista.

'Comitatenses?' Pavo reasoned, noticing the fine scale vests the foot soldiers wore. 'I thought they had all gone east?'

'Not all of them,' Quadratus said with a sigh.

'Sir?' Pavo quizzed.

'Going by the ridiculous plume, I'd say that was *Comes* Lupicinus. He was in charge of the Thracian field armies. I'd heard rumours that he had been left behind with a few centuries of men while his legions were summoned east. And let's just say that Emperor Valens left him back here for a reason,' the big Gaulish centurion rolled his eyes.

'Aye,' Avitus added, 'I've heard of him; an arsehole who wouldn't know the right end of a spatha until you shoved it in his gut.'

Just then, a young legionary stumbled from the training field and into the path of the plumed rider's horse. Then the rider thrashed at the young man with a cane and a sharp crack of wood on skin split the air followed by a roar of pain.

'Just stay quiet, I'll deal with him,' Quadratus insisted.

Pavo watched as the mounted party drew closer and slowed to a trot, the following ten legionaries catching up. The leader wore an antiquated bronze muscled cuirass and a fine, silk-lined crimson cloak. He glared down his nose, his lips pinched and his piercing grey eyes full of scrutiny. A cold bastard. Pavo hoped for a fleeting moment that this was another in the mould of Gallus.

Then Lupicinus lifted a hand in silence and his men stopped behind him. He trotted forward, peacock-like, eyeing the group around the ballista, nose wrinkling as if he had stumbled into an open latrine. He bristled and flexed his shoulders. 'Would Centurion Quadratus make himself known!' The man's tone was sharp and biting.

'Sir!' Quadratus replied, standing to attention.

Lupicinus cocked an eyebrow at the big Gaul. 'You are relieved of your command, Centurion. As Comes of the Field Armies of Thracia, I will be overseeing the limitanei of this region as a whole, and I'll be acting tribunus for the XI Claudia. My two centuries will bolster the numbers of the XI Claudia and will lead your rogues and farmers by example.'

'Yes, sir!' Quadratus barked back, masking any sign of humiliation well – quite a feat for the temperamental Gaul.

'And I'll have my work cut out, it seems; already I have heard word of a missing wage purse, stolen from within the fort?' He eyed each of them like culprits.

'And I'll expect a full briefing on this activity,' Lupicinus continued, flicking his head to the giant ballista, 'for an officer should not be distracted by fanciful engineering. He should be with his men at all times. Inspiring them, encouraging them,' he leaned forward from the saddle and clenched a fist, '*leading* them.'

'Never a truer word has been spoken, sir,' Quadratus replied. 'Indeed, I've just spent all morning on the training field with . . . '

'You'll speak when I say you can speak, Centurion!' Lupicinus barked. 'And you'll sort out your armour before you next stand in front of me,' the comes flicked a finger at Quadratus' rusting, torn mail vest, bringing a chorus of derisive laughter from Lupicinus' riders and infantry. 'You're a disgrace to your legion, and to your empire!'

Pavo's chest stung with ire as he saw Quadratus shuffle on the spot, face burning in humiliation and fury. The big Gaul had forgone the last of the fresh sets of armour to allow those travelling north with Tribunus Gallus to have it. And he was being mocked for the gesture. Pavo stared at the comes; this man was no Gallus.

Then, like an asp, Lupicinus' eyes snapped round to fix on Pavo. 'You have something to say, soldier? Name and rank?' He demanded.

Pavo's stomach fell away and his skin prickled with an icy dread. 'Legionary Numerius Vitellius Pavo of the XI Claudia, third cohort, first century, sir!'

Lupicinus heeled his mount over to Pavo and looked him up and down, then recoiled with a gasp. 'You *reek* of ale, soldier. Drunk on duty? Worse than sleeping on watch! You know the punishment for that, don't you?'

'Flogging at best, sir, or death,' Pavo replied flatly as the rest of the XI Claudia legionaries looked on.

'Aye,' Lupicinus hissed, 'and if I learn that you're the wage thief . . . you know what they used to do to legionaries devoid of honour, do you? They would force them, screaming, into a hemp sack filled with poisonous asps.' The comes was almost purring. 'Then hurl the sack into the depths of a river.'

'Permission to speak, sir!' Quadratus stepped forward again.

Lupicinus spun to him and flared his nostrils, eyes wide in indignation. 'Speak.'

'Pavo was just a moment ago involved in settling a dispute in the town. Drunken locals causing bother. I can vouch for his sobriety.'

'Oh, can you?' Lupicinus straightened up in his saddle again and turned to Pavo.

'And he is a commendable soldier, sir,' Quadratus continued. 'Played more than his part in the Bosporus mission. A campaign bloodier than most I can remember. Helped keep this empire in one piece, sir.'

Lupicinus snorted at this. 'The mission to old Bosporus was a debacle; little more than a cull of half of the border legions.' He jabbed a finger at each of them. 'It's down to you that we're so stretched now!' His face split with a malicious grin as his riders and the ten legionaries behind them erupted in belly laughter. Pavo noticed that one towering legionary in particular seemed to be relishing the humiliation. The man had sunken eyes and pitted skin. Pavo glared back at him, feeling his blood boil. Then he froze, feeling a cold blade slip under his chin.

'What's this?' Lupicinus cooed, having hooked his spatha blade through the leather strap around Pavo's neck to lift the phalera clear of his mail vest. 'Legio II Parthica?'

'My father's legion, sir,' Pavo barked, straightening up, trying to shrug off his anger.

'And now just bones in the eastern sands. Slain in Bezabde were they not? Every last one of them?'

Pavo's teeth ground like a mill, and he struggled to keep his stare straight ahead. His face twisted as he watched Lupicinus rotate his blade on the strap, as if musing as to whether to cut it and take the piece. Pavo tried to stay calm, but rage overcame him and he filled his lungs to shout at the man.

But the breath stayed in his chest as, from behind the riders, one of the comitatenses legionaries gasped; 'Sir!'

Lupicinus turned on his saddle, pulling his spatha away from Pavo. The legionary had one arm outstretched, pointing across the river.

Pavo turned, following the legionary's finger. His skin crawled. There, at the far bridgehead, the bush and treeline seemed to be rippling – the classic prelude to a Gothic infantry attack. He thought of the earlier distant Gothic war horn. What if it had not been civil strife after all?

'Oh, bloody heck!' Avitus growled as he saw it too and started fumbling with the ballista, the crew of three helping him. Then they stopped when Avitus pushed back with a groan. 'We're out of bolts!'

Quadratus turned to Lupicinus. 'Sir, send a rider to the fort or the training field to summon a fifty, enough to cover the bridgehead!'

Lupicinus looked momentarily rattled, but after a few anxious shuffles on his saddle he licked his lips and glared at Quadratus. 'I give the orders here, Centurion, and I will be damned to Hades like a coward if I am going to call for help. Now, ready at the bridgehead!' He waved the group of XI Claudia legionaries and his ten comitatenses forward. At this, Quadratus' teeth ground like rocks.

Pavo rushed into position, shoulder to shoulder with Avitus and Sura, as they had fought many times before. But, caught cold, they were without shields or spears, having only their spathas to fight with. This handful of Roman swords would do well to hold back anything more than a small number of Gothic infantry. The treeline continued to rustle, and the cluster of Romans stood in silence, unblinking, snatching breaths, the roar of the Danubius the only noise around.

'Shy fellows, these Goths?' Lupicinus said, finally. 'Perhaps we should go over there and show them how to launch an attack?'

Quadratus shared a weary look with Pavo, Sura and Avitus on the front line. 'That's how they operate, sir – the Gothic chosen archers. You'll be almost on top of them, think you have the upper hand, then you'll have a dagger in your neck or an arrow in your back. Best thing we can do is use our position, hold the bridgehead. They won't come at us if we stay here.'

'And that is how we gained an empire in the first place, is it? Cowering behind defences and waiting to be attacked?' Lupicinus retorted. His riders laughed again, but this time their laughter was forced and laced with icy tension. 'Nonsense! Advance at a slow march across the bridge. You can still hold your precious bridgehead from the far side.'

Quadratus looked up with a furious expression. 'Is that an order, sir?'

Lupicinus pursed his lips and gazed into the distance as if shrewdly thinking over the move. 'Yes, it is. But let's advance with one of the war heroes at the front. Yes, let's have the drunk,' he stabbed a finger at Pavo.

'Now tell me, why have you been left behind while the better men of your legion are out in enemy territory, eh?'

Pavo searched for an answer. The truth was that he would have been out there too, had it not been for the recent reorganisation of the legion to repopulate the ranks after the Bosporus mission. He had been a proud member of the first cohort, first century. Then, a few months ago, Gallus had insisted that the more experienced legionaries should be seeded through the cohorts as the legion was repopulated with recruits and vexillationes from other legions. Still though, doubt stung at his chest.

'Perhaps you are not as brave as you would have us think?' Lupicinus cut in before he could reply. 'Well come on then, out front, lead us across the bridge.'

Pavo's blood iced at this. All eyes fell upon him. At least his colleagues in the front line offered their sympathy. In contrast, Lupicinus smirked at his discomfort, as did his riders and legionaries. But Pavo had known this was coming and coming soon. With so many officers killed or called out in vexillationes recently, Pavo, like Sura, was only a few steps from being thrust into leadership. And the thought made him nauseous. His one brief spell of leadership had been swift, when he had assumed control of a rag-tag bunch of legionaries – all of them even younger than him – in the Bosporus mission. But here he was faced with men all older and more grizzled than himself, all surely more qualified to lead. *Mithras*, he thought, *surely Quadratus is the ranking infantry officer here anyway?* His eyes moved to the big Gaul.

But Lupicinus spotted his hesitation and pounced upon it. 'Ah, a *coward!*' the comes spat. 'Unable to act without the guiding hand of another, eh? Never a leader. Just like most of the dross in this so-called legion.'

Pavo bristled. He might not be a leader, but he certainly was no coward. He straightened up, readying to shout the men forward, but Lupicinus cut in.

'Centurion Quadratus, lead us forward, show the boy how it's done!'

Quadratus stepped to the fore, his movement disguising a shudder of rage and his face a shade of crimson. Still, the centurion managed to offer a nod of support to Pavo. But Pavo was staring straight ahead, hoping his veneer of steadfast attention would disguise the burning shame inside him. The comes' words echoed in his head.

Never a leader.

'Ready, advance!' Quadratus barked.

As one, the cluster of legionaries stomped forward, the timbers of the makeshift bridge creaking and bucking under their weight, the riders trotting close behind. All eyes were on the treeline. Still it writhed and, as they got closer, it seemed to jostle and judder more violently, as if something was building to a head. But what?

Pavo was almost grateful that his shame was swept away by the nerves that usually preceded a battle or a skirmish. The soldier's curse, they called it: swollen tongue, dry mouth and full-to-bursting bladder, not helped by the thundering torrents of the Danubius below.

Quadratus raised his sword, readying to stop the column as they reached the north bridgehead when, suddenly, the treeline fell still.

'What the?' Sura croaked.

'Halt.' Quadratus spoke his order in a muted tone, frowning.

Ready shields! Pavo screamed in his mind, ears honed for any sound of stretching bowstrings or whizzing arrows, his empty shield arm clenching. A chill wind whistled from upriver, snaking inside Pavo's armour and clothing. He and each of the infantry glanced back to Lupicinus. The comes had managed to stealthily remain some way back from the Roman front; there he sat on his saddle, his tongue jabbing out to dampen his lips and his eyes darting nervously across the forest in front of them. Even from here, Pavo could see Lupicinus' cuirass judder from a panicked heartbeat.

'Orders, sir?' Quadratus asked. 'A member of your cavalry might want to stoke those bushes, flush 'em out? *Show them how to launch an attack?* Or perhaps we should call for reinforcements from the fort?'

Lupicinus scowled at Quadratus' thinly disguised swipe. 'Two infantry, advance and scout,' he replied abruptly.

Quadratus nodded, then made to shout for Avitus to come with him.

But Pavo, still feeling the shame of his reluctance only moments ago, widened his eyes and nodded to the big Gaul.

Quadratus cocked an eyebrow. 'Fair enough then. Pavo, you're with me.'

They stalked off the bridge then across the wide dirt path that hemmed the northern bank of the river. Then Quadratus made a forking gesture with two fingers, each pointing round a side of the thicket.

Pavo nodded, buried his fears and set his eyes on the undergrowth. He held his spatha before him, ready to cut through the gorse bush or any Goth that might try to spring upon him.

'Wait, what's that?' Quadratus whispered from a few feet away.

Pavo squinted through into the gorse and saw nothing but a tangle of leaves and branches. Then his skin froze as he saw the outline of . . . something, something in the shade and foliage. It looked like a figure, crouching in the shadows. He blinked, sure it was a trick of the light, but sure enough, there *was* someone there. A man, a huge man.

Pavo filled his lungs to roar, when a shape burst from the gorse, butting into his chest. The wind was gone from his lungs and he tumbled back, instinctively lashing out at the figure. Then, bleating filled the air and his spatha blade stopped only inches from the neck of a panicked goat. A little Gothic boy in a blue tunic ran out after it.

The boy hugged the goat's neck, eyes wide in panic.

'My oxen! They're trapped in the swamp back there!' The boy cried, pulling the goat back from Pavo by its tether. The lad's eyes were red with tears, his topknotted blonde hair bedraggled and spattered with mud. A bout of pained lowing sounded from behind the gorse.

'It's okay,' Pavo said in a soothing tone, tucking his spatha into his scabbard, his skin prickling in embarrassment.

41

Quadratus closed his eyes, shook his head and muttered a frustrated prayer to Mithras. 'False alarm, sir,' he shouted over his shoulder to Lupicinus.

Pavo looked again into the foliage, frowning as Lupicinus' belly laughter filled the air.

'Perhaps you'll be capable of dealing with this situation, Pavo? You and Centurion Quadratus can round off this business.' With that, he swept his hand above his head in a circle. 'The rest of you, back to the fort. There is much to sort out with this sham of a legion.'

With a thunder of hooves and boots, the comes and the rest of the group were off. Pavo and Quadratus shared a dark look, then the boy tugged on the hem of Pavo's tunic.

'My oxen?'

Pavo nodded and tried to soften his expression. 'Don't worry, we'll see you safely on your way. Show me where they are.'

The boy scampered round the gorse bush and Pavo followed. As he passed Quadratus, the big Gaulish centurion grumbled, his foul glare fixed on the departing Lupicinus.

'If I ever whinge about Gallus again, kick my stones for me, will you?'

The figure remained in the shadows of the thick foliage, his gaze trained on the two Romans as they crossed the bridge into the empire again. With the oxen freed, the boy came to him, holding out a hand.

'I have done as you asked, sir,' the boy said nervously, holding out his cupped hands, screwing up his eyes at the shadows.

'Aye, you have done well,' the dark figure replied.

The boy gulped as the dark figure leaned forward just a fraction, so a sliver of sunlight sparkled on three bronze hoops dangling from an earlobe, then dropped a pair of coins into his hands.

The figure watched as the boy led the animals away, a dark cloud passing over his mind as he thought of his men further up the trail that would slit the youngster's throat. But destiny required ruthlessness and a jealous guarding of knowledge, and that destiny beckoned.

Yes, he mused; the Roman borders were weaker than ever.

It was time to begin.

Chapter 2

'No,' Pavo growled, 'take my hand!' He stretched every sinew in his arm, his fingertips shaking as they hovered only inches from Father's. The dunes all around them shimmered in the white heat of the placid but never-ending desert. The figure in front of him was barely recognisable as the powerful legionary Pavo had looked up to as a child. This man was haggard, his hair wiry and patchy, skin lined and features tired. But most horrifically, his eyes were gone and only empty, cauterised sockets remained. But he was still Father and now, stood only paces from him on the lip of this dune, he just wanted so much to embrace him once more.

'Please, take my hand!' Pavo cried out, but his own voice sounded distant and weak. That was when it always started. First, the sun darkened, then the dunes turned a sickly grey, and then the roaring began. Like a pride of lions at first, then like the cry of a thousand titans, the desert wind engulfed them and the still dunes were coaxed into a ferocious wall of stinging sand. Pavo struggled to resist the urge to blink as the boiling grains stung his eyeballs, but it was no use; the outline of Father grew faint in the storm. Only as he was about to fade completely, he lifted his hand towards Pavo's. But it was too late.

'No!' Pavo sat bolt upright in his bunk, his skin bathed in sweat and his bedding soaked through despite the winter chill in the barrack block. He saw his breath clouding in the air before him in the faint sliver of moonlight that shone through the crack in the shutters above. All around, the exhausted men of his contubernium lay in deep slumber: Centurion Quadratus, Optio Avitus, Sura and the four recruits, Noster, Nero, Sextus and Rufus. He sighed, annoyed that the nightmare had come to him for the second time that night. Then he realised that his hand was trembling, clutching the bronze phalera. He slipped the leather strap from his neck and examined it in the moonlight. His mind drifted back to that day in Constantinople's slave market, all those years ago, when it had first come into his possession.

Then, his thoughts crept to the years of servitude and abuse that had followed. The echoes of slaves screaming in the basement of Senator Tarquitius' villa poisoned his mood and quickly brought the chill through the skin to his bones.

He shook his head and wiped the thoughts from his mind. Then he reached to the bedpost and untied the strip of scarlet silk Felicia had given him. He held it under his nose; it still carried the scent of her perfume. It cleared his mind of troubles, conjuring up fleeting images of her in an inviting pose that finally dissipated into blissful sleep. But only moments after he started snoring, a wail of *buccinas* filled the fort, the Roman horns sounding for morning wake up and roll-call.

Pavo's eyes shot open, the whites bloodshot. He groaned and sat up.

'Bloody Mithras, keep the noise down,' Avitus groaned from the bunk opposite. Then he looked down to Quadratus on the bunk below. 'Mind you, it's less of a din than your farting,' he cackled. Then, when Quadratus poked his head from his bunk and shot him a serious glare, he added, grudgingly, ' . . . sir.'

'Hold on,' Sura croaked from the bunk above Pavo. Sitting up, shivering, still clasping his blanket around him, he nudged open the shutter next to his bunk. 'It's not even dawn – what's going on?'

Pavo looked up to his friend, frowning, then the pair's faces fell into a weary realisation.

'Lupicinus!' They groaned in harmony.

The sky was still jet-black and the torches around the inner fortress walls guttered and crackled. Pavo felt as if he was in some lucid nightmare; frozen, belly rumbling, tired beyond belief. *Still in better shape than some of the recruits*, he mused dryly, hearing their teeth chatter and them stamping their boots to stay warm. Behind the legionaries, the handful of auxiliaries were lined up, and a sorry sight they were: one in three had a helmet and even less possessed a shield. To the rear, the turma of equites and less-than-impressed foederati had mustered also. Then, Lupicinus' two centuries of comitatenses legionaries filed into place in armour that contrasted starkly with their limitanei counterparts. Pavo stifled a snort; so the disturbingly small total of the 'reinforced' XI Claudia – less than five hundred men – had been mustered in the dead of night by the regal arsehole that was Comes Lupicinus. Now, the blend of incredulity and rage on the faces of the front line veterans demanded an explanation.

'By Mithras, I've got work to do,' Lupicinus snorted, striding across the face of the front rank in his pristine dress-armour, his back rigid, 'but I'll make a legion out of you yet!'

His riders, mounted only paces away, glowered down their noses at the assembled legionaries, smirks touching their lips at their leader's wit. In their midst stood a filthy, bedraggled and panting Gothic villager. His hair was hanging loose and was matted with sweat and grime, his bare chest glistened with sweat and his lozenge-patterned trousers were torn and filthy.

'Now, the sharper minds amongst you may have realised that dawn is not yet upon us.' He paused, sweeping his gaze across the ranks as if to add weight to his words. 'But I have roused you for a good reason. While you were sleeping, another incident erupted in Fritigern's lands – in Istrita, a small village near the Carpates and the border with Athanaric's territory.'

A collective groan from the ranks was stifled by Lupicinus' glare.

'A fifty will be sent to the scene . . . '

'Permission to speak, sir!' Quadratus barked before the comes could finish.

46

Lupicinus glared at the centurion. 'Oh, this better be good, Centurion.'

'Including your two centuries, there are less than five hundred men left within these four walls. The remainder of the legion is scattered like chaff over the wrong side of the Danubius. Nobody knows what has become of those vexillationes, sir.'

The skin on Pavo's neck rippled as he heard the big centurion's words, almost reflecting his own thoughts. Thinking like a leader – it gave him a brief glow of warmth.

'Now,' Quadratus continued, 'should something happen here, should the Goths launch a full-scale attack on the bridge then the few hundred here could just about hold them off long enough to give us some thinking time. But if we continue to send out vexillationes . . . '

'That's quite enough, Centurion,' Lupicinus barked over the Gaul.

'But, sir, before Tribunus Gallus left on his mission, he left advisory orders that the vexillationes were to be reined in, to be brought under control – even at the risk of angering Fritigern. Surely you see sense in . . . '

'I see sense in a centurion showing obedience to his superior!' Lupicinus snapped, grappling his cane and raising it to strike, hovering just inches from Quadratus' face.

In his peripheral vision, Pavo saw Quadratus' lips trembling, not in fear, but in barely checked rage. *This could get ugly*, he feared.

But, mercifully, Lupicinus lowered his cane and reset his features to his usual haughty look, peering at Quadratus down his nose. 'Perhaps this kind of cowardly outlook is only to be expected from you . . . *limitanei!*' He spat the last word like a bad grape.

'So perhaps I should excuse Centurion Quadratus from this vexillatio?' Lupicinus mused, then a smug grin spread over his features. 'Maybe a pseudo command is in order. Yes, I seem to remember one of the more junior infantrymen who considered himself a hero.'

47

Pavo's weary mind suddenly focused and his guts turned over as he saw Lupicinus' gaze sweep along the front rank. Sure enough, it came to rest on him.

'Legionary Pavo,' he said gleefully. 'You will lead the fifty.' The comes flicked his finger to the four nearest contubernia of comitatenses and another two from the native Claudia recruits. 'I'll leave it to you to choose your second-in-command. I want you formed up with full marching equipment and rations for two weeks by the time the sun touches the horizon.' With that, Lupicinus turned to the rest of the legion and barked orders to begin double sentry duty.

Pavo's blood felt like icewater in his veins. He looked to the pink tinge on the horizon, then he turned to the forty eight formed up before him. The recruits looked petrified and the veterans of Lupicinus' centuries scowled at him in distaste. The breath seemed shallow in his lungs and his tongue bloated like bread. He opened his mouth to speak, then closed it again, glancing to the comes. Lupicinus smirked at his hesitation. Pavo closed his eyes and thought of Gallus; what would the iron tribunus say to rally his men on a frozen morning, when a treacherous march into foreign lands waited on them?

'Come on, come on! Do I have to get someone to hold your hand again?' Lupicinus abruptly interrupted his train of thought.

Rattled, Pavo turned to the men and bawled, his voice shaking. 'What are you staring at? You heard the comes: get kitted up and get back here. We move out before first light!' His words died in the air and his heart sank as he saw the recruits' faces whiten even more in fear and the scowling veterans' eyes narrow further in distaste.

'Bloody boy telling men what to do,' one of the veterans muttered to the legionary next to him. It was Crito, the towering, sunken-eyed legionary from Lupicinus' comitatenses who had looked on gleefully when Pavo had been ridiculed at the bridge the previous day. Crito sneered at Pavo, the pockmarks on his cheeks emphasised in the torchlight, before he turned and quick marched for the sleeping quarters.

48

Pavo was left standing alone, and he felt colder than ever. Then he realised he needed to choose his second-in-command and looked up, seeking out Sura. His friend was already walking over to join him.

'I'll be watching your back as usual then?' Sura offered.

'Aye, and I'll be glad of it.' Pavo forced a grin, despite the fear swirling in his gut.

As Sura followed the fifty into the barrack blocks, Pavo turned to Lupicinus and his riders. 'What's my briefing, sir?' He addressed the comes, casting a soldier-like stare over Lupicinus' shoulder and towards the horizon.

'The briefing comes in two parts,' Lupicinus replied, nodding to the filthy Goth straggler. 'The first part is as you might expect. Istrita, this man's village, is in the midst of some kind of standoff between the rebel Goths and those loyal to Fritigern. He says much blood has been spilled already, and there is much more to come.' Lupicinus slapped a hand on his shoulder, a condescending smile on his face. 'Then again, I know you'll get by; after all, you're one of the *heroes* of the Bosporus mission.'

Pavo couldn't hold back a frown as he flicked his gaze to the comes. 'Sir, I don't know why you insist on . . . '

But Lupicinus interrupted. 'And then there's the second part of the brief – far more important than slaying a few rebel Goths. You'll have another two passengers coming along for the ride.' Lupicinus opened his arms out to the door of the *principia*. There, in the doorway of the officers' quarters at the centre of the fort, stood a pair of silhouetted figures, one squat and portly, the other tall and athletic. 'Come, ambassadors, meet your guide.'

The two figures walked forward and Pavo's eyes locked onto the nearest of them: short, corpulent and waddling like an overfed goose dressed in purple robes. Then the torchlight revealed a bald pate ringed with wispy grey-blonde tufts, then buttery, pitted skin and a triple row of chins. The man's beady eyes rested on Pavo like a predator.

No! Pavo's stomach fell away.

'Ah,' Senator Tarquitius grinned like a shark. 'So the fates conspire to see us reunited, Pavo?'

Pavo's heart thundered; he hadn't seen his ex-slavemaster since the tumultuous end to the Bosporus mission. Dread gripped him to think what duplicity and scheming had brought the man here to a border fort in the dead of night. He frowned at Lupicinus. 'What is he doing here?'

'The senator is to lead the long-awaited ambassadorial party into Gutthiuda.'

'So it's happening? You're going to speak with Athanaric?' Pavo's mind raced. Despite his cynicism, this peace parley – if handled correctly – could be the key to establishing a truce with Athanaric until the Persian campaign was over and the manpower returned from the east. Yet it was to be headed up by the most odious creature he had ever known.

'Indeed, we are,' Tarquitius replied, smugly.

Then the tall, lean man beside Tarquitius stepped forward into the torchlight. 'We will do all we can to broker a lasting peace.'

All eyes turned to him.

Pavo saw that his expression was earnest, unlike that of Tarquitius. His features were sharp, his cheekbones like blades, and his green eyes alert, delicate lines beside them betraying his age. His brown locks were shot with flecks of grey, dangling on his brow in the old Roman style. He wore an eastern-style, long-sleeved tunic with a high collar, blue woollen trousers tucked into brown leather riding boots and he carried a stuffed hemp satchel.

'Ambassador Salvian,' Tarquitius announced, 'my protégé.'

Poor bastard, Pavo thought.

'Senator, Ambassador, Pavo here will head up your escort,' Lupicinus said, then turned to Pavo, his nose wrinkling. 'Pavo, you will escort the ambassadorial party as far as the crossroads by *Wodinscomba*. That's, what, some ten days march from here?'

Pavo envisioned the map of Gutthiuda, and the terrain between the fort and the rugged hollow that marked the border between Fritigern and

Athanaric's lands. 'Eight days on a quick march, sir,' he replied evenly, sensing Tarquitius' gaze crawling over his skin.

'Very well. But a quick march is less important than ensuring the ambassadorial party goes unharmed at all costs, understood?'

'What happens once we reach the crossroads, sir?' Pavo asked.

'There, the senator and the ambassador will rendezvous with,' he paused, as if he had detected a bad smell, 'Tribunus Gallus and his party. I have sent a rider ahead at full gallop to contact Gallus and his men and divert them to Wodinscomba. When you rendezvous, the tribunus will then escort the ambassadorial party to Dardarus.'

Pavo's heart warmed at the thought; Gallus was to be the man to lead the ambassadorial party into Dardarus, Athanaric's citadel. His only regret was that he could not march with them. 'And my fifty, sir, should we then wait at Wodinscomba for the tribunus and the ambassadors to return?'

Lupicinus sighed. 'Were my orders not clear enough for you, soldier? Make haste to Wodinscomba. Then, as soon as you have rendezvoused, you get your fifty to Istrita . . . and leave the thinking for the real officers and nobles.'

Pavo gulped back the urge to snort at this latest arrogant blast. Instead, he saluted, gazed to the horizon, channelled the anger into his lungs, and bellowed with all his might; 'Yes, *sir!*' Lupicinus and Tarquitius flinched at his blast before correcting their stances. Ambassador Salvian barely disguised a smirk at this.

Pavo instantly liked the man.

The gates of the fortress clunked shut and the fifty set off for the pontoon bridge. They moved at a quick march, two abreast with Salvian riding on a white gelding by their left flank and the copious burden of Tarquitius just behind on an unfortunate black stallion. They passed through a pool of thick, freezing fog that clung to a dip in the hinterland and then crested the clear, frosted ground by the training field, sparkling in the breaking dawn.

Up front, Pavo's breath clouded before him, his lips and nostrils stinging from the cold. Before leaving the fort, they had paused only to throw down some hastily cooked millet porridge and to wash it down with icy water. While the rest had gulped down their meal, Pavo had barely managed to eat half of his ration, his gut churning with anxiety. His thoughts danced with taunting self-doubt and the image of the fifty and Tarquitius scowling at him – or worse, laughing at him – from behind.

He glanced to Sura, by his side; Sura had stuck by him resolutely in his time with the legion. For a moment, a glow of optimism grew in his belly when he thought of Tribunus Gallus and Primus Pilus Felix marching side by side like this.

Then he shot a look over his shoulder, not for too long as he didn't want to arouse mistrust in his men. From his snatched glance, he could see that the comitatenses at the front of the fifty marched well, in formation and at a good pace; Lupicinus' legionaries were obviously well-drilled soldiers. But then there was the handful to the rear – the Claudia recruits; they were ragged, some falling back or marching wide of the column – only to be expected given that they only had a few weeks of legionary life under their belts. He remembered his own fledgling days when a quick march felt like outright torture. It was not so much the pace, but the relentless endurance required to keep it up for ten hours or more every day, especially when laden with the full marching kit: earth shifting basket, hand axe, pickaxe and sickle together with several water skins, a soured wineskin, wraps of hardtack biscuits, millet grain and salted mutton, all pulling at the shoulders. And then there was the mail-shirt, digging into the skin, whilst boots scraped on ankles and helmets chafed on scalps, not to mention the crux of the legionary kit: the spatha sword, hasta spear and the weighty legionary shield.

Despite this, he felt sure they needed a stern word to bring them into formation, but then doubts crept into his thoughts again; would they see it as overly heavy-handed? They were only a quarter mile from the fort after all. No, he affirmed, marching in formation was crucial for the swiftness of the mission. And potentially, he reasoned, for their survival. He would do it for his own good and theirs.

'Keep it tighter,' he roared, then took a breath and turned to finish his sentence; *tighter at the back!* But before he could finish, a voice cut him off from just behind.

'If you think you can march better than us, then drop back here and carry one of these,' Crito grumbled. The rest of the older men muttered in agreement at this.

Pavo fell silent as he glanced at the veterans. They were laden not only with their kit and ration packs, but also – in lieu of pack mules – with the goatskin and timber tent packs doubling their burden. Despite this they were marching in perfect time and formation and Crito was probably the finest example. Pavo's lips trembled as he tried to think of a line that would clarify his order, something that wouldn't sound cloying to the veterans. But too much time passed and the moment was gone.

They came to the bridgehead. There, four legionaries manned the castrum and another two milled around the giant ballista, all stamping their feet and blowing into their hands for heat. Pavo slowed and saluted, just as the vexillatio had done yesterday. 'Vexillatio, coming through,' he called to the sentries.

They straightened and saluted. Then, on seeing that no centurion or true officer marched at their head, they slumped. 'Another vexillatio? Is there anyone left in the fort?' One groaned, his words tinged with anxiety.

Pavo marched past in silence, but he heard the men of his column exchanging gripes about the situation. In the flurry of muttering and whispers, he was sure he could hear his name being mentioned in acid tones. His skin burned. He glanced up to see Tarquitius' eyes fixed upon him, revelling in his ex-slave's discomfort. Then he looked to his side to see Salvian the ambassador watching him with that earnest expression. *Probably shocked by the mumbling boy who's been tasked with protecting him*, he mused, turning to study the ground in front of him again. Then, a nudge from Sura pulled him from his own self-loathing.

'Rider approaching!' His friend cried. Then, after a double-take at Pavo's foul expression, he added; 'Sir!'

Pavo peered to the west. There, bathed in orange from the rising sun, the town of Durostorum shimmered. From the town a cloaked, hooded rider approached, dirt spraying in its wake. He squinted as the figure neared, then a warm realisation grew in his heart.

Felicia.

Her riding style was unmistakable – it was just as he had taught her and just as he himself had learned in this last year. 'At ease,' he called as he heard sword hilts being gripped behind him.

'Ave,' she called, reining the grey mare to a stop by the head of the column. Then she lifted down the black hemp hood to reveal milk-white and delicate features, blue eyes and tumbling amber locks.

'Felicia,' Pavo said, stepping forward, hoping to obscure his ridiculous grin from the fifty. She looked not only beautiful, but fresh too. All that was missing was a smile. 'I've been to the inn three times in the last week and every time you've been elsewhere. Now I find you out here, galloping at dawn near the fort?'

'You sound like my father,' she replied dismissively.

Pavo sighed. 'When will I see you again, properly?'

'When you return from Gutthiuda, presumably,' she replied matter-of-factly. Then she slid from her mount and stood close to him, taking his hands. But she was looking over his shoulder, scanning the fifty with a wrinkle on her nose. 'So . . . the rest of your contubernium – they are not with you?'

He frowned. Why should she care about them? Then he pulled her a little closer. But she continued to avoid his gaze. 'Felicia, what is this about?' He asked, even though he was sure he knew the answer. Ever since he had met her, she had flitted between two personalities: one, a vivacious young lady; the other, a driven, distant woman, far older than her other self. At first he had been confused by her changes in mood. Then he had noticed that these changes came about whenever there was mention of her older brother, Curtius, who used to serve in the ranks of the Claudia. Curtius had died in service and his death was shrouded in mystery and rumour. Pavo could have well understood her sorrow, but not the determination and steel that seemed to overcome her when the subject was raised.

She looked to him. 'Pavo,' she smiled, but it was a cheerless smile, 'when we talk again, I hope all of this will be over.' With that, she pressed her lips to his.

Pavo felt her tears blot against his cheek, but when he opened his eyes, she had already pulled away to her mare. Then she hoisted herself into the saddle, heeled the mount and cried; 'Ya!' With that, she was a hooded rider again shrinking as she galloped back to Durostorum. Pavo's eyes hung on her wake, his thoughts spinning.

'Er . . . Pavo?' Sura whispered beside him.

Pavo blinked, then spun to the fifty. The veterans wore filthy scowls on their faces. Tarquitius examined his fingernails and over-officiously cleared his throat.

'Bollocking us for formation while he stops to chat with a bit of pussy,' one veteran grumbled, nudging Crito with his elbow. But the sunken-eyed legionary simply glared at Pavo, then offered a trademark sneer when Pavo tried to hold eye contact.

At this, Pavo's neck burned. He gulped to find composure and stabbed out his tongue to moisten his lips. The grumbling of the veterans grew, some relaxing out of marching posture and formation, shaking their heads. Sura's brow was knitted in concern and Pavo was sure at that moment that the best thing would be to hand command over to his friend. But then, Salvian the ambassador looked at him, his expression sincere, and then he gave Pavo the faintest of nods, a hint of a smile touching one edge of his mouth.

It was nothing and everything, a drop of encouragement into his pool of despair. He squared his shoulders, pushed his chest out, steeled his expression and sucked in a lungful of air.

'Did I give you permission to fall out? Get back into formation!' He roared.

The men hesitated for a moment, and Pavo's heart seemed to freeze. But, at last, they tightened up into marching formation, though still grumbling. He spun round to face front and, knowing they could no longer see his face, exhaled in utter relief.

Then they set off, boots drumming on the timbers of the pontoon bridge. He noticed that Salvian had ridden level with him and he offered the ambassador a brisk nod of thanks.

Fifty two men, he mused, glancing to Sura and Salvian, and only two would piss in my mouth if my teeth were on fire.

Chapter 3

Over central Gutthiuda, the sky was an unbroken blue, the land was speckled silver with frost, and the tang of woodsmoke and roasting boar spiced the air. Tribunus Gallus and Primus Pilus Felix crouched in the tall grass by a small spruce thicket, examining the nearby Gothic farming settlement. The settlement consisted of a cluster of thatch-roofed stallhouses and a barn, where Gothic families tended to their chickens and goats. All this was set before the backdrop of the grey-black, jagged basalt peaks of the Carpates Mountains, rising from the end of the plain like fangs to mark the edge of Fritigern's territory and the start of Athanaric's dominion, the dark side of Gutthiuda.

Gallus scoured the land around the settlement, his breath clouding before him, his gaunt features drawn and his ice-blue eyes narrowing on every hint of movement. One hand rested on his plumed intercisa, by his side, and he ran the fingers of the other through his dark, grey-flecked peak of hair before reaching down to thumb the small, wooden idol of Mithras in his purse. Silently, he prayed to the god of the legions for two things; glory and death. To lead his men well and meet an honourable end would be perfect. For only death could reunite him with her. *Olivia.*

'Sir?' Felix nudged him, pointing to the north.

Gallus blinked, angry with himself for allowing dark emotion to cloud his thoughts. He turned to his primus pilus; the little Greek stroked his forked beard and screwed up his eyes as the tall grass across the plain rippled briefly. Then a lone rider burst onto the plain.

The pair tensed, readying to run for their mounts, tethered in the trees nearby. Then Gallus held up a hand as he realised it was just a farm boy. 'No, it's not them.'

With a muted sigh, the two sunk down into the tall grass again and Gallus suppressed a curse. Being still like this all morning meant the bitter cold had gnawed through their woollen trousers and tunics and into their bones. He just hoped that if and when the rebel Goths showed up, they would be supple enough to ride, allowing them to carry out their plan.

He examined the map again; the four red dots indicated the pattern of the rebels' movements, and by that logic, this settlement would be their next target. Of course, he mused, there was more than one group of rebels, but all he needed was to catch one of them, to find out more about their cause. But so far it had been like chasing shadows; the rebels would raze or pillage a settlement and then vanish before the Romans or Fritigern's men could get to the scene.

'By the end of today, sir, we'll have one of these whoresons, and we'll get them talking,' Felix said, judging his tribunus' thoughts well.

'I've got a fair idea what they will say,' Gallus mused, his eyes narrowing on the Carpates once more.

'You're certain it's Athanaric's men, aren't you?' Felix asked.

'That dog has been spoiling for a fight for years,' Gallus replied. 'He's had a hand in every modicum of trouble I have experienced in my time with the Claudia. Every single one.'

Felix frowned. 'But what about the reports – that the rebels ride not in Athanaric's colours, but under some ancient banner?'

Gallus turned to him, one eyebrow cocked. 'A distraction, Felix; sleight of hand. That's all it is. Athanaric is at least as shrewd as he is belligerent.'

'Aye,' Felix shrugged, 'this is true. It doesn't bode well for the poor sods who have to go into those mountains when the peace talks are finally arranged.'

Gallus sought his next words carefully; the peace talks with Athanaric were due to take place as soon as an ambassadorial party could be summoned and briefed. Dux Vergilius had advised Gallus that, when the time came, he and his vexillatio would be escorting the party into Athanaric's dominion, to Dardarus, the fortified citadel in the heart of the Carpates. He thought better of discussing this now, instead reaching into his pack to pull a piece of hardtack from it.

'Eat, it will fight the cold from your bones,' he said, crunching into the biscuit and gesturing to his most trusted man to do likewise.

'Agreed,' Felix grinned wryly. Then he lifted his soured wineskin to his lips, 'and a little of this will warm the blood too!' With that, Felix gulped down a mouthful of soured wine and rummaged in his pack.

Gallus folded the map. Then he stopped, his eyes narrowing, touching a hand to the frozen ground. He felt it again, the tremors of approaching riders. He looked up; Felix stared back, wide eyed, the wine-skin hovering at his lips.

'Mount!' Gallus roared.

Felix threw down the wine sack, then the pair leapt onto their horses just as a pack of some hundred Gothic riders burst over the northern horizon and swept down towards the settlement.

It was them: the rebels. They rode in silence at first, braided locks billowing, lying flat over their saddles. Then as they approached the settlement they sat upright, punching their spears in the air, throwing out a trilling battle cry. At this, the Gothic farmers dropped their buckets, tools and bundles and ran for the stallhouses, screaming. One elderly villager's cry was cut short with the swing of a longsword, a crimson spray puffing up and over the rebel who had slain him. Then the rest of the riders ploughed into the slower of the fleeing villagers, hacking, slicing and stabbing.

Gallus heeled his fawn stallion round to the south. He lifted his spatha, waving the iron blade towards a seemingly deserted patch of plain some two hundred feet south of the farm settlement. 'First century, forward!'

Then, like an iron asp, the one hundred and sixty men of the first cohort, first century rose from the tall grass. They had been decked out in the precious remainder of unblemished armour: mail vests over fresh white, purple-edged woollen tunics – with their linen spares underneath to fend off the chill – and woollen, ruby cloaks. They carried freshly painted ruby and gold shields and spathas, spears and *plumbatae* – the lead weighted darts clipped in to the rear of their shields. The iron fins of their helmets split the tall grass like a school of sharks as they marched forward.

'And let them know who we are!' Gallus cried. As he and Felix heeled their mounts into a canter and then a gallop around the flank of the approaching riders, his skin rippled with pride as he heard the baritone roar of the legionaries, backed by the smashing of sword hilts on shield bosses.

'They know all right!' Felix cackled.

Gallus looked over to see the hundred Gothic riders' charge faltering, more than half having halted altogether, heads looking this way and that at this unexpected appearance of the legion. 'Ya!' he roared, squeezing his heels into his stallion's flanks.

'They're turning, sir, they're turning around!' Felix bellowed over the chill rush of air and hoofbeats.

'Then let's make sure they turn in to the valley!' Gallus cried back.

As the first century marched on at a jog, Gallus and Felix galloped round to the north until they were within a few hundred paces of the rebel Goths. Here, just as Gallus had hoped, the rebel riders had reached a forking in the flat land ahead; one path led to the northeast and the forests, the other led into the winding valleys that hugged the base of the Carpates. *And if Athanaric has anything to do with this, then they'll stay close to his beloved mountains.* As the Goths veered left and into the valley, his eyes narrowed. It was time to find out who these rogues were.

He turned to Felix. 'You think he will be ready for them?'

Felix nodded. 'Zosimus? Aye, ready and eager, as always.'

Gallus turned back to the valley. 'Then send up the fire signal.'

A felled spruce trunk was balanced precariously on the eastern ridge of the valley. Behind it, Centurion Zosimus lay prone in the frozen grass. He shivered as he chewed on a strip of salt beef, then rubbed at his anvil of a jaw, numb from the cold, then wrinkled his battered nose as he watched the mouth of the pass.

Still nothing.

The forty men of his century lying alongside him had remained quiet in this frozen wilderness, but he could sense their frustration growing. He glanced across to the opposite ridge and the spruce trunk balanced there; the other forty of his century behind it were no doubt grumbling unchecked over there.

Then his optio, Paulus, broke the silence. 'If the tribunus is wrong about this, sir, we could be waiting here all day in the frozen grass,' he mused, squinting up at the winter morning sun, scratching at his bearded chin.

'The tribunus is never wrong,' Zosimus cast his optio a dark look. He waited until Paulus' features paled, then grinned; 'or so he would have you believe.'

Paulus reflected his centurion's grin.

Zosimus sighed. 'Look, I know how you're all feeling: I can barely feel my own arse anymore, but here, pass this around,' Zosimus lifted up his wineskin, then fell silent, realising it was already empty. His face fell into a scowl once more as he threw it down, then muttered; 'I just hope Fritigern appreciates all we're doing for him. Marching around a bloody frozen Hades to catch the men his lot should be dealing with . . . '

His words trailed off when an orange streak sped into the sky from the plains beyond. Then his eyes grew wide as they fell from the fiery missile

61

to the cluster of Gothic riders who had raced into the valley, blonde locks billowing in their wake.

'Ready yourselves,' he batted a hand across Paulus' chest, scowled along the forty who lined the ridge with him, then waved the other hand at those on the opposite ridge. He grappled at the felled spruce trunk that lay before them, his fingers blue and numb as he searched for purchase. Then, as he and his men took the weight of the timber, he hissed to them; 'Push!'

The Gothic riders raced along the valley floor at pace, and the log seemed determined not to crest the ridge of the valley. He growled, his trunk-like arms shuddering and his boots gouging frozen earth from the ground until, finally, the weight of the log was gone. He and his men rushed onto the lip to see the logs from either edge hurtling down the valley sides, converging on the path of the rebel riders.

The Gothic riders noticed when they had only moments to react. Some leapt clear of the logs, some mounts reared up and their riders fell to the ground, others pulled up short and hurled their riders forward. Those caught in the path of the colliding logs were shattered like kindling; pained whinnying, screaming and the snapping of man and animal bones echoed through the valley.

Before they could reform, Zosimus swept his sword over his head, racing down the hillside at the head of his men.

'Charge!' He roared.

'Yes . . . yes!' Gallus growled, the bitter chill rushing past him as he sped forward at a gallop into the valley. His eyes were fixed on the form of Centurion Zosimus; the big Thracian was leading his century like a lion, silhouetted in the morning sun. The screaming of iron upon iron rang out and the stench of spilled guts was rife.

He flexed his fingers and gripped on his spatha hilt again and again, casting an eye back over his shoulder to see that the hundred and sixty of the first century were not far behind. The jaws of the trap were swinging shut. The truth lay within his grasp.

'Bring them forward, in formation!' Gallus bawled.

'Aye, sir!' Felix roared, dropping back to the right of the approaching line of legionaries. Then, when they were less than a hundred paces from the skirmish, he roared; 'Plumbatae! Ready!'

At once the line rippled, each man presenting one of the three rapier-tipped darts clipped to the rear of their shields. 'Loose!' The pack of Gothic riders was shattered as the Roman hail streaked through the air and smashed into their midst.

'That's it! Break them!' Gallus cried as a second and third volley were loosed. 'Now, Felix, with me!' He roared, heeling his mount into a charge to speed ahead of the rushing legionaries.

He and Felix raced into the flank of the pack of Gothic riders where two of them were hacking at one of Zosimus' bloodied legionaries. The nearest of the riders, a fiery-bearded man, swept the legionary's head clear of his shoulders, then turned, growling, just in time to parry Gallus' strike. Gallus swivelled in his saddle and flicked his spatha up to grasp it overhand, then stabbed down through the Goth's collarbone. Blood jetted from the wound and the Goth's angry grimace melted into a grey, empty stare in moments as he slid from his mount like a sack of wet sand.

Then a longsword swept past Gallus' face, scoring his cheek. His counter-swipe at the attacking Goth fell short due to his mount shuffling back from the fray. *To Hades with this*, he snorted, then slid from the saddle. *This is where the legionary fights,* he affirmed as his boots hit the ground. Then a familiar misty red veil descended over his vision as he slotted onto the end of the approaching legionary line, raising his shield.

'At them!' He bellowed.

The cold seemed to fall away as the legionary line smashed into the Gothic riders. He hacked, stabbed and parried. All around, he saw his

63

comrades fighting, teeth bared, the whites of their eyes bulging. Then he saw one Gothic warrior, nearly as broad as he was tall, grinning like a demon as he drove his longsword through the throat of a legionary. Gallus growled and lunged for the man, sending a left hook smashing into the giant's jaw. The big man turned to face Gallus, but stumbled on the severed leg of a legionary. Crunching back onto the gore-coated ground, the giant scrabbled backwards on his palms and Gallus stalked after him, spatha raised to strike.

The big Goth brought his longsword up with a roar, parrying Gallus' strike. Then he used the moment of respite to stand tall once more, and a terrible grin split his scarred features as he came at the tribunus. A sideswipe with the giant blade came within inches of hacking Gallus' face off, and suddenly the tribunus was on the back foot.

Gallus ducked another swipe of the blade, wincing at the crunch of bone as it took the top off a less fortunate legionary's head. The big Goth stamped forward through the grey mush that toppled from the stricken soldier's skull, then hefted his blade up with two hands and hammered it down at Gallus. The tribunus could only hold his spatha horizontal to deflect the blow, sparks showering and scorching his cheeks as he fell back. Prone, he could only watch as the Goth raised the longsword again for a death blow.

Then, with a flash of iron, the Goth's severed head thudded onto his chest. The giant's body still stood, sword aloft in two hands, blood pumping from the stump that was his neck. A hand grasped the Goth's shoulder and pulled the body back, where it toppled to the ground, legs and arms thrashing. Zosimus stood there, brushing his hands together. The roar of battle died all around him as the last few Goths were slain, and one was barged to the ground and disarmed.

'Job done, sir,' the big Thracian panted, offering Gallus a bloodied forearm.

'Not yet,' Gallus clasped a hand to the centurion's forearm and hoisted himself to standing. The blood was still pounding in his ears and he could only hear his men's victory cries as a dull ringing. Then he turned to see Felix cupping the last surviving Goth by the jaw, frowning. 'But if

Mithras is with us we'll get to the bottom of this rebellion. Let's hear what this cur has to say.'

'Seems Mithras has played a cruel joke on us, sir,' Felix said dryly. 'This one won't be talking.'

Gallus frowned at Felix, then turned to scrutinise the Goth. The man was smiling, but his eyes burned like hot coals, and he clutched a rolled up piece of dark-green hide in his hand, shaking it as if in victory. Then his smile grew until hoarse laughter poured from his lips. Gallus recoiled at the sight of the blistered stump that remained of his tongue. 'What in Hades?' He shot a glance to Felix.

Then, as quickly as the man had started laughing, his face fell into a grimace and he pulled the tip of a plumbata from the hide roll and then leapt for Gallus. Gallus jinked to one side, pulled his spatha from his scabbard once more and swept it up, across the Goth's chest, smashing his rib cage. The man fell to the grass, greying, his eyes growing distant, but fixed on Gallus. Gallus looked to the man, then to each of his legionaries, then to the dark-green banner that unfurled on the ground before them to reveal an ancient Gothic banner.

From the centre of the banner, an emblem of a writhing viper stared back at them.

The orange of dawn cast long shadows across the marching camp, set upon a rise in the plains of Gutthiuda. Gallus eyed his men as they tucked into steaming bowls of millet porridge; uninspiring at any other time, the slop was going down like freshly baked pheasant now. But while his men filled their groaning bellies and warmed their blood, he hadn't eaten properly for two days. An irksome voice insisted he sit and eat with his legionaries, but a sense of unease about this whole mission just wouldn't allow him to comply.

Once again his gaze was drawn northeast, to the looming grey wall that was the Carpates Mountains. Then he turned his gaze down to the banner and the viper emblem, then sat on a log and rubbed his temples; there had to be an answer to this riddle. Yet numerous vexillationes were out here chasing that answer, and the longer they were out here, the longer the major crossing points on the Danubius were left weakened.

He picked up a twig and began tracing out the river in a patch of earth, marking the XI Claudia fort and the town of Durostorum, then the next nearest major fort some seventy miles to the west. Then he moved the twig back to Durostorum and traced a thin line across the river to represent the accursed pontoon bridge.

'Big Quadratus would defend that bridge on his own if he had to, sir,' Felix offered, nodding to the etching in the ground.

Gallus gave his primus pilus a wry gaze. 'Aye, he would. Precious few of his like left in the legion, Felix.'

Felix sat next to him. 'And don't forget Avitus; he'd be fighting by Quadratus' side till the last.'

Gallus nodded. 'But those two aside, we're down to men with little over a year's soldiering experience.'

'And there are only a few of them,' Felix said. 'Pavo has potential. He's a fine fighter.'

'Fighters I'll take, any day of the week, but its leaders we need, Felix.'

Felix nodded. 'Then Pavo will take the route every other legionary has; he'll die a fighter or he'll emerge as a leader.'

Gallus almost grinned at this.

'And what about Sura,' Felix asked. 'He's a slippery bugger. Got an eye for a plan, that one.'

Then a gruff voice butted in. It was Zosimus, licking the last of the porridge from his bowl. 'Sura? You've got to be kidding. That lad's not all there,' he tapped a finger to his temple, 'bloody mental, he is!' With that, the big Thracian sucked a mouthful of soured wine from his skin and emitted a belch that scattered the birds from the nearby spruce thicket. Then, with a chuckle, he wandered off to berate his legionaries.

'And then there's Zosimus . . . ' Felix sighed, grinning at Gallus. 'Sir?'

But Gallus' attention was elsewhere; the sentries by the gateposts were calling down for the gates to be opened. He stood and walked towards the main gate. A rider entered then dismounted and stumbled through the eating legionaries. He came to Gallus, panting, then gulped a breath in and saluted.

'Quintus Livius Ennius, of the *Cursus Publicus*. I bring a message for Tribunus Gallus from,' he took in more air and held out the scroll in a trembling grasp, 'Comes Lupicinus of the XI Claudia.'

At this, the seated legionaries issued a harmonised groan.

Gallus did not react, other than to raise one eyebrow. 'By Mithras, Ennius, that is a double blow. Comes Lupicinus is bad enough, but Comes Lupicinus *of the XI Claudia?*' He took the scroll and snapped the wax seal. Unfurling it, he noticed all eyes were upon him.

'Get this lad some porridge, then break camp and be ready to march before the sun's fully up!' He barked. The men of the vexillatio slunk away to begin disassembling the tents.

Gallus' eyes then darted across the scrawl on the paper.

. . . the parley with Athanaric will take place imminently and takes priority over all activity in Fritigern's lands. Proceed to Wodinscomba, then wait. An ambassadorial party and a legionary escort have been despatched to that location to meet you there . . .

Gallus frowned; the hollow at Wodinscomba demarcated the end of Fritigern's territory and the start of Athanaric's, and was certainly not a place any Roman would want to linger. He looked up at Ennius, brow furrowed. 'When was this order given?'

'Three days ago, sir,' Ennius panted through blue lips and a mouthful of porridge.

'And the escort?' Gallus frowned.

Ennius shook his head. 'A vexillatio levied from the XI Claudia, sir.'

Gallus punched a fist into his palm. 'Mithras!' He spat. So another vexillatio had been gouged from the already husk-like legion. As a soldier, this concerned him. As a man, it felt as though his home was being looted in his absence, and it irked him to think of Lupicinus assuming command of the place so readily.

Ennius looked momentarily startled.

'At ease, rider, my ire is not directed at you,' Gallus said. He gazed southeast to the dark forest, issuing a prayer to Mithras for the vexillatio that was to march from the safety of the empire and into this gods-forsaken land.

Chapter 4

The marching camp was enshrouded in three layers; darkness, freezing fog and then thick forest. Sitting on a log in the centre of the small enclosure, Senator Tarquitius hogged one side of the newly kindled fire. He watched as the legionaries put the finishing touches to the camp, staking their tents to the ground and battering the palisade perimeter into place.

He sighed, his belly groaning as he looked again to his prime cut of goat meat sizzling in the flames. 'Come on, come on!' He muttered and then looked up furtively, anxious that one of the legionaries might catch sight of his ample rations. *But what if they do? They are just dice in my hands,* he reminded himself with a grin. Then his eyes settled on Pavo, their so-called leader. *And this one is a weighted die indeed,* he mused as he eyed his ex-slave, stood alone and silent, examining the fortifications while the rest of the legionaries bantered. He pulled the meat from the flames and sunk his teeth into the tender flesh, juices rolling down his chins. *Yes, this boy is becoming a valuable asset indeed; he just needs to be harnessed.* His eyes fell upon the bronze phalera hanging around Pavo's neck. The piece had been given to the boy, years ago, when Tarquitius had bought him at the slave market. A withered crone had pushed the piece into Pavo's hand and then turned to Tarquitius to hiss a scathing diatribe in his ear. It had chilled him to his core, but in her words lay a sparkling gem, a precious nugget of information that would once again have Pavo in the palm of his hand. He grinned. *Yes, perhaps it is time . . .*

'Your mind is working at all times!' A voice chirped.

Tarquitius bit his tongue, yelped and then looked up to see Salvian smiling back at him – that same open, altruistic expression and half-mouthed grin that he had tolerated for the last six months. He barely disguised a grumble of discontent as he shuffled along to allow his protégé to sit. 'I muse while I sleep, I consider when I am awake,' Tarquitius said, then leaned in towards his protégé, wiping the meat juices from his chin with the back of his hand, eyes wide, 'and at all times, I am leagues ahead of my opponent.'

Salvian nodded and his eyes darted as if a great truth had been revealed to him.

Tarquitius barely suppressed a snort; this man had been through the academies of Constantinople and had learned from the finest thinkers, philosophers and strategists. Yes, he was clever, Tarquitius thought, but his mind was almost too sponge-like, so easily impressionable, lacking that vital spark. *You simply can't teach cunning,* he smirked. Regardless, Salvian would make ideal lapdog in the political world, to go alongside a military puppet like Pavo. Again he grinned.

No, the gift of cunning was only for a worthy few, he asserted. It was just such a trait that had seen Tarquitius rise through the political echelons. That rise had not been without setback and loss of face, he shuddered, remembering the dark dalliance with the Holy See that had spiralled out of control. But, as ever, he had proved indomitable until now, when he was deemed the best-placed official to face the mighty Athanaric himself. Well, he mused, he had at least shown shrewdness and temerity in bribing Dux Vergilius and buying his place on this mission.

'When we travel west, to Dardarus,' Salvian said, carving slices from an apple with his dagger, 'what approach should we take with our Gothic counterparts?'

Tarquitius frowned, his mouth agape, stringy meat dangling from his teeth. Was he being questioned by this upstart? '*We* take the approach that *I* see fit, Ambassador. You watch and learn, and you will be wiser for it.'

Salvian nodded slowly at this. 'And I value the opportunity, Senator. If there is anything I can contribute – perhaps a counter-proposal that seems to play into Athanaric's favour, something to move things along – then I'd be happy to rehearse this with you?'

Tarquitius' eyes narrowed. *Damn, that sounds good.* 'Perhaps, Salvian, perhaps. It is not the most sophisticated approach, but I'll keep it in mind – as a last resort,' he said and then sunk his teeth into his goat meat once more.

Salvian nodded graciously and then stood to leave the fire. Tarquitius watched him go, then turned back to look into the flames. His face grew red from the heat as he gorged on the goat meat and considered what was to come. The talks with Athanaric were what they were and no more. A façade shrouding the plan he and the Gothic Iudex had concocted. Power could be gained readily in times of crisis, and he had lived from meagre rations for too long.

It was time to spawn a crisis that would be remembered for a long, long time.

Pavo shivered, once more scrutinising the wooden stakes, ditch and rampart of the marching camp. Then he glanced out into the frozen night; anything could be out there, he thought, screwing up his eyes, struggling to see more than a few paces beyond the perimeter. Housing only his fifty men, the camp was a miniature of the more defensible counterpart that would be constructed by cohorts and full legions. So it wasn't strictly a marching camp; yes it would give them precious time should they come under attack, but was it acceptable? Again he agonised over whether it would be right to insist that the legionaries – tired, hungry and frozen after the third day of marching – should reconstruct the west-facing side. Then again, he mused, why not? It would be difficult to further sour the relationship he had with these soldiers.

'You have done well for yourself, boy,' a voice spoke, startling him.

Pavo spun round to see the portly figure of Tarquitius, wrapped in a blue woollen cloak, his eyes wide and keen.

'From a slave to, what, a centurion, in just a year?'

71

'I'm no officer,' Pavo replied guardedly; the Senator had witnessed the blatant lack of respect Crito and his cronies had shown Pavo throughout the march so far. 'I'm in charge of this vexillatio, but without official rank.'

'So the legions are bare, then?' The Senator's eyes narrowed and he craned in closer. 'The recruits that are coming in, they cannot backfill the shortage of manpower being sent out into these lands?'

Pavo balked at the stench of the man's breath. 'You saw the fort, the few who line its battlements, the handful at the bridgehead. Supporting this truce with Fritigern is proving as corrosive as warring with any openly hostile neighbour.'

'But how many more are to be levied from the Moesian farmlands – do you know?'

Pavo hesitated; a senator with an interest in military matters was not unusual, but this particular senator had a black history of dabbling in politics that spanned across the borders. There were no new levies scheduled before the spring, but he bit back on this knowledge and shrugged. 'I'm just a legionary,' he replied flatly.

'Ah,' Tarquitius flashed a brief grin that never reached his eyes, 'I see.'

Pavo turned to look out through the fog once more, waiting for the Senator to go away. But Tarquitius did not move.

'Her words would change your life, Pavo.'

Pavo's skin crawled and his eyes darted across the forest. *Her*; the word meant only one thing between Pavo and Tarquitius. It was the day the Senator had bought him at the slave market in Constantinople. He remembered the heat, the stench and the sense of dying hope in his heart. Then he remembered the gnarled crone who had pushed through the crowd and pressed the bronze phalera into his hand. In one heartbeat he had nothing, in the next he had hope once more. Whether she was a demented old woman or a messenger of sorts, it was as if Father had spoken to him. As if neither death nor the thousand miles between Constantinople and Father's bones in the ruins of Bezabde could separate them. He spun where he stood. 'What did you say?'

'You do want to know the truth, don't you? About the phalera?' Tarquitius' eyes glinted.

'About my father . . . ' Pavo mouthed numbly. 'Are you mocking me? What can you tell me of him?'

Tarquitius ignored the plea. 'Give me more detail on the limitanei. How strongly is Sardica garrisoned? Does Gallus plan to send any more men to bolster the barracks there?'

'To Hades with Sardica – tell me what you know!' He said, his voice cracking.

'Perhaps,' Tarquitius' face melted into a vile grin. 'But only in good time. First, you must accept that you are not to deny me any information I may require.'

Pavo frowned, hatred building in his heart.

'Otherwise,' Tarquitius' face fell sour and his lips curled in a grimace, then he tapped a finger to his temple, 'the truth will stay in here!' Tarquitius held his gaze for what felt like an eternity, then he turned to shuffle away towards the fire.

Pavo's blood ran cold with panic, and he loathed himself for what tumbled from his lips; 'There is a half cohort in the city, and another century man the fortlets and watchtowers by the river.'

Tarquitius slowed, turning back to Pavo with a sickly grin, his eyes sparkling. 'Good . . . good. Now tell me, when are the garrison due to return to the XI Claudia fort?'

Pavo frowned, shrugging. 'Whenever a permanent garrison can be founded from the local legions?'

'Ah,' Tarquitius said in resignation, 'not good enough.' Then he raised his eyebrows and fixed Pavo with a stare that turned his gut. 'If you want to know what's up here,' he tapped his temple again, 'then you'll find out the *exact* day when the garrison is to change over.' With that, Tarquitius spun to stomp back past the fire and to his tent.

Pavo's mind reeled as he watched the senator go. Then he looked over to the fire, longing to see a friendly face. But his gaze fell upon Crito; the veteran legionary stared back at him, muttering to his cronies, who looked over at Pavo then laughed. He twisted round and stared out of the camp again, past the palisade and into the fog, his thoughts churning.

'Pavo?' Sura said, coming over to him, gnawing at a piece of barely defrosted salted mutton. 'What did he say to you?' Sura frowned, casting a glance at Tarquitius' tent.

Pavo looked to his friend, his mood lightening just a fraction. 'Just his usual haughty babble – and I'm certain he's digging himself into trouble again.'

Sura nodded, unconvinced, noticing that Pavo was thumbing at the phalera medallion. 'And?'

Pavo looked him in the eye. Sura and Felicia were the only two who knew the whole story of that day at the slave market. He issued a weary smile. 'And something else. I'm not quite sure what, but I'll have to make sense of it first, before I act on it.'

Sura shrugged, nodding. 'Then you can think over it while you eat and get warmth into your veins. Come on,' he beckoned towards the fire.

Pavo gave Sura a weary look. 'I don't think my presence will be welcome.' His eyes traced the line of six goatskin tents and the huddle of veterans and recruits, now sitting as close to the flames as they could get without being singed. Only Salvian the ambassador stood back from the blaze, seemingly drawing warmth enough from a borrowed woollen legionary cloak.

'Come on,' Sura pleaded. 'Just be yourself. They're too busy trying to sink their wine ration to be bothered giving you any more grief.'

Pavo considered declining the offer, then realised the rim of his helmet was now freezing to his forehead, and relented.

As he shuffled over to the fire, the gruff chatter from Crito and the veterans died, and all eyes turned to him. But, to his relief, the Claudia recruits pushed apart to let him in, one offering up his wineskin. Pavo made to step forward, then hesitated and shook his head. 'No, you lads have your fill, I'll get my share later.' His heart warmed at the grateful nods and grins from them, but then he heard a familiar grumbling from the veterans.

'Aye, like you haven't got an officer's wine ration anyway?' Crito barked.

Pavo frowned and made to retort, but halted himself. For this mission he was not a member of the ranks, and could not be seen to bicker with the men. Instead, he sought a way to diffuse the ill-feeling. He reached down to his ration pack and fumbled with his numb fingers until he found the wax-coated disc. He had spent a good chunk of his wage on this cheese and had yet to find the opportunity to enjoy it. He walked over to the veterans and held out the round.

'I've got bugger all wine, actually,' he spoke calmly and with a wry smile. 'I picked up three skins from the warehouse this morning and it turned out they were all water!' He glanced around at the veterans, all of whom returned a stony glance. One broke ranks to chuckle at Pavo's misfortune, but was silenced with a sharp elbow to the ribs. Pavo sighed. 'Look, there's enough of this cheese to go round – get our bellies properly full before we sleep?'

A few of the veterans licked their lips at the thought, and one belly rumbled like thunder, but Crito spoke first. 'Your kind,' he stabbed a finger at Pavo, 'are going to be the death of the army and the death of the empire.'

Suddenly, Pavo felt on trial as all eyes turned on him, and only the crackling of the fire sounded. Chattering voices in his mind told him he should be shouting the soldier down for insubordination, but his tongue felt bloated and useless.

'Boys who have had a nip of blood and think they are heroes,' Crito continued, his pitted skin and sunken eyes lit from below by the fire. 'You've never seen half the action we have, but you step up in front of us when you

75

should be sat over there,' he swiped a finger at the recruits, 'while the real soldiers lead.'

Pavo's mind reeled. He had been through all of this before and had proved himself to Zosimus, Felix, Quadratus, Avitus and most importantly Gallus. He had been a whisper from death more times than he could remember in that nightmare of a campaign to the Kingdom of Bosporus. *And you'll have to do it all again*, he realised, *but this time you have to prove to them not that you're fit to fight with them, but that you're worthy of leading them.* His mind chattered with a thousand voices, each offering opposing advice, then he emitted a weary sigh; 'Think what you like,' he spoke flatly. 'It's double sentry duty tonight,' he continued. 'Finish your rations and settle in your tents. I'll take first watch. Crito, you're on shift with me.' With that, he tossed the cheese round onto the ground by Crito's legs, then turned and walked back to the edge of the enclosure. There, he pulled his grey woollen cloak tight around his shoulders as the cold crept over him again.

A lone owl hooted from a nearby pine, punctuating the random crackle of the now dying fire. Pavo stood watch by the western gate of the miniature camp. Despite the day's strength-sapping march, he found little trouble staying awake, the frost settling on his brow and nose in a fine film and the modest heat from the small brazier glowing by his feet barely registering. He glanced over at Crito again; the towering legionary stood watch at the eastern gate, and the only noise he had made was the occasional thunderous fart or serrated belch.

He touched a hand to the phalera medallion and raked over Tarquitius' words. What truth could the fat reprobate really offer him? From experience, the man was probably just torturing him with some whimsical notion, no doubt invented in the senator's head. Then he saw the withered, puckered features of the crone once more in his mind's eye, and shivered. No, her words to Tarquitius had been all too real.

And what would Father think of him now, he mused? From memory, his father had never been a leader of soldiers. Perhaps this was why he too was also ill-suited to such a role. He calculated how many more days of this torture were left and resolved that as soon as they were back in the fortress, he would explain to Lupicinus how he felt and plead to keep his place in the ranks. Then he imagined the prancing fool's expression and instantly hated himself for being so weak.

'Bloody idiot!' He hissed to himself.

'Being a bit harsh on yourself?' A voice spoke, right behind him.

Pavo turned, wide-eyed. A silhouetted figure stood there.

'Relax,' the figure chuckled, holding up empty hands and walking forward into the faint firelight to reveal keen eyes and sharp features, the mouth lifted at one end in a half-mouthed grin.

'Ambassador!' Pavo spluttered in relief. 'Never creep up on a legionary.'

Salvian cocked an eyebrow. 'Especially when he's had a day like you've had? And please, call me Salvian.'

Pavo frowned and adopted the serious, distant stare that seemed to be the norm for officers.

Salvian nodded with a sigh and a sparkle in his eyes. 'You've taken a battering over these last few days, Pavo, a real battering. I heard Comes Lupicinus crowing about his military record, then deriding the mission to the Kingdom of Bosporus. Then you've had Crito taking every opportunity to destroy you in front of the rest of the men.'

Pavo's chest burned. So he was being picked on now by this stranger. But before he could retort, Salvian continued;

'Yet look at you now; still standing, while the rest sleep, having succumbed to weariness. That tells me a lot about you, lad. You have handled the pressure so well.'

Pavo stammered, disarmed by the statement. 'I . . . I could have done better. I've led lads younger than me once before, but never veterans like this lot, like Crito.'

Salvian chuckled wryly, jabbing a thumb over his shoulder and lowering his voice so the veteran wouldn't hear. 'Crito is what most veterans are: grunts who have put their necks in front of countless enemy swords for an empire that treats them like an expendable resource – no wonder he's a grumpy swine.'

Pavo smirked at this, thinking of Zosimus and Quadratus, both with the tempers of a bear with a ripping hangover. Then he frowned; Zosimus and Quadratus commanded respect despite their gruffness, but Crito seemed spiteful to the core, and this made Pavo uneasy. It was as if the veteran's challenges to his authority were borne of pure hatred and nothing else. 'It feels as if I have a rope round my neck when he challenges me, like I want to swallow my own words.'

Salvian issued another half-grin. 'Ah, yes. Self-doubt is a pox indeed. It plagues me too – more than I care to admit. You're from the capital, yes?'

'Constantinople runs in my blood,' Pavo replied, frowning. 'What of it?'

'Well, you'll know how many pompous bastards call the place their home, pompous bastards who have seemingly been born with an answer to everything.' Salvian deftly nodded to the tent Tarquitius was sleeping in.

Pavo nodded at this.

'Well it's my job to talk with them; debates, negotiations, disputes. Their voices are like war horns and their eyes scrape at my soul as they try to shout me down. My mind screams at me; *I'm wrong*, and I just want to be out of their gaze, away from the conflict. I feel that noose around my neck, just as you do. But you know what I do? I simply hold their gaze and find silence in my mind, allow myself to think back over my decisions, see the strength of my reasoning. With that, my confidence always returns.'

'Aye,' Pavo shrugged, thinking of the pounding heart, the shaking hands and the dry mouth he had felt when Crito and his cronies had all been staring at him in derision, 'but you need composure for that. When Crito is glaring at me it is all I can do to remember my name, let alone revisit my reasoning.'

Salvian nodded. 'True, the nerves come into play when we least want them. It's easily dealt with too,' the ambassador shrugged. 'I learned this from an old senator, right before my first public debate: just breathe in through your nose, slowly,' he spoke, carrying out the action, 'let the air fill your lungs . . . until your belly expands, then hold it . . . then exhale through your mouth,' he whooshed as he breathed out. 'Your heart will steady and your mind will clear of chatter in moments.'

Pavo smiled again. 'So calmness is the key?'

'More often than not. I've lost count of the number of times I have outmanoeuvred a red-faced, ranting opponent in the debating chamber. But don't get me wrong – there are occasions when brute force is the order of the day,' Salvian continued, 'just use it sparingly, when the time is right.'

Pavo frowned.

Salvian chuckled, clasping a hand to his shoulder. 'Ah, me and my advice. Words are all too cheap! Time and experience will bring all this to you. Suffice to say, lad, that I can see in you the makings of a fine leader.'

With this, the ambassador sighed and sat his lithe frame by the brazier, then reached into his hemp satchel and pulled out a crusty round of bread. He tore a piece off and offered it to Pavo.

Pavo took the piece and munched as they chatted. As they talked, he found the biting cold lessening ever so slightly. They discussed their homes and their times in Constantinople. Salvian talked of his old grandmother who lived by the Great Aqueduct and of his adolescent days in the city's academies. Then he spoke of his trips to the West and the East where he had parleyed with the Franks and the Persians alike – and brought back a selection of those collared eastern tunics as well.

In return, Pavo talked of his time with the legion, his tone light as he remembered some of the good times that had spliced the bloodier ones. Then, he talked of his years of slavery. He spoke edgily at first, but quickly opened up after it became clear that Salvian had already guessed his history with Senator Tarquitius. To his surprise, Pavo found his words flowing as he recounted some of his memories from Tarquitius' slave cellar.

Salvian had frowned as he summarised his feelings on the matter. 'No man should be a slave of any other; the very idea is abhorrent. Sometimes I think the empire sees herself as the slavemaster of the world she has conquered, a writhing entity that can control lives and end them as she sees fit.' Then he looked up to Pavo, his eyes narrowed. 'Going by what you've told me of his treatment of you and his other slaves, Tarquitius is the embodiment of such an ethos?'

Pavo nodded and then they fell silent. There was one topic he had not broached, the topic that would surely deprive him of sleep tonight and for many nights to come.

'Now, tell me of your family,' Salvian said, as if reading his thoughts. 'Before those days you spent as a slave.'

'My mother died giving birth to me,' he said, his eyes growing distant. 'My father was a legionary. Lived as one, died as one. I miss him every day,' he said, flatly. He thumbed at the bronze phalera, then looked the ambassador in the eye. They were only to journey together for a handful of days, so perhaps revealing a little more of his past could be cathartic, he reasoned. 'This piece is all I have to remind me of him . . . ' he paused, took a deep breath and told Salvian of that day in the slave market; the crone, the phalera.

Everything.

'By the gods,' Salvian blinked when Pavo finished. 'No wonder you treasure that piece so.' Then he narrowed his eyes. 'But tell me about him,' the ambassador nodded. 'Your father.'

Pavo was hesitant.

But Salvian's expression was keen and sincere. 'You know they say that to speak of the dead is to let them live again?'

Pavo smiled at this, then stooped a little to toast a piece of bread on the brazier. 'Well, there's not much I can say about him, really. He is only a memory now. But when I was a boy . . . ' Pavo sighed as his throat seemed to contract a little ' . . . I used to live for the days when he would come home on leave. We lived in Constantinople, you see, just down from the Gate of Saint Aemilianus. A room in the tenements was our home; the usual crumbling collection of bricks and timber; to me it was just the place I waited until he returned from campaign. Then we would go out every day, at the crack of dawn. I loved to paddle in the warm waters of the *Propontus*, just by the southern shore outside the walls. Then we'd eat, and not just a little,' he realised he was grinning. 'Father would insist that we spend some of his wage on the best grub on offer. I remember one time well: pheasant, lamb, garum dates, honeyed yoghurt and blueberries, washed down with a jug of watered wine.' He looked down at the morsel of bread in the flames, brown and crisp around the edges, and chuckled. 'I can almost smell it and taste it right now.'

He turned to Salvian and was surprised to see the ambassador still regarded him earnestly, hanging on every word.

'I can hear in your voice how much you miss him,' Salvian spoke gently. 'So you are alone in this world?'

Pavo nodded. 'No, there is Felicia, the woman from the bridge. She and I are close . . . at times.'

'Ah, women,' Salvian chuckled, 'it is a struggle to see things as they do at the best of times, Pavo, but that one certainly seemed fierier than most.'

Pavo smirked, then felt a stab of guilt as he glanced back at one of the tents. 'And Sura has been like a brother to me since I enlisted. Then there are the other lads in the legion, the core that have been part of the Claudia since before my time. Then there is Tribunus Gallus,' he started, 'you may take some time to get used to him when you meet him. Despite that iron mask he seems to wear, he has guided me well, and I know he has a heart somewhere in there, but . . . '

81

'But nobody can compare to your father?' Salvian finished for him.

Pavo could only nod, unable to meet the ambassador's eyes, instead scouring the fog.

'When someone is lost to you, sometimes their memory can drive you on through times of adversity,' Salvian spoke, his voice even. 'Sometimes it can shape your entire life.'

Pavo glanced up at him; the ambassador gazed into the dying flames of the brazier, lost in some memory. Pavo frowned. *Every man has a story*, he mused. Then he thought of Tarquitius and this truth he held.

'There is something more, though,' he started, then became suddenly anxious that he would bore the ambassador with the aside.

'Yes?' Salvian urged him.

Pavo shook his head. 'It is late and it is only going to get colder. You should get into your tent and get wrapped up before the worst of it comes.'

At just that moment, a triple volley of thundering farts sounded from the tent nearest them. Pavo winced as he realised it was the tent Salvian was supposed to be sharing.

Salvian half-grinned. 'I think I'd be in more danger in there than out here, thank you. I've never been one for much sleep anyway. Now come on, tell me what is on your mind. We are to part in a few days when we reach Wodinscomba, so what harm is there in sharing our problems?'

Pavo shrugged. 'It's nothing really, well that's just the problem – I don't know if it's nothing. It's Senator Tarquitius,' he nodded to Salvian.

'Ah, yes, my *mentor*,' Salvian rolled his eyes. 'I should have guessed he was still troubling you. Tell me, what has he done?'

'The man has no shame, it would seem, in any of his dealings. But now he is dangling some notion that he knows something, something about my father.'

'How could that be?' Salvian frowned, thinking back over their chat. Then he clicked his fingers, his eyes sparkling. 'Ah! The crone, from the market?'

Pavo nodded his head and shrugged.

'And he hasn't told you what he knows?' Salvian asked.

Pavo looked up with a sardonic expression.

Salvian nodded in embarrassment. 'Of course he hasn't. Sorry, carry on.'

'He wants me to betray my legion. If it was for some small embezzlement or the like, I would not be so troubled by it – but he has a dubious track record; whenever he dabbles, blood is spilled. So I have a choice; to betray my legion and discover a truth that has evaded me since I was a boy, or to uphold my honour and deny myself that precious knowledge.'

They sat in silence for a moment, then Salvian sighed. 'I do not envy you, Pavo. But know this; men face difficult decisions every day, and the merit of their choices only becomes clear once the consequences unfold. You cannot see what lies ahead, so do not agonise over what might come of your actions. If you choose well, you are blessed; if you choose poorly, you will be stronger for it. Consider this, though; you have spent your life serving first a slavemaster and then the empire. Perhaps it is time to serve yourself?'

Pavo latched onto the suggestion. With this hint of encouragement he felt none of the guilt that he had previously when contemplating the senator's proposal. Then he noticed that Salvian was lost in thought, nodding as he mulled over his own words. Pavo sighed, smiling. 'Bet you thought you would get some light-hearted legionary banter out of me?'

Salvian snapped out of his trance, turning to Pavo with a half-grin. 'Aye, lad. Athanaric may prove to be a pussycat in comparison!'

Pavo chuckled at this.

Then, with a crunching of boots on frosted ground, Crito marched up behind them and affixed Pavo with a scowl. 'Right, that's my watch over, *sir!*' The last word was spat rather than spoken.

Salvian and Pavo spun round to see the gruff legionary pull back a tent flap then hiss inside to the two recruits nearest the entrance. 'Right, shift's up, rise and shine.' Then he swung a boot into the tent, prompting a high-pitched yelp from the young soldier on the end of it. With a chorus of swearing and muffled apologies, two recruits stumbled out into the night, shivering.

'Until the morning, *sir!*' Crito barked, gazing over Pavo's shoulder.

Pavo nodded sternly to Crito, considered giving him a word of encouragement, then saw the sneer frozen across the man's face. 'Fall out, soldier!' He barked.

Pavo walked with Salvian to the tents.

'We'll talk again tomorrow,' Salvian nodded with a half-grin, 'sir!'

'Until tomorrow,' Pavo smiled.

Noon on the eighth day of their march saw Pavo's column break free of the silver-shrouded forest and onto the grasslands of Gutthiuda. The fog had lifted, the sky was cornflower blue and unblemished and a fresh winter chill hung on the still air. The tall grass stretched for miles ahead, coated in frost and punctuated only by thatch-roofed Gothic farms loyal to Fritigern, smoke puffing from their chimneys. Wodinscomba was only a short march from here, and then the Gothic village of Istrita was another half a days' march to the north, around the mountains.

Pavo heard Crito strike up a song in praise of Mithras as they pushed through the grass, then two others joined in. There had been something of a lift in the mood of his fifty, a sense of unity. Perhaps it was down to breaking free of the oppressive forest and having a clear vista in every direction for miles, he mused. Then his gaze fell upon the black-grey jagged peaks of the Carpates, lining the horizon to the west; perhaps it was to disguise anxiety. Regardless, it was a blessed relief from the earlier part of the march.

'What's got into them?' Sura asked, nodding to the singing veterans, keeping his voice to a whisper. 'It's the first time I've seen Crito crack a smile.'

Pavo nodded, glancing back to see the veteran's cheeks reddening as he belted out the words to the song with gusto.

'You reckon we can rely on him, if there's trouble in Istrita?' Sura asked. 'He's got a reputation as a fine soldier, but . . . ' His words trailed off as he sucked in a breath through his teeth and shook his head.

Pavo made to reply with his misgivings about the older legionary, then he saw Salvian had drawn level on his mount and was listening in. The ambassador didn't say anything, but he gave Pavo a knowing look, and Pavo couldn't help but smile as he remembered their chats over the last few nights. 'I suppose you have to credit Crito for having served under Lupicinus for Mithras knows how many years without wringing the man's neck. Aye, the man has his flaws, but we all have, eh?'

Sura cocked an eyebrow, then grinned as Salvian dropped back a little. 'I see the ambassador has been filling your head with the one-liners.'

'It's nothing. He's just trying to help, to give me a bit of encouragement.'

'Smooth talker, that one,' Sura shrugged, then grinned. 'Just hope he's not after your arse.'

Pavo chuckled despite himself at this. 'You've got a way with words yourself, haven't you?'

'Finest orator in Adrianople,' Sura replied, bemused. 'I was a herald for a couple of weeks you know, had to carry and read messages to the garrison.' Then he frowned, shaking his head. 'Then they let me go – all because of one spilt skin of wine . . . and a hundred ruined scrolls.'

Pavo chuckled and then looked his friend in the eye. 'I'm glad they did; for now I have you by my side, out here.'

Sura made to reply, then simply slapped a hand on his shoulder. 'Always,' he grinned, then turned to rouse the rest of the legionaries into the chorus of Crito's song.

They marched on until the tink-tink of a hammer striking a nail drew their gaze to one Gothic farmstead: a flame-haired man worked with his boys to erect a fencepost near their thatch-roofed stallhouse, the bleating goats and sheep nearby watching on.

After a while though, the land grew more barren, the settlements thinned and the sky dulled as grey cloud gathered. Pavo examined the trail up ahead. It wound through the patchy grass and then seemed to disappear into a drop in the land between two rocky rises, pricked with decaying tree stumps.

And there were jagged, spindly shapes fixed to the stumps.

Pavo squinted to see what the shapes were, then his face stiffened when he saw them; skeletons, arms splayed wide, nailed to the trunks, the skulls etched with lifeless grins. Gothic warriors, he realised, judging by the rotting, rusting garb that clung to their bones. These would be either sacrifices to Wodin or warnings from Fritigern and Athanaric to any warrior who dared to cross into opposing territory. He realised that the legionary song had fallen into silence.

'Wodinscomba?' Sura asked, his voice tight.

'Aye,' Pavo replied, eyes fixed on the skeletons.

Then something moved, up by one of the rotting trunks; his heart leapt and the fifty behind him rippled in alarm. But then he saw the glinting intercisa helmet and mail shirt the figure wore. At that moment, another such figure climbed up onto the other side of the hollow, waving. Pavo's heart soared at the sight of the two legionaries. 'Up ahead, lads; Tribunus Gallus and his men are waiting on us.'

At this, the recruits of the fifty roared in relief and approval and even some of Crito's cronies joined in despite themselves. Pavo could not suppress a chuckle as one of them tried to disguise his cries by breaking down in a coughing fit.

The trail became ever more strewn with rubble as they descended between the two rocky rises and into the hollow. He turned to Sura. 'Make sure the lads at the back are in good formation – I don't think they'd appreciate a bollocking from Gallus.'

'Aye,' Sura replied, dropping back, 'leave it with me.'

Then, as Sura barked to the legionaries, another voice spoke beside him. 'You're getting the hang of this,' Salvian said, 'and enjoying it, going by the look on your face?'

Pavo disguised his smile. 'Oh, I've no doubt it's only temporary. I might not be smiling when faced with a thousand spears at Istrita,' he said.

Salvian laughed. 'The veneer of the officer; you're learning fast, Pavo.'

Pavo offered him a sincere nod, then smiled.

'And don't let any setbacks knock your self-belief, lad,' Salvian continued, his voice quieter now so only Pavo could hear. 'Remember that you've got what it takes. Lupicinus put you out here because he thinks you will fail, and he wants you to prove him right. Do you know why?'

Pavo sighed. 'Because he hates me?'

Salvian shook his head. 'He doesn't even know you, lad. No, it's because he hates himself. He knows he would fail were he out here as a young lad at the head of a group of grizzled veterans. I may not be a man of the sword, but I have heard much of the empire's commanders at the many feasts and talks I have attended. Lupicinus' early military record is not one to be proud of; he turned tail and fled from the battlefield in his first encounter with the Goths. Then there were tales of how he would use his men as human shields, sending cohorts to their deaths to save his own skin. Nothing was ever proven, of course. But you have seen the bullying veneer he employs today, and that is now his shield. I don't know what made him this way,

Pavo, but something in his youth must have pickled his soul in vinegar and skewed his motives.'

Pavo looked up at the ambassador. He nodded, then faced forward again, acutely aware of an odd feeling in his gut; pity for Lupicinus.

Salvian sighed. 'Anyway, talking of such characters, I'd better fall back to ride alongside my mentor.'

Pavo nodded in appreciation. 'You're a good man, ambassador. I hope we meet again. But be careful around the senator; for all his bumbling and blabbering, he's a snake.'

Salvian's features remained sincere. 'One of many, lad, one of many.' With that, he pulled on his mount's reins and fell back to the rear of the column.

Pavo was alone at the front again, and he allowed himself to smile once more. One more precious good friend in this world, he thought. Then a cry from a familiar voice split the air. 'Ave!'

Pavo glanced up; the hollow was littered with familiar faces from the XI Claudia. The mail vested legionaries were sitting on the inner slopes of the hollow. They had downed their helmets, spears and shields and were hungrily devouring hardtack, salted beef and cheese. One the size of a bull strode forward, a crooked grin etched between his anvil of a jaw and his squashed nose.

'Mithras! We must be down to the bare bones if they sent you out,' Zosimus jibed then thrust out an arm.

Pavo clasped his hand to the big man's forearm. 'Some could say they sent us to save your skins,' he joked back.

'You'd have trouble wiping your own arse, soldier,' another voice called out. Felix, the fork-bearded Primus Pilus cast a stern gaze on Pavo, then flashed a wicked grin.

Then the pair stood to one side to reveal Tribunus Gallus.

Pavo didn't even consider holding out an arm, instead he stamped both feet into the rocky ground and threw a hand up in salute. 'Vexillatio reporting as per rendezvous instructions, sir!'

He stared just past the shoulder of Gallus, but could sense the gaunt and wolf-like features examining him and his fifty. It was a look he had so often mistaken for hatred in his early days as a recruit, but had come to realise that it was just the man's way. Gallus didn't do banter, didn't deal in emotions. A good heart lay inside, but he was pure iron on the outside.

'Legionary,' Gallus said, eyeing the fifty in Pavo's wake, 'or should I call you . . . Optio, or Centurion?'

'Legionary will do just fine, sir, this is just an informal vexillatio. As you have probably guessed, we're more stretched than ever at the fort.'

'Then you'll do well to make haste back there as soon as you've dropped off this ambassadorial party . . . ' Gallus' words slowed as he looked over Pavo's shoulder, eyeing the two figures on horseback, ambling in with the rest of Pavo's column. 'In the name of Mithras, no! Tarquitius?'

Pavo could only nod. 'It came as quite a shock to me too, sir, I can tell you.'

'We meet again, Gallus,' Tarquitius spoke with his usual cloying tone.

'All too soon,' Gallus muttered in reply.

'Pardon?' Tarquitius said, frowning.

'And not a moment too soon!' Gallus spoke clearly this time. Then he turned to behold Salvian, his eyes narrowed and his lips pursed. 'And you are?'

Pavo knew that look – the same look Gallus had cast at him on their first meeting, nearly a year ago, when Pavo lay in the fort jail. The gaze reeked of mistrust and seemed to scour deep into its recipient's soul. Pavo wished at that moment he could tell Gallus of Salvian's good heart and nature, but knew that any trust from Gallus had to be earned. Hard-earned.

Tarquitius cut in before Salvian could reply. 'Ambassador Salvian has been schooled by the finest minds in the capital, trained in the arts of rhetoric, philosophy and diplomacy. Now he approaches the completion of his training, under my tutelage.'

'Unlucky bastard!' Pavo heard Zosimus mutter under his breath. At this, Tarquitius shot the big centurion an icy glare. But, before anyone else could speak, Salvian slipped from his saddle to stand before Gallus.

'Tribunus Gallus,' he saluted, 'Ambassador Salvian. The sight of your column here warms my heart. I was wary that the rider may not have been able to find you out here in these vast plains and hills.'

Pavo watched as Gallus scrutinised Salvian's sincere expression and basic garb. The tribunus' expression softened for a heartbeat, then grew stern once more. 'The rider was frozen and bleeding,' Gallus said, 'he rode like a centaur to find us; you should have more faith, Ambassador. Equally, I knew the men of my legion would escort you to us safely.'

Salvian nodded sincerely. 'They marched well because they were led well.'

Pavo's chest bristled with pride, and it was all he could do not to show it.

'Aye,' Gallus mused, rubbing his chin as he beheld Salvian, 'a master of rhetoric indeed . . . '

Salvian leaned a little closer to Gallus and issued a half-mouthed grin, nodding almost imperceptibly towards the senator. 'Those are his words, not mine. I value some of the teachings of my grandmother more highly than the endlessly-flowing verbal effluent of the pompous togas in the capital.'

Pavo watched as Gallus' gaze remained flinty. Then, for a heartbeat, the tribunus' lips twisted up at the edges into a faint smile. It had taken Pavo the best part of six months to elicit such a response from the man.

'What was that?' Tarquitius squawked, leaning forward in his saddle.

'Right!' Gallus shouted, pretending not to hear the senator. 'There is a Gothic Iudex to be calmed, not half a days' march from here. We march immediately. Then Pavo and his men need to make haste back to the fort.' He spun to Pavo and Sura. 'But be on your guard, for rebel riders are roaming these lands.'

Words of correction spilled into Pavo's throat, but he caught them just in time – experience had taught him it was folly to talk over an officer, especially this one. Then, as the two hundred and forty legionaries formed up into a marching column, aided by Felix's bellowing orders, Pavo sidled up to Gallus.

'Sir, we're not going back to the fort.' He said as the tribunus made to mount his fawn stallion.

Gallus froze, one arm across the saddle. 'Tell me this is a joke, soldier.'

Pavo forced himself to maintain eye contact with the Tribunus. 'I wish it was, sir. It's another disturbance, north of here, around the mountains. Istrita.'

'Rebels?'

'Aye. Quadratus was adamant that we should follow your advisory orders and bed in until we had more available manpower, but . . . '

Gallus held up a hand to stop him. 'But Lupicinus knew better.'

Pavo nodded.

Gallus shook his head, his gaze tracing the frosted rubble underfoot. Then he looked to Pavo, his ice-blue stare intense. 'All these vexillationes out here, scattered and far from home.' He looked up, across the horizon. 'Go to the village, sort out the mess there, and then get back to the fort, Pavo. But by Mithras do it fast. For I fear there is a snake in the grass, and out here,' his expression darkened as he scanned the plain behind Pavo, 'we are in its sights.'

Chapter 5

Gallus squinted ahead and gritted his teeth once more as he beheld the bald-headed, wobbling mass that was Senator Tarquitius, wrapped in a dark-blue cloak over his senatorial toga and sat on some poor bastard of a stallion.

'Comes with his own insulation, that one, eh, sir?' Felix whispered from his side.

'Aye, and his own horseshit,' Gallus nodded. 'It galls me to say it, but he is going to be the difference between war and peace with Athanaric.'

'Then Mithras help us,' Felix replied solemnly.

They fell silent as they approached the base of the Carpates. A rocky corridor led through the mountains, right into Athanaric's heartland. A pair of Gothic spearman stood on the outcrops above, one on each side of the pass. They were dressed in red leather cuirasses and woollen breeches and carried longswords and round wooden shields. They sported long blonde locks tied into the distinctive topknots favoured by their military. The pair glared down on the approaching column and the silence was broken only by a stiff, whistling wind.

'Friendly bastards, eh?' Felix whispered.

'I expected nothing less,' Gallus replied, flicking his gaze briefly up to the sky, now blemished with gathering grey clouds. Then he raised a hand. As one, the column stopped, the mounted figures of Zosimus, Felix, Tarquitius and Salvian flanking him.

'Ave!' Gallus called firmly but without warmth. The Gothic sentries did not reply. 'I am Tribunus Gallus of Legio XI Claudia Pia Fidelis. I have escorted an ambassadorial party here to speak with noble Iudex Athanaric, he has been expecting such a meeting for some months.'

The sentries looked at one another, then glared back down. One of them nodded and swept a finger across the five on horseback. 'You may ride through.' Then he squared his shoulders. 'But the rest of your soldiers can go no further.'

Gallus gripped the reins of his stallion until his knuckles turned white. The land ahead was doubtless garrisoned with thousands of Athanaric's finest cavalry and infantry, yet he was being stripped of his handful of men like some untrustworthy brigand. This whole sortie was getting so one-sided it was almost a taunt.

'Don't give them the excuse,' Salvian whispered by his side. 'I can see it in his eyes, he wants you to react.'

Gallus turned to the ambassador, his teeth gritted, then felt his rage dissipate just a fraction; Salvian seemed a good judge of character and intention.

The colour returned to his knuckles and, reluctantly, he turned to Zosimus. 'Lead the centuries southeast, back to Fritigern's territory, then make camp there. A good, solid marching camp,' he nodded firmly, 'and we'll be back to lead you home by sunrise in two days' time.'

The grinding of Zosimus' teeth was audible over the wind.

Gallus looked to the centurion. The big man was utterly fearless, and the promise of riding into Athanaric's lair thrilled Zosimus as much as it terrified the others. And that was just why Gallus trusted him implicitly. 'I'd rather have you by my side through there,' he nodded to the pass, 'but I need you to lead these men until we return.'

'Yes, sir,' Zosimus relented. 'We've got your back covered, sir. But I want one of my best men with you,' the big centurion replied with a sparkle in his eyes, then slipped from his mount and handed the reins to his optio, Paulus. 'Defend these men with your life, Paulus.' With that, the big Thracian swaggered back past the column, barking orders. Then the *aquilifer* raised the legion standard and the legionaries snaked round behind him to head back down the trail with a rumble of boots, shields and iron.

Gallus twisted back to face the mountains and the Gothic sentries.

'Now you may pass,' one sentry spoke. With that, he lifted a horn to his lips and blew, conjuring a baritone moan that echoed through the pass and all around.

The five riders moved into the pass at a gentle trot. Paulus brought up the rear, one hand on his spatha hilt and his eyes trained on the crevices and boulders lining the walls of the rocky corridor. The basalt-grey passage wove through the mountains for some quarter of a mile in front of them, but they could see the frost-dappled green of a plain at the far end. The clopping of their mounts' hooves on frozen ground echoed in the corridor as if a full cavalry wing followed them. But the stark truth was that five men of Rome were riding into the Gothic heartland alone.

'I feel like we've been stripped of our swords, shields and armour,' Felix muttered.

'That's not all,' Gallus replied through taut lips, staring straight ahead. 'Listen. Don't look up, just listen.'

Felix frowned. 'Eh?'

'Yes, in the gaps between the clopping of hooves,' Salvian joined in, nodding to Gallus, 'can you hear it too?'

Felix's eyes darted across the ground in front of him as he concentrated, then his face fell. Every so often, the juddering vibration of tensing bowstrings sounded.

'They've probably got a hundred chosen archers up there, arrows trained on our necks. We're walking through a perfect kill zone.'

'But why?' Felix hissed. 'We're on a peace mission?'

Gallus shook his head wryly. 'We're at the mercy of Athanaric's whims now, and he's a capricious whoreson.'

'What are you muttering about?' Tarquitius cut in, his high-pitched warbling filling the pass and startling the others.

'Just keep your head and your voice down and ride straight,' Gallus growled, 'if you don't want an arrow in your throat.'

Tarquitius' face paled, his lips flapping as if to speak, but he was mercifully silent.

As they approached the end of the pass, Gallus wondered how a naturally defensible land like this had ever fallen from the grip of the empire. Dacia had been hard won, hundreds of years previously, and the tragedy was it had not been lost to an enemy, but evacuated wilfully. Now the past had come back to haunt the empire, with its fiercest adversary bedded in inside the protective crescent of these great mountains.

Then the ghostly orchestra of wind, hooves and bowstrings dropped away as they rode out of the pass. Another two Gothic sentries eyed their progress from above as they rode out onto the plain enclosed by the mountains.

Gallus gazed in wonderment at the sight: this heartland of the so-called barbarian Goths was thriving and organised. The bulk of the plain was dotted with farmsteads, smithies and workshops. These buildings were surrounded by fields, a patchwork of brown fallow and hardy winter crop, where men, women and children worked the land with oxen, ploughs and sickles. On the wide dirt roads linking these settlements, carts laden with supplies of wheat, barley, peas, beans, flax, linen, leather and iron ore rumbled from place to place. Where the land was unfarmed, horses grazed in their hundreds; tall and strong beasts befitting the image the Goths held as fine horsemen. Then Gallus started at another moan of a Gothic horn. He and the other four darted their eyes to the north of the plain. There, cupped on its northern side by the mountains, stood a thick, stone-walled citadel.

'Dardarus,' Paulus whispered from behind.

'Aye,' Gallus nodded, 'a far cry from mud huts and palisades, isn't it?'

95

The Goths tended not to fortify their settlements, using timber palisade if anything at all, but Athanaric had clearly veered away from that tradition with this place. The walls were sturdy, at least twice the height of a man and broad as a bull as well by the looks of it. Probably built on ancient Dacian foundations, Gallus thought, noticing the huge limestone blocks that formed the lower half of the wall. Six thick stone towers punctuated the bulwark, each stretching another five feet up and capped with timber covered guardhouses, where huddles of chosen archers stood, watching the activity on the plain. Between the towers, the battlements were dotted with the conical iron helms and speartips of Gothic sentries.

The moaning sounded again as the gates swung open and a party of Gothic cavalry rode out.

'Looks like we've got a welcoming committee?' Felix said.

'Relax,' Salvian replied. 'I'll introduce us as exactly what we are – a peace envoy.'

Tarquitius clumsily heeled his stallion forward. 'No, you will not. I will be speaking and you will be watching, learning.'

'Senator,' Salvian spoke evenly, 'would it not be more becoming of you to maintain a dignified, almost majestic silence for now? After all, these are only lowly cavalrymen. Then, when Athanaric is present, and you do speak, it'll lend all the more weight to your words.'

Tarquitius shot a furtive glance around the four of them. 'Yes,' he muttered. 'Perhaps.'

Salvian turned to Gallus and issued a wry half-grin.

For the second time that day, Gallus smiled. He realised that disliking this man was going to be difficult.

The light was almost gone as Pavo's fifty approached the edge of the pine thicket. The night sky was full of thick cloud, and only fleeting appearances of the waxing moon illuminated the flatland ahead.

Then they saw it: Istrita.

The circular, timber-walled settlement was elevated on a small hill and was ringed by a ditch and rampart. Firelight and shadows danced on the thatched roofs of the dwellings inside. Four squat timber watchtowers rose above the walls, one either side of the gate looking south and two on the far side of the village, looking north. Pavo could make out a pair of sentries on the platform of each. As they neared, a heckling of many voices grew louder, then, with a violent smash of clay, a collective cheer erupted.

Pavo's step shortened instinctively at the noise, and he heard the ripple of armour as the fifty behind him did likewise. His eyes hung on one thing; a pole protruding from the centre of the village. From it hung a blackened, still smoking body. At the tip of the pole, a dark-green banner fluttered in the breeze, and a snake emblem was woven into its fibres.

'Lupicinus said there was some standoff between Fritigern's villagers and the rebels?' Sura said beside him, his breath clouding in the chill. 'Well I don't know about you, but I'd say the rebels won?'

Pavo looked to his friend, then glanced round at the clutch of wide-eyed and doubt-ridden faces behind him. His throat dried out as he felt the weight of expectation fall upon him; all of the fifty were glancing at him and then the village. He weighed the next move in his mind and two options materialised: to march on the village, or to wait out here for dawn. Then he remembered Gallus' words.

Go to the village, sort out the mess there, and then get back to the fort, Pavo. But by Mithras do it fast. For I fear there is a snake in the grass, and out here, we are in its sights.

If Gallus' suspicions were correct then waiting for dawn could be a fatal mistake, he realised, as any roaming rebel riders could hack down fifty legionaries isolated on flat ground like this. He looked up to eye his fifty.

'We should leave it till morning,' Crito said before Pavo could speak. 'We'll get a clearer picture of the place then. Besides, we're all tired and hungry – we need to rest.'

Pavo spun to him, angry with the veteran's interjection but also anxious at his decisiveness and confident tone. And all of Crito's cronies were nodding, murmuring in agreement. Pavo felt his heart shrink. Perhaps the veteran was right; despite Gallus' advice, the land around Istrita seemed to be deserted and this thicket offered a modicum of shelter; maybe waiting out here until daylight was the safer option.

No, he insisted in his mind, *Gallus has been out here for longer than Crito or anyone else in the fifty, and he is the far more experienced soldier.* He felt his heart thunder as he tried to assemble the words of his argument for marching on the village here and now. His tongue felt bloated like a damp loaf of bread, and his lips seemed like dry, taut rope.

'We should march on the village to . . . ' he started, the prickling doubt in his chest choking his words.

'What's that?' Crito cut him off, cupping a hand to his ear, exaggerating how little he had heard.

Pavo spun away, humiliation burning on his neck, pretending he was eyeing the village. At that point, the words of Salvian floated into his head, and he saw the ambassador's calm, cool countenance in his mind. *Breathe in through your nose, slowly. Let the breath fill your lungs . . .* Pavo did this, certain it would not be enough. But he felt his heart slow again, and his blood seemed to flow warmer and smoother in his veins, the jitteriness in his limbs subsiding. He turned back to the fifty.

'We march on the village tonight,' he said, his words even and his tone a little deeper.

Crito gasped, shook his head, then his lips twisted over gritted teeth. 'Then you'll be sending fifty men better than yourself to their deaths . . . *sir!*' He spat the last word like a piece of gristle.

Pavo felt his shame of moments ago boil into anger, and realised his own lips were twisting to match Crito's expression. The first words of a

98

bitter retort danced on his tongue, then he heard another smash of clay from the village and saw fear dance across the faces of the fifty. He sighed, closed his eyes and dropped his hands to his sides. He focused his thoughts and worked back over his reasoning. Then he looked up to set a sincere gaze on Crito.

'I want every one of us to return to our homes as soon as possible, safe and well. You make a good point, Crito,' he said. Crito seemed disarmed by this statement, his grimace falling. 'So three of us will reconnoitre the village, while the rest stay out here, safe and concealed.' He looked to the rest of the fifty. 'You can eat your fill and slake your thirst until we return.'

The legionaries looked to one another, each checking for looks of dissent on the faces of the others, but finding none. Pavo glanced to Sura, who wore a look of relief.

'Habitus,' Pavo barked at the beanpole legionary, one of Crito's cronies, 'If we don't return for whatever reason, if anything should happen to us, you should return to Wodinscomba and look to rendezvous with Tribunus Gallus and his men when they come back through that way on their return from Dardarus.' Then he nodded to the two men nearest to him. 'Crito, Sura, drop your shields and spears; you're with me.'

With a grumble, Crito jogged forward to join Sura. Then the three set off, stalking forward in a crouch to stay low and in the shadows as they neared the ditch surrounding the settlement. Mercifully, the Gothic sentries on the watchtowers seemed more interested in the source of the commotion inside the village than the night shadows outside. Pavo and Sura slid down into the ditch and then scrambled up the earth rampart to push their backs up against the timber palisade. There, they fired glances at Crito, still climbing from the ditch, then to the tip of the wall and then to the village gate. Another raucous cheer erupted from within the village along with a smash of iron upon iron.

'Sir!' Crito hissed.

Pavo didn't turn to the veteran, instead locking his gaze on the guard towers. 'For Mithras' sake, Crito, keep your voice down!'

'Sir!' Crito said again, this time in a half-hiss, half-yelp.

Pavo spun to him; Crito was some five paces away, ducking near the top of the earth rampart, eyes wide and mouth agape. He followed Crito's panicked stare and gawped at the dark shape that lumbered towards them.

A sliver of moonlight revealed a hulking Gothic warrior, bare-chested, skin and hair coated with black dirt, spear hefted in his hands. Pavo grappled at his spatha hilt, when footsteps sounded from behind him. He spun to see two more dark shapes rounding the walls on their other flank. Pavo rushed to meet the nearest of them, but the Goth swung his spear shaft like a club. Pavo's nose cracked and a white light filled his head.

Darkness took over.

Chapter 6

In the attic of a stall-house in the heart of Dardarus, Gallus knelt, alone, whispering the last few words of his prayer to Mithras. He clutched the wooden idol to his heart, all the while seeking out the wraith-like memory of his long dead wife, but begging the deity of the legions for the strength to go on without her. He took a breath to begin the prayer yet again, but hesitated on noticing an orange glow of torchlight dancing outside the open shutters. At that moment he realised he had been praying since mid-afternoon.

Enough for today, he told himself, standing. He tucked the idol into his purse, stifling the long-buried, stinging sensation of sorrow behind his eyes.

He firmed his jaw, then wrapped his ruby cloak around his shoulders. Then he glanced around the timber floor and whitewashed stone walls of his room in search of some form of distraction. The room was sparsely furnished; tucked into the corner was a bed topped with a hay mattress and thick woollen blankets. In the other corner, by the open shutters, there was a chair, an old oak chest and a table, stocked with a jug of fruit wine and a jug of water, plus a loaf of wheat bread and a bowl of cherries. He lifted the water jug and filled a pewter cup, before draining it in one gulp. Then he found his gaze was drawn to the shutters and the vista of the winter's night outside.

He rested his palms on the window ledge, framed with thick thatchwork, and studied the scene; it had begun snowing heavily, he realised. The Goths shuffled through the wide streets, cloaked in snow. The jagged tongue of the locals intermingled with the crackling of torches. The firelight

2

222

2

from the city houses and streets cast a haunting glow up the side of the sheer mountain that formed the northern wall of the citadel.

He chuckled wryly; the setup inside the walls of Dardarus only served to further blow away the Roman misconception of the Gothic lifestyle. Yes, the citadel lacked the finesse and architecture of Roman cities, but the streets were wide, the defences sturdy and well thought out. The buildings, although mostly timber, wattle and daub with thick, thatched roofs, were stocky and hardy, their foundations sunken firmly into the bedrock. But there was one aspect of the skyline in particular that kept drawing his gaze: the feasting hall, where the talks were to take place.

That afternoon, when they were escorted through the streets of Dardarus they were, no doubt intentionally, taken past this impressively long and sturdy structure that seemed to be central to the citadel. Outside the hall was what looked like a muster area with a tall pole erected in its centre, bearing a pagan banner depicting a boar on an emerald background. Any doubt that this was testament to Athanaric's firm rejection of Christianity was dispelled with one look at the bloodstained earth around the foot of the pole. How many young women's throats had been opened on that spot in sacrifice and in search of Allfather Wodin's approval of their warmongering? Gallus' eyes grew distant; *and how many poor souls have died on Rome's swords?*

He spun from the shutter and placed his intercisa helmet on his head, the short plume adding to his height. They had been told that Athanaric had chosen to wait until the evening to meet them – a blatant show of power and control, Gallus thought. But now evening was upon them. Any moment now they would be summoned to eat and then talk with the Gothic Iudex and his trusted men. Gallus had never felt less hungry or talkative. He had once dined with Emperor Valens himself and almost felt choked by the formality of it all, but this would be something different entirely. This would be like dining in Hades.

He glanced through the door of his room, lying ajar, and across the corridor to Salvian's room; the ambassador's door lay shut. In the briefing scroll delivered by Ennius the rider, Dux Vergilius had rambled like a poet.

Tarquitius and Salvian are men with gilded tongues and jewels for minds. Gallus was sceptical of the rhetoric as usual, and the description was certainly ill-fitting of the odious Tarquitius. But he liked what he had seen of Salvian so far; a sincere man who could also employ a dry wit when it was called for. Then he remembered the dux's insistence that Gallus was to stay with the pair at all times to ensure their safety. *Their loss would be more costly than an entire cohort of your men, Tribunus; guard them with your life!*

Gallus grimaced, drained his cup of water, then strode across to Salvian's room. He lifted a hand to knock on the door, but it opened silently under his weight on the floorboards. The door swung open to reveal a neatly made bed with Salvian's satchel upon it, and then the ambassador, in the corner of the room, pulling on his white, eastern-style tunic.

'Ambassador, I expect we will be summoned . . . ' Gallus begun.

At this, Salvian started, spinning to face Gallus. 'By the gods!' He exclaimed, wrenching his tunic on. 'You mustn't creep up on me like that, Tribunus.'

Gallus cocked an eyebrow in bemusement; so the man was flappable after all.

Then Salvian composed himself and cocked his familiar, half-mouthed grin as he slid his legs into his woollen trousers. 'You should see about getting new hobnails in the soles of your boots!'

Gallus chuckled despite himself.

Then, without warning, a jagged voice spoke, right by his shoulder.

'Iudex Athanaric is ready for you now,' a granite-featured Gothic warrior spoke in broken Greek, 'follow me.' With that, the warrior turned and strode down the corridor.

Gallus shared a cagy glance with Salvian, then darted back into his room to pick up the rolled-up snake banner before following the big warrior.

When they reached the end of the corridor, Gallus was warmed by the sight of Felix and Paulus, equally adorned in polished armour, with Tarquitius in his senatorial robe.

'The empire's finest, eh?' Then he turned to address Tarquitius and Salvian. 'Remember that we're there by your side. Just give me a nod or a glance if things start to spiral out of control.' He eyed each of them. 'Are you ready for this?'

Salvian gave a subtle nod of affirmation.

Tarquitius wore a tormented expression of bagged-up fear and desperate ambition. 'I was born for this,' he proclaimed, his shrill tone filling the corridor.

As the Gothic warrior led them from the stallhouse, Gallus walked beside Felix. 'I'm more concerned about that overfed snake than the Goths right at this moment,' he whispered, the creaking boards disguising his words.

Pavo's ears were still ringing and his vision was little more than a pool of murky shapes. He felt hands grapple at him, lifting him to standing. He groaned, swaying on the spot, squinting at his surroundings: he was in some kind of stony basin. A ring of blurry shapes writhed and it seemed as if a thousand harpies were screeching all around him. Then, one voice cut through the din, barking in a jagged Gothic tongue, then repeated the message in broken Greek.

'And facing mighty Adalwolf, crusher of skulls, drinker of blood, grinder of bones, is . . . '

Pavo almost spluttered out in dry laughter. As his vision began to clear, he wondered what poor sod was being pitted against such a creature. Then he wondered what the dark mass right in front of him was. Then he realised it was a man. A giant of a man whose bald head seemed to be fused to his shoulders without the need of a neck, and his expression was one of indulgent rage. He was clad in an iron scale vest over a woollen tunic and he carried a weighty longsword in each hand, the veins in his tree trunk arms bulging as if trying to escape from the skin. His eyes were trained on Pavo and his face was split with a predatory grin. Pavo had a distinct feeling that this was Adalwolf.

Oh, bugger!

' . . . the brave but foolish Roman warrior, who comes to storm our village with two men by his side. Ready yourself, Roman; meet your fate with the honour your people talk of as if it belongs to them alone.'

His senses sharpened by this, Pavo blinked at the warrior, then shot glances all around: they were inside Istrita and in some crude stone-ringed gravel pit with a large timber cage at the far edge. A triple tier of timber benches encircled the pit and formed an arena, the seats packed with baying, snarling Goths – the whites of their eyes and their teeth glinting like hungry wolves in the torchlight. All of them were warriors – no women, elderly or children in sight. He glanced up at the Goth who had announced the bout. The stocky man was sitting on a timber chair, erected on stilts about the height of two men above the other benches of the arena.

Pavo made to roar at the speaker, when unseen hands pressed a spatha hilt into one hand and a round, wooden Gothic shield into the other. Then his helmet was pressed onto his head. He spun round to see the two Gothic warriors who had armed him, scuttling away, climbing out of the pit to their seats.

'Pavo, duck!' A hoarse voice called out from his side.

'Sura?' Pavo swayed around to the direction of the voice. Blinking, he saw his friend, bound at the wrist with Crito, the pair kneeling at the edge of the pit. Sura's face was filled with horror. Then a fist that felt like a jagged rock hammered into Pavo's cheekbone. His helmet flew from his head and his vision filled with white light once more and he flailed backwards, until he slammed into the pit wall. A roar of delight poured from the crowd at this.

Shocked back to his senses, Pavo twisted round to behold the giant who had almost shattered his cheekbone. It was only now that he noticed the corpses of Adalwolf's previous opponents – Fritigern's Goths by the look of it – lying in bloody streaks around the arena, entrails dangling from gaping sword wounds. He glanced back up at the big warrior and the bloodied blades in his hands and felt his gut turn over.

The giant lunged for him, swinging one of his swords. Pavo ducked, the blow swiping through the air, skimming his scalp. A chorus of frustrated groans rang out at this.

Pavo rolled away from the lumbering giant, who followed him, cackling, spinning each of his swords as if they were kindling.

'Gut him!' One young Gothic warrior screamed, pointing a finger at Pavo, his face contorted in anger. Pavo glanced to him and then back to his opponent, his mind reeling. If he was to fight, there was a good chance he would be killed by this monster. If he was to fight and win, the Goths would kill him anyway. If he was to refuse to fight, he would be killed. This fine array of choices did little to still his thundering heart.

He ducked under another sword swipe and crashed back against the timber cage by the side of the arena. Hands shot out through the slats, grasping at him. Caught, panic welled in his heart as the giant rushed for him, then a voice hissed from the cage. 'They are coming, Roman, they are coming!'

Pavo shrugged free just as the giant's sword swing smashed into the cage, and he scrambled back to see hundreds of faces in the gloom within the barred enclosure; warriors, women, children and elderly alike – the populace of the village, he concluded. One man pressed his face against the cage from inside, his eyes wide with fear and his shattered nose oozing blood. 'They are coming,' he repeated.

Pavo frowned. Then a hiss of iron cut through the air and he snapped to his senses, leaping back as the giant's blade scythed down on the spot where he had stood. Then he pulled his shield before him. As the giant closed in, Pavo snarled at the man seated on the elevated chair. 'You're a fool if you think this will go unpunished.'

'And who would punish us, Roman?' The man roared. 'The fools still loyal to Fritigern?' He pointed to the cage. 'Or perhaps the fifty Romans cowering down the track in the thicket? I don't think so. If they move a step closer to my walls, then my archers will puncture their hearts! And if they stay outside, then they will not see the morning . . . '

Pavo roared in frustration, then he braced as Adalwolf swung both of the longswords round to smash them into either side of his shield. Pavo's arms shuddered from the impact and the shield splintered on both sides. One more smash like that and the shield would be gone. Then, as the giant heaved his weapons up and round to repeat the move, Pavo saw the opportunity; Adalwolf's chest was exposed. To slide his spatha up under one of the scales would be a death blow, but it would be the death of the three Romans as well. He had to keep the fight going, to gain time to think, so instead he lunged forward, punching his shield boss into the man's breast. The giant's swing was checked by the strike and he staggered backwards, retching, spitting bile into the gravel.

But Adalwolf was stilled for only a moment. Pavo lifted his spatha to parry a downward slash, then the follow-up slash with the second sword, both strikes by the heavy weapons jarring his shoulders, numbing his arms. He staggered round to the man's flank and threw a jab at the binding in his scale vest, just above the kidneys. The strike was weak and Pavo fell back with a yelp, clutching the torn skin on his knuckles.

'No more running, Roman,' Adalwolf purred, 'stand and fight. I will tear out your throat, then those of your friends.'

The giant's words were gleeful, and Pavo's blood ran cold. He braced himself, trying his best to shut out the hundreds of snarling faces all around them. His yell of pain had honed their thirst for blood. Then, for an instant, he froze, realising that even the wall guard had turned to look in on the village, absorbed by the spectacle. He thought of Habitus and the others outside, and prayed they would spot this, prayed they would disobey his orders. Then the giant came at him, roaring.

The warrior's arms and blades were a blur such was the speed and power of the attack, and Pavo could only parry instinctively. With every strike, he realised he was being driven back. First at a stalk, then at a stagger, now he was practically running backwards. The shrill roar of the crowd grew deafening, then he heard skin tear and felt a searing pain across his neck, numbly realising he had suffered a cut across the throat. A cold terror gripped him; if it was arterial then he had moments at most.

Better to go out fighting, he resolved with a grimace. He let his fear swirl into anger, then lunged forward, punching through the sword-swipes of the giant, spatha tip aimed for the man's heart.

But all he heard was the scream of iron as his sword spun from his hand and up into the night sky. Silence fell on the arena. Then, as one, the crowd erupted in a cacophony of laughter. Pavo's vision began to spot over – he was spent and weaponless. The throat wound was superficial, but it mattered little now. Adalwolf stepped forward, placing the edge of each of his swords by either side of Pavo's neck, lining them up carefully, readying to swing them together. Through a grin, he hissed; 'I will keep your head, Roman, to remind me of this day.'

Pavo stared through the giant, numbly, and his eyes started to close. Then something flashed in the night sky, catching the moonlight, silently streaking towards them. Pavo and Adalwolf started, turning to it. Pavo recognised the missile at the last moment, and ducked back. With a meaty punch and a dry cracking of bones, the plumbata burst through the giant's throat, severing his spine and twisting his head to an unnatural angle.

Pavo stepped back, his face spattered in blood and gristle. Adalwolf's body toppled away, the double longswords still clutched in his hands. There was a hiatus of barely a heartbeat as the crowd looked on, stunned, while their mightiest warrior's corpse spasmed in a pool of its own blood. Pavo looked to the timber watchtowers: where the Gothic sentries had dropped their guard for only moments, slumped corpses now lay, impaled by Roman spears and plumbatae. Dark shapes were dropping over the wall and into the village. The fifty had heard his prayers and pounced on the Goths' moment of lapsed concentration.

Then the rebel leader stood, eyes wide, scanning the timber walls. 'To arms, we are under attack! The wall guard have been . . . ' his words were cut off as Sura and Crito, still bound, clambered up onto the arena benches and then rushed at the foot of the chair to barge it back until it rocked and toppled into the crowd. Then there was a hissing and the sky glinted once more, this time with an organised volley of some fifty plumbatae. Chaos erupted as the missiles hit home, striking down the Gothic warriors.

'The legions are coming!' One warrior cried out.

The rebel leader scrambled from the toppled chair and slapped him, then barked and yelled in a vain attempt to rally his men. 'Stay your fear, for the Viper has risen!' He roared. 'And by dawn tomorrow, this plain will be alive with his northern allies!'

Pavo frowned momentarily, blood pounding in his ears. Then, two Gothic spearmen rushed for him and he was jolted from his thoughts. He wrenched the pair of longswords from Adalwolf's corpse, and hacked the tip from one assailant's spear, then punched a sword through the chest of the other. He spun to parry the dagger that the first man thrust at his back, then sliced the man's hand off at the wrist. He twisted round looking for his next opponent, but already, the Goths were outnumbered, the legionaries slicing through the remainder who fought on.

At this, the rebel leader cried out to the last few around him. 'Fight on, you fools, the Viper will come for us . . . '

His words ended with a cry as Crito barged forward and punched his spatha into his shoulder, pushing down until the artery was severed and black blood leapt high from the wound. The rebel leader toppled to the ground, gurgling his last. Crito cackled, eyeing the draining corpse, then sidling over to Pavo. 'Well whoever the Viper is, he won't be coming for this one!'

And with that, the battle was over. Amongst the scattered bodies, Pavo spotted those in legionary armour, entrails strewn on the ground, white bone showing. But he remained calm. Upon first joining the legion, the veterans had described it as 'the soldier's skin', the ability to detach from all emotion in the face of such brutality. All men in the ranks developed this after a few bloody encounters. He looked at the scars that lined his forearm; now he would have to explain it to some of the recruits.

'What now?' Sura panted, wiping his sword on the tunic of a Gothic corpse.

Pavo's eyes darted around the arena, then he strode over to the timber cage and slashed at the rope that held its door shut. The huddle of villagers, starved and dirty, tumbled out, thanking the legionaries. The wide-eyed man from the cage clasped his forearm, introducing himself as the village chieftain, loyal to Fritigern.

But Pavo heard only a voice rasping in his head, repeating the words of the dead rebel leader over and over. *The Viper has risen! And by dawn tomorrow, this plain will be alive with his northern allies!*

He pushed the chieftain away and strode for the northern village wall, but the chieftain followed him.

'Roman, I cannot thank you enough,' he started, following Pavo up the watchtower stairs, 'but you must listen. It may be too late even now!'

Pavo did not reply as he slapped each of his hands onto the timber stakes that formed a balcony atop the watchtower. The forest to the north was still. Then he spun to the man, his face stony. 'Tell me what is happening here!'

The chieftain's expression was grave. 'He has lured you here, just as he has manipulated Athanaric, just as he has brought this darkness from the north!'

Pavo frowned. '*Who* has lured us here?'

The man's eyes widened. 'The Viper! The hooded shade in the green cloak, the one who plots the end for all Rome.' He gestured to the snake banner flying above the village. 'That is his mark!'

Pavo grimaced at this. 'Then that banner will burn tonight!'

'No!' The Chieftain shook his head. 'We must leave it in place – for when they come!'

'For when *who* comes?' Pavo frowned harder, then something in his peripheral vision sent a chill to his soul. He spun to the northern forest. It seemed to be writhing.

The chieftain backed away, eyes bulging, lips trembling. 'It is as I feared. Our lives are already lost, this is a trap, Roman, a death trap. First Fritigern will fall, then your empire will tumble!'

Pavo saw the edge of the forest darken, then glimmer, as a wave of *something* flooded forward. Then a sea of torches sparked to life, illuminating it all.

A vast horde of warriors spilled from the trees, converging on the village.

There were many thousands of them, moving in clusters, each group distinctly armed and dressed. First there was a wave of mounted men. They resembled the Goths with their flowing blonde hair and pale features, but the majority wore scale vests, pointed conical helms and flew banners with emblems that were not of the Thervingi or any other neighbouring Gothic people. And they were fine riders, powerful in the gallop, holding a lengthy iron lance in a two-handed grip, carrying neither a shield nor holding the reins of their mounts, such was their grace. *Alani*, Pavo realised, the horsemen of southern Scythia.

Behind them marched a series of smaller groups of warriors, some mounted, some on foot, and each pocket of men was distinct in its appearance. The men of one group wore blue paint on their faces and bare shoulders and had their scalps scraped clean of hair around the sides and back. Another group wore furs and carried bows as tall as a man. Then another group wore a curious leather - Pavo's eyes strained to see what it was, then his gut lurched as he noticed two red-rimmed holes in the fabric; human eyeholes. More and more groups rumbled towards the village and Pavo could only gaze through them, looking for an answer.

What terrible thing drives these people south?

Sura and Crito ran up to stand alongside him and the three gawped at the approaching mass.

'Mithras, save us!' Sura croaked.

111

'Alani, Agathyrsi, Geloni, Neuri,' Crito frowned, scanning the horde, pointing out each distinct group. Then he jabbed a finger at the edge of the northern forest, 'but who or what are *they?*'

Pavo and Sura craned over the watchtower edge, peering in the direction of Crito's outstretched finger. From the forest, an even larger sea of shapes spilled forth, cupping and dwarfing the many tribes that already filled the plain. Riders. More than they could hope to count. Pavo's eyes danced over the scene, a frown wrinkling his brow.

Then, a horribly familiar war horn moaned and brought with it the jagged cries of thousands of men and the drumming hooves of thousands of beasts. A set of invisible, icy claws walked up Pavo's spine. He glanced to Sura and Sura glanced back.

'*Hunnoi!*' They spoke in unison.

Pavo's stomach fell away. Every night since the torturous mission to the Kingdom of Bosporus, he had prayed that he would never set eyes on them again. But here they were, their fearsome appearance betrayed by the torchlight; stocky and powerful, with flat, yellow-tinged faces etched with three scar welts on each cheek. Their hair was shaved at the temples and forehead and pulled taut on top. They were armed with long cutting swords, composite bows, lassos, nets and daggers and were clad in goatskin and leathers.

'The Huns?' Crito's face paled. 'I thought they prowled far to the north, on the steppes beyond the edge of the world?'

Pavo pinned him with a wide-eyed look. 'So did I. Indeed, I prayed they would remain there.'

'If we'd stayed out there overnight . . . ' Crito started, jabbing a thumb to the plain and thicket south of the village. Then he swallowed the rest of his words, shooting a furtive and defiant glance at Pavo.

But Pavo didn't care about the troublesome veteran or for his own pride; an invasion was coming like a tide, and they were to face it, alone. 'Honestly, Crito, I don't think it would have made any difference. They're coming for us.' He glared at the approaching mass, then eyed Sura and Crito.

'If we are to die, then we die as legionaries,' he spoke solemnly. 'Have the men form up by the village gates.'

He drew his spatha. Sura and Crito did likewise. Then he filled his lungs to roar in defiance at the approaching horde. But the roar stuck in his throat when a hand was cupped over his mouth and another grappled roughly at his shoulders, pulling him down behind the lip of the palisade.

The village chieftain and a group of villagers had wrestled him, Sura and Crito to the timber platform and out of sight of the oncoming horde. He snarled at them, then stopped, seeing the consternation twisting their faces. The Goths jabbered in their own tongue, their tone urgent, pointing to the dark-green banner that fluttered above the village. Then the chieftain himself hushed his kinsmen and then turned to the Romans, pushing a finger to their lips for silence.

Pavo frowned. The marching horde was almost at the walls and the watchtower platform trembled like a leaf. He braced for what was to come.

Then a jagged cry called out from the blackness.

At this, the chieftain stood and waved, calling out, his tone warm. But, behind the palisade, he was waving his other hand at the Romans to stay down.

'Whoresons! They're in league with the rebel Goths and that lot out there!' Crito spat, wriggling free of the Goth who restrained him then clutching at his sword hilt.

'No!' Pavo held up a hand, peering through the sliver of gap between the palisade stakes: the horde was spilling past the village like a river round a lonely rock. And then they continued to the southeast, towards Fritigern's heartland. The Hun rider who had hailed the village was marshalling them in that direction and now stood, watching as the village gates were opened to allow the villagers to scuttle out and heap fresh animal carcasses onto the Hun wagons.

'I might have been wrong about staying outside, but I'll be damned if . . . ' Crito snarled, sliding his spatha from his scabbard.

'No!' Pavo repeated. 'These villagers are on our side and loyal to Fritigern,' his eyes darted across the timbers by his feet as it all fell into place, 'but the horde think this village is sided with the Gothic rebellion,' he glanced to Sura, nodding, 'because of *that*.' He stabbed a finger up at the dark-green snake banner. 'That's the only reason we're not rent with a thousand arrows right now.'

Sura's eyes widened. 'But they're headed for the river. We've got to get word back to Durostorum and the fort.'

The village chieftain crouched beside them, face whiter than snow, eyes wide. 'Roman, there is no going back to your empire now,' he whispered, 'the Huns will fall upon Fritigern's men and it will be a battlefield all along the great river. To travel through that land would be to run onto myriad sword blades and spears. I must implore you to stay here, for outside, the Viper is at large!'

Pavo frowned. 'This Viper, he is a Hun?'

The chieftain frowned at this. 'No, he is Thervingi.'

'Then tell me, for Mithras' sake, where is this man?'

The chieftain shook his head, his face falling grave. 'The Viper is no man; he once tried to unite all the tribes of Gutthiuda and rise against Rome, but he was slain before his ambitions were realised. Slain by Romans. Yet now, many years after his death, some say that his shade still rides on these plains, cloaked and hooded in green, seeking vengeance.' The chieftain stabbed a finger out in the direction of the departing horde. 'This is *his* doing!'

Pavo frowned, searching for the words to reply. He looked to Sura and Crito, who wore puzzled frowns. A shiver of doubt danced across his skin. 'His shade rides on these plains . . . ' he began, then sighed and pinched his nose between his thumb and forefinger, screwing up his eyes as his head thundered with exhaustion and a thousand thoughts. 'We don't have time for this. We will be moving on as soon as we've had a moment to take on food and water.'

'But you must stay, at least for tonight. Tend to your wounded, fill your bellies and rest properly.'

Pavo shook his head. 'We are already behind that horde. Every heartbeat that passes will see them edge closer to the imperial borders. We leave. Tonight.'

Then he turned to Sura and Crito. 'Thoughts?'

'If Fritigern fights,' Sura spoke first, 'he'll lose, surely. His armies are numerous and well-trained, but they are unprepared for . . . that,' he nodded in the direction of the departed horde, then shivered, pulling his cloak tighter.

Pavo nodded solemnly. 'So what if he chooses not to fight? He is no fool – Gallus has always said that Fritigern won't fight unless he knows he can win,' he looked to Sura, his expression grave. 'What if he chooses to run?'

Sura frowned. 'Run, run where?' Then his face fell.

'The only place left for them to go. Across the Danubius. Into the empire.'

The first thick flakes of snowfall danced around Pavo, Sura and Crito as they gazed southeast, eyes wide.

Chapter 7

Iudex Athanaric's feasting hall echoed with jagged laughter and a wasp-like melody buzzed from a pair of pipers. The cavernous interior was bathed in a warm orange from the guttering torches and the roaring log fire in the centre while the shutters rattled from the snowstorm outside as if in protest. All around the hall, a hundred or so of the iudex's finest warriors and an equal number of buxom and fiery Gothic women were packed around the long timber tables. They drained keg after keg of barley beer and fruit wine, growing more rosy-cheeked and boisterous with each one.

At the top table, Gallus sat beside Salvian, Tarquitius, Felix and Paulus. Opposite sat Iudex Athanaric, Fritigern's rival and probably the most belligerent whoreson the empire had known in years. The iudex and the two brutish warriors flanking him cast flinty glares back at the Roman party.

Probably in his mid thirties, a similar age to Gallus, the Gothic Iudex was tall and lean, wearing a silver band to hold back his shoulder length, straight, jet-black hair. His eyes were constantly narrowed and his broad, battered nose spoke of his love of conflict.

Between them, the table was piled with food that could have graced Emperor Valens' table; roast teal and guillemot, herring, cheeses, curdled milk, wheat bread, pears, cherries & jugs of fruit wine; only Tarquitius had indulged though, the others merely picking at the fare.

As the talks continued well into the night, Gallus felt weariness creep over his mind. He saw the same look in the eyes of his legionaries, especially Paulus, whose eyelids were drooping. Even the drunken Goths eventually succumbed to weariness, gradually filtering from the hall until only the eight around the top table remained. But Tarquitius was in full flow, proposing

116

concessions on either side; preferential tax rates for Gothic traders crossing into the empire and an exchange of surplus grain and textiles. Salvian had remained silent at first, but as the talks went on he interjected more and more, deftly steering Tarquitius in his negotiations. Gallus was surprised at how well the talks were going, seemingly concluding with the notion of a yearlong pact of peace. His thoughts started to drift, his eyes dry and heavy.

Suddenly, the chatter ceased when a choking snore from Paulus echoed over them. The optio looked up at Felix and then Gallus, his eyes red-rimmed, his face wrinkled in sleepy confusion and his dark beard tousled and unkempt. 'Eh . . . I, oh, sorry,' he muttered, reddening. Gallus shot him an icy stare, while despatching a prayer of thanks to Mithras that it had not been him who had nodded off.

'Perhaps nature is telling us we have talked enough. Are we finished?' Salvian asked, looking to Tarquitius and Athanaric.

'Aye,' Athanaric spoke in a gruff tone, 'for now.'

Tarquitius scowled at Salvian. '*I* think we are finished too. Therefore *I* propose that we adjourn for the night, then gather tomorrow to read over the summary of our proposed treaty.'

All nodded. Then a violent winter gust rattled the shutters around the hall.

'It promises to be the coldest winter in memory,' Athanaric said, calmly.

Gallus returned the Gothic Iudex's gaze. 'What I have seen of it already it has chilled me enough.' Under the table, he clenched his fingers around the dark-green banner.

Athanaric sat back in his chair, a grin splitting his face, and clasped his hands. 'What is wrong, Tribunus? Your tone is disrespectful given the generous concessions I have made to your empire,' his eyes glinted, 'especially at a time when it is so weak.'

117

'Weak? You are so certain of that?' Gallus replied. In his peripheral vision, he noticed Tarquitius squirm in his seat. He turned to the senator, eyes narrowing.

But Athanaric cut in; 'It is common knowledge that your field legions are in the east, Tribunus, and it is not hard to work out that your border legions are stretched all over Fritigern's lands in search of these rebels.'

'And what do you know of these rebels?' Gallus leant over the table, his jaw clenching.

Athanaric leant forward likewise, then grinned mockingly. 'Nothing other than the reports that have come in. I must say though, it does sound like you are having difficulty in curtailing them. Are they too fast for you?'

Gallus felt the ire boil into his chest. He stood, snatching up the banner, undeterred as the guards flanking Athanaric leapt up and levelled their spears. 'Look me in the eye, you dog, and tell me you know nothing of *this!*' He pulled at one edge of the banner. It unravelled across the spoils of the feast; all eyes around the table fell upon the dark-green, blood-spattered piece, and the snake emblem coiled upon it.

Athanaric gazed at the sight for a moment. 'Well, well. You seek the Viper?' With that, he cast his head back and let out a roar of laughter that filled the feasting hall.

Gallus squared his shoulders.

'Relax, Tribunus,' Athanaric motioned for him to sit, shoulders still juddering with the last of his laughter.

Gallus noticed Salvian frowning, urging him to sit also. 'The Viper?' Gallus held out his arms as he sat. 'If you truly seek peace, then you will tell me what you know, Iudex.'

'I know only the tales that were told around the fires when I was a boy,' he said. 'They called him the ferocious iudex who was to unite the fractured tribes of Gutthiuda. The one who would forge a nation. The one who would slay Goth and Roman readily to achieve his goal; to march upon the empire.'

Gallus' jaw stiffened at this, but Salvian placed a calming hand on his forearm.

Athanaric did not notice this, his gaze growing distant as he spoke, the firelight dancing in his eyes. 'They would say that if we did not behave, then the Viper would come for us in the night, hooded and cloaked in dark green, his face hidden in shadow,' Athanaric paused, raising his eyebrows, 'then rip out our throats. And, by Wodin, did that threat work. I remember lying awake and silent every night, afraid to breathe, seeing him in every shadow, hearing him in every cracking twig, every gust of wind.'

A piece of kindling snapped in the fire, and all apart from Athanaric jolted.

The iudex's face melted into a dark smile, his gaze rising from the fire to settle on Gallus. 'Fear of the Viper's unseen presence had us beaten from the beginning. There is much to be admired in such a creature, do you not think?' The iudex left the question hanging in the air, then his face fell solemn and he continued; 'But you can rest assured that he is no longer a threat, Tribunus. The Viper died many years ago. To seek him is to seek a shade; a lost ideal as ethereal as the morning mists that dapple my plains and mountains.'

Gallus nodded to the hide banner, cocking one eyebrow. 'But this is the Viper's symbol, is it not?'

'It is.'

'Then why do these rebels carry it today, Athanaric? Men do not fight for a shade!'

'What men will do surprises me every day, Tribunus,' Athanaric leaned back, steepling his fingers under his chin. 'You asked what I knew of this marking. I have told you all I know, yet your eyes still narrow with mistrust?' He glared at Gallus.

Gallus glared back.

Salvian interjected. 'Perhaps this discussion is for another time? It has been a long evening, after all.'

'It has indeed,' Athanaric agreed, a cool grin splitting his features. 'Turn your mind from doubt, Tribunus; have I spoke of anything other than peace tonight?'

A tense silence ensued, then Gallus sighed, his head thumping and his eyes stinging with tiredness. 'Aye, perhaps I spoke in haste.'

All around the table stood, and with curt nods of the head, the two parties separated, Athanaric and his guards striding to the back door of the feasting hall and the five of the Roman party heading for the front door.

Gallus led Salvian, Tarquitius, Felix and Paulus out into the dead of night and the roaring blizzard, each pulling their cloaks tight as the bitter cold swept over them. They trudged through the snowdrifts lying in the deserted streets of the citadel to reach the stallhouse. Once inside, they shook themselves down of the snow.

Gallus looked to Salvian and Tarquitius. 'You had him in the palm of your hand. I can only apologise for my outburst at the end.'

'No need, Tribunus,' Tarquitius snapped back, 'I expect little in the way of sophistication from a soldier.'

Gallus firmed his jaw and nodded, burying the reply he wanted to give. He saw Salvian deftly cocking one eyebrow to him, as if thinking the same thing.

'Until tomorrow,' Tarquitius added briskly, then the senator and the ambassador headed for the timber staircase leading up to their rooms.

'Sir?' Felix asked. 'You're not satisfied with Athanaric's response, are you?'

'Are you?' Gallus replied.

'Not one bit,' Felix said, flatly.

Paulus frowned along with them as they looked through the door, slightly ajar, back across the centre of the citadel to the feasting hall.

You chase a shade, Tribunus.

'We won't catch any shades tonight,' Gallus sighed after a moment of consideration, then nodded towards the staircase. 'Come on, let's sleep and hope the rest brings us some inspiration.'

Tarquitius stood in his room, by the door, pulling his cloak tighter. His eyes were drawn to his bed once more. Rest and warmth would have to wait though, he asserted, and once again he stealthily edged his door open and turned one ear to the corridor. There was now a chorus of snoring from one of the other rooms in the stallhouse attic; a grin split his face.

He stalked carefully over the timbers, putting his weight only on the joins. The snoring was coming from behind the closed door of Optio Paulus, he realised. Then he stalked on further, past Salvian's shut door, then that of Felix. Then he froze; Gallus' door was ajar. He peered around the doorframe, his breath stilled. Then he issued a muted sigh of relief upon seeing the tribunus muttering distantly in some nightmarish torment, his face bathed in sweat.

Your nightmares are about to become real, Tribunus, he mused.

Reassured that he went unseen, Senator Tarquitius crept down the stairs and opened the main door and walked out into the night. He muted a gasp as the biting wind of the blizzard shocked his skin. The snow was knee-deep as he plodded through the street then across the open centre of the citadel towards the feasting hall. He pulled the neck of his cloak up and over his head, both to protect his face from the cold and as a guise. A few houses still bore the orange glow of torchlight in their windows, and he looked around furtively, anxious to avoid prying eyes.

Be at ease, he chided himself, *only the sharpest of minds are aware of what is to happen tonight.* The men of the legions had treated him with barely disguised contempt since the rendezvous, but now he wielded the power; it was time to cash in his knowledge of the strengths and weaknesses of the border legions. The sham of a peace parley earlier had served its purpose. Now, a private audience with Athanaric awaited him.

He reached the feasting hall and edged its door open, slipping inside. Merciful warmth enveloped him as he let his cloak slip to his shoulders. The hall was in darkness apart from an orange pool of light at the far end, bathing the top table.

He made to step towards it when, suddenly, from the shadows, two flashes of silver stopped him in his tracks. He felt the cold iron of a pair of speartips jabbing at his chins. White-hot terror raced through his veins as his eyes adjusted to the gloom and he saw the two brutish Goths who held the weapons, their faces twisted in anticipation.

'I . . . I'm here to speak with Iudex Athanaric,' he stammered.

The pair looked at one another, then one sneered, his grip on his spear tightening.

'Ah, Senator Tarquitius!' A voice boomed. It was Iudex Athanaric, who had moved into the pool of torchlight by the top table.

Tarquitius' skin crawled as his name echoed throughout the hall, sure the whole citadel would hear.

But Athanaric continued, striding down the hall. 'There was a point tonight when I thought you had forgotten the true purpose of your visit here, Senator – I thought that sham of a parley would never end! Come, sit with me, let us discuss more pressing matters. Guards, leave us.'

Tarquitius scowled as the two guards lowered their spears and left to stand outside the hall, then he walked with Athanaric to the table.

'You have had some six months to progress our plans, Senator,' Athanaric spoke stonily, his jovial facade dissolving. 'Tell me what you know, and make it concise.'

Tarquitius recoiled at this. The barbarian spoke to him as if he was a dog. 'You stand to gain vast spoils from my knowledge, Iudex. Value my company as you would value those spoils.'

122

Athanaric stared, unblinking. 'Tell me of the border legions.'

Tarquitius shuffled indignantly, then pursed his lips. The iudex was a stubborn whoreson; with too few men to mount a full-scale invasion, he relied on scraps like this, scraps that would open the door of the empire for him. *Perhaps,* he mused, *it would be prudent to play to this dog's delusions of power.*

'The imperial borders are weak, Iudex, weaker than they have ever been. I have spent your funds wisely,' he grinned, lifting a trio of scrolls from his satchel, 'and those I have bribed know only that they talked to a senator; your part in this remains undisclosed.' He flattened the first of the scrolls to reveal a map of the River Danubius, then stabbed a finger at a large dot, south of the river and well west of Durostorum. 'Here is where I propose you strike. The city of Sardica is virtually undefended; barely half a cohort lines its walls and the forts on the river north of it are manned only by a century at most.' He looked up, thinking of how he had wrung that information from Pavo, then felt a sweat break out as he saw that Athanaric looked down on the map in distaste. *Time to sell it,* he realised. 'But even better; that garrison is due to return to the XI Claudia fort before spring. Within the month, I should have knowledge of the exact dates of the garrison changeover.' He leaned forward, towards Athanaric, his eyes glinting. 'Inside the Roman borders, such movements are often lax. A window of opportunity could be created; time it right and your forces could puncture the Roman borders and take this city and the governor's family who reside there with little resistance. The ransom for their heads will be handsome, and *I* can guarantee it will be met,' his eyelids dipped a little, and he purred, 'for a healthy commission, of course.'

He watched as Athanaric sat silently, no doubt mulling over the deal. It was just as he had planned for months now. A controlled invasion where he could be the saviour of that wretch of a governor, gaining esteem from both the iudex and from the empire. A lavish reward, a lofty promotion and a thick slice of the ransom would no doubt be in the offing.

Athanaric looked up and Tarquitius waited eagerly on his praise.

'There will be no raid, no sacking of Sardica.'

Tarquitius cocked his head to one side, frowning. 'I beg your pardon?'

Athanaric's face split into a cool smile. 'I said, there will be no raid. Those ambitions are trivial in comparison to what is to happen now. Much has transpired in these last months that you know little of, Senator.'

Tarquitius snorted. 'What is this? The whole guise of a peace parley took months to organise, just so we could meet here, like this. And now you rebuff my carefully laid plans?' The blood boiled in his veins. 'You would do well to make the best of my services, Iudex, for plenty others would be happy to make use of them!' He stabbed a finger into the table as his words rang around the room.

Then an icy realisation danced over his skin.

They were not alone.

From the corner of his eye, he saw the shadows ripple by the far end of the hall.

Then, like a shade, something drifted forward. Shadows and a dark-green haze.

The hairs on Tarquitius' neck stood on end as he turned to the apparition. A figure, cloaked and hooded in dark green, came straight for him. He felt the beginnings of a squeal build in his lungs as it approached. Then the figure stopped abruptly, only paces from him.

The face was cast in shadows, only the line of a jaw illuminated by the guttering torchlight.

Tarquitius snatched a glance at Athanaric, who was smiling an awful smile. 'What is the meaning of this? We were to talk *alone!*'

'You are alone, Senator,' the figure hissed. 'I am but a shade.'

Tarquitius' eyes bulged and he looked to Athanaric.

Athanaric nodded. 'You should be honoured, Senator, for the Viper stands before you.'

Tarquitius' lips flapped. 'The Vi . . . '

'And you should listen and listen well to what I have to say, Senator of Rome,' the Viper spoke in a rasping, caustic tone. Then he reached out, lifting Tarquitius' scrolls and tearing them in half. 'Iudex Athanaric has told you what will be; no raid will take place. He has no intention of crossing the great river only to bolster your reputation then come scuttling back with a few coins. Your small-minded ambition will serve as a minor pillar in what is to come.'

Tarquitius' throat tightened and sweat danced down his scalp and over his eyes, despite the cold.

'Yes, the Roman borders *will* be breached,' the Viper stabbed a finger into the table. 'But it will be no mere raid. This will be an invasion . . . an invasion that will *end* your empire.'

Tarquitius' eyes bulged, his heart thudding. He glanced to Athanaric. 'But your armies are too few; one spear for every ten of Fritigern's, you said. And Fritigern is in truce with the empire.'

'And my own loyal riders number only a few hundred. This is true,' the Viper agreed.

'So, how . . . ' Tarquitius started.

'It is simple. Fritigern's armies will be pressed into service,' the Viper purred. 'My riders have been disrupting his lands for some months now and drawing the Roman legions from their forts. But that has just been preparative for what is to come. As we speak, a storm readies to smash against Fritigern's lands.'

Tarquitius frowned, looking to Athanaric. 'A storm?'

'The dark hordes of the north, Senator,' Athanaric grinned like a shark, 'remember them? Like a press, they will drive Fritigern's armies onto Roman soil.'

Tarquitius felt his face blanching and a prickly dread rippled across his neck. His past dealings with the Huns had left a black stain on his soul. 'You are making a mistake, a big mistake. They cannot be harnessed!'

125

'Any man can be controlled, Senator,' the Viper spat, 'as you have so ably demonstrated with your actions and your presence here tonight. But now that you know what is to come, your mind may well turn to betraying me?'

Tarquitius shivered as he imagined a thousand more figures waiting in the shadows of the hall. 'No, I . . . '

'What is to stop me from cutting your throat over this very table, right now?' The Viper rasped, lifting a houndstooth dagger from his cloak, placing the point on the table and twisting it round with his thumb and forefinger.

Tarquitius' gut churned and he felt his bladder weaken as the blade glinted in the torchlight. A thousand thoughts flashed through his mind, then one image remained.

Pavo.

'I can still be of use to you,' he nodded hurriedly. 'I have a network of contacts in the legions now. One of them, a legionary, was going to get me the date of the Sardica changeover, but I could steer him elsewhere? I hold a piece of knowledge that he craves; he will do whatever I ask, I know it!'

The Viper's jaw creased in a grin at this and he spun the dagger in silence for what felt like an eternity. 'Then you should continue to deny the legionary this knowledge, Senator. Without this, it seems you would be truly worthless to me, and I would have little reason to keep you alive.' The Viper leaned closer to him. 'Now you will return to your empire knowing that, in a heartbeat, I could expose you as the traitor that you are. I will be watching you, I will see your every move, hear your every word.'

Tarquitius nodded, mouth agape. He had only just avoided disgrace and execution after the Bosporus debacle. Any more tawdry and shameful revelations would surely be the end of him.

'But you must be ready for when I next call upon you to do my bidding. When you see my mark, you will obey.'

Tarquitius nodded hurriedly, then glanced to Athanaric and then back to the Viper.

The Viper leaned forward, a flicker of torchlight illuminating his jaw again for the briefest of moments, the light dancing on his awful grin. He placed his mouth to Tarquitius' ear and rasped;

'Run, Senator . . . '

Tarquitius shot up from his seat, stumbled backwards, then turned and scrambled from the hall.

Athanaric watched the door swing shut, then eyed the hooded figure in whom he had placed so much stock.

The Viper – the demon who had haunted his childhood – now offered him the glory he had sought for so long; for the land to be cleansed of Fritigern and his followers so he could be the one true Iudex.

Now that the reality dangled before him, he felt agitated at the doubts that crept into his thoughts. 'Do you think the senator has a point about the Hun hordes? You are sure they will ransack only Fritigern's lands? And what if Fritigern fights, or seeks shelter in my mountains?'

The Viper was unmoved by this prospect. 'Turn your thoughts from doubt, Iudex. The Huns and their subjects have already been herded to their goal like sheep. And, likewise, Fritigern will be steered, for my finest man is by his side.'

Athanaric could not contain his amusement at this. 'Fritigern. My greatest rival. The one I thought so shrewd. He does not know that a demon has wormed its way into his trust?'

The Viper steepled his hands under his chin. 'Do you not see the beauty in that, Iudex? And that is exactly why we lured the Romans here – for we now need an equal hand in their ranks.'

'The Romans are shrewd,' Athanaric countered, grudgingly. 'As I understand it, trust is hard won in the legions.'

'It is all in hand,' the Viper nodded. 'Trust is forged in the fires of adversity. Now, let me tell you how we will stoke that fire . . . '

Chapter 8

Pavo's breath misted before him as he eyed his fifty, formed up before him in the village torchlight. Night was still upon them and the snow fell silently around them, already ankle deep and coating the men's shoulders and helmets. The Gothic villagers had brought them hot vegetable pottage and bread. They had gratefully and greedily devoured this rich and warming mix before crunching through hardtack biscuits. Then they had washed it all down with fruit beer and fresh water. Their tired, sleep-deprived bodies fractionally revitalised, the veterans and recruits now looked to him in expectation. And he dreaded what he was about to say.

They could not go home. At least, not the way they had come.

Yes, Pavo affirmed, it was only natural to want to flee directly back to the river after sighting the hordes just a short while ago. But it would be a fool's flight, straight into a swarm of Hun arrows and a sea of Alani sword points, or under the trampling hooves of Fritigern's fleeing armies. No, he squared his jaw and nodded, touching a hand to his bronze phalera; the answer lay in another direction. They would have to move southwest, skirting the stony mass of the Carpates where they had left Gallus. This way they were less likely to cross paths with the Hun horde. But that meant crossing into Athanaric's territory. A lesser of two evils by a sliver.

He heard the rustle of iron and a nervous cough and looked up; the eyes of his fifty hung on him. Doubt grew in his breast, so he focused on the impression of the phalera medallion on his skin, and thought of father. But still, his lungs and his throat felt scrambled and knotted at the prospect of what he was to say. He sucked in a breath through his nose and held it in his

129

belly, before exhaling through his lips. He repeated this three times then issued a thank you to Salvian as he felt the tension in his body ease.

Calmed, he clasped his hands behind his back and eyed the ranks. Crito and the veterans stood with their usual torn expressions while the recruits looked to be on the edge of panic.

'Last night, we saw something we were not meant to see. At least we were not meant to see it and live,' he started. 'That horde is right now ploughing through Fritigern's lands. Nobody will be safe there – neither Fritigern's people and his armies, nor the Claudia vexillationes scattered all over his villages. We cannot go back the way we came.'

He looked to Crito, expecting a challenge. But it was a recruit, a boy of barely fifteen by the looks of it, who spoke, his anxiety getting the better of him.

'My wife and my mother are alone back there, in Ad Salices, the town by the willows, only a morning's ride from the Claudia fort. Sir, we've got to get back to them! If we delay or take a longer route then . . . '

'We all stand to lose a great deal, soldier!' Pavo cut him off sharply, pity stabbing at his heart as the young lad shrank, his face blanching at the rebuke. 'And we must not panic.'

The veterans shuffled in disgruntlement, and Crito shook his head. Pavo clenched his jaw at this. 'Legionary, do you have something to say?'

Crito nodded. 'Absolutely.'

'Let's hear it,' Pavo said in a more even tone, hoping his face wasn't as flushed as the prickling heat on his cheeks suggested.

'The lad is right, sir. I too have a wife and daughter, in Marcianople, and they are only safe whilst the borders remain secure. Comes Lupicinus and the dregs left back at the fort cannot stop any attempt by Fritigern to cross the Danubius.'

Pavo nodded, seeing a glimpse of humanity in the big veteran. 'So do we charge blindly into the rear of what must be the largest army ever formed north of the Danubius?' He eyed Crito and the lad. 'Slain, you will be of no use to your families.'

'So what do you propose?' Crito spat.

Pavo braced himself. 'We go through Athanaric's lands.'

'What?' Sura yelped.

Pavo shot him a burning look. 'We must avoid the Hun horde at all costs. Thus we must march round them, and cross the Danubius upriver, southeast of here. And that, I'm afraid, means marching along the base of the Carpates.'

'You've got to be joking,' Crito said with a deadpan expression. 'The march here through Fritigern's woods felt like walking in a wolf's den – and that's supposedly allied territory. But the lands over there,' he jabbed a thumb over his shoulder to the edge of the Carpates, 'are rife with cutthroat Thervingi who would be delighted to bring fifty severed legionary heads to their master. Athanaric has said it openly – murder of Romans is legal and encouraged.'

'This is true,' Pavo nodded.

This time Crito gasped, scratched his head and spat into the snow, and the rest of the legionaries broke out in a concerned murmur. 'You were right, sir, about last night, and I was wrong. We should have marched on Istrita as a fifty. But you're wrong about this.'

At this, the fifty erupted in a rabble of agreement, only Sura declining the opportunity, though he did wear a look of indecision.

Pavo racked his brain for a tactical answer. Then, once again, Salvian's face popped into his mind. *Self-doubt is a pox indeed. When you are unsure of yourself, just think back over your decisions, see the strength of your reasoning. I promise you, your confidence will return.* Pavo steadied himself, thinking back over the flurry of thoughts that had danced in his mind since the horde had slipped into the southern horizon: of all the alternatives, this plan was the only one he could bring himself to ask the others to do –

knowing all other options meant death for them all. He looked up and fixed his gaze on Crito, but addressed the fifty as a whole.

'I don't know if I'm right or wrong, it's as simple as that. Only the fates can determine whether this is the right action. But consider this: why do you think all of these disturbances with the rebel Goths have broken out so suddenly over the past few weeks across Fritigern's lands, yet Athanaric's lands have been apparently untroubled?' Pavo cast a glance at each of them, as if demanding an answer.

Crito sneered as if to dismiss the question, but Pavo saw the glint of realisation in the veteran's eyes. At the same time, Sura sighed in understanding, and some of the other veterans groaned as they realised it too. Crito looked up. 'The disturbances were bait,' he spoke flatly.

Pavo nodded. 'Exactly. Bait to draw out the Claudia piecemeal, where each vexillatio would be snared on some incident like this,' he swept his hands out across the village. 'Then, when the Huns come at the call of Athanaric, or this *Viper*, they smash into not only Fritigern's people, but the tattered pieces of the limitanei. It's not just the XI Claudia – the V Macedonia, the XIII Gemima, the IV Flavia and the I Italica are all scattered around Gutthiuda in tiny vexillationes, tunics up, arses bared . . . the *entire* border army. And the Huns are here to exterminate them.'

'And all that pressure will end up against the imperial borders,' Sura barked, backing Pavo up.

Pavo nodded his thanks, then continued. 'So we come back to it again: take the short route home and certainly die on a Hun arrowhead. Or take the long route home and *almost* certainly die on a Gothic blade.' A wry smile crept onto his face despite his efforts to keep a Gallus-style iron veneer. But some of the veterans seemed to warm to this, breaking out in dry laughter. Then Crito allowed one side of his mouth to lift and issued a gruff chuckle.

'So are you with me?' He called to them, hubris and terror battling in his veins.

There was a mixed grumble, and he shared a nervous glance with Sura.

Sura's eyes darted around him for a moment, then he drew his spatha and battered the hilt into his shield boss. 'For the empire!' He cried. With that, some of the fifty cheered. Others remained silent, looking around uncertainly.

Crito shook his head with a wry grin; a grin that said the veteran was still unconvinced.

Pavo filled his lungs, squaring his jaw.

'Form up, ready to move out!

Paulus woke, saddle sore from his short journey on Zosimus' mount the previous day. The babble of the Gothic populace drifted through the shutters and into his room in the stallhouse attic, rousing his mind from sleep. He stretched his legs and groaned as the chill of the winter morning slipped inside his blanket. Then, cracking open his eyelids, he realised it was not morning – it was nearer noon. He sighed and made to sit up. Then a hand wrapped across his mouth and pushed him prone, and another clamped across his chest.

Panic welled in his heart as at once his eyes darted; two bearded Goths stood over him. He writhed under their grip, twisting towards his spatha – within arm's reach – but they pinned his arms with their knees, their weight simply too great.

'Your Mithras will not save you now,' one of them hissed, then pressed something cold against Paulus' throat.

Then the Goth ripped his hand back. Paulus felt an odd burning on his neck, seeing a dark-red spray of liquid pump up into the air. At once his skin was hot and his insides cool. Then a black veil fell across his vision.

Gallus had fallen into a fitful sleep as soon as he had returned to his room and removed his helmet and vest. Despite the shutter in his room lying open to the bitter chill and the brightening sun, he had remained, neither awake nor asleep, calling out her name as he always did.

'Olivia?' He could see her, stood at the end of his bed. She was smiling, cradling the tiny form of a baby in her arms. He sat up, a pained smile stretching across his face as he reached out with one hand towards her. 'You're here?' Olivia shook her head and her smile faded, then a single tear escaped one eye and stained her cheek.

Gallus shuffled forward towards her, reaching out to stroke the babe's fine hair. But the apparition disappeared before him, like a morning mist. His eyes focused on the reality: a crimson heap that was his cloak, and the tiny, carved idol of Mithras that lay on top of it. He remembered that day, only weeks after she and little Marcus had burnt on the pyre, when he had said his prayers to the war deity, begging to be thrown into conflict, to lose himself in the defence of his empire.

He sensed self-pity writhing in his chest. In disgust, he leapt up from the bed, grimacing, pulling the iron shutters in his mind closed over his moment of weakness. He strode over to the jug of water and splashed a cupped handful of the icy contents over his face and pushed his fingers through his peak of hair, steeling himself for the day ahead. He poured himself a cup of water and moved to the shutters; outside, the town was still cloaked in a thick layer of snow and the centre of the citadel had been set up as a market, abuzz with activity. Then he realised it was not morning, but midday. He scolded himself for sleeping so late, but was distracted when he saw a party of Gothic spearmen pushing through the square. Then he saw another. *Coming this way?* He wondered with a frown. 'Let your mind rest for one bloody moment,' he chided himself with a shake of the head and a weary chuckle.

He reached to the table for a date, when a muffled gasp sounded from across the corridor. Like a cat, he spun to the door, eyes wide, swiping his swordbelt from the back of the nearby chair. Then footsteps rattled on the floorboards and ended when his door juddered from a shoulder-charge.

Gallus ripped his spatha from his scabbard and braced.

The door burst open and Felix tumbled in, eyes wide and chest heaving, shaking his head as if lost for words. He was carrying a sword dripping with blood, jabbing a finger back through the door.

'Speak!' Gallus hissed in agitation.

Felix gulped in a breath. 'Assassins, sir! They've killed Paulus – slit his throat. I've slain the pair that did it, but they nearly had me as well!'

Gallus' mind raced. 'You're sure you killed all of the assassins?' He asked, pulling on his woollen trousers, leather boots and mail vest.

'Certain!' Felix panted. 'Why?'

'Because there are twenty or so Goths coming this way, and I've got a terrible feeling they're coming to finish the job.' He glanced outside; sure enough, the party of Gothic Warriors were filing around the side of the stallhouse, towards the door. 'Quick, wake Salvian and Tarquitius!'

Felix darted across the corridor, and Salvian opened his door before Felix got there. The ambassador's face was pale and his eyes were shadowed under a frown. 'Trouble, Tribunus?' He called across the corridor to Gallus.

'There will be if we're not fast.' He darted a glance to the chest in the corner, then to the shutters; below, horse traders and thriving market stalls filled the space. 'Quick, come in here,' he called to the ambassador. Then he opened the chest and lifted out a pair of wide, cherry-red, lozenge-patterned trousers and slid them over his legs, cursing his fumbling fingers, before pulling a red, hooded cloak around his shoulders. 'Ambassador,' he hissed, 'find some Gothic garments, we're going outside!'

Salvian frowned, then saw the Tribunus eyeing the drop from the shutters to the ground below. 'Ah, right, I'm with you,' the ambassador whispered, pulling on a set of dark grey, rough woollen trousers and a brown

135

hooded cloak. Felix did likewise. Then Senator Tarquitius came waddling in, his face whiter than the snow outside, his eyes distant. Gallus frowned at his odd demeanour, then shoved a rugged hemp cloak into the Senator's arms.

Gallus rested one foot on the window ledge, sheathing his spatha and tucking two plumbatae inside his belt. Then he hissed to the three in the room. 'There; that hay cart – wait till it passes below! Then we jump . . . and be ready to duck and hide – the square is crawling with Gothic spearmen.'

Just then, a floorboard in the corridor creaked, and Gallus knew what was coming next. He and Felix spun to face the doorway, spathas drawn. 'Jump, now!' Gallus roared to Salvian and Tarquitius.

Salvian turned and leapt, slipping down the thick coating of snow on the thatchwork then landing silently on the hay cart. Gallus elbowed at the blubbery mass of Tarquitius, but the Senator took to squealing and clawing at the edge of the shutters like a stubborn cat. 'Will you just bloody jump!' He roared, then kicked out, forcing the senator through the window at last.

Then Gallus and Felix turned back to the doorway just as a clutch of towering warriors spilled into the room with a guttural roar, swords and spears levelled for the kill. Sensing the lead Goth lunge for him, the tribunus swiped his spatha round just in time, the Goth's longsword nicking his cloak and the mail underneath. Gallus grabbed the man's forearm and butted into his nose, the dull crack of facial bones crumbling as a testament to the ever-handy tactic. The lead Goth fell away, groaning, only to be replaced by three more, coming at Gallus like a pack of wolves. He parried their first strike, stumbling backwards, then swiped at the next, inadvertently taking the Goth's fingers clean off with the blow. But three more pushed in to take the stricken man's place.

'Sir, there are too many of them!' Felix cried as he stumbled back from a flurry of spearpoints.

Gallus growled, hacking at one spear, then shuffled back to the window. 'Go!' He barked.

Felix leapt from the room, then Gallus climbed into the window frame and booted out at the Goths who rushed for him. Then he let himself fall backwards. He slid down the snowy thatch in silence and then was weightless for a heartbeat, before he landed on something soft – but it wasn't hay. Then, a pig-like squeal from under him split the air. Gallus writhed round and clamped a hand over the senator's mouth.

'Another noise from you and . . . ' Gallus started.

'Sir, come on,' Felix hissed from the back edge of the cart.

Gallus vaulted from the hay cart and on to the packed snow on the square, then glanced around; in the fervent bartering and shouting, nobody had noticed them, yet. But, above them, the rest of the Gothic spearmen leaned from the open shutters, baying and calling across the square.

'Where do we go?' Tarquitius warbled as he slid ungraciously from the cart and onto the ground.

'Anywhere but here, and let's do it fast!' Gallus spat.

Then Salvian's eyes locked onto a line of market stalls, laden with clothing. 'This way. We can change clothes again and they'll lose us in the crowd. Come on!'

The four barged forward, the crowd parting reluctantly, jostling, shoving and cursing their efforts. But Gallus could see the glinting eyes and speartips of two pockets of Gothic spearmen surging through the crowd towards them like a school of sharks.

'Duck, so they can't see us,' the tribunus urged the three behind him. He reached out and swiped a dyed blue woollen cloak from the nearest stall, and a tent-like red one that would do for the senator. Then he set his sights on a dark and narrow alley up ahead, splitting the horreum and a two-storeyed workshop.

'Yes, we should slip in there,' Salvian nodded beside him. 'If they pass us, then the stables are by the other side of the horreum.'

Gallus nodded. 'Then let's do it.'

They scurried through the crowd as the pursuing spearmen craned and jostled. Finally, they slipped into the shadows of the ally, where the air was thick with the stench of stale urine and faeces. Tarquitius was a shade of crimson, his skin bathed in sweat from the brief exercise and his chest heaved, a hoarse groaning coming with each breath.

'Shut up, you fool!' Gallus hissed, as he heard the urgent clatter of Gothic boots approaching. He fixed his eyes on the end of the alleyway, breath bated.

'We are in the shadows, Tribunus,' Salvian whispered. 'They will not see us.'

The Gothic spearmen clattered past the mouth of the alley, surging on through the market.

'Now, to the stables!' Salvian whispered as the three around him exhaled in relief.

The four pushed through the tight end of the alleyway – Tarquitius having more difficulty than the others. They emerged into a quiet backstreet of the citadel; one side was lined with a stable complex, and their mounts were in the nearest stall.

A young, emaciated Gothic boy stood nervously, holding a grooming comb.

'You are not Thervingi?' The lad said, his voice unsteady.

Salvian crouched, holding the boy's shoulder, fixing him with a friendly gaze. 'You would do anything to protect your family, wouldn't you?' Salvian said, pressing a pair of bronze *folles* into the boy's palm. 'This will see your table heaped with food for a week at least, I would have thought?'

The boy nodded, gawping at the coins.

'All we want is to leave this place with our lives,' Salvian continued. 'Raise the alarm if you must, if it'll save you from punishment, but give us until the sun starts to drop from its zenith, at least?'

The boy nodded shyly, then glanced up at the noon sky.

With that, the four mounted their steeds, darting nervous glances each way down the empty street.

'So now we just have to make it through the streets of Dardarus, then out of the gates unseen?' Gallus asked dryly.

'Fear not, Tribunus, we are merely Gothic traders, passing through,' Salvian issued one of his trademark half-mouthed grins, then pulled up the hood of his cloak. 'If the thousands of Goths between here and the gates are to believe that, then you must too.'

Gallus flicked up an eyebrow and wondered if the ambassador could sell candles to the blind. He, Felix and Tarquitius raised their hoods also – the senator still wearing an expression of a startled cat. *Whatever nightmares that reprobate suffered last night, they were undoubtedly deserved,* he mused dryly.

Then he steeled himself for what was to come and touched a hand to his spatha hilt under his cloak. *To the gates, then. And if the Goths challenge us,* he affirmed, *then Mithras help the bastards!*

Chapter 9

Pavo's legs had numbed long before dawn. Now, past noon, the snow was thigh-deep in places and all around them was a wall of white. His face ached from the roaring, relentless blizzard that seemed to be pushing them back, willing them to stay out of Athanaric's lands.

'We have to shelter,' Sura chattered.

'We can't,' Pavo glanced around; he could see only a few feet in each direction, and still they hadn't sighted the Carpates. Only the occasional groaning of the recruits that broke through the whistling storm told him the rear of the column was still there. He once again tried to orient himself, ever-fearful that they could unwittingly stumble right onto one of Athanaric's hillforts, citadels or camps. Or even into the path of the Gothic Iudex's horsemen, who would delight in an easy kill such as this.

'The men are exhausted, we need to find a place to stop,' Sura tried again.

Pavo shook his head, pulling his snow-coated cloak tighter. 'If we stop, we freeze.'

'Pavo,' Sura said, gripping his forearm. 'I know you want to lead us back to the river and the empire. I know you're afraid you will fail them. But if we don't seek out shelter . . . '

Pavo turned to him with his lips curled in a snarl, then his face fell as he saw his friend's blue-tinged features and snow-coated eyebrows. At that moment, the blizzard changed direction. In the brief lull, he saw his column, shivering, chattering, stumbling like drunk men, minds numbed with the cold, their armour and cloaks almost all white with the clinging snow. He cursed himself for letting it get this bad.

'Stop,' he barked over the gale, then he caught sight of a pile of rocks thirty paces or so to their right. 'We shelter from the winds behind those rocks and then we eat.'

But Sura shook his head and held up a hand, holding a finger of his other hand to his lips, eyes wide.

Pavo frowned at this latest contradiction. 'What now?'

'That is no mere rock pile,' Sura said, leaning in to speak into Pavo's ear.

Pavo turned to the rock pile and the breath stilled in his lungs; the blizzard changed direction once again and, like a huge white curtain being drawn back, the might of the Carpates was revealed, the rock pile lying at the base of the great mountains. And there, right where Sura's gaze was trained, was a craggy corridor that led through the mountains. On either side, a pair of armoured Goths stood like inhuman sentinels on the face of the rock, tucked into nooks to shelter from the storm, shivering in their cloaks.

'The road to Dardarus!' Pavo whispered, his words carried away by the storm.

He turned to Sura, nodding towards the fifty. 'Get them against the rock face. We cannot be sighted!'

The gates of Dardarus swung closed. Gallus, Felix and Salvian cantered through the snow and across the great plain alongside a cart laden with flax and an old man leading a line of donkeys. The crop fields they passed by were deserted, unworkable under the thick blanket of snow. The sky had clouded over, grey and bulging in places. A dark portent of a fresh snowstorm if ever there was one.

They had circled for what felt like an eternity near the gates, waiting on an opportunity to slip out with another party. Gallus had been sure he felt eyes watching them suspiciously when they finally tagged onto the trail of the flax cart. Now outside he wanted with all his heart to heel his mount into a gallop.

He looked ahead, to the opening of the rocky pass that would lead them away from Athanaric's heartland. 'This cart is headed for the farms. When we reach the mouth of the pass, we will be alone, and we will be challenged,' he whispered to Salvian, nodding to the two spear-wielding sentries posted halfway up the rock face, guarding this end of the pass.

Salvian's eyes were already upon the pair. 'It's all about perception, Tribunus. Those sentries will see a group of Gothic riders approaching, nothing more.'

Gallus shook his head. 'Our garb will count for little as soon as they bark at us in their jagged tongue. I speak their language but I sound as Roman as they come; same with Felix.' Then he turned to Tarquitius. 'Senator?'

Tarquitius' face was blue, his eyelids and nose coated in frost. 'He . . . he is a shade . . . ' Tarquitius mumbled repeatedly.

Gallus frowned and looked to Salvian.

Salvian cocked an eyebrow then issued that now familiar half-smile of his. 'It seems that my mentor is compromised. It is down to me to guide us home.'

They trotted through the snow, knee deep to their mounts in places, and the sky was almost black over the pass. Then the gaze of the two sentries fell upon them and the nearest one barked down a challenge.

Salvian calmly lowered his hood, taking care to ruffle his hair as he did so, pushing his locks out of the neat Roman style he wore them in. When Salvian replied, his accent was in perfect harmony with the sentry's.

Gallus cast a furtive glance at Salvian and saw just what the ambassador had said the Goths would see: an unkempt, ordinary Gothic rider in shabby clothes. *You sly dog*, Gallus mused.

The sentry hesitated for a moment, then Salvian barked in an impatient tone, flapping a hand down the pass and then shrugging. At last, the sentry nodded for them to proceed.

The three moved into the pass, and almost as soon as they did so, the dark clouds to the west opened, pebble-sized clumps of snow drifting down in a thick fall.

Gallus felt elation in his veins, but noticed Salvian glancing back to the plain of Dardarus, frowning.

'Ambassador?'

'Be ready, Tribunus,' he looked Gallus in the eye, 'I sensed undue hesitation from those sentries. They were aware of something . . . '

'The boy at the stables – perhaps he has . . . ' Felix started.

Then the wailing of a Gothic war horn filled the pass from the Dardarus end.

Felix and Gallus gawped at one another. Tarquitius was jolted from his frozen malaise.

'Ride!' Salvian roared, the words echoing along the pass.

At once, the four heeled their mounts into a gallop. The thundering of hooves was not enough to drown out the stretching of a hundred bowstrings, if not more, high above them. Then the creaking stopped, replaced by a growing hiss like a thousand asps. Gallus held his breath, wishing he had brought his helmet with him. Then, all around them and in the wake of their gallop, Gothic arrows thudded down from above, tips hammering through the frozen earth and shafts quivering in anger.

'Split,' Gallus roared over the whinny of his terrified beast, 'ride as I do!' The tribunus yanked his stallion's reins, urging her to slice across the front of the other three, veering left and then sharply right in turn, staying just a half stride ahead of the clusters of arrows.

He glanced back to see Felix and Salvian, fortunately skilled riders, following suit without following his path exactly, and Tarquitius struggling to keep up at the back. Gallus grimaced and faced front again – the other end of the pass was still a good few stadia ahead. 'Mithras, give us hope!'

Then, as if the God of the legions had heard his name being called, the wind in the pass grew to a powerful gust. The air around them thickened, not with arrows, but with driving, blinding snow. The arrow hail slowed, and the accuracy fell away as the trail through the pass was rendered invisible to the archers above.

'It seems the Christian God is not all-powerful yet?' Salvian panted through a wry half-smile.

Gallus lifted his dagger from his belt, then tossed the blade, hilt first, to Salvian, while Felix offered his blade to Tarquitius. 'We're not out of trouble yet and we must stay on our guard. I hope you can fight as well as you talk, Ambassador.'

Salvian cocked an eyebrow, eyeing the blade. 'I hope so too.'

A dry chuckle escaped Gallus' lips, but was cut short when the ground around them seemed to quake. From the Dardarus end of the pass, the roar and rumble of cavalry grew louder and louder.

The four shared a look of dread, then Gallus heeled his mount into a gallop for the far end. 'Ya!'

Snatching glances over his shoulder, he saw the grey-white of the blizzard twist and turn. Then it stilled for just a moment to reveal Gothic riders; fifty of them, snarling behind spears, shields and helmets and haring in on them at full gallop.

'They're gaining on us, sir!' Felix roared over the howl of the blizzard.

'Here,' Gallus snarled, pulling the pair of plumbatae he had clipped into his belt that morning, 'slow them down with these.'

He heard Felix's manic cackle over the tumult as the primus pilus loosed the weighted darts at their pursuers. With a pair of distant groans, two Gothic riders were skewered out of the equation.

'Just the rest of them now, sir,' Felix roared.

'And those up ahead,' Salvian cried, jabbing a finger forward at the far end of the pass, now emerging from the blizzard.

Gallus strained his eyes: there, like a row of fangs, stood a line of some forty Gothic spearmen strung across the end of the corridor, spears dug in, faces twisted into snarls.

Gallus growled through gritted teeth, him and Felix flanking Tarquitius and Salvian. There was only one hope, he realised, noticing the spear wall was only one man deep and there was a definite gap between two men in the centre. A sloppy spear wall indeed. *Oddly sloppy,* Gallus reasoned, before washing the thought from his mind. He lifted his spatha and pointed to the opening.

'Ready yourselves. Stay together. Ride for the centre . . . *charge!*'

Pavo and his fifty were pressed flat against the base of the mountainside, and the blizzard battered them relentlessly. Crito and Sura stood nearest to him. He risked poking his head out to survey the scene again. The two sentries remained holed up in sheltered crevices about twenty feet up the mountainside. There was no way his fifty could cut across the opening of this pass without being sighted, he realised, unless the storm thickened enough. But even then his men were exhausted – would they be fast enough to steal across in time?

Then a distant Gothic war horn moaned from the far end of the pass.

The fifty suppressed gasps at this. Then Pavo noticed something move on the far side of the pass entrance – beside a small, dark cavern opening, partly concealed by another rock pile. He squinted to see what had

145

moved, then froze as a line of Gothic spearmen filed from the cavern. They were armoured in conical helmets and red leather cuirasses, wore furs around their shoulders and carried tall spears and round wooden shields.

'Mithras!' Crito growled, craning over Pavo's shoulder as the spearmen formed up in a line across the entrance to the pass.

'They're readying to keep someone out?' Sura chattered, glancing in trepidation to the east. 'The Huns?'

'No, they're facing into the pass?' Pavo replied, frowning. 'They're trying to keep someone *in*.'

Then the spearman at the end of the line barked, and the two at the centre of the line looked at each other, frowning. Their commander barked again and the pair grudgingly took a deliberate half step away from each other. This left a gap of a pace between their shields, while the rest of the line stood, shields rim to rim. Pavo frowned.

'They're not trying very hard – a cavalry charge could easily break through that centre,' Sura said, reflecting Pavo's thoughts.

'Sir, now's our chance!' Crito hissed, jabbing a finger up to the two sentries above; both had also turned away to face into the pass, bows lifted, arrows nocked.

Pavo nodded, then turned to the fifty and hissed; 'On my word!' He glanced round once more, then raised a hand. 'Now!'

As soon as the order was given, the statue-still fifty came to life like an iron centipede, snaking through the snowdrifts. When they were almost halfway across, the blizzard howled with a newfound ferocity, battering them from the east. Pavo turned his face away from its wrath, towards the pass. Through slit-eyes, he saw the line of Gothic spearmen and what looked like a distant blur of Gothic horsemen filling the pass behind, racing towards the spear line. But in between were – the breath stilled in his lungs – *Gallus, Felix, Salvian, Tarquitius!*

'Turn and face!' Pavo bellowed. 'Prepare to engage!'

146

The fifty spun to face the pass, startled, as the fleeing Roman horsemen raced for the Gothic spear line.

Salvian burst through the weak centre of the Gothic line, swiping a dagger down at the throat of the nearest warrior, who pirouetted, blood jetting from his jugular. Gallus and Felix heeled their mounts into a jump, the hooves of their beasts bursting the skulls of two more Goths. Then Tarquitius trundled through the hole that was rent in the line.

They had broken clear of the trap, but outside the pass, Tarquitius whipped at his mount with a cane, terrifying the beast and spurring it into a wild gallop. The beast charged forward and then foundered in the deep snowdrifts. In one flurry of hooves and whinnying, it stumbled, snapping a leg and crashing into the path of the other three. All four riders were hurled into the snow. Behind them, the Gothic spearmen had turned and closed ranks, while the mass of Gothic cavalry rumbled up to join their kinsmen. As one, the Gothic warriors advanced.

Pavo saw that they would be on top of Gallus and the Roman riders in moments. 'Forward, double-line, quick march!' He roared.

At first, the recruits hesitated, eyes wide in panic.

'Forward, as one. Stay together and we can face them down!' He cried.

At this, the veterans echoed Pavo's call, and the recruits were jolted into action. The fifty clutched their spears and shields with frozen hands, and shuffled into a line, two deep. Then they ploughed as best they could through the waist-deep drifts. They spilled around Gallus, Salvian, Tarquitius and Felix like a shield. Then Pavo raised his sword, just as he had seen his superiors do time and again, and called out. 'Plumbatae, ready!'

The vexillatio rippled, each man unclipping one of the three weighted darts from the back of his shield and holding it overhead.

Pavo squinted through the snow, seeing that the Goths would rush into range in a few more paces, then he roared; 'Loose!' The pack of missiles arced through the blizzard, and Pavo steeled himself for the crunching of bone that would follow.

But the plumbatae thudded down harmlessly into the snowdrifts, a handful of paces before the Goths who had stopped dead in the mouth of the pass. The men of the vexillatio looked on, stunned, as the Goths remained there, glaring.

Then a war horn moaned twice. At this, the Gothic riders and the spearmen looked to one another, then cast nefarious grins out to the Romans. With that, they turned to walk and trot calmly back into the pass, vanishing into the blizzard.

The survivors of Pavo's fifty fell from the square, panting, some laughing hysterically, others vomiting into the snow.

'Why didn't they come for us?' Crito hissed. 'They could have butchered us!'

'Maybe they thought a legionary cohort might be waiting out here?' Sura reasoned, squinting over his shoulder into the driving snow.

'No. They were obeying orders,' Pavo replied. 'That double call from the war horn, and the gap in the spear line . . . something smells bad about this.'

His words trailed off as, over Crito's shoulder, Pavo caught sight of Salvian. The ambassador was clutching at his shoulder where he had fallen from his mount. The sleeve of his high-necked tunic was stained with blood, and his face was wrinkled with pain.

'Ambassador!' Pavo gasped, rushing to Salvian's side. 'Capsarius!' He yelled, seeking out the medical man of his fifty. Then he pulled at the neck of Salvian's tunic. 'You're losing blood. Let me have a look.'

Salvian pushed him back, his face etched with agony. 'No!' He snarled.

Pavo balked at the ferocity in the man's voice.

Salvian sighed and shook his head, a weary half-grin lifting his lips. 'I'm sorry, lad, I didn't mean to bark at you. It's a simple scrape yet it hurts like Hades . . . but we must break clear of this place. I will bandage it later.'

Pavo shrugged and nodded, frowning. 'Make sure you do. I've seen too many comrades die of what they've called simple wounds. But you're right,' he realised, the image of the Hun horde pushing to the forefront of his thoughts, 'we must make haste from this place.'

He spun to locate Gallus. The tribunus was kneeling by his crippled stallion, whispering soothing words in its ear as he aligned his spatha blade over the beast's heart. Then, with a rasping whinny, the stallion's pain was ended.

Pavo moved to crouch beside Gallus. Then he spoke in a low voice; 'Sir, I have to tell you something . . . '

But the tribunus, still kneeling, was searching the pass with a narrow gaze, lost in thought. 'Either Athanaric's capriciousness has reached new levels, or something is gravely wrong.'

'Sir, something *is* very wrong,' Pavo started, his tone urgent. 'While in Istrita, we saw . . . '

But Gallus continued with his own musings, cutting him off. 'He could have had us slain at any point when we were within his city walls. Yet he chooses to have the peace talks *then* attempts to cut our throats while we sleep. And now, at the last, he lets us slip through his fingers.' He stood, shook his head with a sigh and cast his gaze all around. 'And why . . . *why* do I feel as if we are being watched in our every step?'

The rest of the legionaries within earshot glanced around likewise, their eyes filled with fear at what might be out there in the blizzard. Then, from the east, a hulking shadow appeared in the wall of white, then hundreds more flanked it. To a man, the legionaries braced, breaths stilled in their lungs.

'Did I miss the fight?' A familiar gruff voice cried over the storm. Centurion Zosimus emerged from the whiteness, his legionaries jogging behind him, faces blue, armour stuffed with cloth for insulation. 'We heard the war horns.'

Curses and gasps of relief rang out at the sight of the big Thracian and his men.

149

Pavo shook his thoughts clear of the distraction and turned back to Gallus. 'Sir, In Istrita . . . '

But Gallus was already striding through the snow towards Zosimus. 'We can talk of Istrita when we are on the march,' he called back over his shoulder.

Frustration welled in Pavo's chest until he could maintain decorum no longer. 'The Huns have marched on eastern Gutthiuda!'

The words echoed in the air, and all eyes turned to him. The only noise was that of the howling storm.

Gallus stopped and spun, then strode back to Pavo, gripping his shoulders, eyes wide. 'Speak, soldier!'

'The Huns have descended on Fritigern's lands, sir. More of them than I could hope to count!'

'Mithras, no! If they fall upon Fritigern's lands then . . . '

'Then Fritigern will be forced onto the imperial borders,' Pavo finished as Gallus' eyes darted. 'But the arrival of the dark riders is no coincidence, sir. The Chieftain of Istrita said that they were summoned from the northern steppes.'

'Summoned?'

The legionaries had gathered round the pair in a tight circle now, hanging on every word.

'The chieftain was delirious and rambling. I don't know if his mind had deserted him, but he spoke of a shade. A shade who rides on the plains of Gutthiuda, cloaked and hooded in dark green. The one who leads the rebel Goths. The one who has summoned the Huns and supports their march on Fritigern's lands . . . '

'The Viper?' Gallus finished with a mirthless laugh.

Pavo frowned. 'You have heard of this creature?'

'I have heard only tales and rumour,' Gallus spat, punching a fist into his palm, 'much as you have; that this Viper is long dead. Yet it seems that entire peoples march for him. How can that be?'

'Athanaric has had dealings with the Huns in the past,' Felix offered, his brow etched with a frown. 'My guess is that it is one of his minions – masquerading as this Viper?'

'No, if you had seen the fear on the faces of the people of Istrita,' Pavo shook his head. 'This is no cheap ruse. Those villagers are certain that it is the shade of the Viper himself who is behind all of this – they say the Viper has manipulated Athanaric. And the rebel riders, they are devoted to the Viper's banner.'

Gallus' gaze fell to the snow, his eyes darting.

The blizzard roared over them, and each of them could offer no more.

Then Salvian spoke at last. 'Out here we can find no answers. And if what you say is true, Pavo,' he glanced around the wall of white in every direction, 'then this land is even more treacherous than ever. We must make haste for the Danubius and imperial lands.'

'Agreed,' Gallus growled under his breath. Then he nodded to the aquilifer, who raised the snow-caked eagle standard. 'Let us get out of this accursed land.'

With that, the tribunus filled his lungs;

'Form up. Quick march!'

Chapter 10

It was noon and the snow fell thick and silently over the town of Durostorum and the XI Claudia fort. The streets of the town were bereft of the usual bustle of market day; instead, there was only the wall guard and a few brave souls shuffling around the streets, buying in what provisions were available. Every home glowed orange with firelight and near the centre, *The Boar and Hollybush* glowed brightest. The traditional vine leaves and ale stirring pole emblem by the door were smothered in snow. Inside, the place was dotted with customers and a muted chatter and crackling of a heaped log fire filled the place.

'Tastes kind of . . . fruity,' Avitus mused, squinting as he beheld the ale cup, smacking his lips together.

'Fruity? It's bloody ale! You're the one who's bloody fruity!' Quadratus gasped, then roared in laughter at his own remark.

Avitus shrugged. 'I just mean, well, you know how wine's got flavour, well ale has too, if you think about it.'

'That's just it. I don't think about it, I drink it.' Quadratus jostled in mirth again.

'Alright, alright,' Avitus said, shuffling in his bar stool indignantly. 'I'm just saying, that's all. No harm in observing, is there? Besides, I'm not sure what I'd choose these days. Wine or ale. Wine's got such a rich . . . '

'Ale,' Quadratus said flatly. 'It's what my ancestors drank, it's what I drink. Ale, every time.'

'Fair enough,' Avitus chuckled, supping his drink again. There was a definite note of cherries in there, but he decided not to bother mentioning this to Quadratus. Sighing, he felt the strength of the drink wash around his mind. This was the golden moment, the sense of elation during the first few drinks and before the mood changes and gradual loss of function that usually followed. It was also the short time in between sobriety and deep drunkenness when memories of times past would leave him be.

He glanced around the inn at the array of rosy-cheeked locals and the handful of recruits who were not on sentry duty that morning. Then he looked to Quadratus and realised how much he had missed times like this. Times when both of them were just good friends, drinking and sharing stories together. That was how it had been, he mused, in these last few years, ever since he had come east from Rome; they had shared a contubernium, marching, camping, eating and fighting together. Simple times and good times.

But things had changed when the contubernium had been broken up to repopulate the centurionate, which had been almost completely wiped out during the Bosporus mission. Zosimus, Felix and Quadratus had all been promoted to lead their own centuries and it had driven a wedge into the group. They could never share the same degree of camaraderie while on duty. And Avitus himself could never aspire to join the centurionate, just as he had explained to Gallus when the post had been offered to him; a mere optio could live out his days as just another face in the ranks, but a centurion's name would be too visible – and then the past would find him, surely. He realised he was no longer smiling. The golden moment was over.

His mind drifted inevitably to the past and the dark times, to the stain on his soul: all those missions he had carried out in the provinces of the Western Empire for his shadowy masters, and that last mission they had tasked him with, sending him east. His only solace was that the Avitus that had been sent out east had died that day, or so his old masters believed. And that last mission had never been completed. Even now the contents of that last scroll brought a bitter gall to his throat. So he had chosen his path, and anonymity and fleeting friendships with those who passed through the ranks were to be his lot. If only that had been the end of the matter, he pondered with a scowl.

153

He shook his head clear of the thoughts, slapped a hand on his knee and forced a smile. 'Right, another one?'

Quadratus held up a finger as he drained his existing cup, then slapped it down in the timber bar top. 'Aaah!' He wiped a hand over his moustache. 'Yep, it tastes sweeter with every one.' Then he frowned. 'Still not fruity, mind.'

Avitus chuckled, turning to the barmaid and rummaging in his purse to produce two bronze folles. 'Felicia, another couple of ales please?'

She looked up, her complexion milky-fresh, blue eyes sparkling and a smile beaming through ochre-stained lips. 'Be right with you!' She chirped, sweeping out from behind the bar with a tray of drinks for another table.

Avitus offered her a warm smile in return. Then the shadow of guilt passed over him, and he quickly turned away from her and back to Quadratus.

'Lucky whoreson, that Pavo,' the big Gaul grunted. 'Seems she's settled on him.'

'Eh? Aye, for now,' Avitus raised an eyebrow. Felicia had something of a rich history of involvement with men stationed at the fort. And he was pretty sure he knew why. He gazed into the crackling log fire, memories of that summer night coming back to him all too easily.

It was only a few months after he had sent false reports of his own death back to his western masters. He had been in the Claudia fort, heading back to the barrack blocks when he had noticed the young legionary, Curtius, creeping in the shadows. The lad was armed with a dagger, moving silently for the door at the end of the first barrack block. Avitus realised to whose quarters he was headed, and at that moment he understood that the boy was no mere legionary. His old masters had hired this lad to complete the mission that Avitus could not. The memory of what happened next stung like acid in his thoughts; the scuffle, the pleading, the hesitation, then the thrust of the dagger. For just a fleeting moment on that dark night, he had justified spilling one man's blood over another's, a logic he had never again understood. His usual justification to himself was that he had been young and foolish. 'Old and foolish now,' he muttered.

'Eh?' Quadratus grunted. 'What're you on about?'

Avitus looked up, realising that Felicia had delivered two fresh ales to them while he had been ruminating. 'Ah, nothing, just thinking aloud.'

'We've all got a lot on our mind these days?' Quadratus nodded to the open door, through which the snow-covered bulk of the fortress could just be made out. 'Lupicinus and his legionaries seem set on breaking the recruits. I mean really breaking them, not just scaring them shitless to see how they'll react under pressure. No, he seems to want to really destroy their spirits. Obsessed with showing them up as cowards . . . obsessed!' The big Gaul snorted in disgust.

Avitus nodded. 'He has no time for the Claudia or the task of keeping the borders safe. It's all about Lupicinus, the big hero.'

'Big, prancing fairy, more like. I've yet to see him in battle, when it really matters,' Quadratus replied, stabbing a finger into the cracked oak bar top. 'And from what I've heard, when it really matters, he goes missing.'

'Let's hope it never comes to that,' Avitus supped his ale, 'If Pavo's managed to carry out his orders, then Gallus and the first century are due back within a week. Pray to Mithras the togas that went with him managed to talk Athanaric round to peace.'

Quadratus shot him a wry glare. 'Now you really have been drinking too much of that *fruity* ale.'

The pair shared a dry cackle.

Neither noticed Felicia slip from the inn, cloaked and hooded.

'Faster, ya!' Felicia yelped, heeling her mount on down the road that linked the town to the XI Claudia fortress, snow churning in her wake. Then she

155

veered from the road, cutting diagonally across the fields. *I only have a short time. The faster I get there, the sooner I find out the truth.*

When she neared the fort, she saw the wall guards stretching over the battlements to identify her. She slowed the beast upon approaching the walkway traversing the ditch that surrounded the walls, then lowered her hood and called up to the guards atop the gatehouse. 'Yeast, for the store,' she said through a forced smile, holding up a hemp sack.

The sentry's stony face melted into a boyish grin upon seeing her, and he called down to the gates. 'Open up; lady Felicia coming through.'

The smile fell from her face as soon as the sentry's back was turned, then it reappeared as soon as the gates swung open. The space inside the fort seemed larger than usual; the garrison was even sparser than she had realised. Still, all that mattered was that one man in particular remained stationed here. And while he was drinking himself into a stupor back at the inn, she had this precious opportunity to seize the truth. The *speculatore*, the bastard of an imperial agent who had murdered her dear brother, Curtius.

'Afternoon, miss,' the burly legionary manning the gates offered with a dip of his head. 'It's a cold one for you to be ridin' around in.'

It's about to get a whole lot colder, she realised, her thoughts darkening as she set her eyes upon the barrack block beside the horreum. She patted the hemp sack. 'Maybe, but the price of this will buy a few weeks worth of firewood for the inn.'

'Ah, but the stuff we brew here tastes like warm ditchwater compared to the amber nectar you pour us up at *The Boar.*'

As she dismounted, she tittered and the legionary grinned lovingly. That was all it took, she found, to get from them what she wanted. That was all it had taken the previous week when she had plied some young recruit with ale. She had hoped that in his inebriation, the youngster would help her distil her theory that one of the veterans was the man she sought. Then, like a ray of sunshine in the dead of night, he had started slurring about a secret, something he had seen in one of the barrack blocks; a legionary, crouched and alone, weeping, holding a scroll with a special seal. She hated herself for using the lad like this, but all that mattered was justice. Or was it revenge?

'I hope to see you up there soon?' She winked. 'Now, I'll just drop this off at the horreum, yes?'

The legionary nodded, still smiling before turning back to the gates.

She made for the horreum doors, then stopped and shot a quick glance around the battlements. All of the wall guard were facing out, keeping an eye on the countryside. *Good boys*, she mused. Then she slipped over to the barrack block and crept inside.

Inside, she wrinkled her nose at the questionable odour of stale sweat. Through the gloom, she performed a quick reconnaissance of the contubernium blocks, darting along the corridor, poking her head into each one, and each one was deserted. Her heart began to thud as she reached the block at the end of the corridor. Inside, eight bunks lay unoccupied, the bedding roughly tidied. This was it.

Then she stopped, seeing the strip of red silk tied to the bedpost of one of the bunks. She moved to it and traced a finger over its softness, remembering Pavo's face when she had given it to him. She could still detect the sweet scent she had put on it to remind him of her. Pavo was a different prospect to the other soldiers; a young man with a good heart. Apart from this strip of silk, all she had given him was mixed messages and violent mood swings. He deserved better than that, and she had known this for some time. But, like everything else, Pavo came second to finding Curtius' killer. She composed herself and turned away from Pavo's bunk.

She scoured the wall at the other end of the room. There it was, just as the young recruit had said; an area of flaking mortar, just behind the head of one of the lower bunks. This was where the recruit had seen the weeping veteran and the scroll. She gathered herself and heaved at the timber frame of the bunk, hauling it back from the wall. Now she could see the outline of the stone that sat loose in the mortar. She wrapped her fingers around it and pulled. With a grating of rock and a cloud of dust, the stone came loose. She squatted to be level with the hole it left behind.

There, at the back, lay a scroll, just as she had been told. She reached in and lifted it out. It was a single scroll, yellowed and torn around the edges. Most importantly, it bore a wax seal. The seal was coded, but Felicia had seen that coding before. The seal of the *Speculatores*, the scum of the empire. Men who would rob, rape or murder at the emperor's request. The man who had hidden this scroll was one of them. *Curtius was one of them too!* A voice rasped in her mind. She screwed her eyes shut tight and shook her head.

He was young and foolish. He did not deserve what happened to him, she affirmed.

Stuffing the scroll into her cloak, she then opened the sack of yeast and rummaged inside, pulling out a smaller sack that jingled with a thick clunk of coins, and bore the XI Claudia bull stamp on its fibres. She placed it into the hole and replaced the stone and then pushed the bunk back into place.

Outside, she heard a babble of voices. Fear gripped her. She scurried for the door then stopped herself, taking a deep breath and standing tall before she stepped outside. The heavy snow was still falling as she passed two recruits who entered the barrack block. Then, she threw one arm over her horse, ready to mount, when a voice split the air.

'You there! What were you doing in the barracks?'

She started, glancing to the centre of the fort. From the principia, a sharp-faced, plumed and ornately armed figure approached her. Squinting, she searched for a viable explanation. Then she relaxed into a beguiling smile as she found one. The perfect one.

'I was looking for one of your legionaries. Numerius Vitellius Pavo?'

'Ah, Pavo, the so-called hero?' The officer chortled.

She had heard of the jumped-up peacock who had come in to rule the XI Claudia, and she was fairly sure this was him.

The officer's expression changed as he beheld Felicia at close range, a glint of lust igniting in his eyes and his tongue jabbing out to dampen his lips. 'Pavo is currently out in the badlands of Gutthiuda, miss. He won't be back here for some time. But perhaps I can help? Comes Lupicinus, at your disposal.'

She suppressed a shudder, then composed herself. 'Well, perhaps,' she looked away, then back to him with a girlish shyness.

Lupicinus puffed out his chest. 'I am in charge of all you see here, and of all you can see in every direction from the top of the walls. What can I do for you?'

'Well, I went into Pavo's bunk block there, and I noticed something. The wall was crumbling.

'Ah yes, the place needs patching up and a good lick of paint,' Lupicinus agreed.

'But there was something behind the mortar,' Felicia tried her best to look puzzled, 'some kind of sack with a legionary emblem on it.' She leaned closer to him, looking to each side as if to share a secret. 'It was full of coins.'

Lupicinus' face paled and he squared his jaw.

Quadratus woke with a groan, rubbing his temples. He felt as if his head had been used for clubbing practice and his mouth was bone dry and felt as if it was coated in fur. His eyes were still welded shut, but he could sense the dawn light upon them. Without opening them, he rolled over, away from the light, shivering, clasping at his blanket – it seemed coarser than usual, and there was a dank, musty smell in the air. Well it would take more than that to rouse him, he mused. All he could remember of the previous night at the inn was Avitus' face growing rosier, the fire warmer, and the local ladies friendlier. When had they left the inn to head back to the fort? His memory was pure, unspoilt, jet-black.

Another wave of agony shot through his brain. 'Oh bugger, I think we overdid it this time, Avitus,' he grunted in the direction of his optio's bunk. But there was no reply.

Then he heard a tinny rattle of keys in a lock.

Quadratus blinked his eyes open. He was not in the barrack block.

'What the? Where am I?'

He shot to sitting, squinting at the orange glare of the dawn sun that beamed through an open door, framing a plumed silhouette and two armed men either side.

'Centurion Quadratus,' the voice spoke.

Quadratus instantly recognised the voice. 'Comes Lupicinus?' He scanned the bare stone room and the iron bars. 'Why am I in jail?'

'You have been found guilty of the theft of legionary wages.' Lupicinus held up a hemp sack with the faded bull emblem of the legion. 'I told all of you I would find the culprit, and I told you they would be dealt with *severely*.'

Quadratus roared with laughter despite his miserable state, then clutched his pounding head. 'Leave it out. Now get out of my way, it must be time for morning roll call.' He stood and scrutinised each of the men stood by Lupicinus, fully expecting one of them to be a grinning Avitus. But both of them were Lupicinus' men, comitatenses clad in their scale vests, and both wore baleful glares and flexed their fingers by their sword hilts.

'You are to be bound in a sack of asps and drowned in the Danubius.'

Quadratus' jaw fell open and he uttered a bemused gasp. The punishment had fallen into folklore such was the rarity of its use, similar to stoning and being beaten to death by colleagues.

Lupicinus nodded to his two men. They both strode forward and grappled Quadratus by an arm each.

'Get your hands off me, you whoresons!' He roared, thrashing his elbows, the left crunching against one man's jaw, sending him spiralling back into the wall. Then, with a sledgehammer of an uppercut, the big Gaul sent the other man flying against the iron bars. Then he turned on Lupicinus, but the comes stood poised, his sword drawn. Quadratus clasped his hand to his missing scabbard, then uttered a curse and balled his fists, stomping forward.

'Guards!' Lupicinus roared down the jail corridor, backing off.

At once, a party of five more of Lupicinus' men came thundering down the corridor bearing spears. They surrounded the big Gaul and pinned him in the circle of their spearpoints.

Quadratus' face grew a shade of plum, and he readied to lash out, despite the odds. Then a cry echoed down the corridor.

'No, Quadratus!' Avitus called as he ran to the scene. 'Don't fight them, I know you're innocent. We can sort this out.' The little Roman turned to Lupicinus. 'I've told you, there's no way he did this, sir. Centurion Quadratus lives, breathes and sleeps for this legion.'

'The money was found concealed by his bunk,' Lupicinus countered, 'we discussed all of this last night. Although you two were in a disgraceful state – it's little wonder you remember none of It.'

Avitus frowned and looked away from the tribunus. 'I know the money was found by his bunk, but that doesn't mean he put it there, surely? Let me defend him.'

Lupicinus turned to him with a sneer. 'Defend him?'

'At the trial?' Avitus cocked an eyebrow.

Lupicinus barely disguised a grin. 'There will be no trial. The execution is to take place today. Immediately.'

One of Lupicinus' men unfurled a large hemp sack. 'The snake keeper is here, sir,' he purred.

'No trial? You can't do that. The tribunus would not allow it,' Avitus stammered.

161

Lupicinus' men barged him out of the way, three of them tethering Quadratus' hands. 'You forget, your precious Tribunus Gallus is not here. I am in charge and I insist that the thief dies before the sun has risen. His drowning will teach the rest of the ranks to think twice should they be tempted to line their purses.'

With a suddenly leaden heart, Quadratus glanced back at his optio and good friend. He knew it would probably be the last time he would see him. Wearing just a tunic and boots, he was marched through the fort and out onto the snow-coated plain. The stark chill searched his bare limbs as he was guided towards the banks of the Danubius. There he felt the eyes of the formed-up and scant garrison upon him; the two sagittarii, the smattering of auxiliaries, the turma of equites, the turma of foederati and the pocket of Claudia legionaries alongside Lupicinus' century and a half of comitatenses. Did they pity him, despise him or fear him? It didn't matter, he realised, nothing would matter in moments. He looked up at the sky, blue in between the gathering clusters of fresh snow clouds. He could hear only the rush of the waters as he searched for the words of the prayer to Mithras. Then he wondered if a prayer to the Christian God would be prudent.

Then a hiss of a snake tore him from his thoughts and, for the first time in years, he felt fear twist through his veins. The snake handler held in his arms an asp that writhed in agitation, and beside him was a timber crate, the gaps between the slats revealing several more of the creatures. His heart thudded and then, like the passing eye of a storm, the fear dissolved and he felt only sympathy for the beasts, for they were to die needlessly as well.

Then, as Lupicinus read out the charges again, he noticed something else, behind the snake handler. A black-cloaked and hooded figure stood, hands clasped. Then the hands moved to lower the hood. It was Felicia the barmaid, but her usual beauty was wrinkled in a cold, spiteful grimace. Quadratus frowned. Then he noticed something else: Avitus had joined the ranks. The little Roman winked at him, then patted the bow slung across his shoulder and nodded.

Quadratus frowned, then realised what his friend had in mind. But all around them, Lupicinus' legionaries stood guard – too many of them. He tried to fire a frosty glare to Avitus. But before he could, a knee barged him forward, to the lip of the bank where the earth had sheared away and a six foot drop into the Danubius awaited.

He eyed the swirling torrents, shivering at the sight of the occasional chunks of ice that clashed together on the surface. With a chorus of angered spitting and clouded breath, the snakes were dumped in the sack. Then he heard footsteps march up behind him. He closed his eyes.

Then he heard the stretching of a bowstring.

Quadratus spun on the spot. 'No, don't do it!' He called to Avitus.

But Avitus, standing with the bow slackening in his grip, stared back not at him but across to the north bank of the river. Lupicinus and the watching ranks did likewise, mouths agape. The snakes sprang from the sack and clamped their fangs into the snake handler's throat and shoulders, but not one person moved to help him or even looked in his direction.

Quadratus blinked, then turned to the north bank. There, emerging from the tree line, were armoured Gothic cavalry and spearmen. First a few. Then hundreds.

Then thousands.

At their head, surrounded by sapphire-blue hawk banners, Iudex Fritigern was saddled on a black stallion and in full battle armour.

A Gothic horn moaned, and the cavalry flooded onto the pontoon bridge.

Chapter 11

The gale had eased and now the snow fell silently over the upper Danubius. Pavo waited in line as each of the weary column hopped from the northern bank, across a gangplank and onto the Roman trade cog that Gallus had abruptly commandeered from the riverside. The portly ship's captain had suffered an apparent loss of hearing when the tribunus had first hailed him, but a few well aimed plumbatae had remedied that.

The already heavily burdened cog sunk lower in the water as each of the legionaries hopped onto the ship. Gallus stood on the deck, waving each of them aboard. 'That's it, lads! As soon as we're off the banks we can eat, slake our thirst and set sail for home.'

Pavo stalked across the plank and thudded onto the deck; treading on wood felt good after nearly seven days of relentless marching through knee-deep snow with only fleeting breaks to rest. They had hunted and foraged along the way, sheltering in caves when the storm grew too fierce to continue.

He trudged past the captain, whose face grew darker the further his vessel sunk into the water. Then he sidled over to Sura, who had already pulled his hardtack and mutton ration from his pack and was chewing on it like a starved wolf.

'Hunger is a spice for any meal, eh?' Pavo sighed as he took off his helmet then set down his shield and pack to sit by his friend, letting the tension ease from his body. Still munching, Sura offered Pavo a piece of hardtack in lieu of a reply. He took it, snapped the piece in two and crunched into one half, then washed it down with a generous swig of soured wine. All around him, the legionaries groaned as they loosened their boots and burdens likewise.

The gangplank was withdrawn and the cog set off downriver. Pavo sighed as he took another swig of wine. The liquid was tart on his tongue and instantly warmed his blood. He watched as Gallus strode around the deck, offering words of encouragement to his men. It had been a seamless and natural transition of command; the survivors of his fifty merging with Gallus' vexillatio. Even Crito and the rest of Lupicinus' men behaved like model soldiers under Gallus' gaze. The mere presence of the tribunus had driven them on, even when they were at their weakest. And, at last, Pavo was back in the ranks. It was what he had craved since Lupicinus had forced command upon him, but now that it had been taken away he felt a stinging shame on his skin. He did not resent Gallus in any way; instead, he loathed himself.

Crito ambled past, groaning, rubbing a hand across the small of his back. Pavo braced for either a sneer or some barbed comment, but instead, the veteran simply gave him a nod. Pavo wondered if he had won some modicum of respect from the grizzled veteran, or if Crito now no longer saw him as some kind of threat or affront now that he was a mere grunt again. His mood darkened.

'You'll get your chance again, lad,' a familiar voice spoke beside him.

He looked up to see Salvian. The ambassador was still lithe and looked comparatively fresh for a non-military man who had just been subjected to such a march. If anything, he looked in better shape than many of the legionaries.

'My chance? I'm not sure I want it,' Pavo spoke in a hushed tone, expecting Salvian to chuckle at this and hoping Sura by his other side would not hear him.

But the ambassador shook his head, his sharp features sincere. 'You were magnificent back at the pass. Your tribunus has commented on this more than once since then. It's not a matter of whether you will be given a leader's role, Pavo, but when. I meant what I said before, you know; your father would have been proud of you,' Salvian continued unabated.

165

Pavo nodded firmly, hoping the moisture welling in his eyes at the sentiment wasn't visible. He realised he was looking at Senator Tarquitius, stood alone at the prow of the ship. The senator still cut a haunted figure and had barely uttered a word since the skirmish at the pass.

Salvian followed his gaze and then smiled. 'Ah, yes, the senator's demands of you. Have you made your decision – will you humour him?'

Pavo frowned. He had barely had time to think over Tarquitius' demands for garrison information.

Salvian sighed. 'I'm sorry, your mind is troubled enough. Think only of where we are headed, the fort, your woman . . . ' he finished with a half-grin. With that, Salvian strolled over to a cluster of legionaries, accepted the offer of a wineskin, then immediately had them roaring in laughter with some quip.

Pavo looked to Salvian, and then to Tarquitius again at the opposite end of the boat. *To betray my legion and learn the truth?* His mind filled with a collage of all the times he had been a whisker from death at the end of a barbarian blade. Father had fallen to such a blade. He thought over Salvian's words in the forest just a handful of nights previous. *If you choose well, you are blessed; if you choose poorly, you will be stronger for it. Perhaps it is time to serve yourself?* He nodded; maybe it was time to sacrifice a sliver of honour.

He lifted his soured wineskin once more and took a generous swig. Then he strode over to Tarquitius, rested his hands on the prow and looked downriver to the same distant point the senator's gaze was fixed on.

'I will do as you ask. But on one condition; you must promise me that no lives will be lost from whatever . . . *initiative* you have planned.'

The senator remained silent, staring downriver. Pavo frowned. 'Senator?' He said, his voice low.

Then Tarquitius turned to him, face ghostly-white, eyes bulging and distant, sweat snaking across his forehead despite the cold. The Senator's lips trembled as he spoke. 'I have no need of the Sardica information now.'

Pavo's blood boiled at this. 'What?' He hissed. 'Is this some kind of game to you? You dangle some truth in front of me and then tear it away! You will tell me what you know of my father!' Pavo snarled.

Tarquitius' haunted expression did not change despite Pavo's ire. Staring through him, the senator muttered; 'I can never tell you.'

Pavo felt his hands tremble, and the urge to wrap them around the senator's fat neck was overwhelming. Then he felt the eyes of the other legionaries on them. 'This is not over,' he snorted in disgust, then took another mouthful of wine and strode to the side of the vessel, his breaths coming short and shallow.

He leant over the side; the rippling water growing hypnotic. Perhaps this was fate telling him he had made the wrong choice, he mused. He felt his mind grow giddy as the wine took hold, and this lifted his spirit just a fraction, pushing the senator's game from his thoughts. But, almost immediately, the grim truth of what might be waiting on them downriver came flooding in to replace it. He longed to learn that Felicia was safe, and he searched the swirling rapids as if looking for some confirmation of this.

He turned from the edge of the vessel and made to take another swig of soured wine, but stopped, seeing Gallus walk over to him.

'Drink your fill, Pavo. Mithras knows you've earned it.'

Pavo nodded, then looked into the mouth of the skin and sighed. 'Perhaps later,' he said, putting the cork back in place. 'I feel it may taste far sweeter once we have set eyes upon Durostorum and the fort and are sure all is well there.'

Gallus frowned.

'It's the Hun horde we saw, sir. Every time I think back over it, I am sure it must have been a nightmare,' he shook his head, 'but it was real, and I fear that we may be returning too late.'

'Then you are not alone.' Gallus looked downriver pensively. 'A game is being played, Pavo. The Huns will show no mercy to Fritigern's people, and I just know Athanaric is embroiled in their arrival.' He paused, shaking his head. 'But this . . . Viper, I fear he is no shade. We have both seen the rebels and their devotion to the Viper's cause. Men do not fight for shades, Pavo. Yet this creature has so far remained invisible . . . and the most deadly enemy is the one you cannot see.'

At that moment, a distant moan of a Gothic war horn sounded downriver. The entire crew of the cog froze.

Pavo and Gallus stared at one another.

Avitus could only stare at the sight; the rush of the rapids and the rapping of hooves filled the air as the Gothic cavalry rumbled over the timber bridge, snow churning in their wake.

Every fibre in his being screamed to run or draw his spatha, but he noticed that the riders did not move at a charge. They looked weary and nervous and their weapons were sheathed. More, behind the warriors on the far bank, many thousands of Gothic women, children and elderly had emerged from the forests, their faces gaunt and staring like lost souls. He glanced to Quadratus; the big Gaul stepped backwards from the riverbank and crouched by the puffy, blue-skinned corpse of the snake handler. His eyes never left the far riverbank as he snatched the long dagger from the dead man's belt.

'What is this? Do they come in peace?' Avitus said.

'Aye, so it seems,' Quadratus nodded as he stood. Then he turned to the rest of the legion; some were stumbling into a run for the fort, others were levelling their spears, eyes wide in panic. 'Sheathe your weapons!' The big Gaul cried. But even as the words left his lips, one legionary roared in a mix of terror and bravado, hurling a plumbata at the foremost Gothic rider who was halfway across the bridge. The dart punched through the man's jaw and sent him sliding onto the pontoon bridge.

'You bloody fool,' Avitus gawped at the legionary who had thrown the dart. It was Ursus, one of Lupicinus' men, and he had already turned to run for the fort. At this, other legionaries hurled their spears and darts at the approaching riders before turning tail. Three more Goths were punched from their mounts by the hail.

On the bridge, a rabble of confusion grew amongst the Goths, then boiled over into a cacophony of anguished cries as word of the slayings spread. The riders around the slain men cried out and drew their longswords. Then, like a porcupine presenting its spines, all those behind followed suit. As one, the Gothic cavalry broke into a charge.

'Oh, bollocks!' Quadratus bundled the recruits back towards the fort. 'Run, you bloody idiots, run!'

Avitus turned to run with the big centurion, then stopped short as he saw Felicia. Her face was torn in a scowl, stalking round to the rear of Quadratus, a curved iron dagger in her hand. He leapt for her, grappling her by the arm so the dagger fell to the snow.

'Get your hands off me,' she hissed, her breath clouding in the air.

'Sorry, miss. No time for manners or we're all dead,' he spoke gruffly, shoving her towards the fort gates.

Her eyes narrowed on Quadratus as she backed away before turning to run for the fort. At that moment, Avitus realised that she knew. Or at least she thought she knew. She had found his scroll and assumed that it belonged to Quadratus, framing the big Gaul for the wage theft.

Then a ham-like hand grappled his tunic collar and yanked him forward as well.

'Move!' Quadratus bawled in his ear.

The pair set off at a sprint, the ground shaking beneath them from the chasing cavalry. Up ahead, Lupicinus sprinted at the head of the Roman retreat, all decorum and smug majesty from moments ago discarded. They stumbled past the four-pronged ballista and Avitus growled. 'Never even got a single shot away!'

169

Quadratus pulled him along. 'Just keep your eyes on the gate, we're almost there . . . ' his words were cut off by the crunch of a Gothic spear ripping through the chest of a recruit who had stumbled just ahead of him.

'Death to the Romans!' A jagged Gothic cry filled the air.

Avitus shot a look over his shoulder; Fritigern and his retinue of riders followed the charging cavalry, but while the lead riders' faces were twisted in fury, the Gothic Iudex was roaring at them, gesticulating, waving them back. 'Stop, you fools,' Fritigern roared at his men, 'the Romans are not our enemies!' But the charging cavalry were deaf to their leader's pleas.

Avitus faced front again. Then his shins thwacked into something, and he and Quadratus tumbled to the ground, ploughing into the deep snow.

Avitus scrambled to his feet and glanced back to see what they had tripped upon.

Comes Lupicinus lay in the snow, clutching his ankle, panic welling in his eyes. He reached out to Quadratus, his lips flapping silently as if stalling when trying to call for help.

Avitus looked to Quadratus, then the pair looked to the cavalry haring in on the felled Roman, spears raised. With a grunt, Quadratus leapt up.

'No!' Avitus yelled. But Quadratus was determined, stomping back towards Lupicinus. With a frustrated growl, Avitus prised a spear from the hands of a dead recruit and hoisted it then hurled it forward with a roar. The missile punched through the lead cavalryman, who was thrown back into his fellow riders' paths and the charge faltered for a precious instant. Quadratus heaved Lupicinus up and slung him across his broad shoulders, then hobbled for the fort gates. Avitus skirted around the centurion, loosing arrows at the reforming riders to cover the retreat. The recruits spilled onto the battlements and began roaring encouragement to the trio.

Quadratus stumbled to his knees as soon as he was inside the fort, dropping Lupicinus to the ground. 'Get the bloody gates closed!' He bellowed at the pale-faced and trembling recruits, twisting to see the snarling Gothic riders just strides from the entrance.

As the gates slammed shut and the locking bar clunked into place, Quadratus and Avitus issued a synchronised sigh of relief.

Then, oblivious to the *capsarii* rushing to surround him, bearing dressings and salve, Lupicinus looked up at Quadratus. 'You saved me?' The comes stammered.

Quadratus shrugged.

Avitus stepped between the two and stooped to glare at Lupicinus. 'And I trust he can consider himself pardoned?'

'Yes,' Lupicinus nodded, his features milky-white with terror. 'Yes, he can.'

Then a jagged cry rang out from outside the fort. Not the cry of a Gothic horde, but the booming voice of one man.

'Sir,' one of the recruits on the walls cried, 'Iudex Fritigern requests parley.'

Lupicinus' eyes widened and his face paled, then he shrugged off the medics and held out an arm to Quadratus. 'Get me up to the walls, soldier!'

Avitus took the other half of the comes' weight, and together, he and Quadratus hobbled up the steps to the battlements. There, they let Lupicinus down. The comes slapped his hands onto the battlements to balance, sending thick snow down into the ditch below.

Then the three plus the meagre garrison of the fort fell silent as they gawped out across the plain. Fritigern's followers were now flooding across the pontoon bridge in a seemingly endless train. All up and down the river, rafts and small boats were being launched to bring over swathes more. Crowds of Goths pressed against the far riverbank, unable to force their way onto the bridge or onto any crafts. They cast frequent nervous glances over their shoulders to the north and moaned in fear at the shadows back there – then huge groups of them began throwing themselves into the raging torrents of the river. They thrashed bravely in an attempt to swim to the southern bank, but few made it more than halfway across before perishing. Already formed up to face the fort were Gothic spearmen in their thousands and

171

cavalry numbering several thousand again. Behind this army, the Gothic women, children and elderly clustered in their tens of thousands. They brought with them emaciated herds of mules, goats and oxen, and drew carts and pulled baggage on timber frames.

The recruits around Lupicinus were quick to offer their insights. 'Fritigern has pacified his men, sir. The riders who charged us have been disarmed,' one said.

Lupicinus seemed to draw confidence from this information and the thick walls that separated him from the Goths. He puffed out his chest and straightened his helmet. 'Good, good. The barbarian knows what a mistake he has made.'

'Sir,' Quadratus hissed beside him. 'We must tread carefully or there will be a massacre here today. Remember, we cast the first dart on the bridge.'

'Don't push your luck, Centurion; leave the thinking to me,' Lupicinus peered down his nose.

As Quadratus turned away to disguise a muted flurry of curses, Avitus noticed something in the comes' eyes; pure terror.

Down on the plain, Fritigern had pushed through to the fore on his stallion. Grey-flecked, fiery red locks and a beard tumbled down his shoulders from under his ornate, silver, full-face helmet.

Lupicinus called out to him, his voice shrill and wavering. 'Iudex Fritigern. By crossing the Danubius, you have committed an act of war against the Roman Empire. You will be shown no mercy by our legions.'

Fritigern removed his helmet, his locks framing deep-set, tawny-gold eyes, flat cheekbones and a narrow nose. He pointed to the handful of legionary and Gothic corpses strewn on the path to the fort from the bridge. 'That Roman and Gothic blood was spilled is regrettable, but you must believe me; I come here not as an enemy, but as an ally of Rome. We had no choice but to hasten across the bridge, for the dark riders are less than a morning's ride behind us!' Fritigern waved a hand back to the far riverbank.

Lupicinus heard this and then stabbed out his tongue to dampen his lips. 'Who?'

'The Huns. The dark riders of the northlands, they have conquered all who have crossed their path so far; the Alani, the Neuri, the Geloni, the Agathyrsi, the Melanchaenae . . . and they almost exterminated our cousins, the Greuthingi! Now they have descended upon my lands without warning or mercy with many more warriors than I have mustered here,' he swept a hand across the ever-swelling sea of armoured men and riders. There were at least ten thousand Gothic warriors and what looked like more than many times that number of civilians, with more still flooding across the bridge. 'My people have suffered terribly in these last days, their families slain, their lands raped and confiscated.'

'So state your case, Goth. What are you here for?'

Fritigern clasped a hand across his chest. 'We come seeking shelter in Roman lands.'

Avitus and Quadratus looked to each other.

'Have we got room for, what, a hundred thousand in here?' Quadratus snorted under his breath.

'We ask for grain and land to settle. In return this mighty army you see before you will guard your borders to the last. The Hun hordes who drove us here will not be able to sweep across the river like they swept across my lands, I am sure of it. Not while all Rome and all my warriors await them. And that is the key; a true alliance between our peoples and our armies. Added to this, we will comply with your emperor's long-standing wish for my people to convert entirely to the Arian faith. What say you, Roman?' A chill wind whipped across the snowy plain and the question hung in the air as Fritigern clutched the Chi-Rho emblem on a chain around his neck. 'Remember that we are in truce and think well on the consequences of your answer.'

Avitus' turned to Lupicinus, whose eyes darted, widening in growing panic. 'We need to preserve the alliance, sir, at all costs. But there's no way we can support these people – there's no way they can support themselves –

the whole province is on the brink of famine as it is. We have to send word south, to Constantinople . . . and east, to the emperor!' He glanced to the imperial messenger by the fort stables.

But Lupicinus was hesitant. He turned to the two. 'This is not your decision to make, Optio, nor is it that of your centurion. No, Fritigern has come to me, and it is up to me to manage this situation.'

Quadratus frowned. 'Sir, we need help.'

Lupicinus raised a hand. 'I will not call for help!' Lupicinus snapped, his eyes wild, his lips twisted into a snarl. 'No, the coward who calls for help is already beaten. I am no coward! I can manage this, alone!'

Avitus looked to Quadratus, the pair sharing a look of weary dread.

Lupicinus shook his head. 'Send a rider to summon the remainder of my comitatenses from the coast – two centuries of the finest soldiers.'

'You talk of centuries,' Avitus uttered. 'Sir, we need legions to deal with this.'

'Your commander has given you an order. See that it is carried out.'

'You're being a fool!' Quadratus spat.

'Watch your tongue, Centurion,' Lupicinus barked, and two of his retinue barged forward, hands on spatha hilts.

Avitus leapt in front of Quadratus, spreading his arms wide between the two antagonists. 'No! We must remain calm!'

Quadratus stepped back, simmering with rage. 'Yes, *sir*,' he grunted to Lupicinus.

The sky greyed and the first flakes of a fresh snowfall began to spiral around Avitus and Quadratus as they flitted down the steps. Behind them, Lupicinus' booming reply to Fritigern rang out, his tone haughty and self-reverent as he invited the iudex and his retinue to come to the fort gates.

Avitus leaned in towards his big friend as they walked. 'Be wary of your words around him; he acts on whims and seems driven by pride. You were moments from having icy river water in your lungs and asp-venom in your veins!'

'But he's a bloody fool,' Quadratus muttered under his breath. 'He's obsessed with proving he is not a coward. All we've worked for, all our brothers who have died over the years. That imbecile will tear it all to shreds. For what – his pride?' He threw his arms up.

'Then *we* need to intervene.' Avitus replied in a hushed voice, eyes darting to make sure nobody else was within earshot.

'Aye,' Quadratus nodded, smoothing his moustache, 'but how?'

'We write the emperor a message, and sign it as if it came from that arsehole up there,' Avitus nodded to the figure of Lupicinus on the battlements. Then he slipped a hand into his purse and produced the neatly broken wax seal he had lifted from the Principia floor that morning. The seal bore the imperial eagle and was ringed with the letters of Lupicinus' name and rank. He felt a twinge of righteousness; sleight of hand and stealth were two skills from his past that he could put to good use for once.

'Eh?' Quadratus grunted, eyeing the piece, then nodding to the Principia. 'You'll be hard-pressed getting the scribe in there to forge a letter – he's been kissing Lupicinus' arse as if Gallus never existed.'

'Then I'll write it myself,' he said.

Quadratus frowned at him.

Avitus shrugged. Men of the ranks could not write, and Avitus had never revealed this skill, burying it with the rest of his past. 'There are things I learned, things I did, back in the West,' he started, feeling the words tumble out like a confession, 'that I left behind. Or that was the plan. Funny how the past just keeps coming back, isn't it?'

Quadratus' frown remained for a moment, then a broad, stump-toothed grin broke out across his face. 'You sly little whoreson! Let's do it!'

The pair ducked into the barrack block, then emerged a few moments later, Avitus bearing a rolled-up scroll of paper with the wax seal melted onto it. He stopped by a tall, dappled gelding and slapped its haunches, then called to the nervous-looking imperial messenger stood nearby, eyeing the battlements. It was Ennius, the rider who had been despatched to Gallus' party in the forest with the order to wait on the ambassadors. 'Oi, forget what's happening out there, get over here.'

'Sir?' Ennius asked.

'You have family in Durostorum, yes?'

'I do, sir. My wife, my elderly father and two baby girls.'

'And do you fear for them right now?'

Ennius gulped and eyed the battlements again. 'I'd do anything to protect them.'

Avitus nodded. 'Good lad. Now get fresh water and rations for a ride. A long ride. I want you to go east, to the port at Tomis. Get a berth on the fastest imperial vessel there that's heading for the Persian front. If there isn't one going there soon, then charter one.' He held out the scroll. 'This should see you right. When you're landed again, ride until your arse bleeds and get word to Emperor Valens. The scroll holds all the detail, but tell him we need legions, lots of them.'

Ennius hesitated. 'But, sir, I overheard Comes Lupicinus; he said he wanted a rider despatched to summon his centuries from the coast?'

Avitus gripped the rider's shoulders. 'To Hades with the comes – we will despatch another rider to do his bidding later, but you must ride now. Save your empire, man, and save your family!'

The rider nodded, grasped three water skins and pulled his cloak around his shoulders, then leapt onto his gelding and heeled it into a trot for the fort gates.

Avitus watched the gates creaking open, and wondered if it would be becoming to issue a prayer to Mithras for the rider. Would Mithras know of his sins of the past? Would he forgive him them should this Ennius reach the emperor in time. His thoughts churned.

Then, as the gates swung fully open, Ennius broke into a gallop. But the gates did not shut behind him. Instead, the gateway was filled by a mass of foreign riders.

Iudex Fritigern and his retinue entered the fort, their faces stony.

Chapter 12

It was nearing sunset when the cog rounded a bend in the river. At last, Pavo recognised the snow-cloaked hinterland on the southern banks and the faint salt tang in the air. He glanced to Sura, who wore a matching grin.

Then, a roar from the crow's nest confirmed it as the stone-walled town rolled into view, bathed in the fading sunlight. 'Durostorum!'

'Thank Mithras!' Felix cried, perched halfway up the mast, punching a fist in the air. 'The imperial banners still fly above her walls!'

The legionaries leapt to their feet, pushing to the edge of the vessel to stand alongside Pavo. There they erupted in a cheer at the sight of the market town that was home to many of them. Then they cheered again, even louder, when they saw one of the few men left in the wall guard waving at them from the snow-coated battlements.

But Pavo's grin faded as they approached, for the sentry was not waving in greeting; his arms were moving frantically, pointing downriver.

'Silence!' Gallus barked.

Then, over the roar of the rapids, they heard the man's pleas.

'Get to the fort!'

All on the cog fell silent as it rounded another bend and the plain east of the town spread out before them.

The XI Claudia fortress was like a lonely rock in an unsettled sea of foreign peoples, tents and campfires.

Goths were everywhere, like a crop field, from the fort and all the way across the plain to the gates of Durostorum. Women, children and elderly swarmed between the tents, campfires and malnourished herds of goats and oxen. Pockets of warriors patrolled the camp, wearing conical helmets and red leather vests, bearing spears and round wooden shields. Others stood watch around the edge of the camp and some tended to their fine mounts, penned in to rudimentary stable areas. In the centre of the camp, the sapphire hawk banner of Fritigern rippled in the breeze.

Then Pavo heard a muttering by his side.

'By Mithras, it has happened. What have I done?'

Pavo frowned, turning to see Tarquitius, flexing his fingers on the rim of the vessel; the senator's face was a deathly white as if he had witnessed an army of shades.

'Fear not,' Salvian said before Pavo could question his old tormentor. The ambassador pointed to the cluster of legionaries who appeared to be helping a family of Goths in setting up their tent. 'It seems that the Goths are here in peace, and that Fritigern upholds the truce.'

'And we can only be thankful it was not the dark riders we found,' Pavo spoke sternly, following Tarquitius' furtive glances over to the shadowy northern banks of the river; then he noticed the pontoon bridge had been destroyed and prayed that meant the march of the Huns had been curtailed.

Then a pair of Goths in the watchtower of the castrum – all that was left of the bridge – cried out then raised their bows and loosed a pair of fire arrows. The flaming missiles streaked into the twilight sky, illuminating a basic timber jetty as they fell silently into the waters.

Gallus glared at the Gothic spearmen who filed to the jetty, beckoning the Romans to the riverbank. 'It appears they are welcoming us home.'

Inside the principia, the air crackled with tension. Gallus and Lupicinus sat opposite one another across the large, scarred oak table, the candlelight casting both of their faces in demonic shadow.

Pavo darted a glance to those around the table: Sura, Zosimus, Felix, Quadratus and Avitus stood with Pavo in an arc behind Gallus, while a group of six grimacing, scale-vested comitatenses stood behind Lupicinus. Ambassador Salvian stood in the middle, a look of bemusement on his sharp features. Tarquitius was seated beside him, his face still milky pale and his eyes bloodshot and weary – seemingly still haunted by his trip to Dardarus.

'I defer to your authority, sir,' Gallus spoke calmly, 'but I must insist on a full debriefing on why I returned from my mission to be escorted into my own fort . . . ' the tribunus paused as his veneer of calm dissolved, his top lip trembling, his teeth grinding, ' . . . by *Goths?*'

'You are correct, Tribunus,' Lupicinus spat back, 'you *will* defer to my authority.'

Gallus sighed, giving a reluctant nod. 'Without question. But, in the best interests of the legion and the borders we are sworn to protect, sir, tell me why Fritigern's armies and people swamp the land from here to Durostorum?'

'Iudex Fritigern and I have come to an understanding, Tribunus,' Lupicinus began, his tone sharp, 'and the crux of it is that our borders are now secure. The foederati are commonplace in the legions these days, and I have simply taken that to the next level.' The comes' words were firm, but his eyes barely masked panic.

Gallus hesitated, his glare speaking a thousand words. 'Foederati have, until now, been employed in manageable numbers. Some of them good-hearted and willing fighters, some of them vile cutthroats. Believe me, I have experienced the best and the worst of them. But we have never opened our borders to an entire *people!*'

Lupicinus sat back, a look of smug contentment in his eyes as he tapped a finger to his temple. 'Progressive thinking, Tribunus. We are now in a new age, an age when the legions alone are not enough.'

Gallus dipped his gaze from the comes, and took a deep breath before looking back up. 'But, sir, I have heard on the way through the fort that you plan to manage this situation alone? I am sure these are just rumours though; surely you intend to engage with the emperor, or at least call on the reserve legions of the Emperor's Presence, stationed in Constantinople?'

'These rumours are fact, Tribunus. I will see this crisis through, alone. The cowardly would call for help to those they see as their betters.' Lupicinus' eyes burned into Gallus and the six behind him, then he punched a fist against his heart. 'And I am no *coward!*'

Pavo winced at the man's words, and the manic look in his eyes.

'So you and your patchwork legion will get behind me in this endeavour. And be warned that, any attempt to engage Emperor Valens will be treated as an act of mutinous intent.'

Pavo darted a glance to Quadratus and Avitus; the pair had intercepted Gallus on the way into the fort and told him of the rider who they had despatched to the east. Zosimus, Felix and Gallus had praised the pair, their frowns at the goings-on easing just a little at this sliver of hope.

But the eastern frontier was weeks away by land and sea, and Pavo feared that Ennius' efforts would be little more than a moral victory over this peacock of an officer.

Then, with a screeching of his stool on the flagstones, Lupicinus stood. 'Now, I will take my leave to eat. Before night watch begins, we are to gather here again, and Iudex Fritigern will be joining us. Watch and learn how I deal with the barbarian, and you could share in my glory.' With that, he left with his six men, and a chill gust filled the room with snowflakes before the door slammed shut.

Gallus stared at the door, his eyes wide in incredulity. Then he turned to Quadratus and Avitus. 'Well you both deserve promotion to emperor for enduring that one for the last few weeks.'

Quadratus saluted with a dry grin. 'You don't know the half of it, sir. But let's just say that my first act in the purple would be to have him measured by a sackmaker.'

181

'I'll let my imagination fill in the gaps there, I think,' Gallus cocked an eyebrow, then he tapped the table and gestured to the empty stools around it. 'Now sit, I need my officers and veterans here to discuss the next steps. And I want to know all there is to know about Fritigern before we speak with him.'

Pavo and Sura made to leave them to their discussions, when Gallus stopped them with a pinning stare. 'Legionaries, draw up a stool. As I said, I need my veterans.' Pavo glanced to Sura, then turned back and sat, rubbing his throat to disguise a gulp of apprehension.

'Well?' Gallus swept his eyes around each of them.

Quadratus started. 'Burns my tongue to say it, sir, but Fritigern is straight up genuine, as far as I can tell. There's a real fear in his eyes; he's not interested in a fight, he's just grateful to have his people across the imperial borders safely.'

'Is it true, sir, about the Huns to the north?' Avitus asked as he sat. 'All of Fritigern's men look like they've seen Hades itself. They say that the forest came to life only days ago, and that the Huns fell upon their villages without mercy.'

Gallus' gaze grew distant, 'I have not sighted them, but Pavo has.'

Pavo nodded, feeling expectation tangle his tongue as the officers turned to him, faces deadly serious in the candlelight. Then he saw Salvian give him a nod of encouragement. He sucked in a breath and began; 'It happened in Fritigern's village of Istrita, near the border with Athanaric's lands. We sorted out another uprising of rebels. That was bloody, but it was a piece of honey cake compared to what came next.' The officers leant in, transfixed on his words. 'They came out of the forest, just as Fritigern's men said. It was dark as pitch, but there were easily,' he paused, spreading his arms wide, 'thirty thousand of them, more than a match for Fritigern's army – if his Goths were prepared. But if they fell upon Fritigern's villages and forts unexpected, then it's no wonder that his people were driven to our borders. That so many of them escaped with their lives is a feat in itself.'

'And all this happens in Fritigern's lands while Athanaric's lands go untouched,' Avitus frowned, piecing it together, thumping a fist on the table. '*Whoreson!*'

Gallus and Pavo shared a dark look, then the tribunus shook his head. 'No, and this is the crux of it all,' he paused, glancing around those in the room as if judging his next words. 'I fear that the Huns and Athanaric are but the puppets in some greater strategy. The rebels, those swift few who drew out our vexillationes so effectively and softened our borders so we had no option but to accept Fritigern into the empire,' he nodded. 'It is their leader we seek.'

Quadratus and Avitus looked to one another, eyes wide. 'Their leader?'

Gallus gazed into the flame of the candle. 'They call him . . . the Viper. He has orchestrated all of this, yet,' he paused, chuckling wryly, 'to the best of our knowledge, he is a dead man, killed years ago in some botched exchange of hostages. Yet his shade seems to command the loyalty of the rebels and is aiding and encouraging the Huns.'

'A dead man . . . ' Avitus replied after a lengthy silence, his brow wrinkling. Then he looked up at Gallus. 'Are you sure, sir?'

'Avitus?'

Avitus' face turned grave, and he took a moment to compose himself. 'A man can become a shade if it suits him, sir,' the optio's voice cracked a little, and he shot furtive glances around the table, 'if his name is sullied, or his life is in danger. Or perhaps if it suits his ambition? And if enough people who seek a man believe he is a shade, then they will lose the heart to find him.'

Pavo frowned. The little Roman had rarely shown such an introspective side to his nature. Something was troubling Avitus, that much was clear. Regardless, the optio had made a salient point.

'Aye,' Zosimus mused, 'you can kill a man, but not a shade.'

183

Pavo looked around the table; all had fallen silent as if the mention of this phantom had cast a spell on them. He looked to the flagstones, searching for that answer, the one thing that would hook it all together; the mysterious Gothic rebels, the Hun hordes, the coming of Fritigern's people. His mind churned, but produced nothing. Even Gallus examined the palms of his hands as if desperately searching for an answer.

Salvian broke the spell. 'In my time I have marched with wise men, razor-witted and shrewd; I have marched with lion-hearted soldiers who have forgotten the meaning of fear. In only the precious few weeks I have been in the company of the men of this legion, I know for certain that you are both.' He sat back from the candle, slapping both hands on the table's edge. 'Let us not be beaten by this Viper before we have even crossed swords with him, shade or otherwise.'

Pavo's skin prickled with pride at the words, and he saw the other veterans straighten up, square their shoulders and firm their jaws.

'The ambassador is right,' Gallus added, 'we can only stay vigilant. The answer hangs somewhere in the fog. And as long as it is there, we will find . . . '

His words trailed off as a set of determined footsteps thudded up to the principia. All braced, expecting Lupicinus to enter.

With a chill blast of air and a flurry of fresh snowflakes, the door burst open. But stood in the doorway was Iudex Fritigern, flanked by a warrior whose silver hair billowed across his face in the gale. Fritigern was dressed in a brown tunic and green woollen trousers. Otherwise he was unarmoured and unarmed, his red locks framing contorted features. 'Where is the comes?'

Gallus stood. 'I am Tribunus Gallus; I will speak for Comes Lupicinus until he returns to duty.'

'Then perhaps you can explain what's going on out there?' Fritigern stabbed a finger towards the plain. 'One of my men has been beaten, a woman has been raped and her children are missing; she claims they were taken by Romans.' Fritigern paused, taking a deep breath before looking

Gallus in the eye. 'We came here as allies seeking shelter, but we are being treated like prisoners.'

'Sit, Iudex Fritigern. We will talk this through as a matter of priority. Felix, will you see to it that a platter of bread and a jug of wine are brought to us?'

Felix nodded and darted outside. Fritigern sat while the warrior accompanying him slunk into the shadows by the door.

'I have not eaten since dawn yesterday, Tribunus. My belly roars and my legs tremble. But I do not care for food, not while my people out there live off only what grain they could carry across the river. They are already running short. When that happens,' he leaned forward, his weathered face etched with pain, 'I will lose control of them. This is not a threat, Tribunus, merely a reality. Insurgency has been rife over the last months. Whole villages have been sacked by these rebels since the summer. My failure to curtail them has seen the mood for change stick to my people's thoughts like a plague. I have no means to police my people in their current state, yet I hear whispers that some of those very rebels are in our midst. Rumour and counter-rumour are rife!'

Gallus paused for a moment, then said; 'Some of these rumours may have more substance to them than you may think, Iudex. What do you know of the Viper?'

Fritigern's brow wrinkled. 'Until these last few weeks, I had not heard that name in a long, long time. I know only of the tales of his brutality, told to me and my brothers when we were boys. A man bent on uniting the Gothic tribes and then leading them to war.'

'And he is dead now, I believe?' Gallus continued.

'Long dead, Tribunus. And the Gothic tribes are the better for it.'

'Are you sure he is dead?' Gallus asked. 'What if I was to tell you that the rebels we engaged fought under his banner?'

Fritigern cocked an eyebrow. 'Nonsense! What would be their motive – fighting for a dead man?'

Gallus swept a hand towards the door of the principia, in the direction of the plain and the Gothic horde. 'Perhaps the same motive as the Viper himself once had. To unite the tribes and march upon the empire.'

Fritigern looked to the door, and for a moment, Pavo was sure the iudex's eyes grew a little wider as he mulled over the possibility. Then, in a heartbeat, Fritigern's face fell into a scowl and he snapped round to Gallus, thumping a fist on the table.

'To suggest my people are any part of an invasion is a dangerous place to tread, Tribunus.'

Tension crackled in the air, until Salvian sat forward. 'This talk will not solve our immediate troubles. Perhaps if we were to start by taking stock of what supplies of grain and livestock we each have, then we could form a plan, perhaps a rationing strategy?'

Fritigern seemed to teeter on the border of agreement. Then, finally, his shoulders dropped just a fraction and he nodded.

Pavo watched as Gallus and Fritigern chatted. Roman scribes and workers from the horreum and their Gothic counterparts scuttled in and out on Gallus and Fritigern's summons to confirm and correct the estimates.

As the pair talked, Pavo tried to piece together the secret of the Viper once more. But it wasn't long before he felt the toll of the past weeks begin to pull on his eyelids, and his weary limbs grew numb. He eyed the other veterans and saw that they, too, were flagging. He looked to the doorway, thinking of his bunk in the barracks, when the conversation caught his attention once more.

'And while we are camped on this plain,' Fritigern said, 'I will focus all my efforts into seeing this rationing is carried out fairly. I will appoint one of my most trusted men to oversee the policing of this system . . . ' he stretched out a hand to the hulking warrior in the shadows. 'This man has been like a brother to me for over twenty years, and has saved my life more times than I can remember. Indeed, without him, we may well have strayed right into the Huns' path on our way here.'

Pavo frowned. As the warrior stepped forward, the shadows slipped from him, revealing a fine scale vest and forearms encased in leather greaves. Then the face was illuminated: long, silver hair and a beard, pointed nose, three bronze hoops dangling from one ear and a ruined eye that was a gnarled patch of scar tissue and milky matter. The figure grinned at him.

Fritigern nodded sincerely. 'Ivo will serve our alliance well.'

Chapter 13

The beetling walls of Antioch shimmered in the late morning sunshine, merging into the terracotta infinity of Syria. Stood on the battlements, Emperor Valens sighed. Under his snow-white fringe, his sharp blue eyes examined the land to the east. Trade caravans speckled the sandy paths leading from the city to the banks of the River Orontes. His gaze passed along the precious waterway that spliced the land, its surface dotted with cogs and imperial galleys, drifting lazily to their destinations. Then his eyes narrowed on the hazy line where sand met sky and remained there for some time.

Reassured by the emptiness of the horizon, he turned to stroll along the battlements. While the centre of the city was abuzz with the usual activity of market day, the legionaries manning the walls were silent and pensive. They knew what lay beyond the horizon, in the eastern deserts. Each of them wore the lightest of linen tunics under their scale vests, skin glistening with sweat in the heat, saluting promptly as he passed.

Wintering in the east would be a pleasant affair, he mused, breathing the warm air in through his nostrils, but for the looming threat of Shapur's seemingly infinite, well equipped and well-drilled armies. The Persian King's advances into Roman Armenia had drawn the empire's every resource to the eastern frontiers: grain, artillery, craftsmen and most importantly every available comitatenses legion either side of Constantinople. And he, as emperor, had neither seen the capital nor set foot west of Constantinople since the summer, and it looked certain that he would not see it for several summers more. He paused, gazing out to the east once more. *Come on, mighty Shapur, make your move. Break me or break against me, before my empire crumbles behind me!*

188

Every night so far he had wakened while all else was still, troubled by the imminent danger he had left behind in the distant Danubian borderlands. Due to the empty imperial coffers, the Moesian fleet had been effectively decommissioned, now numbering a token set of just eight biremes patrolling the river while the rest lay rotting in a pontoon bridge near Durostorum. Added to that the already poorly equipped border legions had been forced to forgo their yearly resupply of armour, arms and clothing. And their numbers had never been fully replenished since the erosive mission to the Kingdom of Bosporus. The great western river itself now presented more of a barrier to the Goths than the Roman defences did. All it would take was for one concerted push.

Despite the heat, he felt a shiver dance across his skin.

Then footsteps thudded up the stone steps behind him, shaking him from his memories. He spun to see a sweating, emaciated man hobbling up towards him. Like birds of prey, two white-robed *candidati*, Valens' loyal bodyguards, sprinted nimbly to shield their emperor, clutching their sword hilts. But, on seeing the sorry state of the man – his hands and thighs bleeding from a long journey on horseback most probably – Valens raised a hand, and the candidati relaxed just a fraction.

'Quintus Livius Ennius of the Cursus Publicus,' the exhausted man panted, saluting, then he slumped to one knee and held out a scroll with a wax seal. 'Emperor, I have sailed and rode for two weeks and have not stopped for rest in the last three days. This message comes from . . . ' his voice trailed off nervously.

'Speak!' Valens demanded.

The man looked up, his face taut with fear and awe. 'This message comes from the west, from Comes Lupicinus in Moesia. The Danubian hinterland around Durostorum and the XI Claudia fort has been breached.'

Valens pushed past his candidati, dipping to his knees as dread gripped him. He grabbed the man by the shoulders. 'What? How?' He tore the scroll from the man's grasp, the wax seal crumbling as he unfurled it. His eyes flitted to the crux of the message.

189

. . . and now the majority of the Gothic tribes have united and marched upon the empire under Fritigern's banner, ascribing the arrival of the Huns as the catalyst. Fritigern claims he still observes our truce, and offers his men as foederati in exchange for food and sanctuary. But the grain supplies are almost gone, and the limitanei ranks all along the river are equally depleted. It is only a matter of time before the Goths' hunger turns to anger. Emperor, I implore you to provide sanction for emergency grain supplies to be delivered to the Danubian frontier. And, as a matter of equal urgency, I beseech you to send legionary support to Moesia . . .

Valens' eyes swept over the rest of the letter and the estimations of the Gothic number, then hung on the signature; the scrawl was much the same as the rest of the text – not the worst he had seen but definitely not the fine, practiced handwriting of a scribe or an officer. Then he picked at the remains of the wax seal; although it bore Comes Lupicinus' mark, it had been resealed, albeit carefully. He fixed his gaze on the rider. 'I will ask you this only once. Know that the fate of the empire may depend on your answer.'

The rider blanched and nodded hurriedly.

'Who gave you this letter?'

'As I said, Comes . . . ' The rider gulped, then blinked, sucking in a deep breath. 'Centurion Qu . . . Quadratus, and Optio Avitus, Emperor.'

'Who?'

'Centurion Quadratus and Optio Avitus of the XI Claudia Pia Fidelis, Emperor.'

Valens snorted. 'A centurion and an optio forged a letter from Lupicinus?'

The rider nodded. 'They thought it was the only way to salvage the situation on the Danubius, Emperor. Comes Lupicinus is in command at the scene and he was refusing to send out a call for help, so Centurion Quadratus and Optio Avitus sent me east.'

'Disobeying direct orders from their comes?' Valens scowled. 'By God and Mithras that legion has some rogues, and thank God and Mithras they do. And Lupicinus, that repellent and wayward character, brash as a lion one minute then as timid as a mouse the next? Perhaps he would have been less hazardous if I had dragged him east with me,' he mused. Then he frowned, his mind replaying the last time he had dealt with the XI Claudia. 'But you said *Lupicinus* was in charge of the Claudia?'

The rider nodded.

'So Tribunus Gallus has fallen in battle?' Valens recalled the tall, lean officer with the gaunt, wolf-like features who had once come to his palace.

'No, Emperor. Tribunus Gallus was on a mission to parley with Athanaric. He should have returned by now, unless . . . '

Valens sighed. 'If Gallus is the man I remember, then he'll have made it back. And if he takes charge of the situation, then all is not lost. But this scroll paints a bleak picture,' he pinged a finger on the edge of the tattered sheet of paper, 'and time is of the essence.' He tried to imagine the entirety of Fritigern's people, camped on the Danubian plain by Durostorum, but found the image dissolving in his thoughts every time. The key to managing this mass migration, he realised, was in keeping Fritigern's masses where they were. They *had* to remain on the plain of Durostorum until military support could be provided. But the limitanei legions in Moesia and Illyricum were threadbare, and it would be a dire struggle to keep Fritigern's men in check as things stood, he realised. But perhaps the Gothic horde could be assuaged, albeit temporarily, with provision of grain. Yes, if the many southern towns and cities could spare just a little from their stores, then it might be enough.

'I'll have my scribe prepare orders to provide food for the Goths. It will be your job, Ennius, to ensure that the order is delivered to Tribunus Gallus, assuming he has returned.'

With that, he snapped his fingers and looked to his pair of candidati. 'Get this rider as much food, wine and water as he desires, then set him up in one of the palace bedrooms, and then send my capsarius to put a salve on his

191

riding sores.' He turned back to Ennius, helping him from his knees. 'You will rest and recuperate until dawn. Then I will provide you with a stallion from my stables and the scroll containing my orders. After that you must ride, faster than you have ever ridden before.'

'Yes, Emperor,' Ennius said.

'And when you've done this, I'll see to it that you're promoted to chief of heralds.'

Ennius gawped. 'Thank you, Emperor. I will ride at speed, heedless of my wounds.'

Valens watched the rider being ushered away down the steps and through the throng of market day. He wondered what he might have had to return to in the west had this Centurion Quadratus not taken it upon himself to defy orders. Not for the first time in his reign, the finest thread of chance was holding the empire together.

Now he had to plot his next move. He turned and rested his palms on the battlements, eyes scouring the sand below, searching for an answer. He visualised the campaign map that would be waiting on him back at the palace, seeing the carved wooden pieces on the eastern border that represented his campaign legions. There were over thirty comitatenses legions facing Shapur's armies. The figure sounded impressive, but the reality was that many of those legions were well understrength and stretched along the vastness of the Orontes, the Tigris and the Armenian borders along with the twenty four permanently garrisoned limitanei legions. That meant there were scarcely enough men to rebuff any advance by Shapur, never mind mount any kind of offensive. The sun burned on his neck as a solution evaded him.

Think, man, think!

He jostled the numbers, but every act of taking any significant number of legions away from the Persian front meant leaving a glaring gap for Shapur to exploit. No, he realised, he could afford to lose only two legions, three at most – some five thousand Romans. Then the nagging doubts started as he remembered the estimate of the Gothic numbers: over ten thousand Gothic cavalry and infantry, plus the eighty thousand who followed them who were no doubt armed as well? And if Fritigern's lot had been driven south then it would only be a matter of time before the Greuthingi Goths and others flooded to swell his ranks further. His chest tightened. Perhaps another limitanei legion could be collected from the upper Armenian borders with limited risk. Then he thought of the eastern heavy cavalry in the palace stables; the swarthy, moustachioed men who rode those fine mounts, man and beast armoured like an iron centaur. Yes, an ala of *cataphractii* could be spared as well, he thought. That would provide nearer nine thousand men.

Still not nearly enough.

What more could he do? The manpower simply did not exist. Then he remembered, from the ancient texts; when the Spartans had sent aid to the Syracusans in the form of just one man, a noble and valorous strategos who transformed their campaign against the Carthaginians. Suddenly, he realised what was needed.

'To my campaign room,' he barked, then clapped his hands. Two candidati rushed to flank him as he flitted down the steps from the battlements.

The midday sun scorched the column of legionaries, cooking their bodies inside their scale vests as they marched across the Syrian plain, the terracotta dust thrown up from the march coating their throats.

Mounted at the head of the column, Traianus' thoughts flitted between his empty water skin and the grim memories of the skirmish back in the dunes. He rubbed at his hooked nose and then his jaw, now broad and stubbled with grey as he approached his fiftieth year. Then he looked at the blood encrusted under his fingernails and was sure he could still smell the entrails of the last of the Persian warriors he had slain. Just as when he had been a legionary, blood and slaughter ruled now that he was *Magister*

Militum Per Orientalis, commander of all legionaries in the extreme east, answerable only to Emperor Valens himself.

Mercifully, the outline of Antioch emerged from the heat haze on the western horizon; rest and refreshment was near. When they reached the eastern gate, Traianus raised a hand in salute to the wall guard.

'Ave!' The sentry called out, then shouted down inside the city. 'Open the gates!'

Traianus felt the cool shade of the gatehouse like a balm on his skin as they passed under it and into the bustle of the city. Antioch was situated just a few miles west of the volatile border between the two great empires of Rome and Persia. It was the first city that could be considered partisan, staunchly Christian, as opposed to almost every other settlement dotted across the border region – riddled with zeal, Christianity and Zoroastrianism clashing as opposing holy truths. Indeed, even the legions here had adopted the Christian God over the previously infallible Mithras. Traianus often wondered not which god to follow, but if there was such a thing at all.

He led his men across the market square, shaded by the baths and the horreum, then past the Column of Valentinian and the Great Church of Constantine. Then they entered the market swell, rich with a stench of sweat and a mixture of camel and horse dung and packed with a sea of faces gawping at their blood-spattered armour.

Then a column of sorry-looking slaves was bundled across his path in chains. Both parties halted. The bald, ageing slavemaster turned round to see what had held up his column. He looked Traianus in the eye with a scowl, then gulped in fear as he realised who he was dealing with.

Traianus cocked an eyebrow at the state of the slaves: dressed only in loincloths, their legs were more bone than muscle, their ribs seemed to be pressing tight against their skin and their faces spoke of the many years that had passed since they had last been free men. Then he noticed a faded stigma on one man's bicep. *Legio II Parthica*, it read. A frown wrinkled his brow.

'Hold on,' he raised a hand as the slavemaster readied to whip his slaves onwards.

The slavemaster stopped, his eyes widening in fear. Around the two columns, the crowd slowed, looking on in hope of a brawl.

Traianus slipped from the saddle and grappled the slave's arm. 'This man was a legionary?' He looked to the slavemaster. 'Is he a deserter?'

The slavemaster made to reply, but the slave cut in before him;

'Never!'

One of Traianus' legionaries lunged forward, raising a balled fist to the slave.

'No!' Traianus barked, then lowered his voice and looked the slave in the eyes. 'Let him speak.'

Under his hay-like, untended hair, the slave's face was sun-darkened and lined with age, his cheeks were sunken and his lips cracked and bleeding. But his eyes screamed defiance.

'I am Caelus Pedius Carbo of the II Parthica, first cohort, second century. I fought for my empire until the last. I shed blood on the walls of Bezabde until I could no longer stand,' he gestured to the network of thick scar welt on his arms and thighs.

Traianus' eyes widened. 'You fought at Bezabde?' The sack of the fortified city on the banks of the River Tigris had sent shockwaves around the eastern frontier, but much time had passed since that incident. 'That was, what, more than fifteen years ago.'

Carbo looked to Traianus with glassy eyes. 'Has it really been that long?'

Nodding, Traianus suppressed the surge of pity he felt for the man, then replied prosaically. 'It was thought that none survived the razing of the city? I was part of the relief column that arrived there, too late.' His mind flitted with the images of the blackened, toppled walls, the blood-slicked streets and the whimpering of the dying.

Carbo shook his head. 'It may have been better that way. When Bezabde fell, the Persians took me along with the captured. There were hundreds of us at first. I worked in the salt mines in heat a man should never

195

know and I was certain that I had arrived in Hades. Days turned into weeks, then months, then years and by then we lost count. My comrades weakened and fell victim to the lung disease of the mines and eventually there were less than half of us left. I started to pray that I would be next. Then one day I was bought by a Persian noble who took me to his luxurious palace. There I had the pleasure of pools and baths and silken bedding. A stark contrast to the mines. Except that he had me horsewhipped for his amusement, every day.' He twisted to reveal the almost unbroken coating of scar tissue that was his back. His shoulder blades were crooked, as if they had been broken and healed many times. 'Then I was sold on to a travelling trader. I have changed hands many times since then and now I find myself here, as a slave to the empire I would gladly die for.'

Traianus frowned, scanning the column of slaves. 'Are there more survivors?'

Carbo sighed. 'Not here. But I fear that some of my comrades still live, back in the desert salt mines.'

Traianus turned his gaze on the slavemaster. The man's bald head glistened as he broke out in a nervous sweat. 'Unshackle this man,' he barked, 'and pray to God and Mithras that you don't cross my path again.'

The slavemaster thought about protesting until two of Traianus' legionaries growled, part unsheathing their spathas. Quickly, the slavemaster fumbled with the shackles, then backed away from Traianus. The slave gazed down with a haunted look to the worn and callused flesh on his wrists where the iron had been clamped for so long. He did not move, even when the slavemaster rushed the rest of his column off into the throng of the market.

'Would you serve again, soldier?' Traianus asked Carbo.

'Gladly,' Carbo nodded. 'Through all those years in the salt mines, one thing kept me and my comrades going: the promise of being reunited with our empire once more. Though I never dreamed I would be in chains when I next set foot in her sweet lands.'

'Then you will serve again. You will be fed and tended to at the city barracks. There you will be assigned one month's light duties and double rations, until your strength has returned.'

Carbo gazed at Traianus, realisation dawning on him that this really was happening. Then one of the legionaries nodded to him, beckoning him into the column. The watching crowds returned to their own business again and the rabble of market day erupted once more.

Traianus wondered if the man's words were true as he climbed into the saddle again. Were there poor beggars from the II Parthica chained together in the notorious Persian salt mines? A bitter gall rose in his throat at the thought; Shapur would pay for this. If Rome could not conquer Persia with her armies, then another route would have to be sought. Emperor Valens had talked of a covert approach to infiltrating the Persian heartlands, but so far those plans lay undeveloped.

Then a voice barked over the rabble. 'Magister Militum!'

Traianus twisted to the voice. A legionary waved at him frantically.

'Emperor Valens requests your presence with the utmost urgency!'

The campaign room in the city palace was blessedly cool, and Traianus had slaked his thirst with a wide-brimmed cup of fruit juice. He looked on at the campaign map and the carved wooden pieces aligned along the borders. Then footsteps grew louder behind him until Emperor Valens and a pair of candidati entered the room.

'Ah, Traianus!' Valens' azure eyes were sharp as always. 'Your return is most timely.'

'Emperor?' Traianus frowned, watching Valens pluck four of the pieces from the map and place them west of Constantinople, near the Danubian limes.

'Let me waste no time with preamble,' Valens spoke evenly. 'The Danubian frontier is on the brink.'

Traianus frowned. 'Athanaric's Goths?'

Valens cocked one eyebrow. 'Perhaps, behind it all. But it is Fritigern who has breached our borders.'

'Fritigern? He has broken the truce?'

'That is not clear. It appears that he comes in peace,' Valens shook his head, 'and I will come on to the detail in a moment.'

'But surely if he has encroached on our borders then he is in breach of the treaty?'

Valens nodded. 'All valid questions that I will need to answer, Traianus. But it seems that the immediate danger is of famine. Fritigern has brought with him little or no grain. If we are still to respect the truce – as we must in the first instance – then we are obliged to aid him. The rider who brought me this news will be setting off at dawn to advise the local tribunus that he can levy grain from the towns and cities far to the south of the river. It'll be a stretch, but I'm hoping it will be enough to ensure that Fritigern and his people stay exactly where they are until I get there. If they mobilise in search of food and fall upon our towns and cities . . . ' his words trailed off as he gazed at the province of Moesia on the map, suddenly so distant. The handful of wooden pieces representing the limitanei looked desperately sparse, and the pieces Valens had moved there from the east did little to bolster their number.

He clapped his hands and a scribe rushed into the room, stopping beside Valens with a reed pen and a leaf of papyrus at the ready.

Eyeing the moved pieces, he spoke. 'Send word to the II Armeniaca, the IV Italica, the II Isauria and the I Adiutrix. Then muster my ala of cataphractii and an ala of equites; they are to mobilise and rendezvous at Trapezus. There, the *Classis Pontica* will take them to Tomis. Make sure they understand that this order is given with the utmost urgency.'

With that, he turned to Traianus, affixing him with a sincere gaze. 'These legions need the leadership of one of my best men.'

Traianus' skin prickled, realising what was coming next.

'And that is why you must lead them, to weed out the truth and to bring our borders back under imperial control.'

West. Traianus skin prickled. It had been twenty years since he had last set foot in those lands. A jumble of memories came to the fore.

'Now,' Valens continued, 'you should also be aware of the other threat; the reason Fritigern pushed south in the first place. It is the Huns; they have moved on Gutthiuda.'

'The dark riders?' Traianus' skin froze. He had heard of their trail of devastation in their inexorable advance westwards from the distant and windswept eastern steppes. But many believed they were still well north and east of the Gothic heartlands. 'Then they have moved south with great haste, it seems?'

'Indeed. Yet they are not the immediate danger.' Valens tapped a finger on the campaign map. 'In all my years, the one thing that has kept our borders safe has been the political fractures in the land of the Thervingi Goths. The rival iudexes have quarrelled and switched allegiance swiftly and often, like leaves dancing in a storm. But now, the arrival of the Huns seems to have forged them together, Traianus.' Valens looked up. '*That* is my grave concern. It is not just Iudex Fritigern and his standing army, or some beefed-up mercenary rabble that has breached our borders. This is almost the entire Thervingi nation, mobilised as one, all the minor iudexes of eastern Gutthiuda following under Fritigern's banner. It seems that only Athanaric's lot have remained north of the river, holed up in the Carpates. I fear it will only be a matter of time before the outlying Gothic tribes, the Greuthingi included, flock south to join under Fritigern's banner. If the tribes unite in such number, the empire will face an unprecedented threat.'

Traianus' skin crawled.

'Traianus?' Valens asked, frowning at his magister militum's suddenly ghostly pallor.

But Traianus heard his emperor's words like a faraway echo, while the words of the one-eyed warrior from that distant day on the wharf rang in his head, as if the giant was hissing them into his ear right now.

This is only the beginning, you dogs. The day will come when the Viper will rise again. On that day, the tribes will be united. And on that day, Roman blood will flow like the Mother River.

Chapter 14

The first morning of April brought with it a bitter chill and a fresh snowfall across the plain of Durostorum, as if winter was determined not to be usurped by the overdue spring. A full month had passed since the arrival of Fritigern and his people and still more Goths had spilled onto the plain in that time, further stretching the meagre grain supplies. Amongst the sea of tents, the number of shapeless bumps in the snow had grown steadily as Gothic elderly and children perished from hunger and exposure. And as their families succumbed to the conditions, the warriors were growing ever more restless. Then, in these last few days, factions of them had called for Fritigern to break free of the camp and march south in search of food.

In the poor light afforded by the snowfall, Gallus stood at the northern end of the Gothic camp near a rudimentary goat pen. He eyed the corpse of a Gothic warrior – this one had certainly not succumbed to starvation. The body was half in the pen and half out, entrails stretched out across the snow, and all around him were the bodies of slaughtered goats. The stench was overpowering.

'And they took the last of our grain!' The old Gothic woman pleaded, cupping her hands together, her eyes wet with tears for her slain son. 'And they were not driven to it from hunger. No, they carried the sacks to the riverbank then slit them, letting the grain fall and ruin in the waters. They *want* us to starve!'

Gallus sighed, his eyes tracing the trail of grain-speckled hoofprints in the snow to the riverbank and then to where they dissolved into the snowdrifts. *Like shade riders. Absurdly fitting*, he realised, clenching his teeth. He had now lost count of the number of attacks that had happened like this over the last few weeks, in the dead of night. He looked to the woman. 'So tell me again, you say it was *them?*'

The woman nodded, choking back a sob. 'Yes, the Viper's riders! They mask their faces then strike in a pack, like wolves. Then they disappear into the night.'

At that moment, her elderly husband came from a nearby tent to stand by her. His expression was different; his eyes were darting and his lips thin, his demeanour agitated. 'That's enough, Oda, we cannot change what has happened.'

Gallus' eyes narrowed.

The Gothic woman turned to her husband, frowning, annoyed. 'Erwin! How can you be so . . . *calm!*' With that she broke down in a fit of sobbing, covering her face with her hands. Her husband held her to his chest as she shuddered with grief.

Gallus caught another furtive glance from Erwin the Goth. This man had something to say, he was sure of it. Then a wracking sob from Oda split the air.

Now was not the time.

He sighed and handed the old man a linen wrap. The bread loaf inside was the last one to have been fired in the fort ovens. 'Fill your bellies. Your son would not want you to suffer. Perhaps we can talk later though?'

The man closed his eyes, nodding as he took the offering. Then Gallus turned to walk away.

'Tribunus,' Erwin called after him.

Gallus turned. The old man's brow was now wrinkled, and there were no more snatched glances, his gaze locked on Gallus.

'I am old now, but I . . . ' he paused, his gaze drifting into the dancing snowflakes, ' . . . I remember the atrocities the Viper committed. These night-slayings brought it all back to me. And then this,' he gestured to his dead son's torn body. 'Fritigern may scoff at the idea of the Viper being at large amongst his people, but the threat is very real.'

'You have something to tell me, old man?' Gallus' breath stilled and all his senses were primed.

Erwin's jaw stiffened as he looked to his dead son and then back to Gallus. 'Perhaps, Tribunus.' Then the old man clenched one fist, hugging his wife closer, his eyes moistening. 'But first, and for Wodin's and Mithras' sake, put an end to the equally foul behaviour of your legionaries!'

Gallus bit back on an instinctive response, for the man made a very valid point. Reports had been rife of Lupicinus' men abusing their authority while policing the Goths; beatings, extortion and threats, all going unpunished as Lupicinus looked to demonstrate his authority over Gallus. Then, three days ago, the wife of a Gothic noble had been raped in front of her children by a comitatenses legionary named Ursus. The few hundred extra Claudia legionaries – the vexillationes that had escaped the turmoil in Gutthiuda and returned to the fort in these last weeks – would have to be put to work in policing Lupicinus' men as well as the Goths, it seemed. He nodded sincerely to Erwin. 'They are not my men, but I will do all I can.'

'Then perhaps we will speak again,' Erwin said, his gaze dark as he turned and ushered his wife into their tent.

'Perhaps?' Gallus replied even though he was alone in the swirling snow. 'Most certainly, I would say.'

With that, he turned and strode from the pen to pick his way through the sea of tents on the snow-packed track that led back to the fort. His mind spun with thoughts of the Viper, of Lupicinus and his unruly centuries, of the Huns lurking north of the river. To add to these woes, imperial communications had fallen silent; Mithras alone knew how many or how few legionaries remained in the other limitanei forts up and down the river. Worse, there was still no word or sighting of the messenger, Ennius, despatched over a month ago to gather orders from the emperor. Without intervention from Valens, this situation could only get darker.

These troubles were plentiful enough to fill the minds of ten men, he mused, but it was the unseen presence of the Viper and his men that threatened to tip the balance and shatter the truce with Fritigern. The Viper's riders seemed bent on driving the Goths to starvation. *But they won't suffer starvation for long,* he realised, *they will rise up. This is what the Viper seeks!*

He looked up, and his gaze fell upon Salvian. The ambassador shivered under his cloak, blowing into his hands for warmth as he waited, holding the reins of his and Gallus' stallions. The man could easily have washed his hands of this affair and rode south to Constantinople, or to the port cities where a ferry would have taken him home, no doubt to a luxurious villa in the capital. Instead, he had remained in the frozen north, and Gallus was glad of his company.

Gallus took the reins and gave Salvian a nod. 'It appears that the Viper was at large again. Or at least his riders were.'

Salvian's brow furrowed and he cast his eyes over the snow-capped timber watchtowers that had been constructed to demarcate the Gothic camp; the legionaries stationed in them had a clear sight of most of the plain, in daylight at least. 'Then these riders must be within the Gothic camp, they *must* be,' he spoke through chattering teeth.

Gallus cast a quick glance back to the tent circle of Erwin and Oda. 'Perhaps we should appeal to Fritigern to question suspects?'

Salvian turned to him and pinned him with a sober gaze. 'Unless you have something solid to put forward to Fritigern, any speculative arrests are liable to spark trouble. The Goths want to break from this camp and rampage south in search of food. The iudex is inches from crumbling to their will.' Salvian mused over his own words and then nodded. 'You need proof, Tribunus.'

'Then it is simple,' Gallus replied, 'we will find proof.'

Thundering through the moonlit forest, east of Durostorum, Ennius and his stallion had both passed the stage of exhaustion, the mount frothing at the mouth.

The two week journey had been frantic, and the world had changed around him day by day. The air had turned cool and fresh on the ride to Trapezus. Then, on the galley to Tomis, it had grown bitter. Then, the white-cloaked land that he disembarked onto felt like another realm entirely from Antioch and the Persian front. At first he had been grateful of the cold as it soothed his chafed skin and weary limbs. Now, though, even his thick woollen cloak could not fend off the violent shivering.

But he was only a few miles away from the end of his journey. He longed to see the XI Claudia fort, to hand over the scroll. He could hear the praise ringing in his ears already, taste the ale in the inn, feel the warm comfort of his bunk. And then there was his promotion. His wife would be overjoyed and maybe, at last, they could afford to buy a small landholding where their two baby girls could grow up and his father could live out his days in comfort.

Inspired, he lifted the scroll from his cloak and kissed it, then clutched it tight in his grip and leaned flat on the saddle, heeling the beast. 'Come on, boy, not long to go now. Ya!'

Focused on the last rise before he would break clear of the forest and onto the plain of Durostorum, he did not notice the figure lurking in the shadows by the trackside, hands cupped to the mouth.

Ennius heard a shrill bird call and frowned; it was the first note of birdsong he had heard since returning to this snowy land. He glanced over his shoulder.

Nothing.

He turned back to set his sights on home, when two dark figures darted from the trees ahead, a rope held across the track between them. Ennius' eyes bulged and a scream caught in his throat as the two pulled the rope taut, lifting it so it caught Ennius around the chest and pulled him from his saddle. A sharp crack rang out as he tumbled, head over heels across the snow and bracken of the forest floor.

Then everything came to a standstill. Groggily, Ennius saw his panicked stallion gallop off into the distance. He struggled to sit up and glanced around; the two figures were nowhere to be seen. He saw the scroll beside him and gratefully snatched it up from the ground. He made to stand then buckled and collapsed again with a scream as white hot agony coursed through his left leg: a shard of pure white bone jutted from the shin, poking through his leather boot, and the lower shin and foot hung at an absurd angle. He twisted away and vomited.

Then footsteps crunched through the snow, right behind him.

Retching the last of the bile from his belly, Ennius looked up. Two Gothic spearmen grinned like sharks, their topknotted locks billowing in the chill breeze, features illuminated in the moonlight. Ennius clawed at the dirt, pulling himself away despite the agony of his leg. But then he froze, hearing the gentle clop of hooves just behind him.

He twisted round to see a figure, in a dark-green cloak and hood, face in shadow, mounted on a black stallion. One of the Gothic spearmen plucked the scroll from Ennius' hand as he gawped at the dark rider.

'This is what you wanted, Master?' The spearman asked, holding up the scroll.

'Indeed,' the dark rider replied, pulling another, identically sealed scroll from his cloak. Then the shadows within the hood turned to behold Ennius. 'Orders will reach the legionary fort, rider. Just not the ones you have carried all this way,' he unfurled the original scroll, nodding as he read the contents. 'No, this scroll will be little more than ashes in a matter of moments, as will you, Roman. As will your empire, before too long.' With that, the figure raised one hand and extended a finger, then swiped it down.

Ennius gawped, fear stiffening him at once. Then he twisted back to the two spearmen just in time to see the nearest of them draw a longsword to hold it two-handed, then swing the blade towards his neck.

The forest echoed with Ennius the rider's scream until it was abruptly cut short.

Moonlight illuminated the plain as Senator Tarquitius made his way from the fort back to his rented room in Durostorum.

'What have I done?' He raked frozen fingers over his bald pate, muttering to himself as he crunched through the carpet of snow, past the crackling torches and fires of the nearby Gothic camp. Then, on seeing a family of emaciated Goths walking towards him on their way to the camp, eyeing him nervously, he straightened up and cleared his throat to stride in his best senatorial fashion. But as soon as he had passed them, his shoulders slumped again and he rubbed at his temples.

He had been used, like a puppet, like a stepping stone. Again. Power had been dangled before him, like a carrot before a donkey, to lead him into this mess. All the expense, all the effort, all the lickspittle behaviour he had employed – all to ascend the ladder of imperial power. Yet it had all blinded him to the reality; *he* was the die in another's hand. And if this Viper's desires were to be realised, then there would be no empire. For the first time in so long he wanted to confide in someone, but he no longer knew who he could trust. And there were few if any who trusted him.

The men of the legion barely disguised their contempt for him, and Salvian, his protégé, had seemingly sided with them. Then there was Pavo. His ex-slave glared at him like a demon every time their paths crossed. *But I cannot tell him what he wants to know*, he affirmed, remembering the Viper's threat. *You should continue to deny the legionary this knowledge, Senator, for without it, it seems you would be truly worthless to me, and I would have little reason to keep you alive.*

And then there were the Goths. Every one of the towering warriors who cast him a cold look could well be one of the Viper's riders. Rumour had been rife that those very riders were secreted within the Gothic camp, and were the ones behind the numerous midnight slayings of noble Goths and ruination of what little grain supply they had. Perhaps, he gulped, looking around the plain, he might be their next target.

A chill wind whipped up, blowing snow over him.

'Why do you mock me,' he shook a fist at the night sky, then wondered at which deity he cursed. Wealth and power had been his gods since his earliest days as a politician, and both had served to humiliate him. He felt a fresh wave of despair creep over him, then pursed his lips and balled his fists. 'Bury your self-pity, you fool,' he affirmed, 'it will bring you little providence.'

'Speaking to shades, Senator?' A voice spoke from the darkness, startling him.

He spun to scour the shadow under a lone snow-cloaked oak. There stood a dark figure beside a pair of tethered geldings. His nightmares rushed in for him as he remembered the green-cloaked apparition in Athanaric's feasting hall. *The Viper?*

The figure stepped forward, and he heaved a sigh of relief upon seeing not a green cloak but a scale vest. It was Fritigern's aide. 'Ivo! What are you doing here?'

The giant warrior stepped forward, bronze hoops sparkling in his earlobe, the milky matter in his ruined eye glistening in the moonlight. 'I have come to summon you.'

Tarquitius frowned. 'Fritigern wants to see me, at this time?'

The big warrior shook his head, a cool grin splitting his face. 'No, my *true* master has deemed it time to call upon you. He is nearby.'

Tarquitius scowled as Ivo carefully removed the two leather greaves on his arms. Then an icy horror raked across his skin as he set eyes upon the blue ink snake stigmas that coiled around the giant's forearms.

The Viper's words hissed in his mind.

When you see my mark, you will obey.

Pavo and Sura walked the snowy track through the Gothic camp on the first of their night patrol circuits. Their brief from Gallus was simple; to catch the Viper's riders at large and to ensure that no innocent Goth was harmed. However, the passing Goths who carried firewood between the tents saw them as intruders rather than protectors, casting them steely glares and uttering low growls.

But Pavo's mind was elsewhere. He wondered just how far he was prepared to go to weed the truth from Senator Tarquitius. Just last night he had found the nightmare of Father replaced by one where he was drinking a cup of warm blood, draining it before gleefully asking for more. Then he had looked down to see that in his dream he wore a senatorial toga. That had been enough to waken him, panting, bathed in sweat.

He shook his head of the memory and cast a glance across the plain to the dark outline of the Durostorum. At this, another cloud was quick to settle over his thoughts. They had visited *The Boar and Hollybush* earlier that evening. Felicia had been there, and once again, she had been distant, distracted.

'You think she's after a bit of Quadratus?' Sura chirped, blowing into his hands.

Pavo's face wrinkled and he turned to his friend.

'Well she did ask more than once when he was due to patrol the Gothic camp?' Sura shrugged. 'I'd say there was a chance she was after a bit of . . . ' he looped one forefinger and thumb and prodded his other forefinger through it vigorously.

'Did she look as if she was in that kind of mood?' Pavo snapped.

'Ach, she has a reputation . . . ' Sura started, then stopped, seeing Pavo's scowl.

They walked on in silence, and Pavo thought of his bunk, praying tonight would be the night when he would fall into a dreamless sleep. The phalera tingled on his chest as if to remind him that hope was futile. He rubbed at his eyes; perhaps another night of chatting with Salvian was in the offing. They had spent many nights in these last few weeks talking and drinking watered wine while the rest of the fort slept. Conversation was always so easy with the ambassador, and offered a pleasant alternative to the nightmares. Pavo felt the beginnings of a smile lift his lips.

Then a high-pitched scream and angered voices rang out from a nearby cluster of tents.

Pavo looked to Sura and Sura stared back.

The Viper? Sura mouthed silently.

Then, without another word of deliberation, the pair clasped their hands to their scabbards and ran to the noise, their mail vests chinking.

From the corner of his eye, Pavo saw tent flaps ripple, Gothic heads poking out, frowning.

'Every Goth in the camp must have heard that scream,' Sura hissed as they ran.

Then they stopped, mouths agape at the scene before them, lit by the dancing orange of a campfire. This was not the work of the Viper.

A golden haired Gothic lady, ageing but still beautiful, cowered in the centre of a circle of eight legionaries. She whimpered, holding a hand to her face, unable to stem the flow of blood where her teeth had been knocked out. The legionaries were scale-vested comitatenses and carried blue shields; Lupicinus' men. They had their spears levelled, keeping at bay a pack of five Gothic men, all of the same family going by their hair and features.

Then the lead legionary kicked a dark piece of matter, clearly crawling with maggots, towards the woman. 'You got your meat, now eat it, before it rots!'

Pavo recognised the voice instantly; it was Ursus, the snub-nosed and scowling ringleader of the group accused of raping the Goth noble's wife. Ursus rubbed at his knuckles, red with the woman's blood. The rest of the men were those of Ursus' contubernium, and they wore the same sneers of malice.

A wave of ire and nausea swept over Pavo as he eyed the scene, and his mind echoed with Salvian's words. *There are occasions when brute force is the order of the day.*

'What in Hades is going on here?' He roared.

Ursus stopped, then turned to Pavo as if he had just punctured his wineskin. 'You've got no business here, limitanei. Move on.'

Pavo and Sura stepped forward together. 'Aye, but we do. This is our plain, our fort, our town,' Pavo growled. 'And these are our allies.'

Ursus snorted. 'Our allies? They're dirty, stinking, barbarian whoresons. Legionaries like you pair of pussies are the reason we are in this state in the first place. The whole of the Claudia are just the same.' His cronies rumbled in laughter at this. 'Now be on your way or you'll be sorry.'

Pavo laughed a mirthless laugh, feeling his heart thunder. 'No, you'll tell us what you're doing.'

Sura clasped his spatha hilt and added; 'Or believe me, *you'll* be sorry.'

Just then, one of the male Goths with striking green eyes stooped to pick up the rotting piece of meat and held it out. 'We begged and begged them for food. Grain, flour, barley, anything that would fill our children's bellies. They said they'd provide more boar meat, but only if we gave up . . . ' the man's words were interrupted by a howl from the cowering woman, ' . . . only if we gave up our eldest child for the slave market. We gave up our boy, knowing that we would buy him back one day when all this is over. I haven't cried so hard in all my life, Roman, as I did on the day they took him away.' The man's eyes were glassy and his expression lost, then it curled up into sheer hatred, and he hurled the stinking, maggot-infested meat onto the snow. 'Then they brought us this; foul scraps of dog meat. And we are but one family of many that these whoresons have destroyed.'

Pavo gawped at Ursus and the contubernium. 'Have you lost your minds?'

'Are you trying to spark an uprising?' Sura added.

211

'Watch your mouth,' Ursus spat back.

Pavo's blood iced as he noticed from the corner of his eye a crowd of Goths emerging from the darkness, agitated, many armed. There were at least fifty of them. 'Ursus, we can arm wrestle later, but for your own sake leave, get back to the fort.'

Ursus' grimace faded when he noticed the ring of Goths that grew around them. 'I have nothing to fear from these animals,' he swept his sword derisively at the gathering Goths. 'You barbarian dogs can scurry back inside your tents!'

Then, one Gothic boy leapt forward from the ring to grapple at the injured woman's shoulders in an attempt to hoist her clear of the Romans. Ursus instinctively swept his spatha down. The boy toppled to the ground, his head cleaved at the crown, grey mush dribbling from the wound. Ursus looked up and round, his eyes wide in panic. 'I thought he was coming at me with a blade!'

A silence hung in the air. Then a jagged Gothic cry rang out.

'Kill them!'

'No!' Pavo roared, but his words were lost in the tumult as the crowd of Goths fell upon the contubernium. He and Sura tried to claw the Goths back, but were pushed away. At the centre of the circle, spears, axes and swords were battered down on Ursus' contubernium again and again, the thud of shattering shields ringing out. Then, when the Roman shields were ruined, the punch of ripping meat and the crunch of snapping bone filled the air, accompanied by the final screams of Ursus and his men.

Then, without warning, a pair of Gothic warriors grasped Pavo and Sura, pulling them back from the incident. One of the Gothic pair hissed in Pavo's ear. 'Thank your Mithras that you have shown some valour today, Roman, otherwise you would have met the same fate.'

Pavo shrugged free of the man's grasp.

Then a voice split the air. 'Cease! By God and Mithras, cease!'

Pavo twisted round. Out of the darkness, Gallus, Lupicinus, Fritigern and Salvian emerged, side by side on horseback. Either side of them, the first century of the XI Claudia formed a line: Felix leading them and Quadratus, Zosimus and Avitus flanking them on the right. The legionaries edged forward, shields and swords ready, their crested helmets jutting forward like fangs. Pavo and Sura fell back to join them.

Fritigern heeled his mount forward and the Gothic circle parted immediately. 'What have you done?' He cried, seeing the sop of gristle and blood that was once Ursus and his men. 'Comes, Tribunus,' he called back to Lupicinus and Gallus, 'You must believe I had no wish for this!' Then he turned back to his people. 'You have been warned!' He roared at them. 'You will pay for this.'

The Goths looked back with stunned faces, and more and more flooded to the scene. Then one Goth shouted back. 'We have paid dearly as it is, Iudex Fritigern.' It was the green-eyed Goth who had spoken to Pavo. 'They have sold our children into slavery and mocked us by giving us rotten dog meat.' At this, hundreds of voices chorused in agreement.

Fritigern's face changed at that moment from panic to disgust. The Gothic Iudex twisted in his saddle and shot a burning glare at Lupicinus. 'Is this true?'

Lupicinus' lips trembled wordlessly, his tongue stabbing out to dampen them, his eyes darting around the gathering Goths.

Then Fritigern looked to Gallus, exasperated, his arms out wide. 'Tribunus?'

Gallus' nose wrinkled at the claims and he shot a fiery glare towards Lupicinus. 'It appears so, Iudex Fritigern. But clearly, like you, I had no knowledge of these men's intentions before their deeds were done.'

Fritigern looked from Gallus to his people, once, twice, then again. He panted through gritted teeth, his fiery locks whipping over his wrathful eyes, and pointed a shaking finger at Gallus and Lupicinus. 'You cannot hide behind ignorance much longer, Romans.'

213

At this, the Goths rallied in a cry of support; thousands of them had now gathered, swelling around the first century. Fritigern seemed to flinch as he realised the effect of his words, and he turned to address his people, hands raised in a calming gesture. 'Turn your minds from trouble, my people.'

'Trouble is all around us!' One voice roared back.

'You will obey your iudex!' Fritigern roared in riposte.

'Then give us food! Give us food and we will follow you! Otherwise, step aside and let us fight for our lives!' Another lone voice cried out. At this, a thousand more voices agreed. Then, with a rasp of iron, a thousand longswords were drawn and then held overhead.

'Oh bollocks,' Sura hissed, seeing Fritigern's face fall, and Gallus' arm rise to give the order to ready shields. 'This is it!'

Pavo readied to draw his spatha. 'I've got your flank, brother.'

But then a rumble of hooves grew from the south of the camp, accompanied by a cry. The Romans and Goths hesitated, turning to the south to scrutinise the two riders who thundered towards the confrontation.

Senator Tarquitius rode at the fore, clutching a scroll, and Ivo followed close behind. 'Emperor Valens has sent word! We have grain, we have plenty grain!'

At this, the Goths lowered their swords and their roar died. All eyes fell upon the senator.

Quadratus and Avitus broke from the Roman line, stalking over to Tarquitius, the little optio grabbing at the senator's sleeve. 'Ennius the rider, he made it back? The man's got a knack for timing!'

Tarquitius avoided his gaze. 'The emperor's orders are here, and that's what matters.' With that, the senator unfurled the scroll and Fritigern and the gathered Goths hushed to hear as he puffed out his chest to read aloud.

As Tarquitius let the first few words from the scroll spill from his lips, Gallus noticed something; Erwin the Goth stood, face pinched in hatred. His gaze was fixed not on the senator, not on Fritigern, but on Ivo.

Gallus' breath stilled as he looked to Fritigern's giant aide; Ivo's good eye sparkled under his brow, and an inappropriate, shark-like grin curled under his arrowhead nose as the scroll was read aloud. A cool dread gripped Gallus' heart as he looked to the broken wax seal on the parchment. He remembered how easily Quadratus and Avitus had forged the outgoing scroll. He glanced to Ivo again. *What if* . . . He leaned over in his saddle towards Tarquitius. 'Senator . . . stop,' he hissed.

But Tarquitius was in full flow and his voice filled the air.

'. . . and while military support may be some distance away, an imperial reserve of grain is available for just this eventuality, just a short distance south of Durostorum . . . '

Gallus' hopes were momentarily lifted. Perhaps his fears were unfounded. If the grain could be gathered up from the southern towns and brought back to this plain then there was a chance that the Goths could be placated. Keeping them on this plain was vital.

But Tarquitius' next words chilled him to his core.

' . . . Iudex Fritigern and the Thervingi will find grain at Marcianople, and should proceed to the city. No Goth or Roman will starve as long as . . . '

At this, the Goths cried out joyously, drowning out the rest of the message. Ivo, however, did not so much as blink.

Gallus stared at the giant warrior and then at the senator. There was no imperial grain reserve left in Marcianople. He knew this because he had requisitioned the last of it some months ago to fill the empty horrea of Durostorum and the fort. More, there was no way Emperor Valens would invite the Goths to march south. He looked up to see Ivo ride over to

215

Fritigern, then whisper in his ear, gesticulating to the south, urging and prompting the iudex as always.

But this time it took little effort, for Fritigern's features were tinged with the same glow of hope as his people. The Gothic Iudex heeled his mount round to face his people, then swept a hand to the south.

'Wake all in the camp, tell them Rome has promised us salvation. We will march with haste!' Fritigern cried. 'Cavalry: form up at the head and ride at full gallop. My infantry and archers, you will accompany the families and what animals we have left. The sooner we reach this city the sooner we are saved, as by the emperor's solemn promise.'

Gallus tried to heel his mount towards the iudex, to correct him, to quell his expectation. But he and the first century were blocked by a surge of Gothic bodies; the cavalrymen rushed for their mounts and the people broke away from the scene of the standoff, hurrying back to their tents to douse their fires, tear down tents, collect their belongings and ready their wagons. Gallus felt control spinning away from him. He glanced to Lupicinus; the comes gawped at the goings-on with the expression of a boy lost in a busy city street.

'Marcianople? That can't be right,' Felix stammered over the rabble, 'The horrea of the city were near empty the last I heard.'

Gallus eyed him gravely, shaking his head. 'Not a grain left in them, Felix.'

Quadratus' face fell. 'Fritigern will snap if he gets to Marcianople and there is no grain.'

Salvian sidled up next to them, watching Fritigern and Ivo at the head of the Gothic exodus. 'Do the people of this city know what is coming for them?'

Gallus spoke in a hiss; 'The gates of Marcianople will be closed when Fritigern arrives there. When this happens, I can only pray Fritigern's wisdom and dislike of fighting against city walls still holds true. But I fear that his thoughts will be twisted towards conflict by the man who rides by his side.'

216

Salvian's brow wrinkled, following Gallus' gaze to the front of the Gothic migration. 'You suspect Ivo, Tribunus?'

Gallus nodded, then drew his icy gaze around the gathered legionaries. 'Ivo is no aide of Fritigern or ally of Rome. He knew what was on that scroll before it was read.' He cast a foul glare at Tarquitius, who avoided eye contact. 'Every misfortune that has occurred in these last months has pushed Fritigern's people towards this; the arrival of the Huns, the tyranny of the rebel riders and their leader, the Viper – that shadowy creature who remains unseen yet seems to be ever-present in all of this like a vile stench – and then the ruination of the Goths' food supplies. It has been a blessing that, despite this litany of disasters, Iudex Fritigern has held good to the truce until now . . . but that scroll has just pushed us to the brink of war!'

Gallus twisted to Ivo. 'Senator!' He barked. 'I can only hope that there is record of Ennius the rider bringing that scroll into the fort.'

Tarquitius' features blanched and his jowls quivered. 'I . . . '

'Don't test me, you fat fool!' Gallus roared over the snowstorm. 'Where did the scroll come from?'

'It came from the rider . . . ' Tarquitius stammered, ' . . . I think.'

'Who handed it to you?' Gallus pinned him with a glare, heeling his mount over to Tarquitius and grappling the neck of the senator's robes, yanking him from his saddle so they were nose to nose.

'Ivo. He brought it straight from the rider and then the rider made haste to Constantinople. Ivo thought that haste was imperative and so came straight to me,' Tarquitius lied, his eyes darting wildly over Gallus' enraged features. 'So there will be no record of Ennius the rider's arrival at the fort.'

Gallus snorted, shoving the senator away again. 'Then we are to believe that the words on a scroll delivered by a Goth are those of our emperor? This is a nonsense – we must ride Ivo down and take him from Fritigern's side!'

Salvian placed a hand on the tribunus' forearm. 'Be wary, Tribunus – we are on the brink of war. Remember, we need proof!'

217

Gallus closed his eyes, his shoulders heaving as he took in a series of calming breaths. 'Then we must shadow Ivo's every move,' he spoke at last. With that he heeled his mount into a turn and barked at the watching legionaries. 'Form up the legion; we march south immediately!'

Chapter 15

Dawn broke over southern Moesia, and with it came the babbling of scores of meltwater brooks. The thousand men of the XI Claudia spliced the land, marching south in an iron fin topped column towards Marcianople. Then, as the morning wore on towards noon, the snow gradually became dappled with patches of green where a thaw had begun. For the first time in months, the air was mild. But in every Roman heart, the ice had yet to thaw.

They had overtaken huge trains of Gothic women, children and elderly headed for Marcianople. But they had little hope of catching the huge sprawl of some seven thousand of Fritigern's spearmen, miles ahead, let alone the vanguard of some three thousand Gothic riders that would already be at the city's walls.

In the Moesian countryside all around them, Roman landworkers, slaves and estate owners stood together as one; frightened and confused by the massive horde of Goths that had swept down the Roman highway that morning, fully armed and unchecked. They called out to Gallus, Lupicinus, Salvian and Tarquitius at the head of the Roman column, pleading to be told what was happening, before rushing to join the rabble of Roman citizens in the column's wake.

Pavo marched near the front of the third cohort, first century, alongside Sura. He cast frequent glances over his shoulder to the rear of the column where this rabble of Roman citizens followed. He prayed that Felicia and the folk of Durostorum were either in that rabble or had heeded Gallus' hasty orders. *Take word to Durostorum and the outlying towns and farms; they are to head south, to seek shelter in Thracia. The walls of Adrianople and the surrounding cities will protect them.*

Pavo had scanned their faces again and again, but there was no sign of Felicia and her father in that lot.

'She'll be safe,' Sura said, beside him. 'She's a smart one.'

Pavo gave his friend an unconvincing smile. 'Too smart for her own good.'

Then they slowed as the column narrowed a little to filter across a fragile-looking timber bridge. The structure straddled the River *Beli Lom* – a narrow, twisting and deep waterway with spruce and beech thickets dotting its steep banks. Pavo frowned as he saw Gallus despatch a group of five legionaries from the head of the column to the rear, where they stopped the driver of the slow and cumbersome wagon at the tail end. He watched as the wagon slowed to a halt at the northern bridgehead, and the legionaries began unloading its contents; coils of rope and lengths of timber. The kit looked familiar, but he couldn't quite place where he had seen it before.

Then an elbow jabbed him in the chest, and he twisted to face front again.

'We must be near, look,' Sura pointed to the columns of what he prayed was hearth smoke just over the rise ahead.

Pavo fixed his gaze on the plumes. His stomach shrivelled and he felt his bladder swell – the usual prelude to any battle. 'Perhaps the ambassador can still find a diplomatic route to bring Fritigern back from the precipice?'

Sura looked up. 'Eh? Salvian? I doubt he'll get the opportunity. The time for talking is past.'

Pavo shook his head. 'I'm not sure. Fritigern still has a good heart. If he can be persuaded to talk, there might be a chance.'

They marched until the rise fell away to reveal a verdant plain, frosted but mercifully snow-free. To the east, the hills tapered to reveal the distant blue waters of the Pontus Euxinus. To the west, patchwork farmland hugged the hills, punctuated by thickets of pine forest. Then the shimmering limestone hulk of Marcianople rose into view with its tall, sturdy walls and towers, and the hardy but few limitanei legionaries lining the battlements. It would have been a sight to warm any Roman heart had it not been for the swarm of thousands upon thousands of baying Goths pressing around the base of those walls.

Wrapped inside the walls, domes and red-tiled roofs jostled for space, an indication of city's rise to prominence in recent years. The church dome towered higher than any other, a gold Chi-Rho cross extending into the clear sky. Pavo wondered if the Christianised Goths amongst those surrounding the city might hesitate upon seeing the symbol. But already, timber and vine ladders were being passed forward and leaned against the walls, reaching the battlements. The Goths were riled, just waiting on the order to fall upon the city. Before the main gate, Fritigern was mounted and as ever Ivo was by his side. The pair seemed to be berating the wall guard, gesticulating towards the high-arched and iron-studded gate, shut tight. Then, to add to their leader's voice, a Gothic roar caused the land to shake and many of the rawer recruits to shrink, such was its ferocity. Then it fell sharply into silence, as Ivo raised his hands.

'The empire has betrayed us!' Ivo roared. 'They promised us food and let us march on our last trace of strength. The Romans must be punished!'

As they neared the Goths, Pavo noticed Lupicinus and his riders slowing, dropping back down the column. He frowned, seeing the comes' face etched with fright, knuckles white and trembling on his mount's reins. Then Lupicinus shuffled in his saddle as if readying to . . .

'Mithras, no!' Pavo gasped in realisation.

Lupicinus' blood ran cold and panic welled in his heart as he gawped at the baying Goths staining the plain, wrapped around the city like a noose. *So many of them. So many sharp blades. They're going to cut us to pieces. They will slice the flesh from my bones!*

In the few battles he had fought in his time, the odds had never been this grim and he had managed to remain safely tucked into the rearmost ranks. Victory and survival had lifted him to his current post. Yet today, there would be no hiding, he realised, his limbs quivering. And his tarnished reputation would no doubt live on. The shame and ridicule from his early career would be his legacy.

At that moment he felt a surge of regret. Why had he let the bitterness of his childhood follow him through the rest of his life like a vile stench? Why oh why had he not ignored his father's jibes and pursued a career in the senate regardless? He remembered that childhood day, on the shore outside the city of Odessus, when he had first gauged his father's disgust at his craven nature. He had been playing happily in the sand, collecting shells and splashing in the shallows. Then, a scowling, pug-nosed boy had picked a fight with him, butting him back with the palms of his hands. Lupicinus had first felt the terror on that day; his breath short, his skin clammy and cold, his mind awash with confusion. He had looked to his father, sat nearby on the shingle, supping wine by the skinful, face red from inebriation and sun. 'Help!' He had cried out, reaching one hand to his father. 'Fight back, you coward!' Was all the help he received. The pug-nosed boy had beaten him to the ground and then rained blow after blow upon him unchecked. When at last the boy had finally grown bored and left, Lupicinus had squinted through swollen eyes, tasting the metallic tang of his own blood washing down the back of his throat. His father had stood over him, sneering, breath reeking of stale wine. 'You're no son of mine if you can't fight, you *coward!*'

Something stung behind Lupicinus' eyes and he felt them moisten. Then reality pushed the memories away as he heard Iudex Fritigern's voice pierce the air.

'Your emperor granted us access to your horreas and all the grain they hold, so you will open the gates, or we will smash them from their hinges. Do not presume that you could resist my armies. We may not possess siege engines, but I have enough men to pull your walls down by hand. And when my men fall upon your people, I can no longer be held responsible for what will happen to them.'

Lupicinus' guts turned over at this. He realised that he and his riders were dropping back as the marching legionaries kept up the pace set by Tribunus Gallus. Then, as the column approached the rear of the Gothic swell, the warriors there turned, braced and ready for conflict, presenting a wall of spears to the Romans. Behind them were Gothic women, children and elderly; gaunt, pale and with black-ringed eyes, their usually well-groomed hair tousled and dirty. They reeked dangerously of desperation. Then, they split apart like curtains, opening up a spear-walled corridor leading to Ivo and Fritigern.

At the head of the column, Gallus did not hesitate, leading them into the corridor. Lupicinus and his riders were the last to enter. He could feel the baleful glares of the Goths burning on his skin and the speartips hung just an arm's reach away on either side of him. Every muscle in his body twitched, longing to pull the reins and heel his mount into a turn and then a gallop out of the Gothic mass and far from this plain. *Yes,* he affirmed, *my men will understand, they will ride with me.* He stabbed out his tongue to dampen his lips, then glanced over his shoulder. But the faces of his men were stony. They were not for turning. In each of their eyes he saw his father roaring at him. *Make your mark, you coward!*

Worse, the Gothic corridor had closed up behind the column, like a predator devouring a meal. Panic rippled through him, and he shuffled in his saddle, wide-eyed. There was no going back. His heart thundered until he thought it would explode from his chest, when suddenly, an idea formed amongst the chaos in his mind.

He looked to the walls and saw safety behind the timber, iron studded gates. He filled his lungs.

'Forward!' He bellowed, digging his heels into his mount's flanks and tearing his spatha from his scabbard, pointing it directly at Ivo and Fritigern. 'Take down the leaders!' Lupicinus roared. As he set off, his riders threw their confusion to one side and followed their comes.

And while they fight, I can reach safety, Lupicinus affirmed, before shouting up to the gatehouse. 'Open the gates!' Then he lowered himself in his saddle. The sea of stunned Gothic faces gawped as he hared forward. The men in the Roman column yelled out in anger and confusion, while those atop the gatehouse frowned at his calls for the gates to be opened. *But they don't understand; I'm not a soldier, I'm not meant to be here.* The gates were growing closer and closer. All he had to do was swerve past Fritigern and Ivo and he was there. Surely they would open the gates for him? Inside the city he would be safe. *To Hades with you, Father!*

Then the iron-clad, mounted figure of Gallus swung into his path, face burning with ire. Three legionaries flanked him on either side, presenting a Roman spearwall to protect Fritigern and Ivo.

'Halt!' Gallus roared.

Lupicinus' heart leapt and he reined in his mount, the beast skidding and the riders behind him toppling from their saddles. The comes' wild gaze swept over Gallus and those flanking the tribunus. Then his eyes locked onto Pavo.

Pavo returned the stare, his top lip curling to reveal gritted teeth, his spearpoint resting by Lupicinus' heart.

Lupicinus' hands grew slack on the reins and his shoulders slumped. His mind drifted and his eyes grew distant.

Then a lone voice taunted him in his mind.

You coward!

Gallus raised a pleading hand to Fritigern, then trotted over to Lupicinus, grappling his wrist, shaking the sword from his grip. 'You imbecile! You could have killed us all!'

But Lupicinus' face was ghostly white and his gaze was far-off.

Gallus frowned. Then, finally, the comes twisted his head round to look straight through him, his lips moving but the words carried no feeling. 'Dux Vergilius . . . will hear of your . . . insubordination.'

Gallus gripped his wrist and hissed in his ear. 'That fat sot hears only the gurgle of wine disappearing down his throat. Here and now our actions could save the empire . . . or end it!' He glared at Lupicinus, anticipating another retort, but the comes was lost somewhere behind his own eyes. Then, the reflection of Ivo grew in Lupicinus' pupils.

Gallus steeled himself and turned to face the giant warrior.

'Odd behaviour for an ally?' Ivo sneered. 'I feared we would have to slay you and your column in self-defence, Tribunus.' The sea of spears and arrows poised around the scrawny Roman column creaked and rippled as if in agreement.

Gallus hesitated for a moment, then looked Ivo in the eye. 'This was a dreadful miscalculation by my comes. Just as some of your riders broke rank when you first crossed into the empire.' Then he turned to Fritigern. 'I apologise unreservedly for this incident. Thanks to Mithras and Wodin that no blood was spilled.'

'Yet the gates are shut, Tribunus. My people will still perish from hunger,' Fritigern spoke coldly.

Gallus held the iudex's gaze. 'Grain *will* be delivered to your people.'

Fritigern frowned. 'You will open the gates?'

Gallus shook his head.

Fritigern snorted. 'Then don't waste your breath, Tribunus.' He looked around his people, then up to the walls. 'This reeks of trickery; perhaps Rome thought she could spring some kind of trap upon my armies here, below your fine city walls?' Fritigern spread out his arms to the surrounding countryside. 'Well I see no reason to be fearful. My armies could shatter anything the empire was to throw at it,' he leaned forward, wagging one finger at Gallus, 'and you know this.'

'It does indeed reek of trickery,' Gallus replied, his eyes narrowing on Ivo. 'Unfortunately, I fear both your people and mine have been tricked.'

Ivo looked back, his face expressionless.

225

Gallus glanced to Salvian, a few ranks back; the ambassador almost imperceptibly shook his head. One word rang in his thoughts. *Proof.* He suppressed a growl of frustration. To obtain proof would require time, and they had precious little of that.

'But let us put this to one side and focus on the vital issue – your people need grain, as do mine. And I can assure you, Iudex Fritigern, that we are still bound as strongly as ever by our truce.'

'No,' Fritigern hissed, 'this has gone too far. Too many concessions have been made. We came to you under truce, seeking refuge. Yet we have been subjected to rape, murder, starvation and humiliation!'

'I beg for your patience, Iudex Fritigern. Grain could be here, in front of you, by morning,' Gallus said, the tension tight in his voice. 'Surely the promise of peace is worth one more night of patience?' At this, the surrounding Goths fell silent.

'Do not make promises you cannot fulfil, Tribunus. It will be worse for all your people in the longer term.'

Gallus looked Fritigern in the eye, his face gaunt and unsmiling. 'I do not make false promises.' A breeze whistled over them as they eyed one another in silence. 'It is possible. Difficult, but possible,' Gallus continued. 'You would have to provide wagons and riders though, say two hundred of each. My turma of cavalry will lead your men to the settlements nearby. We could pull together enough to see us through a few more weeks.'

Fritigern made to reply, then stopped as Ivo whispered in his ear. Gallus' eyes narrowed at this. Fritigern seemed to mull over the giant's words for some time, before finally shaking his head, drawing a barely disguised sneer of disgust from Ivo.

The Gothic Iudex looked up, then beckoned a tall rider with topknotted locks and a decorated red leather cuirass. 'Gunter, muster your riders.' The rider nodded and wheeled away on his mount, then Fritigern looked back to Gallus. 'You have until sunrise, Tribunus.' Then he placed a hand over his heart and pointed to the Chi-Rho above the church basilica, then pointed to the wooden idol of Mithras Gallus was clasping in his hand. 'After that, no god can help you and your empire.'

The waxing moon flitted between the scudding clouds in an otherwise pitch-black night. Mercifully, spring had taken hold of the land at last and the air was pleasant. Amidst the sea of Gothic tents and campfires surrounding Marcianople, a small, neatly aligned block of contubernium tents offered a semblance of order to the chaos of the day just passed; the XI Claudia legionaries were posted here outside the walls whilst Lupicinus and two centuries of his comitatenses had quickly volunteered to bolster the city garrison.

Inside his contubernium tent, Pavo lay stretched out on his cot. He had lain there for what felt like an eternity, studying the shadows cast by a guttering candle on the roof of the tent. He struggled to see how tomorrow could be anything other than his last day; the end of the XI Claudia and perhaps the beginning of the end of the empire? On and on his thoughts churned until, almost surreptitiously, sleep crept across him. He felt the jabbering of his ruminations become distant, and his eyelids grew heavy. Then the nightmare came to him again.

'Father?' He called out, reaching for the hunched, tired old man before him. His heart wept at the sight. The once-proud legionary seemed to be fading before him. 'Take my hand, before it is too late!' He roared, glancing nervously around the peaceful dunes. The sandstorm would come any moment now, and when it did, Father would be gone again.

But this time, the sandstorm did not come.

Then Pavo realised that Tarquitius was standing by his side. The senator carried a writhing viper on his shoulders; the beast's scales glistened as it wrapped around him, as if soothing him.

'Senator?' Pavo said uncertainly.

But Tarquitius' eyes were glassy and distant. He did not hear Pavo's words.

Then the viper slipped around Tarquitius' neck and its head rose up behind him, tensing, broadening. Its jaw dislocated and stretched wide, fangs bared and dripping venom, throat gaping, ready to devour. Yet Tarquitius was oblivious to this.

'Senator!' Pavo stumbled back, horrified. The snake readied to sink its fangs into Tarquitius' skull. The man would die and the truth would die with him.

Suddenly, Pavo felt the weight of a spatha in his hand. At once, he hefted the blade towards the creature, but the snake slipped free of the senator at the last moment. With a punch of ripping meat, the blade scythed halfway through Senator Tarquitius' neck. Blood pumped from the wound like an ocean, flooding the sands until Tarquitius' body was shrivelled and shrunken to the size of a peach stone. Pavo stared, repulsed at the sight. Then he saw the tip of the viper's tail slip under the sand.

The first stinging grains of the sandstorm danced against his face, and Pavo remembered where he was. He shot his gaze back to the nearby dune, looking for Father.

But the dune was empty. Father was gone.

Pavo's thoughts raced. Then he filled his lungs and clasped the phalera.

'If there is a truth about you that I must know, then I will find it!' He cried out over the empty dunes.

Pavo blinked, realising he was sitting bolt upright, slick with sweat. The candle had burnt out, and it was still dark outside. He rubbed at his temples as the angst of the nightmare slipped away. Then he sighed at the sight of Sura in the nearby cot, snoring like a boar, as if tomorrow was just another day. Apart from Sura, the tent was empty; evidently many of the legionaries had found sleep hard to come by. He lay back in his cot, determined to sleep again.

It seems the Viper is even infiltrating my nightmares, he stifled a wry chuckle as he shuffled into a more comfortable position. As he did so, his drowsy gaze fell upon a shadowy shape by the tent flap. *Did it just move?* He rubbed his eyes, sure it was just the residue of sleep in his mind. But his nightmares swirled with all that had happened in these last months: the Viper's riders, embedded within Fritigern's horde, operating under cover of night, slipping into Goth and Roman tents to slit throats and pillage grain.

Then the shape glided forward like a shade, cloaked and hooded. Panic gripped Pavo's every sinew.

Was this the Viper himself? The hooded shade in the green cloak, the one who plots the end for all Rome?

Pavo scrambled backwards from his cot, clawing out for his spatha and hopping up to standing, pointing the blade at the figure. Then he smelt a sweet, floral scent, saw the slender shoulders and curve of hips. He hesitated, sword in hand.

'I was going to surprise you by slipping into your cot,' Felicia whispered, stepping into a patch of dull torchlight from outside and lowering her hood. Then she let the cloak fall from her shoulders and her amber locks tumbled down her back and chest. She wore a close-fitting blue tunic and brown leggings. 'I thought you might be pleased to see me, but not this pleased.'

Pavo frowned then blushed, realising that he held the spatha hilt near his groin, the tip hovering near Felicia's breasts. 'I . . . oh, sorry.' Then he sheathed the sword, and a dreadful realisation crept over him. 'Felicia, it sickened me to think you might not have got out of Durostorum safely, but this is the worst place you could have come to.'

'But I am here,' she spoke flatly. 'I followed the column, rode alongside the wagons.'

'Then I should never have taught you to ride,' Pavo spoke in scorn, but then couldn't resist melting into a smile when he saw her eyes sparkle in the gloom.

'I think we've taught each other a thing or two in the last year,' she cocked an eyebrow.

Pavo chuckled, then composed himself, gripping her by the shoulders. 'I'm serious, Felicia, it's dangerous here; if grain does not come by morning, war could be upon us. The enemy are wrapped around us and Marcianople like a noose, ready to snap shut. You should head further south, to Adrianople.'

'I will, when the time is right. Father is already there, looking for a place for us to stay. Yet I fear for what might happen there – the city will be like a hive in a few days and grain is surely as sparse there as anywhere else?'

Pavo slumped to sit on his cot. 'Aye, trouble lies in every direction, it seems.'

Felicia sat next to him, clasping his hand in hers. 'Perhaps we should forget about what happens next, if only for a short while?'

Pavo saw that she eyed the empty cots around the tent with a frown. Then she checked herself and the sparkle in her eyes returned and she pouted, her lips full and soft. 'Perhaps,' he leaned closer.

Then a grunt from behind broke them apart.

'What's going on?' Sura propped himself up on one arm, squinting, a foul look on his face. 'Felicia? What're you doing h . . . ' then his face fell and he sighed. He picked up his cloak and stomped for the tent flap. 'I'll be outside.'

Pavo smirked at this. Payback, he reckoned, considering the number of times he had spent the night trudging aimlessly while his friend 'entertained' the local women of Durostorum.

Felicia pulled him back to her.

He held a hand to her shoulders. 'Just promise me that you will ride from here, before dawn.'

She glanced again to the empty cots, eyes narrowing. 'I promise.'

With that their lips pressed together. They kissed hungrily and Pavo smoothed his hands over her curves, cupping her breasts, caressing her buttocks. It had been so long since they had been together like this. She pulled off her tunic and leggings and Pavo slid off his tunic. In the dim light, they pressed together, then fell back in a tangle of lust.

Gunter the horseman sucked in a breath of fresh night air and looked back to the orange glow emanating from the Roman port-citadel of Odessus. The wall guard had braced in alarm at the sight of his Gothic riders approaching, their bows stretched, ready to unleash on the foreign cavalrymen. Fortunately, the escort of Roman equites sagittarii cavalrymen had raced to the front to explain that they were friendly. And so, despite stubborn resistance initially from the Roman governor, they had completed their mission and acquired the precious grain – just enough to stave off hunger and war for now.

He thought of his wife, skeletal and feverish after weeks of starvation since their flight from Peuce Island on the Danubius delta. She had simply refused to eat, giving everything over to their son. Young Alaric possessed a sharp mind and was growing into a tall and powerful boy for his age. But even he was flagging after a sustained diet of boiled grass and indigestible root.

'But now the famine is over!' Gunter spoke aloud, looking up to the sky, touching a hand to the bronze Christian Chi-Rho amulet around his neck and allowing himself a smile for the first time in so long. Perhaps this religion that was spreading from the empire like wildfire was the true faith after all? At this, habit kicked in and he whispered a word of apology to Allfather Wodin.

With that, he heeled his mount into a turn and then a gallop. His topknot swirled in his wake as he entered the forest to catch up with the train of mules and wagons. The grain sacks heaped on the beasts and vehicles had taken on a treasure-like quality, with Roman and Goth riders alike eyeing the haul with wide eyes, no doubt scenting the fresh-baked bread it would soon become.

The forest floor was cool and damp and mercifully almost clear of snow. The pace had slowed a little due to the terrain, but so long as they pushed on, nothing could stop them reaching Marcianople before dawn. He raised his hand and punched the air as he galloped to the fore of the column, filling his lungs, ready to emit a roar of encouragement.

But that breath stayed in his lungs.

Up ahead on the forest path, a figure loomed.

A lone rider shrouded in a dark-green hooded cloak, mounted on a jet-black stallion.

'Who goes there?' Gunter called out, squinting at the ethereal figure.

The rider remained motionless, head bowed. The mount's breath clouded in the night air.

Gunter held up one hand, slowing the column. 'I said, who goes there?'

The rider's hood shuffled, looking up. The shadow where a face should have been seemed to pierce Gunter's armour. Then the rider raised a hand only a few inches from the reins of the mount and extended one finger. All was silent for a moment. Then the figure swiped the finger down.

Gunter's eyes grew wide as the treeline either side of the column rippled. He caught sight of hundreds of speartips that emerged. Then he saw the dark-green snake banner the rogue warriors carried. *The Viper has come for us!* His stomach fell away as he realised what was about to happen. He mouthed the first words of a prayer for his wife and little Alaric, then a cloud of arrows tore through his face, neck, thighs and arms.

Gunter of the Thervingi slid from the saddle, the life gone from his body as it hit the ground like a sack of wet sand. All around him, screaming rang out as a wave of the Viper's Goths sprang from the woods and clamped onto the column like wolves, longswords raised. The riders of the grain column, Romans and Goths, fought for each other in vain as the jaws of the trap slammed shut upon them.

When the last of the felled riders' throats had been slit, a chant broke out from the victors. *'Vi-per! Vi-per! Vi-per!'*

The green-cloaked rider trotted forward.

'Now burn the wagons, burn the bodies, burn the grain . . . let them starve . . . '

Then the rider raised a clenched fist and pulled on the stallion's reins so the beast reared up.

'Bring me war!'

Pavo stirred from a second bout of sleep, blessedly nightmare free. He rubbed one leg against the other in the warm comfort of his blankets as he came to. Then, patting the other half of his cot, he realised he was alone. Felicia was gone.

He sat up; all around him, the rest of his contubernium were present in the form of slumbering shapes under blankets. The usual chorus of rumbling emissions of gas and grating snores punctuated the stillness, Centurion Quadratus being the main culprit.

He crept from his cot and pulled back the tent flap: it was still dark outside, though a purple band on the eastern horizon, beyond the forest, heralded the first coming of dawn. His gut shrivelled as he stepped outside, rubbing his arms at the stark chill. The grain column was nowhere to be seen.

'Tomorrow is almost upon us,' a voice spoke.

Pavo spun round. Salvian was standing just behind him, hands clasped behind his back, dressed in a clean, high-necked tunic, woollen trousers and muddied riding boots. The ambassador's face betrayed no fear, despite the weighty truth behind his words. 'Are you frightened, Pavo?'

Pavo shook his head, realising that he was not; all his ruminations had been for the safety of Felicia, for Sura, Gallus and the veterans. For Salvian. 'I have a duty,' he patted his scabbard. 'And that's not haughty talk, ambassador.'

Salvian smiled at this. 'You have faith in Tribunus Gallus' plan; the grain column?'

'I would march with that man until the bones in my feet crumbled,' he replied.

'That's not an answer,' Salvian chuckled.

Pavo looked to Salvian. 'Let's just say I have come to expect the unexpected, to prepare for the worst.' He looked to the first sliver of sun that appeared over the horizon, then turned to the ambassador with a frown. 'You could ride from here you know, if things turn nasty. Nobody would expect an ambassador to stand and fight with the legion.'

Salvian issued a wry half-smile. 'I don't run from my problems, lad, never have.'

Pavo sighed at this, and held the ambassador's gaze. 'You are one of the wisest, shrewdest men I have ever known, but you should not underestimate how fast a battle can spread – it is like wildfire. I'll be fighting at the front with Gallus and the veterans, but should we fall . . . '

Salvian cut him off, placing a hand on Pavo's shoulder. 'Your father would have been proud to know the man his son has grown to be.'

A silence hung in the air, and Pavo felt his heart swell with pride.

'Now,' Salvian said, 'put my safety from your mind, for Gallus has other plans for me anyway. He wants me to help organise the Roman refugees. To lead them north, back to the far side of the River Beli Lom.'

'Then make haste, and I wish you safe passage,' Pavo nodded. 'Until we meet again.'

The pair shared a wistful gaze and then went their separate ways.

Pavo turned to head back to his tent, passing the centre of the Roman encampment and the silver eagle and ruby bull banner of the XI Claudia standing proudly near Gallus' tent. Dawn would break soon and there would be one hundred thousand starving Goths expecting a delivery of grain. He mused over whether there would be any point in starting a campfire for his contubernium to cook breakfast upon, given that most of them only had quarter rations of hardtack left.

Spotting some discarded kindling, he stooped to pick it up anyway. When he stood upright again, a cloaked, hooded figure flitted past the tents before him. The figure was tall and the cloak was . . . he froze.

The cloak was dark-green.

Pavo's blood iced.

Calm yourself! He tried to brush it off – many Goths wore green and there were a few Goths and Romans up and about already. He affirmed that it was just some residual unease from last night's nightmare. But something wasn't right: the movement of the figure was odd; stealthy and swift, and it stopped every so often, casting a glance this way and that, like a hunting predator.

Pavo peered through the gap between the tents; the figure seemed to be making for the city gates. The wall guards above the main gate gazed to the eastern horizon in hope of sighting the grain column, and were oblivious as the figure crept up to the well-bolted, iron-studded gates.

Then the figure halted at the gates and shot a glance around, the shadow where a face should have been scouring the camp for observers.

Pavo ducked behind the tent, his heart thudding until he heard the noise of knuckles gently rapping on wood. He risked a glance up; the figure waited by the small hatch near the edge of the gate, a section about half the height of a man used to allow controlled access without opening the gates in full. Pavo frowned, then his heart froze as the hatch opened, and a hand beckoned the figure inside. As the green-cloaked figure slipped into the city, the blubbery features of Senator Tarquitius poked out of the hatch, etched with guilt and fear, snatching a glance in every direction.

'You treacherous dog!' Pavo hissed under his breath, 'what ruin are you concocting now?'

The hatch swung shut and he stayed behind the tent and watched, hoping for more activity, something of substance to follow up on. He suddenly felt conspicuous as the horizon changed from purple to dark orange and a few more Romans emerged from their tents. Frustrated, he pushed away from the tent and headed for his own. He glanced round once more at the walls, sure there was something more to deduce, but all was normal, sentries gazing east in silence.

Then he saw it.

For just the briefest of moments, the dark-green hood appeared behind the battlements, just above the gates. The sentries were oblivious to the figure's presence, the twin gate towers blocking their view. Pavo watched as the figure wrapped its fingers over the crenellations, shaded features scanning the ground outside the gate. He froze as the figure's gaze snagged on him. At that moment, Pavo felt as if he was in the sights of a master archer.

'Morning, sir,' a croaky voice spoke next to him.

Pavo started, turning to the red-eyed legionary who had shuffled from a tent nearby. It was one of the younger recruits – barely sixteen by the looks of it – from the now disbanded fifty he had led to Istrita. Pavo nodded stiffly, embarrassed and proud of the salutation at the same time. 'Morning,' Pavo replied. 'Glad you're in our ranks for what lies ahead today, soldier.'

'Likewise, sir.' The young lad smiled and saluted, then marched off to the latrine pits.

Pavo's smile faded and he spun back to the battlements. The space between the gate towers was empty. He squinted, sure he had seen someone up there. *Perhaps my many nights of demi-sleep have finally caught up with me*, he realised with a wry shake of the head. He walked through the Roman tent rows and turned into the one that would lead to his. He welcomed the thought of the scathing banter that would no doubt break out between the contubernia over yet another scant breakfast. It was the way the soldiers dealt

236

with the brutal realities of their work; when you served in the limitanei, every morning could be your last, and this morning especially so. He glanced sombrely to the treeline to the east: the tip of the sun had pierced the horizon and still no sight nor sound of the grain column. And the Goths were gathering. He frowned, clutching the phalera medallion, detecting the first needles of trepidation in his gut that usually came in the hours before conflict.

His tent and those around it were still free of activity. *Lazy bastards,* he thought to himself with a chuckle. Then he froze where he stood.

A figure was crouched by his tent flap – this time in a black cloak and hood. Pavo's breath stilled when he saw the glint of a dagger in the figure's hand. The figure reached out to open the tent flap, the dagger held overhand.

Pavo rushed forward, throwing himself at the figure. With a thud, the pair were interlocked, tumbling in the dewy grass. The dagger flew from the figure's grasp and landed paces away. Pavo sensed victory as he pinned the figure down with his knees, then pulled a fist back to strike the face, semi-obscured by the hood. Then a floral, sweet scent curled up his nostrils and he heard whimpering. His fist relaxed and his face fell as he saw the milky-white skin of the figure's face, the end of an amber lock tumbling free of the hood.

'Felicia?' He groaned, pulling the hood back. Behind it, her face was wrinkled with emotion, the kohl staining her eyes having run across her cheeks in a flurry of tears, smearing her beauty.

'Will you *please* do away with that cloak!' He said as he helped her to her feet.

But she briskly shrugged him off, teeth gritted and bared, nostrils flared.

Pavo searched her tormented expression for some clue as to what to say. He stepped forward, arms outstretched to clasp her shoulders, but she stepped back as if he was a stranger. 'Felicia? What's going on? Why were you going into the tent . . . with *that?*' he gestured to the dagger.

Felicia was sucking in deep breaths now, composing herself. She wiped her eyes, further smearing the kohl over her cheeks, then stood straight, fixing her hair behind her ears. 'You wouldn't understand, Pavo, and it's best for you that you don't.'

Pavo dropped his arms to his sides with a sigh. 'All those times when I came to visit you at the inn and you had that dark look in your eyes and you would ignore me. Each time I would leave, thinking we were through, but I'd still go back. You know why? Because sometimes, just sometimes, I'd be lucky enough to catch you when you were yourself, smiling, joking. That's the girl that caught my eye when I first joined the legion. Yet I feel like that girl is lost somewhere . . . ' he raised his hands and glanced all around in frustration, then back at Felicia. 'Now this?'

She looked down to her left with firm lips. 'Perhaps that girl has been a guise?'

Pavo felt her words like a blow to the guts, but he didn't let it show. 'No, you're lying. Every time we've lain together I've seen true happiness in your eyes. It's like you've set down a massive burden from your shoulders for those moments. Don't you want to be that girl more often?'

Her lips trembled and she covered her face with her hands. 'How can I?' She whispered, tears escaping the cracks between her fingers. 'How can I when my brother's killer walks free?'

Pavo's heart sank and he closed his eyes. *Curtius – of course.* His mind reeled through all those times Felicia had seemed so interested in the whereabouts of certain veterans. He'd never linked it with her dark moods, until now. Of all the soldiers he shared the tent with, only Quadratus and Avitus had served in the Claudia long enough to have been there when Curtius was in the ranks. His eyes widened.

'You think it was . . . ' he started.

Felicia blinked the tears away and held his gaze. 'I *know* it was Quadratus.' She clenched her fists.

Pavo shook his head, an incredulous smile growing on his face. 'Felicia, you're wrong. Quadratus is a gruff big whoreson, but probably one

238

of the best-hearted men I've ever fought alongside. He'd be more likely to throw himself in front of a dagger that was aimed at a fellow legionary than to harm one of them.' He gripped her wrists, holding her gaze. 'I know this!'

She offered him a pitying, almost apologetic look. 'I'm sorry, Pavo, but it was Quadratus. Of that, there is no doubt.' She rummaged in her cloak and pulled out a yellowed, frayed scroll and held it up as if to underline her argument. 'This memo came from none other than the Speculatores.'

'The emperor's agents?'

She nodded. 'Curtius was working for them too – that's why I know the seal is from them.' Her face fell stony. 'Pavo, Curtius was killed by another agent – in the XI Claudia fort.'

'You think Quadratus is a speculatore?' Pavo pulled back a little. 'He's a fine soldier, a lion on the battlefield, but he's about as stealthy and subtle as an *onager* being pulled down stairs.'

Felicia did not flinch. 'Then why did I find this scroll concealed in the mortar by his bunk?'

Pavo's face fell. He raked over his thoughts. Surely Quadratus was no imposter? He had shed blood with the big Gaul on the battlefield and the giant had saved him on more than one occasion. She was mistaken, surely. Then his thoughts spun to a stop on one unremarkable day in the fort. Pavo had walked in to find Quadratus and his good friend Avitus playing dice on the floor. The rest of the contubernium were stood around them, coins clutched in their hands, placing bets. When he had asked Zosimus what was going on, the big Thracian had replied: *Avitus wants the top bunk, Quadratus told him where to go, I suggested a wager and so here we are!*

'That was Avitus' bunk,' he muttered absently and his heart sank. The little bald Roman was one of the trusted few, the core men of the legion that Gallus had built around him. He had got to know Avitus well in this last year, but only well enough to know that there was some dark core that pulled and twisted at his moods, especially when they drank together.

'Pavo?' Felicia frowned, grappling at his tunic. 'Say it again.'

Pavo's face fell. 'They swapped bunks about six months ago, not long after the mission to the Kingdom of Bosporus.'

She clasped a hand over her mouth. 'Then I would have . . . '

Pavo wrapped an arm around her, pulling her head into his chest. 'You have done nothing, Felicia. Be thankful for that.'

She pushed back. 'But now I know who must pay for Curtius' death.'

Pavo reached out to her, but she stepped away, looking for her dagger. 'Felicia, please, don't do anything, at least not now. Please, let us talk over this more when,' he stopped as an amber light washed across them, the sun was now half-risen. 'Just promise me one thing,' he pleaded, 'that you will do nothing until we have talked over this later?'

She neither nodded nor shook her head. Instead her eyes grew distant as if in thought.

Then, the still and quiet of dawn was torn asunder by the wail of the Gothic horns.

Pavo's skin crawled at the clatter of iron weapons and armour being donned. He looked all around the camp to see that the Goths were mustering. His thoughts spun; the green-cloaked figure on the battlements, Felicia, the missing grain column. Then he grappled her firmly by the shoulders. 'Get to your horse and ride, Felicia, ride as fast as you can and don't look back. Get to Adrianople, get to your father and stay there.'

He held her cold glare firmly.

'All Hades is coming to this plain!'

Hearing the war horns, Gallus hurried to buckle his swordbelt, then slipped on his plumed intercisa helmet. The grain column was nowhere to be seen and this day would see much blood.

He hesitated before leaving his tent, lifted the idol of Mithras from his purse and kissed it. 'Let today bring me one step closer to you, Olivia,' he whispered.

Then he spun as someone pushed into his tent. Pavo. The young legionary's face was wrinkled in consternation.

'Sir, this may be nothing, but . . . '

'Speak!' Gallus barked.

'I saw something, a figure, stealing into the city. Only moments ago.'

Gallus cocked an eyebrow. 'What of it? The gates are well guarded. Only trusted men would be allowed in and out.'

'But this figure was dressed in a hooded, green cloak, sir,' Pavo replied, his face grave.

Gallus hesitated for a moment. The green cloak and the myth of the Viper had haunted his dreams for weeks now. But half-sightings and rumour were but a distraction on a morning such as this. 'Ah,' he feigned disinterest and waved a hand dismissively, 'I have scrutinised every man, woman and child in green in these last weeks. Don't let it distract you.'

'But, sir,' Pavo continued, 'It was Senator Tarquitius who let the figure in . . . '

Gallus' brow furrowed at this, unable to hide his interest, but the clatter of iron and drumming of boots outside shook him back to the more pressing matter. 'Walk with me,' he nodded to the tent flap.

He pushed open the tent flap and froze. Outside stood Erwin the Goth.

The old man's face was drawn and weary. 'This has gone too far,' Erwin muttered, 'and I fear it is already too late.'

Gallus frowned, gripping the man's shoulders. 'For the love of the gods, speak!'

Erwin looked up, eyes weary. 'I feared him so much I let my son's murder go unpunished. Yet I was once loyal to him. I rode with him, you know.'

'Him?' Gallus' heart thundered.

Erwin's gaze was distant now. 'Ivo is the one you seek. He was the Viper's right hand man. He bears the blue snake stigma under his arm greaves. He carries on the Viper's legacy – I am sure of it. It is he who has brought us to the brink of war!'

Gallus looked to Pavo who returned his wide eyed gaze. His eyes darted and a thousand voices babbled in his mind. Then he felt a plan forming in the chaos. He gripped Erwin by the shoulders. 'Make your way to the north of the plain. You could save many lives today, old man!'

With that, he turned back to Pavo. 'This could be the answer, Pavo; no more grasping at rumours and chasing shades!'

Chapter 16

The Gothic war cries were deafening as they punched their weapons into the air, demanding that Iudex Fritigern act. Those nearest the city waited with their siege ladders, eager to push them up and against the city walls. The acrid tang of doused campfires spiced the air and offered an ominous portent to what the day ahead might hold.

'Stand firm, men!' Gallus bawled as he marshalled the cohort into a line, hemming the rear of the Gothic swell. Gallus glanced to each side, heartened somewhat to see the redoubtable grimaces on the faces of his most trusted men; Felix, Zosimus, Quadratus, Avitus, then Pavo and Sura. If things went awry, then he would be glad to fight his last alongside them.

'Sir, I fear we should either be within those walls or far from them,' Felix started. 'The grain column is nowhere to be seen, and they're on the brink.' He pointed to Fritigern and Ivo at the head of the Gothic mass. Ivo, resplendent in his broad scale vest and conical helm, was remonstrating with his iudex, fists clenched, urging him to act.

'No, there is another hope,' Gallus replied, once again scanning the Gothic swell, seeking out Erwin the Goth; *where are you, old man, come on!*

He shuffled in his saddle, teeth grinding in frustration. But they had to wait, it all rested on the old man now. He remembered Salvian's words of caution; *You need proof, Tribunus.* It warmed Gallus to know that Salvian was already headed northwards from the plain with the Roman refugees and would be safe from what was to come. *And, by Mithras, Ambassador, I'll embrace you like a brother if the proof I present to Fritigern staves off war.*

Then, like a ray of sunshine splitting dark clouds, a lone figure wandered from the rear of the swell.

'Sir?' Felix said as Erwin the Goth stumbled towards them.

'All is in hand, Felix.' Gallus replied, ushering Erwin into the Roman line. But then he frowned, noticing that the old man was trembling and his face was pale. Then his gaze caught on little spots of *something* around the neck of Erwin's robe. *Blood?*

A Gothic war horn echoed across the land and it shook Gallus from his doubts. He filled his lungs. 'Stay your fears, men. The day can still be saved.' He flicked a finger to the aquilifer, who raised the silver eagle standard until the ruby bull banner caught the cool breeze. 'Form a column and advance,' he barked, 'and not a man is to draw his sword unless I give the word.'

Pavo squared his shoulders as they marched forward, blocking out his fears. The rear of the Gothic crowd turned to them, gaunt faces scowling in disbelief. Then a confident and predatory glare replaced that look. Just as they had done yesterday, the Goths parted like a venus flytrap sensing its prey, opening up a path to Fritigern and Ivo.

Pavo suppressed a shiver as they marched into the midst of the enemy ranks, blanking out the restless speartips and the sea of faces that eyed them hungrily.

'We could have done with Salvian at right about this point,' Sura spoke, his voice cracking, his eyes darting around the Gothic onlookers.

'He's played his part, and I fear that this time, talking will be inadequate,' Pavo shook his head, saddened and heartened at once. He prayed Salvian and the Roman refugees were already well on their way to safety across the Beli Lom. Then he glanced up to the city walls, seeing that the pale-faced Tarquitius stood there with Lupicinus and the governor; the senator had made a last minute bid to join the evacuation, slipping from the gate hatch, only to stumble back in terror at the sight of the Gothic horde marching on the walls. Again, a bittersweet jumble of emotions flitted across Pavo's heart; if the Goths were to fall upon this city, then the senator would have carried out his last traitorous act. But the truth of his father would die with the fat swine.

Then a dry realisation settled his worries as they marched deep into the Gothic swell; *if the Goths fall upon the city, then I will be in Elysium by evening.*

The column slowed to a halt before Ivo and Fritigern. The rabble of the Goths died to a silence, leaving only the whistle of the gentle wind.

All eyes fell on Gallus.

'Iudex Fritigern, I ask you and your armies to stand down,' Gallus spoke in a flat tone.

Fritigern glared at him, eyes burning like hot coals, a look of utter disbelief etched on his features.

Ivo roared in laughter by his side. 'Their words insult us, Iudex! The Romans have mocked us for the last time.'

'I addressed Iudex Fritigern of the Thervingi, noble ally of Rome,' Gallus shot a glare to the big warrior, then turned back to Fritigern.

The iudex's expression was one of weary resignation. 'You give me no choice, Roman. I have given you chance after chance to prove that the empire was good to her word, that you would treat us as allies and feed and shelter us. I offered you my armies in return; my men could have bolstered the imperial borders, fought and bled for the empire.' His eyes were red-rimmed now. 'Instead, I must turn my swords on your city walls.'

With that, Fritigern raised his hand.

Gallus braced and the legionary column instinctively bunched up with a rustle of iron as mail vests ground together and hands clasped to spatha hilts.

As Fritigern's lips parted to bark the order, Gallus slid from his mount, hands in the air by way of supplication. 'Iudex Fritigern, think this over just one last time, I beg of you.'

Gallus studied Fritigern's face, praying to Mithras that the wrinkle in his brow meant there was a chance he could be persuaded. Fritigern's eyes were glassy now, and the situation was like a spinning folles; the fate of the empire hanging on which side the coin would fall.

'He wants another chance?' Ivo mocked. 'More time for our people to die, for our armies to weaken,' he leant forward on his saddle, his good eye bulging as he pointed a finger at Gallus, 'for Roman legions to gather and attack us?'

At this, Gallus snarled; 'We have trodden lightly in your presence for too long, Ivo, out of respect for the iudex. Now, you leave me no choice.'

Ivo's eyes narrowed.

'Ivo is not who you think he is, Iudex,' he continued.

Fritigern frowned. 'Ivo? He has been by my side for over twenty years, Tribunus, armed and ready to protect me with his life. Please, do not insult me with some weak diversion.'

'Then do not take my word for it, Iudex. Hear it from one of your own!' Gallus spoke firmly, then turned, waving Erwin the Goth towards him. The old man ambled forward, dark lines now staining the skin under his eyes.

Gallus clasped a hand to Erwin's shoulder, then frowned as he noticed a trickle of blood snaking from the old man's lips. Erwin opened his mouth, and blood poured from the stump that remained of his freshly severed tongue.

Gallus recoiled and a gasp of disgust rang out. The old man slumped to his knees with an animal moan, sobbing.

'What is this, Tribunus?' Fritigern scowled, his nose wrinkling.

Gallus realised at that moment that subtlety was useless. 'It is simple, Iudex,' he stabbed a finger at Ivo as his next words formed in his throat. 'Ask your most trusted man to remove the greaves from his arms.'

Fritigern frowned, shooting a glance to Ivo, then back to Gallus. 'Have you lost your mind?'

Gallus stood firm. 'It is a simple request, Iudex. One that could save thousands upon thousands of Gothic lives.'

Ivo began to roar in laughter at this.

But Fritigern held up a hand. 'Ivo. Humour the tribunus.'

The laughter died, and Ivo's face fell. 'Iudex?' He spluttered.

'The tribunus is right; it is a simple request. You have nothing to hide – show him!'

Ivo bristled at this, his shoulders squaring. Then, with a low growl, he reached to untie the laces of his greaves and all surrounding them looked on.

Gallus' eyes were fixed on Ivo as he loosened the knots. Behind the leather would lie the answer, the irrefutable proof in the form of a blue-ink snake stigma.

That Ivo is loyal to the Viper's cause!

But then Gallus frowned as Ivo slowed. He noticed the giant warrior glancing up to the battlements to give an almost imperceptible nod to someone up there. Gallus followed his line of sight and frowned; only Comes Lupicinus and the wall guard stood there now. Then he saw a figure emerge behind them; almost wraith-like, face in shadows under a dark-green hood. His blood iced.

A shout rang out from the battlements and Lupicinus and the wall guard broke out in some kind of scuffle. Above the crenellations, only limbs and flailing fists could be seen. As one, the legionary cohort, the Gothic mass, Fritigern and Ivo looked to the fracas in bemusement. Then, in a flash, an arm rose above the scuffle and a plumbata dart was hurled from the walls. Straight at Fritigern.

A collective gasp rang out as Fritigern shuddered in his saddle and the weighted dart punched into the ground behind him, dripping with blood. Gallus' eyes snapped from the dart to the Gothic Iudex, who was touching fingers to his cheek, gashed wide open to the bone, sinews of flesh dangling and dripping with blood. Fritigern's eyes were bulging.

The coin had fallen.

In the surreal hiatus that followed, Gallus backed away, lost for words. He turned to the cohort and motioned for them to back out of the Gothic swell.

Ivo leapt on the moment. 'The plumed Roman on the walls has tried to kill our leader again, bold and unashamed, here before you all. The Romans are no allies! To arms!' He roared. 'Spill a gallon of their blood for every drop of Iudex Fritigern's that has been shed today.' He smashed his longsword onto his shield boss and orchestrated a roar from the Gothic armies.

Fritigern drew his longsword from his scabbard and held it high above his head.

'Back, back!' Gallus urged his men back along the narrow corridor in the Gothic ranks.

'Death to the empire!' Fritigern boomed swiping his sword down, the point aimed at a wide-eyed Lupicinus on the battlements. 'To the walls! Bring me his heart!'

As one, the horde roared until the earth shook, then swarmed forward with a cacophony of battle cries. The ladders were raised up and clunked into place against the battlements and at once spearmen scurried up their rungs, eager for blood.

Gallus glanced in every direction. The narrow corridor in the Gothic ranks vanished as warriors rushed to slay the XI Claudia cohort.

'Shields!' He cried.

With a wooden clunk the legionaries were little more than intercisa helmets, spears, eyes and snarls behind a shield wall. Pavo felt the air being forced from his lungs as the Romans pressed together. There was no time for a plumbatae volley as the noose snapped tight, Gothic spearmen falling upon the Roman square with a smash of iron and a chorus of screams. Some Gothic warriors skated over the shield wall and into the midst of the cohort, such was their fervour. Some ran at the Roman spears unshielded, grappling the spear shafts, wrenching legionaries from the lines and onto the ground where they were hacked into little more than bone and gristle in a heartbeat.

Pavo's shoulder jarred as the Goths smashed against his shield. Then he punched out with his spear, the tip plunging into one Goth's eye socket, showering his face with hot blood, exploded eye and grey matter. Blinking the gore away, he saw that the charge had barged some legionaries from their feet; the Roman square was bent out of shape and close to collapse.

When his spear was torn from his grasp, Pavo butted his shield out again and again, smashing bones of those who attacked him. Then he ripped his spatha from its scabbard and parried furiously.

A few paces from the square, one red-haired brute wielded a two-headed axe, swinging it round his head, teeth clenched in a manic grin. Then, beside him, a hand clawed at his knee. He looked down to see Sura being dragged out of the square by two Goths, his friend's face agape with terror. The Goths dropped Sura before the axe-giant then backed off as the giant hefted his weapon, readying for a swing at Sura's skull.

Pavo pushed free of the disintegrating Roman square. He pulled his shield round like a scythe to clear a path before him, then headbutted one eager opponent who rushed at him. The fin of his intercisa helmet pierced the Goth's forehead dead centre, a neat triangular hole framed by white bone was quickly filled in by spouting blood. As the giant swung his axe for Sura, Pavo leapt forward, hacking his spatha down at the axe shaft. With only inches to spare the shaft was sheared and the axe head clunked onto the ground. Sura was left, face drained of blood, staring at the irate snarl of the bearer.

'With me!' Pavo roared, heaving his friend up by the forearm, then roaring as the giant ripped a dagger down his bicep and thigh. Fuelled by rage, he thrust his spatha forward, stabbing the giant in the gut.

With that, they tried to fall back. But the rest of the cohort had disintegrated into pockets of legionaries. So the pair circled, back to back, hacking at the Gothic swell. Every direction Pavo looked there were more and more spear shafts and longswords coming for them.

'To the last!' Sura snarled, kicking out at one Goth's gut.

Then there was a jagged Gothic cry from Marcianople. 'We have the walls!' At this, a war horn moaned across the plain, and a cheer rang out.

Pavo blinked in disbelief as the swell around them eased, many warriors turning, rushing past them.

'The city's defences are breached. They're going for the ladders!' Sura spluttered. Then, as if to underline Marcianople's fate, a sharp crack of timber rang out as a battering ram shattered the city gates.

Pavo parried at the thick pocket of eighty or more Goths who remained, set on finishing the Roman cohort. A white-hot, fiery pain shot through his bleeding bicep as he swiped his spatha around him, panting. 'But there are still too many of them, Sura!'

Then, the pair were sprayed with hot blood and a Gothic head bounced past them.

'Have that, you *whoresons!*' A familiar voice rang out.

Tribunus Gallus had pushed through to the pair. With him were big Zosimus, Quadratus, Felix and Avitus, fighting in a tight pack. Crito and a smattering of others were close by.

At this, the Goths nearby backed off, uncertain, glances darting to the pack of hardy Romans and to the rest of their horde, swarming into the city. One turned and ran to the walls, then another. In moments, they were streaming for Marcianople, leaving the bloodied remnant of the Roman cohort behind. At last, the frenzy of battle eased.

Pavo's blood iced as he beheld the city; it looked like some grotesque anthill, the few pieces of stonework not covered by ladders and clambering, red-armoured warriors were spattered with blood or draped with broken Roman corpses. A garrison legionary was hurled from the battlements and fell, thrashing and screaming, then landed head-first with a bony crunch on the ground. Black plumes of smoke belched out over the walls and a chorus of screaming rent the air. He felt shame at his failure to save those poor souls inside the walls.

'Come on, you pair of bloody idiots!' Zosimus roared at him and Sura. 'Marcianople is lost. Make for the north!'

He turned to run with the pack of survivors, when, from the corner of his eye, he noticed that one mail-shirted figure instead ran towards the city, for the rear of the Gothic line, sword aloft. His heart froze. 'Crito!'

Before he could think it over, he was off and after the grizzled veteran.

He heard Sura yelping behind him. 'Pavo? Pavo! Oh for f . . . '

He caught up with Crito just as the veteran was about to take on four Goths on his own. He clasped a hand to the man's shoulder. 'What are you doing?' He roared. 'Didn't you hear the order? The city has fallen!'

Crito's face was twisted in a snarl and soaked with tears as he shrugged Pavo away. 'I can't leave them!' He bellowed, sinking his spatha into the neck of one Goth, who roared in pain then greyed and crumpled as his lifeblood fountained from him.

Pavo parried a strike from another nimble-footed warrior. Then Sura joined them just in time to finish the Goth off with a slash across the belly, emptying the man's grey-red, steaming pile of guts onto the plain. 'Who? Everyone in those walls is dead, if not right now then before noon they will be.'

'My wife, my little girl!' He roared, lunging wildly into another pack of three Goths who came at them. With a flurry of hacking, Crito felled two of them, but then leapt back with a yell as his helmet toppled to the ground, a scarlet stump left where his ear had been. But Crito rushed back into the fray

251

immediately, roaring as he drove his spatha through the Goth's chest, before twisting his head this way and that to look for the next opponent.

Pavo pulled the veteran back and pointed to the walls. 'Crito, they are gone. Listen.'

Crito glared at him, but then his face fell as he heard it: the terrible wailing inside the walls had stopped. Now there were only Gothic roars of victory, and all but a few Gothic stragglers had poured inside the city.

'You can only help them now by living on to remember them, to honour their memory.'

Crito slumped at this. 'I should have defended them. I should have been inside the city.'

Pavo pushed Crito back towards the rest of the fleeing cohort and nodded for Sura to watch their backs. 'Every one of us did all we could, you can't blame yourself. If you had been inside the city then you would have died too.'

Crito's face was expressionless momentarily, then a scowl grew upon it. 'No!' He spat, tears dropping from his snarling expression. 'If you and the rest of them had not run we could have saved them. They're dead because of you, you whoreson!' He thrust the palm of one hand at Pavo, catching him on the spliced flesh of his bicep. 'You may as well have slain them yourself!'

Pavo winced, but bit back the battle-fuelled urge to retaliate. 'Then you can hate me for it, but please, come with us.'

Crito spat at Pavo's feet, then turned and jogged off to catch up with the cohort.

Pavo and Sura followed him.

Behind them, the city suddenly fell silent. Pavo heard the whinnying of horses, a whip being cracked, and then a familiar voice crying out in unearthly pain somewhere within those walls. Then a dull, fleshy clunk ended the cry abruptly and a euphoric Gothic roar rang out.

Lupicinus gawped down from the battlements; the plumbata was still quivering in the earth behind Fritigern. A dreadful realisation crept over his skin as Fritigern looked up to the battlements, stunned, touching a hand to the gash on his cheek.

Lupicinus backed away from the iudex's glare, then spun to the fleeing, green cloaked figure who had appeared from nowhere like a shade to throw the dart. 'After him!' He roared. But the figure fled like a leopard, barging legionaries from his path. Lupicinus raced along the battlements after him, hurdling the stumbling soldiers left in the stranger's wake, eyes trained on the green cloak. *So this Viper is more than just a myth!*

'Stop him!' Lupicinus roared again. But the wall guard were gawping in horror at the goings-on outside, and every cry Lupicinus made went unheard, or by the time the sentries reacted, the figure had fled past them.

Then Lupicinus tripped on the heels of a legionary and fell to his knees, skidding to a halt as the tail of the green cloak disappeared down the stairwell of the gate tower. He punched the battlements and roared in frustration, cursing as he wrenched himself to standing. But then a clutch of sagittarii burst from the gatetower, pushing Lupicinus back like a river as they rushed to take up their positions. After that, the green cloak was nowhere to be seen on the walls or on the streets below.

Then his anger drained when a Gothic war cry filled the plain. He turned to look out over the battlements; the horde outside had come to life. Now they flooded for the walls, streaming up the ladders bearing swords, axes and spears, screaming for blood. Out on the plain, Gallus' cohort resembled a morsel of bread being swamped by ants, Gothic warriors tearing the square to pieces.

His skin prickled and his blood felt like ice in his veins. A violent death awaited him today, he realised, his limbs quivering. He felt his bladder expunge its contents under his armour, and hated himself for it, hearing his father's gruff and mocking laughter. 'I'll show you, you old bastard,' he cursed his father's shade, his voice cracking in terror.

He squared his jaw and scanned the wall guard. The two centuries permanently garrisoned in the city had been detached from their parent legion, the V Macedonia, for more than seventy years, and they knew little more than day to day policing. So his own two centuries of comitatenses would have their work cut out today. To a man, they grappled their weapons with white knuckles, almost as pale as their faces, darting glances to their leader.

'Sir?' A nearby soldier croaked as the howling from the ladders grew closer, iron blades glinting as the Goths neared the top. 'Shall we loose our darts?'

Lupicinus looked back. It was too late for a dart volley; the Goths would be upon the battlements in moments. He stabbed out his tongue to dampen his lips, then filled his lungs and bellowed the best words he could find. 'Brace yourselves, men. Steady your nerves and prepare to show these barbarians the way to Valhalla!'

A perfunctory cheer was cut short as the first of the Goths reached the lip of the walls and had his skull cleaved by a legionary. Then another legionary was punched back from the walls in a shower of blood, bone and teeth, a hand-axe embedded in his face where his nose used to be. The body plummeted to land on the flagstones of the city streets below with a dull crack. With that, the tide of Goths spilled onto the battlements and their cry was deafening.

Lupicinus pulled his spatha and shield up. He poised himself just as he had been trained to all those years ago when he was a terrified recruit; scared of his colleagues but even more so of returning home to his father. A spark of anger flared in his chest at this and he fixed his eyes on the Goth nearest to him. Time seemed to slow as two of his legionaries pressed up to flank him, the trio forming a Roman island in the sea of enraged Gothic spearmen. He jabbed out at the nearest foe, nicking the man's neck, pulling out a piece of arterial wall. The snarling Goth fell silent, eyes bulging in bewilderment as his neck pumped blood. Then he fell like a toy, limbs flailing before crunching head-first into the city streets. At this the nearby Goths hesitated momentarily and hubris coursed through Lupicinus' veins. Perhaps he was a valiant soldier after all.

'For your empire, men!' He roared. Now this was honour! This was glory!

He butted another Goth from the walls and then slashed at a pair who rushed at his flank, slicing one's ribcage wide open and lacerating the sword arm of the other. His two legionaries closed up beside him every time he struck out, but for every Goth he felled, another ten poured onto the battlements to replace them. He glanced down to the streets: the citizens and civilian militia who had been poised behind the gates, armed with hoes and clubs, now scrambled back from the splintering timbers. Some were running for the centre of the city, no doubt looking to take refuge in attics and basements. *To Hades with them*, he thought, *they are the cowards, not I!* He growled and stabbed out at a Gothic spearman, swiping the spear shaft away and driving his spatha deep into the man's guts. Then he slowed: over the dying Goth's shoulder he saw swathes of legionaries toppling lifelessly into the city. The battlements were dripping in a crimson carpet and the count of Roman helmets still active in the fray was now fewer than one hundred, he reckoned.

'We have the walls!' One Gothic voice cried out.

Then the air reverberated to the wail of a Gothic war horn. Moments later, the battlements shuddered under his feet as a sharp crack of splintering timber rang out, followed by a Gothic roar. Lupicinus fought on numbly, seeing the wave of red-armoured bodies wash into the city through the shattered gates, topknotted blonde locks and speartips bobbing like a cornfield. Beside him, one of his legionaries slumped to his knees and then toppled into the city, an arrow having exploded through the back of his throat. Lupicinus pushed back to back with his last man, then felt the man fall away, cleaved in the shoulder. He glanced around the battlements and could see no other Roman standing. His moment of hubris was gone, and his old friend panic clawed at his heart. He could see Gallus and the surviving cluster of the XI Claudia outside the walls, fleeing, and he so much wanted to be with them.

From the heart of the city, pockets of orange flame burst into life and thick black smoke plumes coiled from the red tiled roofs and the narrow alleys. But the worst thing was the screaming; women and children had the most piercing screams, and the enraged and starving Goths cut them short like farmers at harvest.

Suddenly, Lupicinus realised that the Goths around him had stopped fighting.

'Come on, you dogs!' He snarled, swiping out at them, disgusted at the tremor in his own words.

But they backed away, grins splitting their faces. He looked up to see that he was in the sights of chosen archers on top of the gate towers. They winked behind their bows, arrows nocked and trained on his throat. His bowels turned over and his legs took to trembling violently. Why were they hesitating?

Then one spoke in Greek, hissing like a snake as he removed his conical iron helm. 'We have him – Iudex Fritigern's would-be assassin!'

Lupicinus' eyes widened and his mouth fell open. 'No!'

The Goth who had spoken nodded his head. 'Yes. We saw you. Mighty Ivo saw you!'

The others around him nodded and echoed in agreement.

'No, it was not me. It was an intruder, a treacherous intruder.' Lupicinus spun on the spot, searching for respite in the sea of malevolent, grinning faces.

'Ivo and Iudex Fritigern will hear your plea,' the Goth purred, then clicked his fingers. 'Seize him!'

Lupicinus swiped his sword at them, but a jarring blow to his back sent him sprawling and his spatha and helmet clattered down into the city.

Defenceless, Lupicinus scrambled back from the Goths on his heels and palms of his hands. But then he was grappled by his shoulders and hoisted up, then another pair of hands clutched at his ankles and within moments, he was being carried down the stairwell like some prize boar. His lips flapped uselessly, his voice gone. His mind conjured up a flurry of horrific possibilities that lay in store for him as he was carried out of the tower and onto the bloodstained streets.

'Ah, the assassin?' A voice cooed.

Upside down, Lupicinus saw the one-eyed, smirking Ivo, mounted and leading a wing of Gothic cavalry into the Roman city.

Then, Ivo's face fell baleful and he lifted his sword and bellowed to the Gothic swarm around him. 'Here he is! Here is the man who thought he could strike down mighty Fritigern!'

The people slowed, turning to Lupicinus, their faces bent with rage.

'Gut him!' One voice screamed.

'Tear out his heart!' Another cried.

Lupicinus' heart shrank. 'No! It was the one in the green cloak! It was the Vi-'

But his words were cut short as Ivo trotted over and clamped a hand across his mouth. His eyes bulged as Ivo then drew a dagger.

The giant fixed his good eye on Lupicinus' terrified stare. Then he used the blade to prise the comes' teeth apart and then to hack into his thrashing tongue, his arm jerking as he sawed at the flesh. A serrated, burning agony coursed through Lupicinus' mouth as blood spurted from his lips. His cries for help came out as a gurgling, tortured, animal moan.

Ivo pulled the severed chunk of tongue free and held it aloft. 'Now take him to the centre of this fine Roman city. The forum would be a fitting place for his life to end.'

Lupicinus thrashed in vain as he was swept forward on the tide of hands until everything slowed as they entered the forum. He was let down and only four warriors remained clutching his limbs. All around him, the

Gothic warriors and people pushed to get closer, but spearmen held them at bay, forming a circle around him. Directly before him stood Iudex Fritigern. Something had changed about the Gothic Iudex's face; it was his eyes, they were deadly cold where once he had seen some warmth.

'You think yourself a god, Comes Lupicinus?' Fritigern spoke softly.

Lupicinus trembled, unable to reply due to his mutilated tongue, his face soaked in his own blood.

'You tried to break my people on the plains by the river, treating us like animals. You tried to slay me yesterday and again today. You have either the heart of a lion, or the mind of a babe. You have set in motion a revolt against the empire, a revolt that will tear apart her armies, raze her cities, lay waste to her lands.' Fritigern spoke through gritted teeth, holding a clenched and shaking fist inches from Lupicinus' face. Behind him, Ivo stood, grinning like a shark at the Iudex's words. 'Now it is time to show you the power of my armies. My cavalry, archers and spearmen will be the death of your legions, Comes, starting with you.'

Lupicinus gawped as Fritigern stepped back with a nod. He croaked in terror as ropes were tied around his ankles and wrists. Then he glanced around him to see four muscular stallions facing away from him, their topknotted riders sneering back over their shoulders as they fastened the other ends of the ropes to their mounts' harnesses. Then, the men holding his limbs dropped him and walked away. He fell to the ground, the ropes lying loose on the flagstones.

Then, Fritigern flicked a finger towards Lupicinus. 'Destroy him!'

With the cracking of whips, the four stallions were heeled into a trot, and Lupicinus was wrenched from the ground and spread-eagled, his torso bucking and thrashing.

'Ya!' The riders called out as the horses strained, their hooves slipping on the flagstones.

Lupicinus' body stopped thrashing as it was pulled taut. Then, with a rhythmic popping, each of his limbs jolted from their sockets. Next, his muscles and sinew shredded and then disintegrated. He stared at the smoke-stained sky in search of escape from the horrific, white-hot agony that coursed through him. He heard a guttural moaning and realised it was his own. Then, he saw his father's sneering face. *You can't call for help now, can you? You coward!*

He blinked the image from his eyes. The blackness was creeping over him, as if he was being dragged backwards into a dark tunnel. In the remaining circle of light before him, all he could see was Ivo in the watching Gothic crowd.

But there was something else.

A few ranks behind Ivo stood the dark-green hooded figure from the battlements, face in shadows. There and not there at once. Then the figure lowered the hood for a heartbeat, revelling in Lupicinus' suffering.

Lupicinus' maelstrom of agony dulled for that instant as he realised he was staring at the face of the Viper. Confusion laced his final thoughts.

Then, with a wet clunk, Lupicinus' spine disarticulated and his body tore apart at the waist. Guts and organs poured from both halves of his body and at last the blackness took him.

Senator Tarquitius loped through the southern streets of Marcianople behind a handful of Roman citizens. The stench of burning flesh and woodsmoke followed them and the smashing of clay and cracking of wood told of the destruction taking place all around.

The screaming from the north of the city had stopped and now these few citizens who had escaped the influx of Goths were headed for the southern gate. Tarquitius' lungs burned as he tried to keep pace with them. *Got to get out, got to get away. Back to Constantinople. I'll be safe there.* He shot a glance over his shoulder and saw the wall of Gothic spearmen who were sweeping the streets north to south, only a hundred paces away. *The Viper may still have a use for you,* a nagging voice spoke in his mind. *No, with Pavo surely slain before the walls, you can offer him nothing, nothing! He will be the death of you, and you know this!* Another voice countered.

'They've taken the southern walls too!' A man cried out shrilly from amongst the fleeing citizens.

Tarquitius skidded to a halt, lips flapping, blood chilling in his veins as he saw the Gothic spearmen spill around the battlements and the southern gatehouse. Whimpering and wailing, the citizens dispersed into buildings like rats scattering before a bright light. Suddenly, Tarquitius felt more alone than ever before. Then he saw two elderly Roman women at the door of a smithy, tugging at the handle in vain, glancing back in terror.

Tarquitius rushed forward, barging the two to either side of the door and shoulder-charging it open. He tumbled into the soot-blackened room, still hot from forging and the floor still lined with sword racks. His eyes darted around the space for a place to hide. Then he saw the faint outline of a trapdoor in the filthy floor.

'Jupiter bless you!' One of the women croaked behind him from the doorway.

He spun to see the pair coming in to hide with him. Then his eyes bulged as he saw a wave of Gothic spearmen rounding the corner, roaring. Their spears were lowered for the kill, eyes manic with bloodlust and sweeping the street for victims.

Before he realised what he was doing, Tarquitius charged back against the door, slamming it shut once more, pushing the two women out into the street. *Better one of us lives than all three of us die!* He consoled himself as he lifted the trapdoor, heaved out the crate of tools in the small space underneath, then crouched and lowered the trapdoor on top of himself. He screwed his eyes shut tight and bit into his wrist as he heard the thundering footsteps of the Goths approaching, then the tortured screams of the women. Mercifully, they were cut short. Then the footsteps grew distant.

He waited in the floorspace for some time. His legs grew numb and his bowels and bladder creaked. *But I have survived!* He realised. At once, his mind began to turn over the possibilities. Perhaps the Goths would bypass this insignificant smithy? There was bound to be a water bucket in here somewhere. He could hold out for a few days without food and then he could slip out of the city once the Goths left or reduced their presence within the walls. *Yes,* he enthused, *the Viper will assume I perished in the sack of the city. I can slip back to Constantinople, I can resume my role in the senate, then put my mind to my quest for power. Nothing stands in my way . . .*

Then, the door of the smithy creaked open.

Tarquitius' heart froze.

A single, slow set of footsteps trod slowly into the smithy. Then they stopped, right by the trapdoor.

'He came in here, master, our men swear they saw him,' a voice spoke from further away, near the doorway.

Then another, horribly familiar voice rasped, and it felt to Tarquitius that the speaker was right by his side; 'He is in here. We just have to draw him out . . . ' Then a rasp of iron sounded from one of the sword racks.

In the silence that ensued, Tarquitius' eyes darted this way and that in the darkness of the floorspace.

Then, with a thunder of shattering timber, an iron blade plunged through the trap door and scythed past Tarquitius' neck.

At once, the breath spilled from the senator's lungs, and he burst from the trap door, wailing, clasping at the scratch on his neck. He beheld the two figures that stood in the smithy, and knew what a mistake he had made.

'Close the door, Ivo,' the Viper hissed from the shadows of his hood, clutching a dagger in one hand, his cloak damp with blood from the slaughter.

'Aye, master,' Ivo said, the door creaking then clicking shut.

'I . . . I have done as you asked! I let you in to the city,' Tarquitius croaked, crawling from the floorspace, then creeping backwards from the Viper on the palms of his hands until he clashed against a sword rack.

'Aye, you have,' the Viper nodded, drifting forward. 'But I must ask myself; are you still of use to me?' He said, flexing his fingers on the sword hilt. 'Now, I have other places to be; let's make this quick.'

Then the Viper reached a hand to either side of his hood.

The shadow slid away and the poor light within the smithy fell upon the Viper's face.

Tarquitius' eyes bulged and his heart froze. 'Gods, no!'

Salvian galloped from the ridge and into the plain north of Marcianople. He caught up with the head of the Roman refugee column then slid from his mount, panting, and turned back to face the sea of terrified faces. The handful of scouts and non-combatant legion staff who had led them this far were struggling to curtail the panic of the group.

'They want to run, ambassador,' one scout gasped, his eyes wide, barging the crowd back with the shaft of his spear. 'They want to scatter and break for the trees.'

Salvian shook his head. 'No, they must stay together.' Then he waved them forward pointing to the timber bridge over the River Beli Lom, a good mile in the distance, and bawled; 'Pull together, once over the river we will be safe.' To his relief, the authority of a single voice seemed to stay their fears somewhat, and they moved forward together.

But when they reached the centre of the plain, Salvian stopped, feeling the ground tremble. *Riders.* He looked to the eastern end of the ridge behind them. There, in the distance, a cloud of dust rose, growing closer.

Then, a wing of several hundred Gothic riders burst into view, helmets donned, spears lowered, their leader carrying a dark-green snake banner. The Romans broke out in a panicked wail, turning to run in the other direction. But on that side another Gothic wing raced into view, equally readied for slaughter. The two wings cantered forward to encircle the Roman refugees, then stopped.

'Ambassador! What do we do?' The scout was trembling, his face ghostly white.

Salvian looked to the scout, his face grave. 'This is for me to handle. All my years of learning have been for this moment.' With that, he turned to look up in silence at the lead rider. Then he stepped forward, unarmed, palms extended by his side in a gesture of supplication.

But the lead rider's face curled into a predatory grin at this. Then a rasp of iron rang out as he drew his longsword.

'Once we're over that rise, there's less than a mile to go to the bridge; keep the pace!' Gallus bawled to his legionaries, eyeing the grassy ridge that marked the northern end of the plain of Marcianople.

As he ran, he took to firing glances back over his shoulder at the now distant city. It glowed orange, the walls were blackened, flames licked above the battlements and smoke spiralled out across the sky. The acrid tang of destruction stung in his nostrils. The die had been cast; Fritigern had been turned irreversibly. The truce was shattered. He issued a silent prayer to Mithras for the legionaries and families inside the burning city.

He dropped back to the rear of the column to perform a head count of the bloodied, tattered rabble, many having lost helmets, shields and weapons in the action. He counted sixty and frowned, then counted again. Still only sixty. The cobbled-together cohort had been all but extinguished only days after being formed. All those unfamiliar faces he had led from the fort yesterday had slipped into the army of shades that marched in his memories. It warmed him ever so slightly, however, to see that the core of his best men were still with him. Felix, Zosimus, Quadratus and Avitus formed the front of the retreating column and Pavo and Sura brought up the rear. He picked up the pace to join the head of the column again as they crested the rise, then he sucked in a breath to rally them once more.

Then the sixty stopped. Not a single breath escaped as they gaped at the scene before them.

The top of the ridge and the near side of the plain on the other side was carpeted with slain bodies. The Roman refugees. Eyes staring, mouths agape, hands reaching out, frozen in death.

Thousands of them.

Gallus' eyes bulged at the sight, and he heard some of his men vomiting around him. He saw the corpses of the few non-combatant legion staff tangled in the mire of blood and bodies. *Mithras save us,* a voice whispered in his head, *they've been slaughtered like cattle.* He craned his neck to gaze over to the end of the plain; the tip of the bridge over the Beli Lom was just visible. *And they were but a mile from safety.*

He felt all eyes fall upon him. Looking up, he saw glassy determination in each of his men's eyes, except Pavo; Pavo shook his head in denial as he gawped at the carpet of dead, the knotted limbs, the shorn flesh. Gallus frowned, then he realised who Pavo mourned. *Salvian.* Gallus closed his eyes, his heart sinking. *I pray you have a swift journey to Elysium, my friend.*

Then, when he opened his eyes, he saw a hoofprint in the earth, still fresh and swirling with pooling blood. The iron veneer came crashing down once more. 'The horsemen who did this must still be nearby. Get to the bridge!'

As one, the sixty rippled into a jog, down the ridge to make their way across the northern plain. Up ahead, the timber bridge beckoned. Then, a few hundred yards after that, a forest stretched for some distance.

'Whoa! What's that, sir?' Felix skidded to slow down, then nodded forward to a shape positioned at the far bridgehead. It was about as tall as a man and as broad as four, covered with a large cut of hemp cloth. The rest of the sixty slowed likewise.

Gallus' eyes glinted. 'That's our last hope. A four-fanged creature . . . '

Felix cracked a dry grin. 'The giant ballista?' Then he turned to the sixty and bellowed; 'Come on, did I say you could stop?'

Gallus gazed past the device and up ahead. He frowned as he searched the grass around the shape for sight of the four legionaries he had left there, but not a soul was to be seen. He leaned in towards his primus pilus; 'Well hopefully we won't need it,' he said tentatively, darting a glance around the deserted plain. 'We get over the bridge and we get ourselves into those trees. Then we can take stock, see to the men's wounds, check our rations and equipment . . . '

Gallus' words trailed off as he felt it; the ground was rumbling beneath them. He twisted round as he ran.

'Mithras, no!' Felix hissed, sharing the glance back to the grassy rise.

A dust plume billowed from the plain they had just left, then a wing of some one hundred Gothic cavalrymen burst over the rise, the lead rider carrying a billowing banner bearing the mark of the Viper.

'Make for the bridge, break ranks!' Gallus cried.

At this, the legionaries afforded only a heartbeat of confusion before they turned and saw what was coming for them. At once, the column disintegrated and the men ran, throwing down remaining shields, spears and helmets. To a man they knew that to be caught in an open plain, outnumbered by cavalry meant certain death.

Gallus twisted to look back as he ran. The cavalry had closed in on them, only a quarter-mile behind. He could now see their red leather cuirasses, conical helmets and their spears, pointing for the sky. Then, on the jagged bark of the cavalry commander, the iron tips were lowered in one fluid motion for a charge. Gallus glanced over his men; they would never reach the bridge in time, he realised. He dropped back to the aquilifer at the rear; the man was struggling for breath. Gallus clutched the silver eagle standard and wrenched it from the man, who refused to release it at first.

Gallus hissed at him. 'Your honour is intact, man, give me the eagle, and get yourself to that bridge. Go!'

Gallus spun to face the Gothic cavalry, and staggered back on seeing them only twenty paces away, at most. The riders bore the rapacious grins of men who knew victory and an easy slaughter was theirs, their blonde locks billowing, their mounts frothing, glistening with sweat from the charge. He felt a twinge of an old feeling, terror, then swatted it away like a mayfly. With that, he lifted the standard and waved it to the treeline either side of the plain. The lead Goth roared out a baritone war cry, training his spear on Gallus' throat. Gallus closed his eyes and searched for memories of Olivia.

Then, a thick twang rang out, and at once, the trees either side of the plain spat forth a ferocious hail. Gallus opened his eyes just in time to see the Goth before him being punched from his mount by one of the missiles, body shattered like a clay figurine, a cloud of crimson puffing on the spot where he had been saddled. All along the Gothic cavalry line, riders and mounts were swept from their course by the flanking fire of ballista bolts.

'Mithras bless the ballista!' He roared, then grappled the reins of one riderless horse and swung up onto the saddle. Galloping for the bridge, he lay flat along the beast's back and twisted to see the Gothic charge falter under the ballista hail, horses stumbling over the fallen, riders reining their mounts in. He reached down to pluck the struggling aquilifer up by the scruff of the neck, hoisting the man into the saddle behind him.

'Excellent idea, sir!' The aquilifer cried.

'Don't get too excited yet,' Gallus growled, just as the rhythmic twang of the ballistae slowed, then stopped.

'Why have they stopped?'

'The ballistae are out of range,' Gallus confirmed with another glance back; the Gothic cavalry had been thinned, maybe by half, but now the charge was on again and they would still sweep over the legionaries before they reached the bridge. He turned to face forward again, and pointed to the mass on the far side of the bridge with the hemp cloth upon it, 'but that one most certainly is not!'

'Sir?' The aquilifer frowned.

Gallus ignored the man's confusion and roared to the far bridgehead. 'Ballista crew! Ready yourselves!'

Heeling his mount, he kept his eyes trained on the hemp-covered device, waiting for the four legionaries he had left to man the giant ballista to burst from the undergrowth, or leap out from behind it. He had been clear with his orders when he had posted them here on the march to Marcianople. *Keep watch on the bridge from the trees, and be ready to man the device if the Goths turn to war.*

Instead, four topknotted Gothic spearmen scrambled from a beech thicket near the device, then tugged the hemp cloth away, and readied themselves to fire.

Gallus pulled on his mount's reins in horror. The ropes on the device were taut, the weapon loaded. Only now could he see the faint trace of red in the grass around the bolt-thrower, the last remnants of the four poor sods he had left there. Ahead of him, the column had stumbled into an impasse, glances darting from the onrushing Gothic cavalry to the giant ballista. Gallus searched for the orders that would make it all right. But there was nothing.

His heart froze as the giant weapon shuddered and, with a crack of thick rope releasing its furious tension, spat out its four bolts, each twice as tall as a man, with the girth of a young oak and a rapier-like head. A blur of bodies shot past him; three of his men, pinned together on one of the giant missiles which hurtled on across the plain for another hundred feet before ploughing into the earth. From the corner of his eye, he saw the other three missiles wreak similar destruction.

When the ballista fell silent, the crew started to load up the first of the next batch of four missiles. The Gothic cavalry had slowed from their charge, sensing victory. They closed up to form a crescent, penning the legionaries in to the bridge and the riverbank. Then they trotted forward, drawing their swords, eyes glinting as they beheld their kills.

Gallus shook off his momentary hesitation, slipped from the saddle of his mount and then waved the eagle standard. 'Around me!' He roared, pacing backwards from the noose of riders. The straggle of legionaries staggered over to stand with their tribunus, levelling what weapons they still carried. Behind him, he heard the clunk of the second ballista bolt being loaded into the device. This was it, he realised, anger boiling in his chest. His men would die, he would die. But he would die like a trapped animal, without honour. Then, the most innocuous of sights caught his eye as he glanced over his shoulder to check his men's positions; a red squirrel scuttled across the underside of the timber bridge, terrified by the commotion. His spine tingled as a sliver of hope dawned on him.

'I want two men. Good climbers!' He hissed over his shoulder.

The men looked to him and to each other, terror and puzzlement etched on their features.

'Sir?' Zosimus croaked from behind the veil of gore on his face.

Gallus glared at the veteran centurion. Now was not the time for detailed explanations.

'I'm in,' a voice spoke.

Gallus turned to see the wiry form of Pavo. The young legionary was still bleeding from the wounds to his bicep and thigh, but his face was etched with a bitter determination.

'I said, I'm in,' Pavo repeated, taking off his helmet and tossing it to the ground along with his mail vest. Then he backed out of the tightly packed pocket of Romans.

Gallus saw the glint in Pavo's eye, and the faint nod to the Goths busying themselves loading the third missile into the giant ballista. He was already up to speed with the plan. A sharp lad, Gallus thought, not for the first time.

'Me too,' Sura croaked. 'Best climber in all Adrianople!'

Gallus eyed the pair, then nodded. 'Get to it!'

As Pavo and Sura slipped from the rear of Roman cluster, down the riverbank to the water unseen, Gallus turned back to the Gothic cavalrymen. The one in the centre held Gallus' glare and returned it with a smirk.

'The land beneath your feet is now Gothic dominion, Roman!' He spat. 'You are trespassing on foreign soil.' He raised his sword, his eyes narrowing. 'Now you must be slaughtered, like vermin!'

With that, the Gothic riders rushed forth with a cry.

Gallus and the legionaries pushed together, shoulder to shoulder. He readied himself to leap for the big rider who had spoken, and his heart thundered like a kettledrum. He sucked in a breath and roared.

'For the empire!'

Pavo turned from the skirmish and dropped from the lip of the riverbank, then skidded and slithered down the scree of the banking by the side of the bridge.

Every last one of those bastards will bleed their last today, a voice in his head rasped as he saw only the image of that carpet of dead. Salvian, you will be avenged!

The swirling rapids of the narrow river rushed up at him as he slid. When he clawed out to slow his descent, the stones bit into the flesh of his palms. Then, with a thud, his leading foot jarred against a boulder, and he was catapulted head over heels into the water.

The chill water numbed him instantly and his lungs seemed to shrink in shock as he thrashed, fully submerged. Then panic gripped his heart as the current dragged him downstream, away from the cover of the bridge. If the Goths manning the ballista on the opposite bank saw him, then the Roman ploy was doomed. He kicked down to find purchase against the riverbed, but there was nothing there, and the weight of his spatha was pulling at his belt like a rock.

Then something grappled at his collar and he was hauled out of the water like a fish.

'Off to the coast for a break, were we?' Sura grunted, pulling Pavo back to the bank.

'Aye, something like that.' Pavo shrugged Sura away with a frown. Then a bloodied legionary toppled from the bank just above, a crimson gash across his neck. Both of them looked at the corpse and then one another.

'Let's move!' Pavo hissed. With that, he grappled one of the posts supporting the bridge, shinning up then looping his legs around the diagonal beam that stretched out across the underside of the structure. His spatha dangled below him and he felt the beam bowing and creaking as Sura followed close behind, then he looked up; flitting between the gaps in the slats of timber, he could make out the Goths loading the giant ballista. Then he heard the fourth and final ballista bolt clunk into place and his heart thundered.

He let go a few feet short of the opposite riverbank and splashed into the shallows. Then he scrambled up to the bridge side and ducked to peek over the timbers at the Goths; there were four of them, all built like oxen. Crucially though, they had all downed their swords, spears, shields and helmets to operate the huge bolt thrower.

'Ready?' Sura slapped a hand on his shoulder.

Pavo nodded hurriedly as the screaming of legionaries grew more frequent from the skirmish on the opposite bank. 'Two each?'

'Let's go!' Sura hissed. At the same time, the ropes of the giant ballista creaked and groaned as the Goths tensed the device for the next volley.

The pair scuttled out from the banking, looping round to come at the Goths from behind. Pavo slid his spatha from its scabbard silently, then leapt at the nearest Goth. The man spun at the last moment, his mouth agape. He managed to utter the first half of some Gothic exclamation, before Pavo sank his sword through the warrior's shoulder, deep into his chest. 'How does it feel, murderous whoreson?' Pavo snarled, then placed a foot on the felled man's shoulder and wrenched the blade free again, blood spurting from the wound.

The next Goth was stunned for a heartbeat, then scrambled to the pile of longswords nearby, but Pavo flicked his spatha up to grasp it by the blade, then hurled it at the warrior. The blade spun through the air and burst through the Goth's chest.

Pavo didn't wait for the man to fall, instead ripping his dagger from his belt and rushing to Sura, who had slain one Goth but was at an impasse with the last one. The pair's swords were locked and Sura was trying in vain to headbutt the man despite the stark difference in height. Pavo roared. At this, the Goth leapt back, darted a glance over his slain comrades, then bolted for the trees.

When Sura stormed after him, Pavo grasped his friend back. 'Leave him! Get to the ballista!'

Sura spun away from the fleeing Goth, panting in fury, then grappled the right ballista winch as Pavo gripped the left. Gallus and his men at the far end of the bridge had been thinned to a mere handful now. The pair groaned as they pulled at the wheels, veins bulging in their arms, Pavo's wounded bicep slick with blood. At last, each winch clicked – the bowstrings were fully retracted. 'That's it, it's ready!'

Sura stood back from the device, eyes glinting in bloodlust. He cupped his hands to his mouth and roared across the river. 'XI Claudia!'

Gallus spun round after slashing one Gothic horseman from belly to neck. The tribunus' eyes snapped onto the pair behind the bolt-thrower. He relayed the order again and again, until the straggle of legionaries that remained realised what was happening, and barged away from the bridgehead to slide down the riverbank.

The Goths were momentarily bemused by this, some laughing, some throwing gleeful curses, watching as the Romans seemingly fled for the waters. Then their leader looked up to the northern bridgehead, his mouth agape, eyes bulging.

Pavo dipped his brow, his gaze trained on the leader with a steely conviction.

'Loose!'

The giant device bucked as the ropes unleashed their tension, hurling the four colossal bolts directly across the bridge. The riders had not even a heartbeat to react, before their bodies were ripped asunder like wet rags, man after man skewered on the same bolt. Limbs spun free of torsos, heads disintegrated, mounts were smashed like insects, and the air was blotted with puffs of crimson. Then all was still.

The riders who had been moments from exterminating the Roman retreat now numbered only a handful, the rest gone from the world or moaning, their bones shattered or their mounts pinning them to the earth.

Pavo felt no joy, no glory at the sight, only disgust. Yet they had to die for their deeds. Then, he wasted no time in sealing the victory. 'Load the next set of bolts!' He roared.

At this, the Gothic survivors looked to one another, eyes wide. Then they heeled their mounts into a turn and a gallop, back to Marcianople.

He slumped against the ballista, panting, limbs shaking, wounds burning. Then he looked up to share a weary glance with Sura, the pair's relief going unsaid.

Then, a drumming of boots on the bridge sounded as the surviving legionaries came hobbling across, Gallus at their head. But only eight men came with him. The core of the legion still lived; Felix, Zosimus, Quadratus, and Avitus were followed by Crito and Noster.

'Pavo! What are you waiting for? Get the next set of bolts loaded up!'

Pavo looked up to see Gallus frowning at him. He shrugged to his tribunus. 'There are no more bolts, sir, I just said that to scare them.'

Gallus slowed, as if searching for a rebuke. Instead, his face settled into the usual ice cold expression. 'Good thinking, soldier,' he nodded briskly.

Pavo would normally have felt his heart swell at this; drawing a tepid acknowledgement from Gallus was a rare feat – like a bear hug from any other. But he could only think of Salvian, lying back on the ridge, tangled somewhere in that bloody mire of dead.

His gaze was drawn back to the southern horizon and the ridge that lay beyond it; framed by the smoke plumes from the city, a dark cloud of carrion birds circled in the sky over there, waiting to swoop and pick the flesh from the Roman dead on the ridge. Sorrow stung behind his eyes. Then he noticed something move on the sides of the plain.

He tensed, grappling his sword hilt.

'Relax,' Quadratus grunted, clasping a hand to his shoulder. 'They're ours!'

The ballista crews that Gallus had planted in the treeline stumbled up the track towards the bridge. Some thirty men, all having cast off their heavy armour and weapons. All around him, the weary legionaries cried out hoarsely, urging the artillerymen on.

But Pavo's brow dipped as he sighted the lead artilleryman's face; wrinkled in terror.

'Something's coming for them!' He cried, and the rest of the legionaries spun to look.

At that instant, a fresh wing of fifty Gothic riders thundered into view from the treeline, in pursuit of the artillerymen. Pavo instinctively looked to Gallus for an order, his gut shrinking as he realised what that order had to be.

'Take the bridge down!' Gallus barked, his voice grave.

Crito was the first to gasp a reply. 'But, sir, the artillerymen?'

Gallus shot Crito a look that would surely have scorched the veteran's soul, but before the tribunus could add words to the glare, a trilling battle cry sounded from behind them. The legionaries spun to see the big Goth who had fled the giant ballista, bursting from the nearby trees, leading another seven spearmen.

Gallus' head twisted to the threats haring in from the north and the south, then he barked; 'Zosimus, Quadratus, Felix, Avitus, with me, we'll take on those spearmen.' Then he glanced around the four remaining legionaries. 'The rest of you – take that bridge down!'

As Gallus rushed forward to intercept the spearmen, Sura, Crito and the young recruit, Noster gawped after him. Then Noster and Sura gulped and pulled their axes from their belts. They cast hesitant glances at the bridge, then at the fleeing ballista crew and then the Gothic cavalry less than a quarter mile behind.

Crito cast a foul glare upon them. 'Drop your axes!' The veteran snarled. 'We're not condemning our own men to death!'

Pavo wanted to agree with the veteran's words wholeheartedly. But the cold reality was that if they left the bridge standing, the Gothic riders would race across the river and slay the artillerymen and the rest of the legionaries on the northern banks anyway.

'You heard the tribunus' orders!' Pavo barked in reply. 'Do you want to live, or die?'

Noster lifted his axe again, but hesitated, eyes wide with indecision. Pavo growled, then strode over to the bridge, hefting his own axe as he slid down the banking to the supporting pillars. He hacked at the nearest one, then again and again. The bridge shuddered and sagged at one side. Sura was already skidding down the opposite side of the bridge to chop at the other pillar. He looked up at Noster and Crito. 'Come on!' He roared.

At this, Noster slithered down the banking to chop at the remaining pillar. The three hacked furiously, blocking out the wails of confusion from the artillerymen, now only a few hundred strides from the bridge.

The bridge juddered and sunk in the middle. Timbers toppled into the water. Then Pavo swung his axe back for a blow that would surely smash through the last of the supporting pillars on this side. But a hand grabbed his wrist.

'You've gone too far this time, you spineless bastard!' Crito spat, inches from his ear. 'You're too keen to see your comrades die, just to save your own neck.' His face was a shade of crimson from the gore of the fight and pure, boiling rage. 'I could have saved my wife and my daughter if it wasn't for *you*!'

The words bit at Pavo's chest, and he affixed Crito with a firm stare. 'I lost my family, years ago. The few who have ever come close to replacing them have been slain too.' For a heartbeat, Salvian's face appeared in his mind's eye. 'And as for the ballista crew? I've never met them, but they are like brothers to me!'

The pair glared at one another, then they were shaken back to the present by a cry from Noster. 'The pillar on the far side needs to be hewn!'

Pavo glanced across; the bridge would not fall away without that last pillar being smashed. He thought of all that was lost to him, and all he would give to have it back. With that, he leapt up, hauled himself onto the sagging bridge, then rushed across the timbers.

'Pavo?' Sura yelled after him.

Pavo skidded down onto one knee and smashed his axe at the main pillar supporting the southern bridgehead. Once, twice, and again, each time seeing the fleeting images of Tarquitius' haughty expression, of Father stood on the dunes, of Salvian, lost in the tangled carpet of dead. Then, with a groan and a crack, the pillar was gone, and the bridge slid into the waters, disintegrating, pieces being washed downriver by the furious current.

It felt like a great weight had been lifted from his shoulders. For there was no doubt now. He was to die.

As the thundering of the Gothic horsemen grew closer and closer behind him, he saw Crito. The veteran gawped at him from across the river, eyes wide in disbelief. Then he gave Pavo an earnest nod. Pavo nodded back, then glanced to Sura and Noster, before grappling his axe in one hand, spatha in the other.

Then he turned to face the riders.

The Gothic cavalry were but strides away, and the artillerymen skidded to a halt, clustering around Pavo and the ruined bridge, wailing. Pavo saw the Goths through a crimson veil, and the blood pounded in his ears, the phalera pressing into his chest. For an instant, he realised he would now never know the truth of his father. Then he gritted his teeth. *Perhaps Father himself can tell me of it when I meet him in Elysium.*

With that, he barged forward and let out a roar, lining up to leap for the central Gothic rider. He barely realised that the fleeing artillerymen had rallied behind him and rushed in his wake, daggers drawn, echoing his cry.

Like a handful of gazelles turning on a pack of lions, the battered Romans leapt up at the riders, butting, punching, stabbing, pulling the Goths from their mounts. Pavo shouldered the leader in the gut, knocking the man from his saddle, the pair crunching to the plain. He smashed his sword hilt into his foe's jaw, then spun the blade and drove it down into the warrior's chest. As the warrior vomited a thick bloody soup, Pavo stood, ripped his sword free and spun to face his next opponent. At that moment he realised numbly that they had only heartbeats; the small band of brave artillerymen were being butchered around him, despite their bravery. Then he twisted to face the pair of Gothic riders who circled on him, longswords raised to strike. He snarled and raised his spatha, braced for the end.

But a Gothic war horn wailed across the plain. At once, the riders relaxed their sword arms, before calmly sheathing their weapons and heeling their mounts into a canter back across the plain in the direction from which they had come. Pavo's heart thundered and his limbs trembled with fatigue, but his mind was awash with confusion as he watched their withdrawal.

Then he saw it.

On the plain, a good four hundred paces away, the backdrop of beech forest rippled. A solitary figure was there, just before the treeline, watching them. A rider, saddled on a jet-black stallion, draped in a dark-green cloak, the hood throwing shadow over the face, clutching a war horn in one hand. The hood twisted towards the clutch of bloodied Romans.

Pavo felt the figure's unseen eyes rake on his skin.

Chapter 17

In the distance, a cock crowed and the deep orange of a new day spilled over the horizon, illuminating the forest clearing and the babbling brook that spliced it. A handful of bloodied legionaries lay strewn across the clearing floor in deep slumber. Besides the three sentries, only one other man was awake.

Gallus gazed into the embers of the campfire. His face was black with soot and his peak of hair was tousled and unkempt. He lifted a stick and poked at the ashes, eliciting a weary burst of flame. As the heat grew again, a rich and charred meaty aroma wafted across him from the morsel of cooked rabbit that lay by his foot, uneaten despite the nauseous hunger in his belly. Twisting the stick in his hands over and over again, he glanced around the ragtag band of legionaries who lay deep in exhausted sleep around him. *Too few*, he winced. *Where have you taken my legion, Mithras?*

His mind had ploughed over the same jumble of thoughts time and again, and night had come and gone like a passing shadow, with no conclusion to his ruminations. He was sure of only what he saw around him; this smattering of blood-encrusted, wounded and weary men was all that was left of the XI Claudia. After yesterday's desperate fight at the bridge over the Beli Lom, the nine survivors had wasted no time in hobbling northwards for the beech forest, eager to escape the killing fields. Once under cover of the trees, few had spoken; many simply scouring the woods for a source of water and a place to make shelter. Indeed, many had remained mute until they had found this brook, where they had crumpled to their knees and slaked their thirst like dogs.

'Like dogs!' Gallus snorted. 'For that is what we have become!'

277

Over the rest of the day, bloodied bands of legionaries had stumbled across their path, some from the XI Claudia and some from local forts and waystations, all sacked and put to flame, apparently. So much had been lost in a single day of Gothic fury. Again, the image of the carpet of dead on the ridge flitted across his thoughts; those citizens and legionary staff who had looked to him as their saviour. Then his thoughts settled on the face of the one he had come to know best of all; *Salvian*.

He screwed up one fist upon feeling pity snake into his heart. *Stay focused,* he chided himself, *fret over only that which you can change.*

He rubbed at his jaw, spiky with stubble. Including the stragglers, there were now less than forty men at his disposal, and he had lost count of the number of times he had thanked Mithras that one of them was a capsarius. The man had prepared dressings and salves as best as he could, using leaves and roots as a substitute to his normal range of medicines. Yet, despite the man's best work, Gallus was sure that many of those forty would not rouse from their sleep, their wounds being distinctly grave.

He stifled a groan as he stood, his limbs stiff and weary, then placed his helmet on his head, and walked for the edge of the clearing. As he crunched over the bracken, a salmon leapt from the waters of the brook; the plentiful supply of food in these woods was one minor blessing for his small group, he mused wryly, the gentle turn of the season into spring being the other.

He decided to walk upstream, his thoughts churning again. Which Roman cities and settlements still stood? If they had not been besieged already, then surely the nearby coastal citadel of Odessus and port town of Tomis would come under Fritigern and Ivo's gaze today. And the border legions, or what was left of them; would they have gathered, would they already have joined together in preparation for some counter-offensive, or at least in some attempt to contain or track the Gothic hordes? *Of course they won't,* he cursed inwardly. *Some of those tribuni would make Lupicinus appear brave and noble in comparison.*

Then something caught his eye. There, just ahead, was a trail through the forest, and the path seemed to be speckled with something, the colour of sand. Curiosity piqued, he stalked towards the trail, crouching, scanning the undergrowth in suspicion. Pushing through the foliage, the fullness of the trail was revealed, and his heart sank. The yellow grain that speckled the forest floor contrasted starkly against the charred remains of the rest of the grain column and their cavalry escort; crumbling, black timbers were mixed with charred flesh and the blackened bone of man and horse. Numbly, he squatted near one pile of grain that had survived incineration, lifting it in his filthy hands, letting the crop spill slowly through his grip. Nearby, he recognised the Chi-Rho necklace looped around the neck of one charred and arrow-pocked skeleton. It was the rider, Gunter.

So salvation and a continued peace had been barely a handful of miles from reaching Marcianople.

He thought of the forged scroll that had drawn the Goths here. He saw the face of poor Erwin the Goth, his tongue sliced from his mouth when he could have unmasked the devil behind these events – the one who bore the mark of the Viper. Fury boiled in his chest, and the name echoed through his thoughts as he saw the grinning, scarred features in his mind.

Ivo!

He threw down the rest of the grain with a roar, then sucked in breath after breath to calm himself.

Perhaps this was it, he mused. Perhaps it was the end of it all; the empire, his ideals, his self-imposed solitude, encased in iron at the head of the ranks. 'I will be coming for you soon, Olivia,' he spoke in a low tone. Then he squared his jaw, trembling.

'But first, Ivo will die for what he has done.'

Pavo felt warm and comfortable in his fresh tunic, sitting by a fire in a small cave. His wounds were dressed and cleaned and his belly was full of meat and wine. He looked around, confused, unable to remember how he had got here. Then a figure entered the cave and sat opposite him, breaking bread and offering half.

'Salvian?'

The ambassador nodded with a half-grin and then he sat. They munched the bread in silence, and Pavo shot frequent, furtive glances at the ambassador. A wriggling doubt told him this was not real, though he so much wanted it to be. Then he noticed that the fire was dimming. Salvian was brushing his hands of breadcrumbs as if readying to leave. Pavo knew he had to say something, but what?

'Don't go,' he said at last.

'I must, lad.' Salvian shook his head. 'For a shade cannot walk in the land of the living.'

Pavo felt sorrow thicken his throat. Then he felt a stinging on his bicep and looked to see that the wound was there after all, dirty and seeping blood. He frowned, then noticed that his skin was filthy, his tunic torn, and his belly once again groaned with hunger.

His head dropped. This was not real.

As Salvian stood to leave, Pavo stared into the dying fire.

'I will avenge you,' he said without looking up.

Then he felt the phalera on his chest tingle. It grew hotter and hotter until it burned like fire on his skin. Startled by this, he roared, pulling the leather strap from his neck and hoisting it to throw it to the ground. But then he stopped, realising it had grown cool again. More, Salvian was gone.

And the phalera reflected the last of the dimming firelight, casting a faint orange glow on the spot where the ambassador had stood. Something lay there in a heap; delicate, translucent and smooth.

Something lifeless.

Slowly, Pavo plucked the dagger from his belt, then reached over to it, eyes fixed on . . .

'Pavo!' A voice called out.

Like a stone dropping into an icy pond, he was wrenched from his slumber. Panting, he realised he was sitting bolt upright on the clearing floor, arms outstretched, his dagger extended in one hand. He glanced around to see Sura by his side, frowning.

'Bloody Mithras, Pavo, I thought you had lost your mind,' Sura hissed, wrenching the dagger from his friend's grip. 'Stick to the normal nightmares, eh?'

Pavo looked around, blinking. It was dawn and all around him the rest of the legionaries, bar the few on sentry duty, lay in exhausted slumber nearby. This was reality. The legion was all but gone and Salvian was dead. And Felicia? *Mithras tell me she escaped!*

He wriggled from his blanket, then shuffled to the brook at the edge of the clearing. There, he peeled off his tunic, then stepped into the waters gingerly. He shuddered as he cupped water from the stream and bathed his wounds in it, at last washing off the crusted blood. Then he braced himself and ducked under the surface, the shock tearing away any traces of grogginess. Bursting clear of the surface, he scooped water over his bristly scalp again and again. Parts of the dream began to fade from his thoughts with each scoop – even the lifeless thing on the cave floor. But his last words to Salvian echoed endlessly.

I will avenge you.

He stared into the rippling waters as he mouthed the words, seeing the foul grin of Ivo in his mind's eye. And behind the giant warrior, he saw the rippling, dark-green cloaked figure, there and not there at once. Hatred built in his heart, and his teeth ground together like millstones.

He was only ripped from the memories by the snapping of twigs near the edge of the clearing. Gallus had pushed through the trees, his face set in a baleful grimace.

He looked to Pavo and Pavo looked back.

'Gather your weapons, legionary, and rouse the rest of the men. It is time to catch a snake.'

281

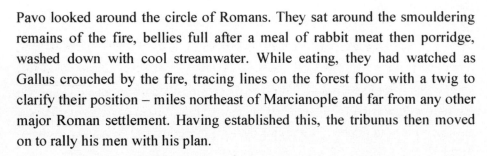

Pavo looked around the circle of Romans. They sat around the smouldering remains of the fire, bellies full after a meal of rabbit meat then porridge, washed down with cool streamwater. While eating, they had watched as Gallus crouched by the fire, tracing lines on the forest floor with a twig to clarify their position – miles northeast of Marcianople and far from any other major Roman settlement. Having established this, the tribunus then moved on to rally his men with his plan.

'So we could flee like scolded dogs to the south, behind the walls of the cities. There we might be safe for a short time . . . but Ivo will not stop.' The tribunus let this last statement hover in the air as he eyed each of the men. 'When a viper slips through the grass, readying to strike, you must skirt around it, unseen, then cut off its head,' the tribunus slapped the edge of one hand into the palm of the other. 'The Gothic invasion was spawned by one man, and it can only be stopped with that same man's demise. Ivo must die.'

Pavo's brow furrowed at this, and his mind conjured up the image of that shadowy, green-cloaked figure that had appeared on the plain. What if Ivo was not actually the head of the snake? His heart needled with a desire to interject and remind Gallus of this, but what was there to work on, other than these fleeting and insubstantial sightings? And earlier, when Pavo had put forward his suspicions while the men roused, Gallus had been insistent that Ivo was the key to it all. No, he affirmed; they had been chasing the myth of the Viper for too long. Gallus was right, Ivo was the living, breathing enemy that they could seek out and bring down. He looked around the other legionaries to see their reactions to the proposal.

'I beg your pardon, sir, but what you are proposing is almost certain death for us all,' Crito spoke out, breaking the silence.

Gallus cocked one eyebrow, then cast his flinty glare around the other men. 'Aye, that it is. Ivo's blood will not come cheaply.'

Zosimus cast an uncertain glance to the veteran of Lupicinus' centuries, then curled his bottom lip and nodded as if in concession. 'To wander into the midst of some hundred thousand Goths unseen. By Mithras, sir, we've been through some scrapes together, but . . . '

Gallus glanced at him, frowning.

Zosimus paused momentarily, then his face split with a broad grin. ' . . . but this one will top the lot!' With that, the big Thracian drew his spatha, then stabbed the blade into the earth and rose to stand by Gallus.

Felix stroked his beard. 'To even get close enough to assassinate Ivo would be some feat.' The little primus pilus looked up with a solemn frown. 'But if we do it, if we bring him down and Fritigern sees him for what he is then thousands and thousands of lives, Romans and Goths, could be saved.' With that, the primus pilus stood and joined the two in the centre. With a dry chuckle, Quadratus and Avitus stood to join them.

'I won't stand in the way of any man who chooses to flee to the south,' Gallus eyed the rest of the legionaries. 'Mithras knows every other cur in our sister legions has taken that path.'

At this, a murmur rippled around the circle.

Pavo's mind had been made up since he had awoken that morning, and Sura's was too. The pair stood to join the veterans in the centre. 'I don't know if what you suggest is possible, sir, but I'd gladly die trying.'

Then he turned to look the undecided men in the eye. If they were to have a hope of succeeding, they needed every man they could get. But the rest of the legionaries seemed to be sheltering behind Crito's doubt.

At that moment, he remembered how Salvian had put him at ease with a few light-hearted words. He took a deep breath and cocked a wry grin. 'Who knows, if we succeed, we may even find ourselves promoted to lead our own legions?' He looked to Crito with a sparkle in his eyes. 'Though Hades knows I'd make a piss-poor officer!'

Crito cast a hard glare back at him for what seemed like an eternity, but was unable to stop a broad grin creeping across his pitted features. The

283

veteran stood, nodding and chuckling, then joined the group in the centre. There, he clasped his arm to Pavo's and gave him a sharp nod.

With that, the tide had turned, and the rest of the legionaries flocked to the centre.

In unison, nearly forty spathas were slid from scabbards and held high in the air. Then, a flock of nesting doves were scattered from the trees as a lung-bursting cheer rang out from the clearing.

Chapter 18

Governor Drusus was a cold-hearted and miserly man, the kind of man who would stride up to the pyre and prise the coins from his dead mother's eyes. He rested one hand on the balcony and stroked the end of his pointed chin with the other, his narrow eyes scouring the northern horizon, stained with black plumes. Then he drew his gaze in over his magnificent city; Adrianople, the pride of central Thracia, the sea of domes, red-tiled roofs, marble and timber, all blanketed by a haze of gentle spring heat. But then he looked to the streets, swollen with low-life, and his nose wrinkled.

The city had descended into chaos in these last few days, with thousands of citizens from the northern cities and towns flocking through the gates. They carried with them all they had salvaged from their homes before fleeing from the Gothic invasion. Now he had a choice to make; the city needed its garrison to police this lot, but more than half of that garrison were Thervingi.

He spun round and strode back into his meeting room, eyes fixed on the two tall, blonde-locked Gothic Centurions before him. Suerdias and Colias had Roman names, and dressed in mail shirts and intercisa helmets they looked every inch like Roman soldiers. And they had served him loyally.

But they were Goths.

And he had his suspicions that the pillaging of his country villa last summer had been carried out by men known to the pair. Now that Fritigern's masses rode unchecked across the countryside to the north, how long would it be before these rogues would join forces with the iudex, razing the country villa and everything else in sight? Yes, they had to be despatched, one way or another.

He affixed them with a hard stare. 'You will take your men and move to the coast. Four imperial galleys are moored south of Tomis. They will take you east. Emperor Valens will employ you against the Persian dogs that lie in wait there.' He held their stares. *And with any luck they will rip your barbarian throats out.*

Suerdias looked to Colias, frowning, then turned back to the Governor.

'But we have homes in this city . . . '

'You will be gone from my city by nightfall, Centurion, or you will be forcibly removed.'

Colias sighed. 'At least give us a few days to wind up our affairs, pay our debts and then move on?'

Drusus thought on the idea for a moment. No, he reasoned, Fritigern's forces were reported to be moving closer to Thracia every day, edging south across Moesia. 'Guards!' He bellowed.

Six Thracian legionaries marched into the room.

'Escort the centurions to the barracks. See that they and their men have left the city by sunset.'

Colias and Suerdias' faces wrinkled, first in confusion, then in ire. Colias shouted over his shoulder as they left. 'You are a fool, Governor. You will be leaving your city with a half garrison at a time when it will need every man available!'

'Oh, you are so sure that Fritigern will bring his armies to my walls?' Drusus cocked an eyebrow, taking this as confirmation of their black blood. But Colias had a point; more men would be needed – first to expel these Gothic legionaries swiftly and then to repel any Barbarian assault. Perhaps it was time to call on the dregs of the populace. Yes, the cutthroat street gangs and the filthy warehouse workers owed him this, he mused.

He clapped his hands, a narrow grin splitting his face as a messenger came running to him.

Tullius swigged another mouthful of ale and then leaned back in his chair, stretching his arms out to behold the drunken rabble that packed the inn and the streets outside. 'And so here I am, in mighty Adrianople, with only a purse and a dagger. Meanwhile my inn lies abandoned, probably drunk dry and being pissed in by brigands and barbarians!'

The ruddy-faced man across the table from him nodded, eyes dull with inebriation. 'Durostorum? *The Boar and Hollybush*, you say? I've been in there when I was trading along the borders. Nice place, but I always felt I'd be likely to lose an eye whenever the legion decided to visit for the night.'

'Aye, made me a fine living, they did,' Tullius mused wryly. 'But, by the gods, did they make me work for it!'

'Well, we've all lost whatever we had,' the man replied, staring through Tullius. Then he seemed to perk up. 'Another ale?' He asked, and was up and staggering to the bar before Tullius had a chance to answer.

Alone, Tullius swirled the ale in his cup. Then a maudlin cloud drifted over his heart. He pulled a leather and gemstone trinket from his purse and held it to his lips. It was the Gothic piece the young lad Pavo had bought for his daughter. Felicia had worn it every day since. He chuckled at this, remembering the many times he had felt for the lad; Felicia made him fight like a dog for scraps of affection. Then, after Pavo left in resignation, she would always have this glow – a mix of satisfaction and happiness, he reckoned. She liked Pavo, that was for sure. So Tullius had been surprised when his daughter had given the piece to him. It was on the last night he had seen her, the night before the exodus of the limitanei and the citizens.

His throat thickened again at the thought. *Why . . . why did she go there?* He grappled at the trinket now, his knuckles whitening. Yes, she was concerned for Pavo, as she had stated in the sheaf of parchment she had left explaining her overnight disappearance. But he knew there was another, darker reason for her rushing headlong into the Gothic crisis. He thought of his dead son and the bitter ire the boy's murder had evoked in his daughter. He closed his eyes. *Curtius, I miss you dearly, but it seems your sister is set on avenging your death, or joining you.*

Then, a smash of clay outside shook him from his thoughts. He looked up; outside, angry shouts rang out, some Roman, some Gothic.

'Get out of our city, Gothic scum!' One voice cried.

Tullius stood and pushed through the crowd. On the street, the drunken rabble and the swell of refugees had been pressed to the sides as, in the walkway, a mob of grim-faced men swaggered forward bearing clubs, daggers and rocks. Workers, Tullius reckoned, going by their grease-stained tunics. There were nearly five hundred of them. Backing away from this rabble were over two hundred legionaries. Three pure Gothic centuries, judging by their height, fair skin and blonde hair. The two centurions who led them seemed to be trying to pacify both the mob and their own legionaries.

'You will not harm any citizen,' one of the two centurions roared to the nearest of his soldiers. But the legionaries bore foul grimaces, swords already drawn.

'But our people have risen, the tribes are uniting!' The nearest of them yelled back. 'Fritigern is out there, this is our calling. Goths in Roman service all across the land are going over to him, you know this! What loyalty do we owe the people of the empire? They mean to cast us outside their walls anyway, or have us murdered should we resist!'

The tall centurion stifled a frustrated growl. While the other one desperately pleaded with the oncoming mob. Then a rock was thrown, smashing the nose of one of the Gothic legionaries, who slumped to his knees, moaning, blood soaking his armour.

Tullius felt the ale clear from his mind. He stepped forward, before the mob. 'You fools, don't you see what you're doing?'

'Out of our way, vagrant!' The mob leader snarled.

'If you drive these men from the city, then they almost certainly *will* turn to Fritigern! And you will have a paltry garrison left to man the walls!'

The mob leader barged forward, shoulder charging Tullius out of his way.

Tullius thudded to the ground, scraping his elbows.

Then, just as the mob leader roared, waving his men forward, Tullius stood and leapt in front of the man once more. 'You fool, stop this madness!'

Tullius felt a sharp tearing in his ribs. He swayed where he stood, then looked down to see the dagger hilt jutting from his chest, his tunic sodden in dark blood. At once he moved a trembling hand past the hilt and to his purse, fumbling to open it, to find the trinket. Then blackness engulfed him and he toppled to the ground.

Colias gawped at the Roman lying on the flagstones, his lips blue and the last of the lifeblood pumping from his chest. Then a hand gripped his shield arm.

'Shields!' Suerdias barked.

Colias raised his shield to the hail of darts, rocks and stones the mob hurled at him. He looked to Suerdias. Suerdias looked back at him.

'We have no choice,' Colias roared over the tumult.

Suerdias nodded, his face grave. 'We slay these dogs, then we plunder the imperial warehouse. We take all we can. Then we seek out our people.'

Colias nodded, then twisted back to shout at his men. 'Iudex Fritigern awaits us, brothers,' he spoke through trembling lips, 'and Allfather Wodin will see us safely to him.'

With that, the pair pulled their shields down and stabbed forward. 'At them!' Suerdias cried, and the Gothic legionaries roared, rushing forward to butcher Governor Drusus' ramshackle mob.

Chapter 19

Fritigern heeled his stallion again, and at last he burst clear of the curtain of fog to crest the foothill, bathed in dawn sunlight. He slowed his mount, stroking her mane as he surveyed the land; the surrounding hilltops and the Haemus Mountains looked like islands in the sea of fog that clung to the lowland. He sucked in the air, crisp and clear. Then he lifted the iron helmet from his head and closed his eyes, welcoming the warmth of the sun on his skin.

For the briefest of moments, he tried to imagine that he was alone up here. His thoughts had been jabbering and jumbled in these last weeks. It felt as though the hand of Wodin had swept him and his people through the recent happenings, and the pressure of being a leader had never felt greater. Then, from behind him, the clanking of iron and thundering of footsteps and hooves in their thousands jolted him back to this reality. He twisted in the direction from which he had come to see the fog swirl and part.

'Iudex, you must not ride ahead like that,' Ivo said.

The scarred warrior rode at the head of a wing of one thousand cavalrymen. These riders, like the rest of his people, looked well-fed and refreshed, their armour polished and clean, their hair washed and groomed, their weapons sharp, their minds focused. It was the first time his people had looked healthy in months, ever since the Huns had driven them from their homelands. Perhaps, he thought, he should be grateful for this blessing. For now his destiny was clear; just like the parting fog, all doubt was gone. The empire had to be punished.

Ivo sidled up to him. His loyal aide wore his grey locks braided into tails and wore an old, bronzed helmet that covered his face to his cheeks.

Fritigern cast his mind back to that day, twenty years ago, when they had first met. It had been on a journey home from a parley with a Thervingi rival. He had been riding with his twenty finest horsemen, men whom he trusted like brothers to fight by his side to the last. And they had. The masked brigands who sprung his column from the trees were like starved wolves, pulling his riders from their mounts. His men fought with all they had, slaying any who came for their Iudex, but there were too many of them. Then, when the last of his men was felled, the twelve surviving brigands had turned to him, bloodied blades readied to strike him down. It was then that the lone warrior had appeared at the end of the track. All eyes had turned to the one-eyed giant. Then the warrior had stalked forward with the confidence of a lion, spinning a longsword in his grip as if it was a twig. At this, the brigands hesitated. Then a few to the rear broke and ran for the trees. The giant smashed his sword into that of the lead brigand, shearing the blade. At this, the rest of the bandits had turned and fled. That moment had forged a friendship that had grown stronger with every day since.

Fritigern's thoughts came back to the present and he looked to his most loyal aide once more.

Ivo's milky eye and the good one peered from the eye-slits, examining the hills ahead.

Fritigern followed Ivo's gaze. 'You are certain that they will come, Ivo?'

'Absolutely,' Ivo nodded. 'Any past disputes pale in comparison to what lies before their people and yours now, Iudex. It is time for the tribes to unite.'

Fritigern nodded, gazing around the hilltop; so this was the place and the time for it to happen. Then he frowned, remembering the tales his mother used to tell him; tales of the one they called the Viper, the Iudex who would unite the tribes and bring bloody war to all. He looked up to the sky; *yet it is me who brings about this brutal reality.*

A needling voice in the back of his mind would not fall silent. Like a trapped man pleading from the bottom of a well, calling out for him to open his eyes, to see what was going on around him. He remembered the claims of

Tribunus Gallus and his gaze drifted to Ivo's leather arm greaves. *What if . . . no!* He shook his head clear of the doubts, remembering the number of times this man had bled for him. A firm voice and a true leader was needed now.

Then Ivo grasped his shoulder.

Startled, Fritigern looked to his aide.

'It is time,' Ivo said, nodding to the far side of the hilltop.

There, the mist swirled and parted and another army marched into view. Thousands of Gothic spearmen and hundreds of cavalry. These were the Greuthingi Goths of northern Gutthiuda. Leading them were Alatheus and Saphrax, the dominant Iudexes of their people.

Alatheus heeled his mount forward.

'Noble Fritigern,' he clasped a hand to his heart, 'Having spent so many weeks fleeing from the demon horsemen from the steppes, it warms me to see you and your kin.'

Fritigern nodded, placing his fist over his heart in reply. 'Aye,' he replied tentatively, thinking of their past quarrels and bloody wars. 'Yet it pains me that it has taken a catastrophe like this to bring us together.'

Alatheus nodded solemnly. 'Know that my men will shed blood for your cause. Over the coming weeks, more of my kin will join us and swell the ranks. But it is not just kin from the north that flock to join you . . . ' he held out one hand to the curtain of mist.

Fritigern frowned as the mist swirled again. Then, like an iron serpent, a column of Roman legionaries marched forth onto the hilltop. A century became two, then they were a cohort, then nearly a thousand.

At this, Fritigern's men rippled to arms, panicked shouts splitting the air.

'At ease,' Alatheus bawled, raising both hands. 'They are with us. Look! They wear Roman armour, but they have Gothic hearts.'

Fritigern's men watched, still uncertain as the legionaries came closer. Then they saw it. Blonde and red locks tumbled from their intercisas and blue stigmas spiralled on their jaws.

The two centurions leading the legionary column stopped short of Fritigern. The nearest pulled off his helmet to reveal narrow, handsome features. He clasped a hand to his heart. 'Suerdias of the northern plains, loyal to the Thervingi, sons of Allfather Wodin!' He boomed. Then he swept a hand back over the wagons they brought with them – laden with Roman arms and armour. 'We will fight alongside you until the last.'

As Fritigern eyed the two armies, a tense silence crackled in the air.

Then Ivo heeled his mount into a canter and halted between the three armies.

'Feel the sun on your skins, my people!' He roared out. 'For today is a great day. Today we see, at long last, the unification of the tribes. Armies will flock to our cause. Iudex Fritigern will lead us to greatness!'

A murmur broke out across the ranks, some of Fritigern's men started to cheer. Then all eyes fell upon the iudex.

Fritigern felt the weight of expectation like an anvil on his shoulders. There was no turning back now, he realised, steeling himself. He drew his longsword, held it aloft and addressed his followers;

'We cannot allow this moment to pass us by. We stand by our common enemy's artery. Our blades are sharp. Let us cut through it with all our combined might!'

Then Ivo punched the air. 'Let the blood of the Romans flow under our feet like the Mother River. The time has come!'

To a man, the Goths roared like lions and the earth shook beneath them.

Pavo ducked back from the ridge, his heart pounding, his skin rippling at the tumultuous roar. Was this really happening? Had the thin air and the mist played tricks on his senses? He glanced up again, over the lip of the ridge. No, it was all real; Goths innumerable cried out in fervour as Fritigern and Ivo stood amidst the three united armies. But there was another figure, mounted and flitting between the masses of spears being punched into the air. Pavo's skin crawled; was it the hooded, green cloaked rider from the plain? He blinked and rubbed his eyes, and the rider was gone, consumed in the sea of warriors . . . or perhaps never there in the first place? He turned away from the ridge, flushing the thoughts from his mind.

Lying flat beside him, Gallus punched a balled fist into the grass. 'Whoresons!'

All along the line of legionaries, similar muted curses and laments rang out.

The handful – just over thirty – who had survived these last few weeks since the sack of Marcianople had tracked the Gothic column vigilantly. They had stalked along the ridges of the foothills, hidden in dells, slept in caves, melted into the forests as though they were the barbarians, waiting on the moment, the sliver of opportunity when they could get at Ivo. In all that time, hope had ebbed on an almost daily basis as they had passed burnt-out forts, razed settlements and scorched lands. Now it all appeared to be for nothing.

'It's over,' Sura said, his tone that of a lost child. 'The Goths have won.'

Pavo ran his fingers across his scalp, his dark locks curling and his beard thick after so many weeks without shaving. 'And we didn't even get a chance to fight them properly.'

Felix gathered the group together, then turned to Gallus. 'We need a new strategy, sir,' the primus pilus' voice was steady, but his eyes urgently searched the tribunus for a response.

Gallus looked across his weary band of men. 'No, we still have a chance. You all saw how cold Fritigern was with the Greuthingi Iudexes and the renegade legionaries; it was Ivo who bound them together and brought that cheer from their armies. The strategy still holds good. Until a viable alternative becomes apparent, we must stay honed on getting to Ivo.'

'We need hope,' a lone voice spoke up.

Pavo turned with the rest to the voice. It was Crito. The veteran had become withdrawn in the weeks since Marcianople, and was surely a portent of where the morale of the rest would be headed.

'I'll stick with the plan, to the last,' he spoke steadily, 'but I fear the last is not too far away. That's what I mean, when I say we need hope. Something has to go our way.'

Pavo felt for the man, and his words seemed to resonate around the group as some heads nodded, some went down, and shoulders sagged. He turned to Gallus, but even the iron tribunus was struggling to find the words of inspiration Crito sought.

Then, the ground rumbled with the thundering of hooves, approaching fast from the misty lowlands behind them.

Instinctively, the thirty spun away from the ridge and the meeting of the Goths. They snatched their spathas from their scabbards and leapt to readiness, eyes wide as they scrutinised the misty curtain down the hill. Gallus signalled frantically but in silence for the thirty to gather together as a square.

Pavo stumbled into position on the front line, Sura pushing up beside him. The pair only had a single shield to share between them, and barely half the front presented spears. Mutterings of despair started across the Romans as they waited on the Goths to burst from the mist.

'Been a pleasure fighting alongside you,' Sura said.

'Aye, likewise,' Pavo replied.

'Cut out the chit-chat, you couple of bum-boys,' Zosimus cut in abruptly, 'and get ready to fight as I taught you!'

A panicky chuckle spread across the line and then the group fell silent, and then braced as a shape burst from the fog.

'Mithras on wine!' Zosimus gasped, his mouth falling agape.

Pavo's eyes bulged at the sight.

A turma of thirty Roman equites rode in a wedge on fine, muscular mounts. But the lead rider was mounted on the finest of them all as he trotted forward to examine the thirty. The man's jaw was broad and speckled with grey stubble, his nose narrow and hooked and his skin sun-darkened. He was no renegade Goth – this man was Roman through and through.

Gallus stepped forward and saluted. 'Manius Atius Gallus, Tribunus of the XI Claudia Pia Fidelis.'

'Appius Velius Traianus, Magister Militum Per Orientalis,' the man replied with a salute. 'Now tell me, Gallus, what in Hades has happened here?'

The Roman cavalry turma and the straggle of legionaries spilled down a shrub-coated hillside into the dell, where a trickling stream would make a fine and secluded site for rest and refreshment.

Traianus sighed, flexing his grip on the mount's reins, his chest tightening as he tried to take stock of the sorry state of affairs. Every town, city and fort from the Danubius to Marcianople had been razed or was braced for such an assault. The limitanei legions were in disarray and he and his cavalry had encountered ragged bands like this dotted all across the countryside. But this band was different; they were not fleeing south. It had come as no surprise to him that these thirty were led by the fastidious Tribunus Gallus. Valens had warned him of a selection of unworthy dogs who held sway in the limitanei, but had described Gallus in stark contrast as a pithy and iron-hearted man who would fight until his heart burst. Indeed, Gallus was insistent that they should stay close to the main Gothic horde, despite Traianus' plans to withdraw to the south.

'We cannot fall back,' Gallus insisted again, marching ahead of his straggle of soldiers to draw level with Traianus' mount. 'We are on the cusp of bringing down the man who has orchestrated all of this!'

Traianus' eyes narrowed at this. The chatter since they had stumbled across Gallus and his men that morning had been swift and chaotic, but he had heard a name mentioned several times now.

And he longed for it not to be true.

'This Ivo . . . you say he was behind the rebel uprisings in Fritigern's lands, and now he rides at the head of the united Gothic army?'

Gallus nodded. 'Yes, sir.'

A cold shiver danced up Traianus' spine. *It is him, it has to be.* 'Describe him to me.'

'Three hoops in his ear, a nose like an arrowhead and . . . ' Gallus started, then touched one hand to his eye.

'. . . one ruined eye, milky and scarred?' Traianus finished for him.

Gallus' eyes widened. 'Then you know of him?'

Traianus nodded. 'I do. I once crossed swords with the man.'

Gallus frowned. 'If you know of Ivo, you must surely know of the Viper?'

Traianus nodded. 'Iudex Anzo was a callous whoreson, Tribunus. Yes, he lived for this to happen: to see the tribes united and the empire cowering before them.'

Gallus lowered his voice to barely a whisper; 'You speak of him in the past tense, sir? I have heard much rumour and legend about his death, long ago. But something needles at my thoughts. What if . . . '

Traianus shook his head. 'I saw Iudex Anzo die on a wharf in Constantinople, Tribunus; an arrow ripped out his throat and he bled his last on the flagstones, twenty-five years ago. And on that day, Ivo swore to see out his slain master's destiny.'

Gallus' gaze fell to the ground, eyes darting as if to make sense of it all.

Traianus leaned in closer as the legionaries began setting up a perimeter around the dell for their camp. 'Do not dwell on whatever smoke and myth Ivo has blown up to cover his tracks. Know only this; a relief column is on the way.'

Gallus looked back, eyes burning, eager.

'Three full legions of comitatenses and one of limitanei are on their way to these foothills along with two alae of cavalry. They move northwards as we speak. Used wisely, they could tip the balance. Your determination to hunt down Ivo is admirable, Tribunus. But tomorrow, at dawn, we must withdraw to rendezvous with our army.'

'And these men you see here today will fight at their head, sir,' Gallus replied evenly, hiding his frustration well. With that, the tribunus turned and strode around the dell, barking orders at his legionaries.

Traianus allowed himself a wry smile at this iron-skinned soldier's fortitude. Then he looked to the horizon again. His mind replayed those last moments of the wharf on that blood-soaked summer day, all those years ago. Gallus' words of doubt prickled at his thoughts.

Could a shade come back to life, he wondered?

Chapter 20

'Wake up!' A gruff voice pierced the air.

Pavo grunted, pulling his cloak tighter to keep in the warmth.

'Ivo is within our grasp!' The voice continued.

Pavo sat bolt upright, as did the rest of the legionaries in the ditch and palisade encampment, blinking sleep from their eyes, squinting at the halo of sun creeping over the horizon.

Crito and Noster were standing in their midst, having been on scouting duty overnight.

'Is it true?' Traianus asked, a frown wrinkling his forehead.

Crito nodded excitedly, his gruff veneer dropping for once. 'We stole past their sentries, to the tip of the Gothic camp; Ivo was there.'

Noster nodded hurriedly. 'We overheard him talking by their campfire.'

Crito scowled at the interruption, then continued. 'Ivo will be riding, later this afternoon, alone! Well, he and a small clutch of riders are to go hunting in the woods just northeast of here. They talked of visiting a gully where deer can be cornered and slain.'

Gallus stepped forward. 'You are certain that they will be separated enough from the main body of the Goths?'

Crito nodded. 'We heard it all; Fritigern is keen to press south, while Ivo hunts.'

'Then we have our opportunity,' Gallus looked to Traianus, 'we cannot pass it up.'

All eyes fell on the magister militum as he hesitated. Then finally, he nodded.

Gallus' chest swelled at this and he turned to the legionaries and riders. 'Let's make it count. We eat and then we pack up. Be ready to march by the time the sun's fully up.'

The group of legionaries – starved of decisive action for weeks – cheered at this and the equites joined in. Then the men set to work; some kindling fires to cook breakfast, others saddling the mounts and gathering their arms and armour.

Pavo dropped a handful of millet grain into his cooking pot, then added a splash of water from his skin. All around him the legionaries bantered in nervous excitement. This was the chance to avenge the murder of all the Roman citizens of Marcianople. Pavo thought of Tarquitius; surely slain in that massacre and now utterly gone along with that last truth about his father. Then he thought of Salvian.

The phalera medallion tingled on his chest, and he could not help but recall the dream where it had burned on his skin; the cave; the dead thing.

The afternoon sky over the Moesian foothills had greyed and a fine rain began to drift down over a red-earth gully. It was humid, and a whiff of damp vegetation hung in the air. All was sedate in the gully but for darting rabbits, grazing deer and swifts circling overhead. Then, like an asp, a column of legionaries emerged silently from the nearby trees.

Gallus led the column while Pavo and Sura followed, some four ranks back. Those who still possessed helmets, shields and armour had left that equipment back in the dell, choosing to wear only linen tunics, boots and swordbelts.

Pavo's breath stilled as, suddenly, Gallus slowed, raising one hand to halt the column and placing the other on the grass. They all felt it at that moment, the distant vibrations of approaching cavalry. 'Down!' Gallus hissed over his shoulder.

As if playing dead, the column collapsed to their bellies on the lip of the gully, eyes peering through the grass, down into the red-earth bowl. It was empty, and there was only one level path in or out – an earth walled corridor pierced with gnarled tree roots.

Pavo looked across to the far side, but the opposite lip was deserted. Traianus and his riders were supposed to be there to complete the trap. 'Where are they?' He whispered to Sura.

'Something's wrong,' Sura whispered beside him. 'I can feel it too.'

Then the sound of hooves grew, echoing through the bowl of the gully. It sounded like every last Thervingi rider was coming towards them. Pavo sunk even lower in the grass, eyes fixed on the entrance corridor as the cool rain soaked his face.

Then, muted gasps were snatched back into mouths as four terrified doe raced into the gully, one with an arrow trembling in its bloodstained flanks. Then a foreign roar filled the air and Roman hearts froze.

'Ya!' A jagged voice cried.

The lead rider came into view first; a Goth wearing a red leather tunic with a thick beard and blonde hair flowing loose. Still moving at a gallop, the rider winked as he stretched his bow and then loosed. With a twang, the arrow zipped through the air and ripped into the wounded doe's throat. The animal fell, hooves thrashing, blood bubbling from the wound.

Three more riders followed the archer into the gully. Ivo was the last to enter, his grey hair scooped back into a topknot, his good eye sweeping around the basin and his bronze earrings and scale vest glinting.

Pavo's eyes hung on the vest. He frowned. It reminded him of something. *Like the scales of a snake.* Images of the dream came to him again, and he searched for meaning.

'Four . . . five.' Sura whispered beside him. 'There are only five of them!'

They watched as Ivo slid from his horse, taking up the bow from his saddle and training his sights on a terrified fawn that skipped around its mother's corpse. The grizzled warrior loosed his arrow and then roared, punching the air in delight as the fawn's body crumpled, its ribs shattered and its heart ruptured by the shaft. The Goths gathered up their kills, then struck up a campfire, before skinning the largest of the deer, splicing it on a spit to roast.

Gallus stared down shufflings of impatience from the legionaries, all the while darting glances to the far side of the gully; still empty. 'We wait for the magister militum!' The tribunus hissed.

Ivo circled the campfire, patting his men on the shoulder. Then the giant warrior carved off four slabs of meat from the animal's haunches, handing a slice to each of them.

'Taste the flesh, taste its sweetness, its succulence,' he enthused. 'Satiate your hunger on it as if it were the very corpse of the empire. For now is the time to reap the rewards for your loyalty.' As the giant warrior spoke, he slowly untied his arm greaves.

'This is it,' Pavo whispered to Sura, eyes fixed on Ivo as the segments of leather armour fell to the ground. There it was, as stark as daylight; upon each of his forearms, a blue, winding snake stigma curled around his flesh.

'The Viper!' Sura hissed. The phrase echoed along the line of watching legionaries.

But then Ivo drew his sword and held it aloft. 'My master and I have drawn the disparate Gothic tribes together, blending them like ore in a furnace.'

My master? Pavo's brow wrinkled. He shared an anxious frown with Sura and Gallus.

Down below, the Goths nodded in approval, all apart from the bearded one. Ivo continued; 'Neither Fritigern, Alatheus, Saphrax nor Athanaric for that matter, is strong enough to seize destiny alone. Thus they will be driven through Roman lands like war dogs. When they have served their purpose, they will be knocked from their thrones by the Viper, my master, the rightful iudex! Then we will be invincible!'

The Goths burst into a joyous roar at this. All apart from the one with the thick beard and flowing hair.

'I will have no part in this,' the Goth grunted, standing, throwing his meat into the fire. 'A united Gothic nation is a fine aspiration, but I am loyal to Iudex Fritigern and Iudex Fritigern alone.'

'That,' Ivo twirled his long sword in his hand as if it was a twig, 'is why I summoned you on this hunt. You will make a fine example.'

At once, the other three Goths shot to standing, ripping their swords from their scabbards.

The bearded Goth backed away. 'What is this?'

Ivo stepped forward. 'This is where you choose between Valhalla and heaven!' Then, with a swing of his knotted arm, he brought the longsword round to hack clean through the bearded Goth's neck. The head spun onto the ashes of the fire, eyes bulging, lips fluttering soundlessly as the man watched his own body stand, headless and spouting crimson from the stump that used to be his neck. Then the body crumpled to the ground like a felled tree and the head was consumed by flames.

With that, Ivo stabbed his sword into the ground. 'It is time!' He held clenched fists to the darkening clouds.

At this, Pavo looked to Gallus. The tribunus cast one last forlorn stare to the far side of the gully, then squared his jaw.

'Ready yourselves,' Gallus hissed, 'surround them and make sure none escape.'

Right on cue, Pavo's bladder seemed to swell with liquid and his mouth drained of all moisture. He and Sura glanced to one another – affirming that tacit vow that they would protect each other's flank.

'Go!' Gallus hissed, rising from the grass, flicking his spatha up. At once, the gully lip rippled as the thirty legionaries – the last straggle of limitanei resistance – spilled into the crater in a wide line. They sped down the red-earth sides, racing in to the campfire in the centre.

They bit back on their usual battle cry and rushed forward in a mute charge. Pavo's vision jostled as the form of Ivo and his men grew closer. Then he stepped on a piece of slate that snapped under his weight, and the Goths spun to the source of the noise. The three with Ivo cried out in alarm, snatching up their swords and stumbling back. At this, the Romans broke out in a roar.

In a flash of iron, the Goths were snared – spatha tips hovering at each of their throats. But Ivo did not move or go for his sword, embedded in the earth. Instead, he wore a wretched grin, bent across his face under that arrowhead of a nose. His calm gaze was trained on the approaching Romans.

The one-eyed giant waited for the Roman cry to die to nothing, then spoke with a calm voice; 'My master and I have been aware of your scouting of us for some time. That is why we lured you here.'

'Your poisoned words are useless now, Ivo,' Gallus barked, then nodded to his legionaries. 'Bind them!'

Pavo grabbed for the lengths of rope on his belt. But then he froze. His gut shrivelled as he heard the creaking of bows all around them. He looked up; the lip of the gully had darkened.

Gothic archers lined the crater; some two hundred of them, faces smeared in woad, earth and root. Their arrows were trained on the legionaries and a dark-green viper banner flitted in the breeze above their heads.

Traianus and the equites were already dead, he realised.

Traianus stilled the breath in his lungs and pressed back against the tree trunk as a band of Gothic archers flitted past the dense thicket. He stroked his mount to soothe her, anxious that a snort or a shuffle would betray his turma's position. Then his hand flexed near his spatha hilt as he looked ahead in frustration – the lip of the gully they were supposed to be lining right now was so close yet so far.

'They're everywhere, hundreds of them - we're pinned down!' The decurion hissed behind him.

Then a roar rang out from the gully, accompanied by the iron screeching of spathas being drawn, just as the archers spilled into place around the lip. Traianus' heart sank. They were too late. He closed his eyes, searching for a plan.

'We can still break free of this, sir, then ride like Hades to the south,' the decurion whispered, grappling Traianus' arm, his grip cold and clammy with terror.

Traianus twisted round to scowl at the decurion, whose face was etched with guilt. 'Soldier, you do not know the measure of Ivo. Long ago, when I last faced him, he slew my centurion and my contubernium. I have known many soldiers who have killed in great number – but never have I seen a man revel in bloodshed like Ivo did that day. I will not leave those legionaries to die at that man's hands.'

But the decurion's face had paled and his mouth hung agape as he gazed past his superior's shoulder.

Traianus frowned. Then, a crunch of bracken sounded.

Traianus spun to face forwards again, then his blood froze.

He beheld the dark-green cloaked and hooded figure that had materialised, barely an arm's length from him. Instinctively, he grabbed for his spatha.

But his hand froze as, all around the thicket, Gothic archers dropped down from the trees silently. Like the others, their faces were smeared in dirt, stained with woad and root, and they held arrows nocked to their bows, trained on the equites.

Traianus' gaze darted all around him, then fell upon the shadows under the green hood. His heart hammered. 'This cannot be real; I saw you die . . . '

Then a voice rasped from within the hood. 'Yes, I remember that day on the wharf well. You fought bravely, Roman . . . '

Pavo stared numbly at the ground before him. The legionaries around him were equally silent. On Ivo's word, they would be rent with hundreds of Gothic arrows.

Then, from the corner of his eye, he saw something move, up on the lip of the gully. Pavo looked up to see that the chosen archers had parted. A clutch of Roman corpses were pushed forward through the gap, throats slit, mail vests and tunics stained crimson, limbs flailing as they tumbled down the gully side. So Traianus' equites had fought their last. But there was one survivor; one Roman was bundled forward, hands bound, teeth gritted, snarling like a caged animal and shaking with rage as he skidded down the gully side.

Traianus.

But Pavo saw the magister militum and the chosen archers as just a blur, for his gaze snapped onto something else. It was as if the undergrowth had come to life; a dark-green shape rippled, emerging from the green of the forest to step down into the gully. An icy finger traced Pavo's spine as the hooded and cloaked figure strode across the gully floor. The shadow where a face should have been seemed fixed on them as it approached.

Now there could be no doubt; the Viper was all too real.

Then the figure stopped before them. Ivo and the three Gothic hunters knelt before it.

'Master,' Ivo whispered, clutching a hand across his heart.

The green-cloaked figure lifted a finger and then swiped it down. At once, the Gothic archers lining the gully rushed forward to begin binding the hands of the legionaries.

Pavo's thoughts spun.

Traianus was barged to his knees before the Viper. 'It cannot be – I saw Iudex Anzo slain, his throat torn out and his body drained of blood!' He croaked, squinting up at the shadows under the hood. 'Who are you?'

At this, a rasping laughter poured from the shadows. Then the Viper carefully took hold of each side of the hood, drawing it back.

Gasps rang out from the legionaries.

Pavo's breath caught in his throat, and his mind refused to believe what he saw; the fawn locks, the blade-sharp cheekbones and the piercing green eyes. And then the half-mouthed grin. Then the cloak dropped from the figure's shoulders and fell to the ground. He was bare-chested underneath, with a lean but muscular torso, and a spiralling snake stigma curling round his shoulders, one of which bore an old, gnarled spatha wound.

'Salvian?'

Salvian's gaze was baleful, and then he shook his head, ever so slowly. 'The guise of a Roman ambassador was an expedient facet; one of many I have grown like a skin since my early years. I have been Peleus the trader, Vetranio the smith, and Leptis the gladiator.'

Pavo frowned; his thoughts grew hazy and the ground beneath his feet seemed to sway. Then he looked to Gallus, whose face had paled. Then he glanced to Traianus; the magister militum stared at Salvian, brow deeply furrowed, eyes haunted.

'No!' Traianus uttered. 'It cannot be . . . '

'Cannot be what?' Gallus gasped, shooting glances to Traianus and then Salvian. 'What is this?'

'Tell them, Roman,' Salvian spoke evenly, his gaze fixed on Traianus.

Traianus cast a distant and defeated gaze. 'This man is no ambassador and certainly no Roman. He is Draga the Goth, son and heir of Iudex Anzo. He *is* the Viper.'

'Now you know,' Draga spoke softly, turning to Pavo.

Pavo felt his heart grow cold. A bitter sorrow stung behind his eyes as he turned back to this man he had, only weeks ago, grieved for as he had done for his father. Then his eyes fell upon the discarded cloak. Suddenly, that dream of the cave came back to him. Where the man he had known as Salvian had been standing, the slippery, lifeless, segmented sheath that had been shed was just that; one of the many skins of the Viper. 'Draga . . . ' he muttered, numbly.

Then Gallus erupted. He barged towards the Viper but was hauled back by the Goths binding his wrists. They kicked at his legs, forcing him onto his knees. 'The forging of the emperor's message, the slaying of the grain column, the assassination attempt on Fritigern, the murder of the Roman citizens I entrusted to your care,' Gallus snorted, 'it was all your doing. And the sortie to and flight from Dardarus, it was all a sham, wasn't it?'

Draga nodded gently, as if he had just been paid a compliment. 'Before Dardarus, I was nothing to you and your legion; afterwards, I was at the heart of your every move, trusted like a veteran. I knew that shedding blood with you that day would buy me this trust, just as I knew that you would not pass up on the opportunity to come here today, to snare Ivo.'

Gallus' top lip wrinkled and betrayed a low growl. 'So . . . you are in league with Athanaric?' He spat.

Draga's grin sharpened and he shook his head. 'Athanaric was but a die in my hand, Tribunus, just as you were. I harnessed his hatred for Fritigern and ensured he would not stand with his equal against the Huns.' He stepped forward and rasped; 'And now Fritigern too is another die in my

309

palm. His armies will fight for my wants, even if they do not realise it. Every day their ranks swell – as does their appetite for conquest!'

Gallus twisted his face away from Draga, his teeth gritted in impotent rage as his hands were bound.

With that, Draga turned and clasped forearms with Ivo and then the pair embraced. 'I have longed for this day since I pulled myself, weak, freezing and bloodied, from the waters of the Golden Horn. Every day I spent, exiled in their city in the guise of a Roman citizen, witnessing their arrogance, the vileness of their nobility, their heinous crimes of war against my people,' he stopped, wide-eyed, to stab a finger at Traianus, 'or what would you call your legions' spilling of oceans of Gothic blood – valorous, glorious . . . expedient?' The veins in Draga's neck pulsed against his skin, bringing the snake stigma to life. His teeth were bared like a hungry predator as he spat these last words, trembling with rage; 'Every time . . . I dreamt of this moment.'

'And I promised you I would devote myself to realising that dream,' Ivo replied.

Steadying himself with a few deep breaths, Draga nodded. 'And it will be even greater than we had imagined.' He swept a hand across the circle of legionaries. 'For not only am I on the cusp of scything into the heart of the empire, I now also have the commander of the eastern legions.' He sneered at Traianus. 'You are a fool, Magister Militum, for you have wandered into my grasp. Now you will tell me of the legions your emperor has sent from the east. Then they will be swept to their deaths like kindling in a rainstorm.'

Pavo gazed at the ground and felt one of the Gothic archers fumbling to bind his wrists. In his peripheral vision, he saw Ivo and Draga punch the air, rallying their men. At once, the gully was filled with Gothic victory cries and the green viper banner was pumped in the air. Then Pavo's gaze settled on Ivo's longsword, still dug into the earth. The phalera on his chest weighed heavily as he realised that all hope was gone. But a thought sparked in his mind;

If all hope was gone, then what was there to lose?

310

With a roar, Pavo threw his head back, his skull crashing into the archer's jaw. Then he pulled his hands free of the rope and lunged forward, plucking the sword from the dirt, swinging the blade up towards . . . Salvian?

A gasp rang out from the watching legionaries as the sword tip halted, resting against Draga's neck. Through gritted teeth, Pavo panted, gaze fixed on the sharp eyes, the half-mouthed smile and the earnest expression. 'Why?' He uttered, before Ivo batted the sword from his grasp, pressing a dagger to his throat.

'No,' Draga said.

'Master?' Ivo twisted round, frowning.

A distant hope sparked in Pavo's heart. Then Draga's face curled with an awful half-grin and at once, the hope was gone.

'Let him live for today. Let them all live. They will be marched like cattle at the head of our people, and their flayed bodies will serve as a portent of what will become of those who resist. Then, perhaps those who do not die of thirst can be slain for our amusement or,' his eyes glinted as he fixed his gaze on Pavo, 'perhaps they can serve as our slaves?'

'Yes, master,' Ivo grinned.

Pavo heard the words as a distant echo. Then he felt the wind being knocked from his lungs as a spearshaft butted into his back. He crumpled to his knees, spitting bile. This time a group of the Gothic archers set about wrenching thick rope around his wrists and tied him to the chain of the other Romans.

Draga stepped forward and looked to the horizon as a warm wind whipped the spray of rain across the gully. 'And now we march south, for there is a harvest to be reaped.' He glared at Pavo and the legionaries with a manic sparkle in his eyes.

'Yes, the empire will pay for its crimes.'

He grasped the viper banner and held it aloft.

'The Viper has risen once again. Now Roman blood will flow, and it will flow like the Mother River!'

Chapter 21

The plains of southern Moesia basked in early spring serenity, baking in the warmth of the sun. The land was punctuated with pine thickets and gentle green hillocks, and scented with spring blooms. On the southern horizon, on a sizeable piece of flat ground, a small farming village lay amidst a network of barley fields.

Then, from the Haemus Mountains in the north, a dust plume rose up like a storm cloud as the Goths spilled onto the plain, the land behind them left churned and ruined. Over one hundred thousand men, women and children marched as one, in a mass stretching almost a half-mile across and many miles in length. The Gothic cavalry formed the wings and rearguard of the mass movement, with the chosen archers and spearmen providing a formidable vanguard, whilst the families marched and rode their wagons in the protected centre. At the head of the Gothic march, Traianus and the legionary prisoners were harried along. They were roped together at the wrist, wearing soiled and ripped imperial tunics, their faces caked in dust and burnt from the sun, their lips cracked and bleeding and their feet blistered and swollen. Behind them, Gothic spearmen threw curses, spitting and roaring with laughter as the beleaguered prisoners walked on in silence.

Then one Goth jabbed his spear butt forward and into Traianus' spine. A joyous Gothic roar filled the air as the magister militum crumpled to his knees, then a fresh hail of spit coated his back.

Traianus bit into his lower lip, knowing fury would do him no good now. Blood spilled from the gash to his knee where he had fallen, seeping into the earth. Just another wound to add to the collection. Ivo and Draga had seen him tortured every night, searing his flesh, twisting the nails from his fingers, salting his wounds. Pain untold. Until, at last, the information they had sought came tumbling from his lips. Now he was being kept alive as some kind of example. He gazed into the dust as the spittle rained down over him. What could he do, other than bleed out in front of his enemy? Then, as if by a divine wind, he was lifted, the rope around his wrists tightening as the men either side of him hauled him up.

Gallus and his veterans wore bitter grimaces on their faces. He looked to them, nodding firmly, eager to hide the fatigue in his limbs. Then they continued at the head of the Gothic migration. As they walked, he wondered at the hardiness of this clutch of XI Claudia legionaries; more pithy and brash than any others he had encountered, either in the border legions or even in the field armies.

But it was from the east that his last hope lay; for that was where he had sent the lone eques, moments before the Viper had captured them. *Ride southeast, hug the coastline and you will find them.* He glanced at the horizon, his eyes narrowing. *Come on, come on, where are you?* He repeated over and over in his head. Then, noticing that a Gothic spearman was watching him closely, he looked down again quickly.

Then a clopping of hooves sounded and two horsemen sidled up to ride with the Roman line. It was Ivo and Fritigern. Traianus stared at Fritigern, ignoring Ivo. The Gothic Iudex stared back, his eyes cold and distant. Traianus recalled the times when Fritigern had been more than a tentative ally. But the man's mind had been twisted to hatred and a hunger for conquest. And all this by the hand of Draga and Ivo.

Ivo and Fritigern cantered off ahead, shielding their eyes from the sun, looking to the settlement up ahead. Then Draga cantered up to take their place. The Viper turned his glare upon Traianus, but Traianus looked away.

This creature had slipped into the Gothic ranks unnoticed, posing as one of Ivo's retinue. His hair was tousled and the beginnings of a fawn moustache coated his top lip. The resemblance to Anzo was stark now.

Draga slid from his saddle to lead his horse by its reins and to walk alongside Traianus.

313

'I watched you, you know,' Draga hissed in his ear, 'ever since that day when you and your men slew my father.'

Traianus stared dead ahead.

'While I was incarcerated in my Roman guise, I watched your rise to power with interest. I heard tales of your ascension through the ranks, your victories across the Danubius and then your victories in the east,' Draga shook his head, grinning malevolently. 'What a bloodthirsty soldier you have been. My hatred of you and everything about your empire has grown every day; from the moment as a boy, when I watched my father slaughtered like a pig, when I pulled myself shaking and lost from the waters of the Golden Horn.' At this, he wrenched his cloak down at the shoulder to reveal the gnarled scarring of the spatha wound, splitting the snake stigma. 'In all that time, I have drawn every last drop of knowledge from your libraries, your great thinkers and your strategists . . . I have bled your empire like a *cut* of *meat*. Now I stand, like the pig-slayer, blade in hand, pressed against the empire's throat.'

Traianus turned to glare at Draga. 'You are a fool, Goth. You think I sought out blood in my time as a leader of the legions?'

'The mass graves on Thervingi lands would suggest you did,' Draga spat.

'You are so blinded by hatred that you are drowning in hypocrisy!' Traianus growled. 'For how much blood will be spilled now – Roman and Gothic – to satiate your thirst for revenge?'

Draga's top lip curled into a sneer. 'Well, Traianus, you can see for yourself. *You* will be the first to see each of your cities and forts burn. The wretches cowering behind their walls will lose any hope in their hearts when they see the great Magister Militum Per Orientalis and his men being herded like cattle by the enemy.'

Traianus suppressed a shudder as Draga grappled him by the collar of his tunic, then pointed ahead;

'Observe, Roman.'

Ivo and Fritigern were signalling, waving a wing of cavalry and spearmen forward. Traianus frowned, squinting at the farming village up ahead, square in the middle of a patchwork of barley fields. Around forty houses lay open and unprotected by wall or palisade, the townsfolk believing they were safe inside Roman lands. Traianus' heart ached as he heard the tinkling of cattle bells and lowing of oxen, along with the high-pitched shrieking of children at play. The ground trembled as the detachment of Gothic cavalry cantered forward. Then they split into two halves, forming a pincer formation. When only a few hundred feet from the village, they broke into a charge.

The playful squealing of the children turned to terrified moans, cut short by the Gothic war cry and then the smash of iron. Before long, the village glowed fiery orange and the sky darkened with smoke. The legionaries bristled, growling through trembling lips, some looking on with glassy eyes, others turning away to weep. It was over all too quickly, the Gothic riders coming away laden with sacks of grain, and the spearmen herding the village cattle to join the huge Gothic flock. The village lay husk-like, silent and still apart from the crackling flames and a handful of twitching corpses. As the raiders rejoined the main Gothic column, one bloodied survivor appeared from the wreckage, crawling, reaching out a hand.

Traianus stared at the old, bald man, face lined with age, gums decorated with only a few teeth. The man froze, mouth gawping, when he saw Traianus and the legionaries bound at the head of the Gothic column. Then the man seemed to lose the will to live, the light in his eyes dimming.

'See the look of realisation in his eyes,' Draga hissed in Traianus' ear from behind him. Just then, the old man slumped to the earth, a last breath rattling from his lungs. 'He knows there is no hope. I have manipulated your empire for years, and now I turn my dagger upon its heart.'

But Traianus looked to the southeast, where the beginnings of a dust plume snaked above a rise in the land. 'You forget, Goth,' he spoke with a trembling breath, 'that you can be deceived, just as you deceived others.'

Draga stalked forward, squinting at the horizon, frowning.

'The torture you subjected me to was brutal, Goth, but I would never betray my legions! The locations I gave you were false,' Traianus growled. 'My trusted man, Profuturus, leads many legions to these lands. But from which direction, only I know. You think I would be so foolish as to reveal this – to anyone? You underestimate your enemy, Draga!'

At that moment, from the dust plumes behind the rise, an eagle standard pierced the horizon, a purple and gold Chi-Rho banner hanging from the crossbar, flitting in the breeze. Then, two alae of other-worldly cavalry burst into view, more than five hundred riders and beasts in each ala. They were clad head-to-toe in iron. Each rider was dipped in the saddle and bore a huge lance.

All along the line of bound Romans, one word rang out as the two packs hurtled forward, converging on the tip of the Gothic column.

'Cataphractii!'

Draga spun back around and stabbed a finger at Traianus, then swept it along the Roman line. 'Slay them!' he bellowed. Then he yelled back to the Gothic cavalry, who were still unaware of the approaching Roman riders. 'Riders! To the fore!'

Traianus twisted to see the Gothic riders looking forward in confusion. Before Draga could bellow a repeat order, he kicked out, sinking his boot into the man's chest. The Viper was sent sprawling in the dirt. But, at once, the spearmen surged forward, blades jabbing out towards Traianus.

'Protect your leader!' Gallus boomed.

At once, the roped-together prisoners bunched into a circle, kicking out, swatting at the frenzy of speartips. Roman limbs were sliced off with ease, unarmoured torsos were punctured all too easily.

Ringed by his legionaries, Traianus glanced over his shoulder to the cataphractii. They were closing in, but still some distance away. He saw another legionary fall, a glistening crimson mush where the man's jaw should have been. Then he roared, pushing forward and to the fore of the circle, kicking out with all the strength left in him.

Pavo headbutted one Gothic spearman who stumbled forward, too eager to stab his lance into the Roman circle. The Goth's nose flattened and he fell to the ground with an animal moan. Then Pavo ducked down to wrest the weapon from the felled man, straining as the ropes binding him to his comrades grew taut.

When he stood up, he realised that Traianus had pushed out from the centre of the Roman circle to stand alongside him. He wasted no time, swiping his wrists down over the spear tip to cut his own bonds. Then he hacked through the ropes binding Traianus and Sura before passing the shaft on for the others to do likewise.

'Pavo!' Sura cried out beside him.

Pavo spun round and jinked to one side, just as another spear punched through the space where his face had just been. He looped his hands up and over the spear shaft and yanked it down to snap the head of the shaft across his knee. Then he grappled at the spear tip, wielding it like a crude dagger. His limbs were numb and the strength was seeping from him as he ducked and dodged the flurry of spear points, stabbing out in riposte. Beside him, Sura cried out as a blade ripped across his shoulder, pulling muscle and sinew from his flesh. Then, the legionary on Traianus' other flank roared as a spear burst through his ribcage and into his heart. The circle shrank, and Pavo felt the wet gore and the grinding bones of slain comrades under his feet.

Death seemed a certainty, when, suddenly, Traianus gripped his wrist and that of the legionary on his other side. 'Ready yourselves!'

Pavo glanced this way and that; the Goths were dropping their spears and turning tail, pushing and scrambling back into their own ranks. Then a foreign, ululating battle cry pierced the air.

317

He spun to see the two groups of cataphractii, just as they smashed into the backs and flanks of the foremost Gothic spearmen, pincering the head of the enemy column. Clouds of crimson vapour burst into the air as bodies were shattered under a flurry of hooves or ripped asunder and lifted from the ground, pierced on those terrible lances. While the front of the Gothic column was shredded, the rest of the Gothic army was too slow to react. Their cavalry foundered as they tried to organise their wings, man and beast stumbling into one another. Meanwhile, the spearmen were pressed back, ranks toppling upon ranks.

Pavo roared out in encouragement as he watched the dark-skinned and iron clad riders plough through the Gothic ranks, lancing spearmen, trampling them underfoot or sending them hurtling through the air. Then, in the gap rent by the riders, he saw something far behind the Gothic front line; a rabble of people, roped together at the wrist. Roman citizens. Then he saw a flash of tumbling amber hair.

Felicia? No!

He was almost thrown from his feet as a clutch of the riders swooped past Traianus, scooping the magister militum up and onto the saddle. All around him, the rest of the legionaries were plucked from where they were stood, many crying out in shock and euphoria, hurling insults back at the Gothic column.

Pavo blinked through the dust cloud, straining to see Felicia again. But when the dust cleared, the Gothic mass had closed up and he could see nothing of her or the Roman prisoners.

'Come on!' A gruff voice roared beside him. It was Centurion Zosimus, beckoning the last few legionaries over to the onrushing cataphractii. The eastern riders leaned to one side on their saddles, hands outstretched.

Each man was pulled from the ground and carried to safety, until only Pavo, Zosimus and Crito remained on foot. Pavo shot a glance back across the horde; the Gothic cavalry and spearmen had now organised themselves, and were pouring forward in a counter charge. As if this wasn't enough, a chorus of groaning bows and then twanging bowstrings rang out as the sea of chosen archers loosed a cloud of arrows.

'Move!' Zosimus roared.

Pavo turned and sprinted after Zosimus, haring for the last of the cataphractii. Then, all around them, the arrow hail hammered down. It punched into the earth and danced off the shell-like backs of the cataphractii, but plunged into the unarmoured flesh of some of the rescued Romans, whose bodies slipped from the saddles and fell under the hooves of the riders behind. Then, behind Pavo, Crito cried out; Pavo turned to see the veteran clutching his ribs, pierced with an arrow. Strides away, the whole Gothic horde rushed for him like wolves to a stricken deer.

'You go first!' Pavo yelled to Zosimus, darting back to the veteran.

Zosimus turned, then scowled. 'Leave him – he's done for!' The big Thracian roared, then he growled like a bear on seeing Pavo scoop an arm around Crito's back to hoist the veteran to standing. 'Oh for f . . . ' The big Thracian ran back to grab the veteran's other shoulder. Together they hobbled forward, the arrow hail zipping past their ears and a thousand Gothic blades at their backs.

Crito glanced at Pavo. The veteran's face was greying, the light in his deep-set eyes dimming. 'You're a bloody fool . . . ' he rasped, ' . . . but I'd march into Hades with you . . . *sir!*'

Pavo glanced over their shoulder at their pursuers, only paces behind. They would never make it, he realised. 'Save it for later, soldier!'

Zosimus wrenched Crito onwards. 'Move!'

Crito cackled, blood rasping in his lungs. 'I don't think so,' he said, shrugging free of Zosimus and Pavo. 'Now run, save yourselves!' With that he turned, took up the sword of a fallen cataphractus, and spun to face the Gothic line.

'No!' Pavo roared as Crito lunged into the Gothic front. The Gothic charge slowed for but a heartbeat as a flurry of blades scythed down on the lone legionary. Then the veteran disappeared under the stampede of Goths.

319

'He's gone! Now get your arse on horseback!' Zosimus bawled, bundling Pavo forward as arrows zipped down all around him and a spear scythed past his ear. Then the big Thracian leapt up onto the saddle of the next to last cavalryman.

Pavo scrambled forward to get to the last cataphractus as longswords swiped at his back, tearing his tunic and scoring his flesh. The Roman rider beckoned him, eyes wide and darting back to the onrushing Goths. He clasped the rider's forearm and swung up and onto the saddle, and at once they sped away from the wall of Gothic blades. As the wind rushed over them, Pavo twisted round on the saddle to scour the rear of the Gothic horde, desperate to sight the rabble of Roman prisoners again. But a huge dust plume covered everything behind the first few ranks.

I will find you, Felicia.

Then an arrow zipped past his cheek and, with a sickening thud, punched through a sliver of the rider's neck, momentarily exposed between the iron aventail and the scale vest. Blood pumped from the wound as one half of the iron creature slid to the ground. Pavo shuddered, momentarily frozen. The he slid forward on the saddle, grappling at the reins to control the panicked mount. As he did so, a rasping voice called out behind him, rising over the tumult of the furious Goths.

'Your empire will soon be in ashes, Legionary!'

Pavo turned back in the saddle, his heart pounding. Draga stood at the front of the horde, a bow in his hands.

'I watched my father bleed his last at the hands of Rome's legions. And now *you* will never know the truth about *your* father, Roman . . . *never!* Tarquitius is dead and the truth died with him!'

Pavo gritted his teeth, then hefted the splintered head of the spear shaft in his hand and hurled it back over his shoulder with all the strength he could muster. The makeshift missile sclaffed from Draga's face, then ploughed into the dust.

Draga touched a hand to his bloodied cheek, eyes burning.

'And you will not see another spring,' Pavo roared.

With that, Pavo turned and lay flat in the saddle. His knuckles trembled, white on the reins as he rode, and the wind whipped at his face.

Chapter 22

In the baking spring heat, Pavo crouched by the brook to fill his water skin. He slaked his thirst and washed the dust from his throat, then cupped water in his hands and threw it over his freshly cropped scalp and shaven jaw.

With a groan, he stood and adjusted his linen tunic, slick with sweat, then trudged over to the oak where he had tethered his chestnut mare in the shade. He took an apple from his satchel and bit into its cool, sweet flesh. Then he slumped against the tree trunk to finish the fruit before washing it down with another swig of water. When he felt the strength returning to his limbs, he stood to feed the apple core to his mare. Then he stroked the beast's mane, whispering comforting words to her as he looked northwards, over the foothills to the limestone giants of the Haemus Mountains. At this, his thoughts darkened; Draga was out there, holding Felicia captive, manoeuvring Fritigern and honing the Gothic horde like a giant blade.

The Goths had pursued Traianus' cataphractii for many miles on the day of the frantic rescue. They had broken off the pursuit only when they had come within sight of the four legions levied from the east – the comitatenses of the II Isauria, the IV Italica and the II Armeniaca, plus the limitanei of the I Adiutrix – here, at the southern edge of the foothills. Traianus had hurriedly organised the legions into a wide front only ten ranks deep to exaggerate the Roman strength – the dust plume behind the legions disguising the paucity of depth. With the two forces only a half mile apart, a tense standoff had ensued, the Goths eyeing the Roman lines and the Romans praying their opponents' resolve would weaken. And at last, the war horns moaned and the Goths had melted back into the foothills and the mountains. That had been weeks ago, and the Goths had not been sighted since, despite these daily scouting patrols.

The Romans had taken this period of respite to re-establish a foothold in their own land. A huge fortified camp had been constructed in a plain to the south to serve as a command centre. Smaller forts had been established at all the southerly passes and routes that led from the mountain range.

While this fragile border was constructed, rumour had become rife that more Goths were flooding over the Danubius unchecked, fleeing southwards from the Hun raiders in Gutthiuda, swelling Fritigern's armies as he readied for a decisive push southwards. Some in the camp whispered that Traianus had sent an appeal for support to Emperor Gratian in the West. However, few expected that the besieged legions on the Rhine and northern Italy could do anything other than pray to Mithras for their eastern brothers.

Pavo was jolted from his ruminations when a lone rider burst over the crest of the nearest foothill, red-cheeked and furious, galloping on a white gelding.

Sura! About time . . . fastest rider in all Adrianople, indeed! He chuckled wryly, standing as his friend and scouting partner slowed to a trot and then slid from the saddle.

'There's no way you'd beat me in a flat race. You're mare's obviously a hill-runner!' Sura insisted as he drew level. Then he pulled the purse from his belt to rummage and produce two folles, dropping them into Pavo's extended palm with a scowl.

'Aye, and yours obviously isn't,' Pavo replied. Then his face fell stony. 'You saw nothing, I take it?'

Sura shook his head, wiping the sweat from his brow. 'Nothing apart from traces of where they have been. The valleys are maze-like.'

'Aye, Salv . . . ' Pavo started, then bit his tongue, 'Draga will have them moving camp every day.' He stared out at the mountains again.

'Tomorrow, Pavo,' Sura said, reading his mind. 'We will find the Goths . . . and Felicia . . . tomorrow.'

The pair remounted and set off southwards at a canter. As they descended the last of the foothills, they entered a plain stained bright yellow with wild rapeseed. To the east of this plain, a small brook ran around a willow grove and the small town of Ad Salices, known by most as 'The Town by the Willows'. The town was tucked in behind the trees and surrounded only by a light timber fence, more to keep the village goat herds in check than anything else. The settlement lay only a quarter of a mile from the edge of the foothills and mountains. Traianus had considered this plain around the town as a site for the Roman camp. Pavo himself had wondered as to the wisdom of this, imagining how the Goths could come within a fraction of a mile of any such camp and remain unseen. Fortunately, Traianus and the senior officers – Tribunus Gallus, Tribunus Profuturus plus the tribuni of the eastern legions – had come to the same conclusion, resolving to set up camp a further two miles to the south on the next plain, over the ridge.

Pavo glanced across at the sun-baked settlement as they cantered past; the townsfolk busied themselves with their daily lives, farming and weaving. Men loaded hay bales, scythes and sickles into a wagon, readying to harvest the early crop, eager to fill the near-empty horrea. One amber-haired woman was stooping by the brook, drawing water into an amphora while her children splashed in the shallows. It was a picture of serenity. But every few heartbeats, she would glance up to the north, her features wrinkled in concern.

And these townsfolk were right to worry, despite Traianus' assurances. The century of legionaries the magister militum had garrisoned there was a gesture and no more. It was the turma of equites sagittarii stationed with them that seemingly mattered more. These thirty men, mounted on the fastest steeds from Traianus' stable, would relay any sign of a Gothic advance back to the main Roman camp.

And the villagers would be left to the whims of Fortuna.

He glanced over his shoulder again as the town slipped into the distance behind them, and whispered a prayer for those people.

'We'll be ready for them this time,' Sura said as they approached a slight rise at the southern end of the plain.

Pavo welcomed the grim look of determination on his friend's face. It was a look that each and every legionary in the camp had worn over these last few weeks, as the scale of the Gothic destruction had come to light. The limitanei legions had been crushed or scattered, leaving the towns, cities and forts of Moesia undefended. While Durostorum had been evacuated, Odessus and Marcianople had been part-razed and plundered, and every settlement and fort in between had suffered the same fate.

'But do you not fear that – after so much scheming and subterfuge – no matter what we do, we're always going to be undermined? What if Draga has planned all of this as well? And what of the Huns? We worry about the Goths in the mountains when the darkest souls the empire has ever faced gather across the river, unchecked.'

Sura sighed. 'We can only fight those that stand before us. And Draga is blacker-hearted than any Hun.'

Pavo frowned. He thought of the long conversations he had shared with the ambassador; the sharp, knowing look in the man's eyes as he had talked of his father, telling him things he had shared only with the few in life he trusted. And then the man had betrayed him like no other. He avoided Sura's gaze.

'You still long for things to be as they were, don't you?' His friend asked, tentatively. 'Draga . . . Salvian, he really meant a lot to you, didn't he?'

At last, Pavo steeled himself and straightened in his saddle as they crested the rise. 'Salvian? The façade? The man who we knew has evaporated like a morning mist, Sura. I don't have time to pine for some sham friendship. None of us do. There are an untold number of war-hungry Goths back there and we need to be ready for them.'

They crested the rise and Sura broke out in a trademark beaming grin. 'Aye, that we must, and we will be!' He swept a hand across the vista on the next plain;

The vast Roman camp dominated the land, bristling with legions, cavalry, archers and artillery. A few slivers of silver marched to the fort from

325

the south. These were the precious few cohorts from the garrisons of the southern cities and the recruits from southern Thracia, mustered to bolster the Roman ranks.

Pavo's skin tingled at the sight. 'Mithras, but that warms my heart every time I see it.'

Despite the size of the encampment, the traditional layout was instantly recognisable. A rectangular ditch was the first line of defence, followed by a tall earth rampart, bristling with stakes. Atop the rampart, a tall timber palisade had been erected. Watchtowers punctuated this barrier at regular intervals, with sagittarii archers and legionaries packed onto their platforms, scouring the northern horizon.

Inside the walls, a sea of goatskin contubernium tents were laid out in grids; one grid per cohort of each legion. Each tent was surrounded by tiny figures, some in their red or white tunics and others glistening in their armour, as the ranks kindled their fires and cooked their rations and catches from the local countryside. Two paths split the camp in a north-south and east-west axis, each connecting with one of the four main gates. At the junction of these paths, five silver eagle standards were staked in the ground at the centre of a cluster of larger tents. This temporary principia was where the officers had been locked in strategic discussions for days.

Outside the camp, intensive drilling and training was underway. The barking of officers and rustle of iron armour filled the plain, drowning out the cicada song. A thick line of sagittarii lined the practice range, emptying quiver after quiver of arrows into painted targets. Equites circled a stretch of plain, swooping past timber posts from which hung sandbags in the shapes of men. Then there were the legionary cohorts, practicing marching drills, plumbatae volleys and shield walls.

The warm air was spiced with sweet woodsmoke and roasting meat as Pavo and Sura cantered down the rise and towards the north gate. As they neared the earth bridge that crossed the ditch, the sentries on either watchtower flanking the gate shuffled bolt upright. They levelled their plumbatae at the pair, and two sagittarii archers stretched their composite bows. Then one sentry called out to them, lifting a buccina to his lips, ready to sound the alarm. 'Identify yourselves!'

Pavo looked to Sura, each of them cocking an eyebrow. Then Felix barged up and onto the leftmost tower, grasping the lip of the balcony, eyes wide. Then he sighed. 'Oh, for Mithras' sake! Let them through!'

'Yes, sir!' The sentry barked back in an overly-officious tone.

The gates creaked open and Felix darted down the timber ladder to greet them as they passed inside the fort. 'Anything?' He narrowed his eyes and pulled at his forked beard.

Pavo and Sura saluted their primus pilus, then shook their heads.

Felix punched a fist into his palm and grimaced, stifling a curse.

'We went over a mile into the hills this time, sir,' Pavo sighed. 'I know our orders were to stay within half a mile of the plains, but we were so sure we'd sight them.'

'Aye, and I'd be first to buy you an ale if you had. But tomorrow, stick to your orders, eh? If you go getting skewered out there then we learn nothing of the Gothic whereabouts.'

'Yes, sir!' The pair barked.

They dismounted by the stables, Pavo patting his mare on the nose and feeding her a handful of hay. He surveyed the goings-on in the camp: siege engineers worked furiously to cobble together ballistae and onagers, their hands blistered and bleeding; smiths smelted and shaped spearheads, spathas and mail; fletchers piled quiverfuls of freshly-hewn arrows and bows by the archery range. Yet Pavo's mind still dwelt upon those lonely hills and rugged mountains, two miles north.

'Pavo,' Sura slapped a hand on his shoulder, nodding to the goatskin awning nearby that offered shady respite from the blistering sun. Zosimus and Quadratus were sitting there, supping from their wineskins and munching on joints of charred and juicy meat. 'Refreshments?'

Pavo nodded and followed his friend. But his mind was set on one thing and one thing only.

To Hades with the orders, he affirmed. Tomorrow, we ride into those hills until we find them! I'm coming for you, Felicia.

Chapter 23

Pavo hesitated for a moment, panting. His hands were bleeding and coated in grey dust and his neck was burnt from the sun. He eyed the peak of the mountain; a jagged limestone ridge some fifty feet up. Though it felt like it hadn't got any closer for the last hour. Then his gaze locked onto a lone mountain goat stood near the peak, munching on a shrub, eyeing him with disdain. He closed his eyes and rested his forehead against the rock face.

'Pavo, come on; we should have turned back long before now!' Sura rasped from below. 'The sun's dropping.'

They had set off from the base of this, what had initially looked like a modest mountain in the Haemus range, at mid-afternoon, and not for the first time since then, doubt danced in Pavo's mind. But again from the other side of the mountain a clash of iron rang out, along with cheering and a jagged Gothic rabble. Above the craggy limestone peak, woodsmoke plumed into the orange-tinged sky.

'Then let it drop!' He spat back, flushing the doubt from his thoughts. 'I'm not turning back now; they're right over that crest.'

'And?' His friend replied dryly, shooting nervous glances to the noise. 'We need to get back, to alert the legions. If we are killed then the legions will never know the whereabouts of the Gothic camp!'

Pavo twisted round, a foul expression on his face. 'You climb down and ride back, then, and report that Pavo is being a stubborn whoreson. But I'm not leaving until I've found her.'

Sura groaned and wiped his hands over his face. 'Felicia? Look, Pavo, I'm with you in that I want to see her safe. But do you really think we have a chance in Hades of freeing her from the horde that lies in wait over that ridge?'

Pavo held Sura's pleading gaze in silence. Then he drew his dagger, clamped the blade between his teeth, turned back to the rock face and scrambled on and up.

A groan sounded behind him. 'Slow down, will you?'

He turned to see Sura scurrying after him, scowling.

'I can't leave you to get skewered, can I?' Sura fumed. With that, the pair continued their climb.

They halted for breath momentarily when at last they reached the top of the mountain. There, a welcome, stiff breeze hit them from the east, ruffling Sura's blonde locks and cooling Pavo's freshly shorn scalp. After this brief rest, they stalked over to crouch behind a large limestone cairn and peeked over the top.

The land in the valley below was awash with Goths.

Soldiers carried piles of longswords, composite bows and armour, stacking them high, while others groomed their warhorses. It was coldly reminiscent of the Roman camp – except there were far more Gothic warriors. Amongst it all, families milled around, cooking stews, pleating hair, darning and scrubbing clothes. Pavo winced as he saw one Gothic woman washing a pile of robes in a barrel of water, her children tugging at her hem demanding she played with them; it was all too similar to the amber-haired Roman woman at the brook by Ad Salices, yesterday. Many innocents would die in what was to come.

Then an elbow jabbed his ribs. 'I'd wager that that's where you want to start looking,' Sura growled, solemnly.

Pavo followed the line of Sura's outstretched finger; the Gothic camp was so vast it spilled through the grey-green pillars of the mountains into the next valley, where a huddle of bedraggled Roman captives were being marshalled across the flatland towards a group of assembled wagons. His heart stilled as he saw the bald, stocky man who owned the wagons handing over a hefty purse to the Goths who herded the sorry figures.

'Slave traders! Romans! Buying their own kind when the empire is crumbling around them!' Sura gasped. 'Have they no shame?'

Pavo bit into his lower lip as a bitter boyhood memory flitted through his thoughts; that day in the slave market in Constantinople when he himself had been paraded in front of nobles and senators like a cut of meat before that fat reprobate Tarquitius had bought him. The very idea of Felicia being subjected to some lecherous, abusive master sent a wave of fire through his heart.

Then Sura slapped a hand on his shoulder, jolting him from his thoughts. 'Sentries! Get down!'

Pavo ducked, then peeked over the rock pile to see the Gothic spearmen dotted along the narrow, high mountain paths that wove around the camp. There were two every few hundred feet, and a tall and broad-shouldered pair were approaching the cairn. He sized their red leather tunics and conical helmets, his eyes narrowing as he noticed how the helmets shaded their faces. 'Right, if they come this side of the cairn, they're out of the line of sight of the rest of the sentries and we can take them. If they go the other side, we wait.'

Sura nodded, flexing his fingers on his dagger hilt.

The pair of sentries strolled closer, joking in their jagged tongue. Pavo readied himself to spring like a cat. But the sentries veered away from the cairn, staying within view of their people. He stifled a curse and dug his nails into his palms. He looked to Sura, then the dropping sun. Doubt laced his thoughts.

Then, an impatient snort from the mountain goat pierced the air. The banter of the two Goths stopped dead at the sound. Then sharp words were hissed, laced with suspicion. Then footsteps ground on the dust either side of the cairn and they heard the sentries' shallow breaths. Pavo looked to Sura. They nodded in unison, then each turned to an edge of the cairn.

The two sentries stalked past the stone pile, eyes wide, spears reaching out as they looked down the mountainside. One laughed, pointing to the goat, visibly relaxing. 'Dinner!' He bellowed. But the other Goth's eyes were locked on the mare and gelding tethered far below. 'Romans?' He uttered, glancing around for the missing riders.

Pavo leapt at him, wrapping one arm around his neck. The pair fell onto the ground, entangled and thrashing. Pavo brought a sweet right jab down on the Goth's cheekbone and the man's head thudded against a sharp rock and he fell still. Then he spun to Sura, who was locked in a struggle with the other Goth, each of them wrestling for control of Sura's dagger. Seeing Pavo come for them, the Goth forced the dagger towards Sura's throat. But Sura flicked his head to the side and headbutted the man, who staggered back, dropping the dagger. Sura caught the weapon by the blade, flicked it over to grasp its hilt, then sunk it into the Goth's heart.

Panting, Sura wiped his blade on the grass.

Pavo eyed the dead pair, then glanced left and right. His heart thundered as he saw two more sentries, only a few hundred feet away. He kicked grey dust over the spilled blood and in the dusk light it was disguised, but the corpses lay stubbornly before him. He glanced around; down the mountain, near the troublesome goat, an outcrop of limestone offered a slim chance to avoid detection.

He stooped and wrenched one Goth up and over his shoulder. 'Grab the other one,' he wheezed to Sura.

As the light faded in the mountain valley, Felicia watched the latest slave cart depart. It was packed with Romans, some nobles, some freedmen, all levelled to slaves now. She pulled at the filthy and frayed hem of her robe and eyed the two who stood before her in the line: a young lad and a pretty Roman woman. Then she would be next, she figured. Before dusk another cart would come and she would be taken away. Yet she cared little for her future. It was

332

the memories of the past few weeks that consumed her every waking thought, and her chest still felt raw and hollow from weeping. She had set out to avenge her brother's murder. Instead she had lost everything.

Everything.

She had fled the plain of Marcianople when it was clear the city would fall. Her mount was small but swift, enough to outride the handful of Gothic horse archers who had pursued her some of the way. Then, upon cresting the rise and entering the plain north of the city, she spotted the chain of thousands of Roman citizens – the refugees from Durostorum and all the northern towns. They were headed for the timber bridge across the River Beli Lom but they looked this way and that as if in search of a leader. Then, a rider on a jet-black stallion had burst over the ridge from the city to take his place at the head of the column. At this, the citizens had cheered. It was the ambassador, Salvian – Pavo's good friend.

The man had immediately set about marshalling the column manfully with only a handful of legionary scouts, scribes and heralds to aid him. Hope had danced in her heart as she had raced to join the exodus. But then she had slowed her mount, seeing Salvian halt the rabble in the centre of the wide plain, a long way from the bridge. Then her veins had filled with dread as Gothic riders appeared from nowhere to encircle the refugees. She had barely been able to watch as Salvian stepped towards the lead rider, but she frowned when the ambassador wordlessly raised a hand and extended one finger. He had held it there for a moment, then swiped it down. As soon as he did so, the Gothic cavalry noose snapped shut. She had turned from the sight as the blades struck home and the screaming had started. Then, when she had heeled her mount round to flee the plain, the breath had stilled in her lungs: Salvian remained where he had stood, unharmed and watching the massacre. Then he had drawn a blood-soaked, dark-green cloak from his satchel and slipped it over his shoulders, raising the hood, before taking up a longsword and joining in the slaughter with the Goths.

Numb, she had fled from the plain at a full gallop and let up only when her mount was exhausted. Then she had hidden in a cave in the foothills, wary of the numerous columns of smoke in every direction and the

333

distant din of battle that seemed to dance on the spring breeze. On the first night she had caught and skinned a rabbit, then roasted the animal over a small fire before devouring it and washing it down with streamwater. The next morning, she had readied to ride for Adrianople, to find Father, when a group of Gothic cavalry had thundered past her hideout, roaring gleefully, severed Roman heads mounted on their speartips like trophies. So she had hidden for another two days. Then, on the third day, the chaos across the land seemed to have lessened just a little. So she leapt on her mount and rode without pause until Adrianople came into view.

Its proud skyline of domes and marbled columns dominated the verdant flatland, and her heart had soared when she saw the city was intact. But something was wrong, she realised. The thick, towering walls were devoid of the usual generous garrison. Instead, only a handful of intercisas were visible. And then she caught scent of it; an acrid tang of burning flesh. Her heart slowed as she approached the gates, and the cluster of limitanei rushed to the gate top to challenge her. 'I'm looking for my father,' she had said, 'he came here from Durostorum to escape the Gothic incursions.'

The drawn, weary look of resignation on the lead soldier's face told Felicia what had happened before he said the words to confirm it. They had let her inside the city, where the trail of destruction was still fresh, as was the massive pile of ash where the pyre had been lit. 'Aye, the innkeeper from the northern limes? He was a brave soul – tried to stop the riots,' the limitanei legionary had said, resting a comforting hand on her shoulder, 'but the Goths and the Roman mob were merciless.'

And so she had walked from the city, numb to her core. Then she had mounted her horse and set off at an aimless canter, unaware of time, heat and cold, hunger and thirst, staring through the horizon as she moved. She barely noticed the group of Gothic riders who circled around her until they wrenched her from the mount and roped her wrists together. 'Another Roman bitch – she'll fetch a few coins!' The rider had joked with his comrades.

A pained shriek pulled her back to the present; the slave line had shrunk once more. She looked up to see the pretty Roman woman being dragged away from the front of the line by the hair, her protests silenced when the slave trader balled his fist and smashed it into her jaw. Felicia felt numb.

With her father dead, Pavo surely slain, and her world torn asunder by the invasion, her heart had grown weary of aching. She stared through the ground before her and sought out her father and Curtius' faces from her memories. She barely flinched when a Goth came over and sliced a dagger through the rope joining her wrist to that of the young Roman. The young man protested angrily, the fear causing his voice to crack.

'You're needed,' the Goth snarled. Then, eyeing the man's finely manicured nails, he grinned. 'Time to learn how to shovel dung!'

As the panicked young man was bundled away like a dog, Felicia realised she had not muttered a word nor tried to wrench free of her bonds in days. Then, when she heard the next slave cart approach, its wheels grinding on the scree, she simply shuffled forward.

'Pick out the ones who will make good whores!' The slavemaster called out to his helpers in a broad Greek accent. The Goths erupted in a chorus of laughter at this.

Felicia didn't even have the will to despise the man. She held out her wrists, readying to be taken away, gazing to the ground through a veil of stale tears.

Then a hand grappled at her wrist.

'Hold on, we'll have a bit of fun with this one first,' a gravelly voice muttered, then sliced the ropes binding her to the others.

In a flash, she was pulled past the slave cart and back through the sea of tents and crackling campfires, towards the southerly edge of the camp. She frowned and looked up to the pair who pulled her on; they wore red leather tunics and conical helmets – spearmen. Suddenly, a spark of fear ignited in her heart and she pulled back. 'Where are you taking me?' She spat, sickened by the trembling in her voice.

The two simply dragged her onwards.

335

Then she felt it; the old fire in her veins – it felt good. She yanked back on the rope and kicked out at the backside of the nearest of the two. 'I said – where are you taking me?'

The Goths all around burst into a rabble of laughter at this and at last, the pair slowed, then turned to her. Her skin crawled as their shadowy faces beheld her. Then her heart skipped a beat and her lungs froze mid-breath. *Pavo, Sura!* She mouthed.

'Stay quiet,' Pavo spoke in that forced, gravelly tone, his head bowed a little and the rim of the Gothic helmet casting his dark eyes in shadow.

She nodded quickly and dropped her gaze to the ground.

'Good little whore, eh? What did you say to her?' One Goth called out gleefully, swigging from a wineskin.

Felicia sneaked a look up to see Pavo giving the man a furtive nod, while Sura glanced around, checking who was watching. Of the two, Sura could possibly pass as a Goth, but Pavo's dark features and beaky nose clearly distinguished him as a Roman. Indeed, a few of the nearby warriors seemed to be frowning, scouring his features. She looked around in vain for something, anything to distract them. Then her eyes fell on the bronze pin holding her tattered robe together. Father had given her that pin, and she whispered a prayer to him as she pulled it from the cloth. Her robe fell to the ground, leaving her wearing only a short linen tunic that barely covered her buttocks.

'My robe!' She whimpered.

At once the Goths' frowns dissolved, their stares flicking to Felicia's ample, bare thighs.

Never fails, she mused.

And they were at the edge of the Gothic camp now, she realised, looking up to see the cairn on the crest of the mountain before them. Pavo and Sura glanced around, then the three made to ascend the rise. But although Pavo and Sura carried on and started climbing, pulling her with them, she felt an odd burning on the skin on her back.

Someone was watching them.

She turned and swept her eyes across the sea of warriors and families, bustling in the torchlight, all busying themselves with their own affairs. Then her gaze stopped, like a tunic caught on a nail, on one figure.

The one they now called Draga – the dark creature who had slain those Roman refugees on the plain before the River Beli Lom – was standing in the midst of the Goths, wrapped in his dark-green cloak, hood lowered. He was staring at them, the firelight dancing in his eyes.

His lips were curled up in an awful half-grin.

In the centre of the darkened tent, Senator Tarquitius touched a finger to the cracked blisters on his lips, his chains clanking as he did so. Then he pulled out the folds of his tunic that hung limply from his body. He had not been this slim since he was a boy, he mused bitterly. Weeks of eating what scraps Draga had brought to him had seen the rolls of fat wither, leaving sagging layers of empty skin in their place. Perhaps it would have been better had he been slain in Marcianople, he wondered. The thought lent him a modicum of dignity. It felt strange to him after so many years of immorality.

The muffled laughter of a Gothic warrior outside startled him. This reminded him just how lost he was – here in the middle of a sea of tents and an army that would raze everything Roman within its path. He looked at the chains on his wrists and felt a mix of bitterness and self-pity tug at his heart.

Then he stiffened his jaw as he mulled over it again; the chain of events that had tortured his every moment in this tent, the face of the man who had led him like a stray dog in his every action.

Salvian . . . Draga . . . the Viper. The protégé who had in fact been the master.

He searched for some caveat that would dampen the shame he felt at being fooled so readily, but found none. Then he heard the voice of some girl outside.

'My robe!' She squealed.

Tarquitius' ears perked up as he recognised her Greek twang. Welcoming the distraction, he shuffled on his hands and knees to the tent flap, as far as the chains would allow him. Then he pushed his nose and eyes through the flap and squinted into the dusk light. There, near the base of the mountain, two Gothic soldiers seemed to be leading a flame-haired girl towards the mountainside. But, some thirty paces away, he saw it; the green cloaked figure drifting wraith-like between the tents, following the trio. Unhooded and now sporting a thick fawn moustache and flowing fawn locks, Draga looked like any other Goth. Apart from the cold, green eyes – something about them was inhuman.

He watched in a mix of interest and terror as the Viper was careful to stay some distance behind the three, one hand on his sword hilt, the other seemingly ready to shoot in the air as if to raise the alarm. But something was stopping him from doing so.

The two soldiers and the girl disappeared on up the mountain path, and Draga remained, watching them for a moment. Then he spun round, eyes snapping onto the tent and Tarquitius' filthy, drawn features.

Tarquitius yelped like a kicked dog and scrambled back inside the tent. As footsteps approached, he muttered to himself, eyes screwed shut, praying that the darkness inside would hide him. Then the flapping of hide and a blast of fresh air was followed by the hissing of the Viper, right by his ear. Tarquitius could feel the man's breath on his skin, but refused to open his eyes.

'It seems I have a use for you after all, Senator.'

Campfires and torches lit up the dusk like a cloud of fireflies across the Roman encampment. Inside the stable compound, Pavo helped Felicia down from her saddle while Sura fed a clump of hay to his mount.

'He saw us, I swear it!' Felicia repeated.

'Why would he let us escape?' Pavo replied, stroking her hair to comfort her. *Because he's playing a game, because he's still in control.* Pavo shuddered and batted the nagging doubt from his thoughts.

Felicia shook her head. 'I've never seen a man look so . . . driven. He'll do anything, Pavo, anything it takes. I saw him turn upon all those citizens. He was merciless . . . '

'Forget about him,' he said, trying desperately to rid his own mind of Draga's image, 'You're here now, you're safe.'

She pushed away from him, her voice cracking. 'I'm alone, Pavo. Apart from you, I have nobody.' She choked back a sob.

At this, Sura gave Pavo a knowing nod, and led both the horses away to the feeding trough, leaving them alone.

Pavo turned back to her, his heart aching. 'Your father would have gladly died to be sure you were not harmed, Felicia.'

'And now he and Curtius are both just memories,' she said, her voice hoarse.

He pulled her close again. 'You have me, Felicia. I'll not rest until you are safe, and clear of this conflict.'

She looked up to him, her eyes red-rimmed, face glistening with tears. 'I cannot avenge my father's death, but my brother's killer walks free, within the walls of this camp.'

Pavo's heart sank.

'I don't care what becomes of me anymore,' she continued, her lips curling to reveal gritted teeth. 'I *must* take vengeance so that Curtius' spirit can rest in peace. Avitus must pay!'

He grappled her arms and shook her. 'Felicia!' He barked.

339

At once, her eyes widened in shock at his tone, as if she had been snapped from a trance.

Pavo pinned her with his gaze. 'You saw the might of the Gothic army, didn't you? When they come to war with us,' *when Draga decides the time is right,* the doubting voice rasped in his mind, 'then everyone, *everyone* in this camp will be at the mercy of their swords. Come the new moon,' he swept a hand around the Roman camp, 'every soul within these walls could be carrion.'

She nodded. 'For some, that would be deserved.'

Pavo sighed. 'Then let the coming battle decide who lives and who dies, please! Do this for me?'

She closed her eyes and gulped back a sob. Time seemed to stand still. Then she nodded.

Pavo felt sweet relief flood through his veins. 'You're doing the right thing,' he affirmed. 'Now, for Mithras' sake, I'm begging you to leave here tonight, for Constantinople. All that lies south of this camp is still firm imperial territory – you will not meet trouble from any Goth.' He pressed his purse into her hand. 'There is enough coin here to buy you a room; go to Vibius, the landlord of the tenements near the Saturninus Gate. He is a decent man . . . well, better than most.'

She breathed deeply, composing herself, blinking as she wiped the tears from her eyes. 'So in the end I am to leave it all behind, let the Goths take vengeance on my behalf?' She said wryly, taking the purse. Then, at last, she nodded. 'Aye, perhaps Father and Curtius would have wanted this.'

'I know they would, Felicia. I didn't know Curtius, but your father used to give me this look like a serrated blade,' he stopped and shook his head, cocking an eyebrow. 'You meant everything to him.' He then grasped the tether of a medium bay stallion and led the beast from its stable. 'Now ride; ride and don't stop.'

She looked into his eyes. 'Find the truth for me, Pavo, I beg of you.'

He nodded.

She wrapped her arms around his shoulders and he cupped his hands around her waist, and they pressed their lips together. Despite her bedraggled state, her scent was still sweet as honey to Pavo, and her tousled amber locks felt like silk, whispering on his bare arms. At last, they pulled apart. 'Now ride,' he insisted, helping her onto the saddle. 'When this is all over, I'll come for you.'

She looked back at him wistfully. He bit back the hard lump in his throat.

Then, her face broke into a partial grin that pushed through her sadness. For the first time in so long, she looked every inch like the mischievous, carefree girl he had fallen for. 'You'd bloody better,' she winked, gulping back a sob, 'or there'll be trouble.'

With that, she heeled the mount into a canter, off through the Roman camp, towards the South gate.

Pavo watched her amber locks dance in her wake, and realised her grin had been infectious.

Then, as the sound of the stallion's hooves faded, he heard barking officers and a smashing of iron; based on he and Sura's sighting of the Gothic camp and their readiness for battle, extra combat training and formation drills were taking place in torchlight all across the camp. The grin faded from his face.

Every soul within these walls was readying to face the Viper's wrath.

It was the dead of night and Pavo's mind would not rest. He shuffled from his cot to drink from his water skin, then headed for the tent flap. He stopped for a moment to glance back into the tent, casting a jealous eye over the snoring soldiers – Sura being the worst offender in Quadratus' absence – then he slipped outside into the night. It would not be long until dawn, he realised, gazing at the waxing moon. The air was fresh and the cricket song was in full flow. He breathed deeply and slowly, in through his nostrils, holding the breath in his lungs for a count of four and then exhaling through his lips, hoping the exercise would calm the circus of angst in his mind. And it did, momentarily, until he remembered that it was Draga who had taught him the technique. He shook the thought away with a low growl.

He saw big Zosimus, Felix and Quadratus sitting around one campfire, the three murmuring in conversation whilst absently toasting bread in the flames. Rest had clearly evaded them too.

'Can't sleep, soldier?' A familiar voice spoke from the shadows.

Pavo turned to see Gallus. The tribunus was standing, looking up at the moon. His gaunt features were semi-illuminated, and one hand grappled a small, carved wooden idol of Mithras. 'Not a wink, sir.'

Gallus issued a dry chuckle and turned his gaze from the moon to Pavo. 'I don't think I've ever slept when danger has been this close.'

Pavo nodded in silence, recalling the rumours from some of the legionaries. They reckoned that Gallus slept rarely – regardless of the presence of danger – plagued by nightmares that would see him waken, screaming, calling some woman's name. He thought of his own recurring, tortured dream of his father, and the lost truth that was surely buried with Senator Tarquitius' ashes in the ruins inside Marcianople. They each had their own troubles, he realised, but one was common to them both.

'You're still troubled by him, aren't you? Salvian, Draga, the Viper,' Gallus asked as if reaching the same conclusion.

Pavo nodded. 'Aye, troubled and ashamed. I once thought I was a sound judge of character.'

Gallus turned to him with sadness in his eyes. 'That creature fooled us all, Pavo. And not just the legions; it seems he has dined and dealt with the empire's finest for years, and all of them saw only a charismatic man and a fine speaker,' he snorted at this. 'Traianus says some of the senators who have visited the camp in recent weeks swear blind that he was a passionate Roman.'

'Then I'll perhaps find room in my thoughts to pity them, either once this is all over, or when I'm walking in Elysium,' Pavo muttered.

Gallus cocked an eyebrow. 'A year in the ranks has dried you to the core, I see.'

'Aye,' Pavo replied, thumbing his phalera medallion, thinking of the grizzled Crito, 'another hardened veteran with a sorry tale to tell.'

Gallus nodded to the fire, where Zosimus was now mid-flow through some tale of the time he caught his wife's brother having a romantic evening with a goat. 'I'll be glad to have them in the ranks beside me, when it comes to it.'

Pavo looked over to the veteran legionaries, grinning as the sordid detail poured forth from Zosimus' lips. The big centurion's eyes were bulging, his tongue poking out as he made a pelvic thrusting gesture and grappled at an imaginary goat. Quadratus roared in laughter at this while Felix winced.

'They were like you and Sura when I first soldiered with them; reckless, all-too-eager, seemingly never happy unless mired in trouble.' Gallus hesitated momentarily. 'So I thank Mithras you pair will be on my side as well.'

Pavo turned to him, emotion swirling in his chest. 'And I thank him that you'll be leading us, sir,' he replied after a pause. Gallus cocked an eyebrow at this, but Pavo was sure that through the shadows he could make out a hint of a smile on the tribunus' lips.

'Anyway, I came here to find you.'

'Sir?'

'You may be interested to know that a refugee arrived at the camp, not long after you returned from scouting,' Gallus continued. 'He claims to have been released by the Goths.' Gallus' features hardened. 'Senator Tarquitius has returned to us, Pavo.'

Pavo's stomach fell away. 'He's alive?'

'He must have been suckling on Fortuna's tits; it seems he can either cheat death . . . or he's still tangled in all of this.'

Pavo's gaze darted across the ground before him. For all Tarquitius' failings, the news of his survival was like a sweet cordial. The key to the riddle of his father was not lost after all. He looked up to Gallus. 'But he was . . . *is* in league with Draga and Ivo, I'm sure of it. He's the one who delivered the forged scroll, he's the one who let the Viper in to Marcianople.'

Gallus nodded. 'Of that, no doubt remains. A litany of evidence is piled up against him; remnants of the garrison of Sardica have claimed he tried to bribe them into deserting the city's defences. And a scroll he sent to Athanaric tells of what he had planned after that. He reeks of treachery. That's why he is in chains right now, as we speak.'

'Then surely he will be executed?' Pavo frowned.

'I assure you, he will be. But not yet.' Gallus looked to him, searching Pavo's eyes, then glancing to the phalera. 'I asked for a stay of execution; I believe you and he have unfinished business?'

Pavo's heart swelled. 'We do.'

Gallus nodded to him. 'Then finish that business tonight. Whatever happens, happens.'

Pavo nodded, the blood thundering in his veins. 'Yes, sir!'

Pavo crept through the cluster of contubernium tents, then crouched as he reached the centre of the camp. The tent up ahead, a stone's throw from the principia, was guarded by two legionaries. Inside he would find Tarquitius. *And the bastard deserves everything he gets,* Pavo affirmed, teeth gritting, his fingers flexing on his spatha hilt.

He took a deep breath, slipped the spatha under his tunic, then stood tall and approached the tent.

'Ave,' he greeted the two shadowy legionaries tentatively.

The smaller of the two legionaries stepped forward. It was Optio Avitus – just as Gallus had arranged.

'Ave, Pavo,' Avitus replied, the light falling on his stony features.

Pavo saw the weary sadness in the little optio's eyes – a similar look to that Gallus wore only moments ago – and wondered if troubled thoughts were endemic within the camp. The difference was that Pavo was almost certain that he knew what Avitus' troubles were. Felicia's words rang in his mind. *Find the truth for me, Pavo, I beg of you.* But now was not the time to broach the subject.

He nodded to Avitus. 'Gallus said you'd be expecting me?'

'Aye,' Avitus replied, then nodded to the wide-eyed legionary who stood guard with him. 'Noster, go to the north gate and wait by the watchtower.'

'Sir?' Noster replied, frowning.

'That's an order,' Avitus replied evenly.

As the young legionary trudged off, Pavo nodded to Avitus and then made to duck inside the tent. But the optio grappled his bicep, pulling him back.

Pavo frowned, his heart racing, locked in a gaze with the optio.

'You're a good lad, Pavo,' he said, his eyes moistening. 'Be aware that what you do in there tonight will live with you forever.'

Pavo's gaze drifted away to the tent flap and then back to Avitus. He nodded slowly and in silence. With that, Avitus released his grip and followed Noster to the north gate.

Pavo turned to the tent and entered. Inside it was warm, silent and bathed in shadows. A shape sat on a bench at the far end. In the gloom, Pavo saw a haggard, drawn, sagging caricature of the man who had once been his master.

Tarquitius was lost in a muttering monologue, his eyes distant. 'I've dined at the imperial palace. I've advised the emperor in matters military and civilian.' He pinched his thumb and forefinger together. 'I've had the empire's fate in my grasp, like an insect. But still I was bested by him. The man is a *demon!*'

Pavo stood before the senator, then pulled his spatha from his tunic. At this, the senator looked up as if awakening from a deep sleep.

'Pavo?' Tarquitius spoke softly. Then his gaze fell on the spatha and his eyes bulged. 'Pavo!' he squealed.

Pavo clamped his palm over the senator's mouth, then with his free hand he hefted the sword overhead. He fixed his gaze on the terrified eyes of Tarquitius, then brought the blade smashing down.

All was silent, and then the cleaved chains slithered from the bench, and Tarquitius held up his hands, mouth agape. 'You've freed me?'

'Ironic, isn't it?' Pavo sneered. 'But do not get any ideas – I will slice out your heart if you do not do exactly as I say. Now, walk with me!'

Pavo bundled the emaciated figure from the tent. Then he drove him on with the tip of the spatha towards the north wall of the camp, picking a path of shadows amongst the tents. They came to a halt by a patch of darkened ground near the palisade. Pavo glanced around; they were out of sight of each of the nearest watchtowers. This would be perfect, he affirmed.

'Now,' Pavo said, steadying himself, squaring his shoulders, 'tell me of my father.'

Tarquitius' eyes widened, and he shook his head regretfully, the slack skin of his jowls wobbling. 'I will die if I do.'

Pavo brought the spatha to rest against the senator's neck, ready to swipe. 'You will *certainly* die if you do not – by my blade here and now or by execution for your treachery in a matter of days.'

'Then I am to die . . . ' he muttered, his gaze growing distant again.

'No, there is another option.' Pavo clapped his hands three times. From the darkness, Sura appeared, stony-faced. He led a chestnut gelding by its tether over to the pair, then disappeared again, leaving the beast. As the senator's brow wrinkled in confusion, Pavo continued. 'The guards have been told to expect that a lone rider will be leaving the camp tonight,' he held out the reins to Tarquitius. 'Tell me and you live.'

Tarquitius' face creased in panic. 'But Salvian . . . Draga swore that if I told you, he would kill me. He sees everything, hears everything . . . ' The senator shot glances in every direction, eyes bulging.

Pavo's breaths came short and shallow at this, the words twisting like a dagger in his heart. 'The Viper played you, just like he played me . . . just like he led the whole empire and all of the Gothic tribes into this, like gladiators being led to a death bout.' He grappled the spatha with both hands and fixed the senator with a dark glare. 'Now, do you want to die?'

Tarquitius looked all around him, then to the ground. His shoulders slumped. 'I have torn off more meat than I can chew in these last months.' Then he looked up to Pavo. 'Does it interest you to know that I despise myself, boy? Does it?' His voice was cracking.

In that instant, Pavo felt a twinge of pity for this man, then steeled himself. 'Through all those years I spent in your slave cellar, I saw a man soured with political ambition, devoid of charity or empathy. A man who revelled in the torment of his slaves. Do not talk to me of remorse, Senator. Tell me of my father!'

Tarquitius' gaze grew distant, and he nodded.

Pavo's heart pounded.

'That day, at the slave market, when I bought you. You remember the crone who accosted me?'

Pavo nodded, eyes narrowed. He had never forgotten the white-haired old lady, wraith-like in appearance, who had given him the phalera. He clasped one hand to the piece.

'She foretold that if I harmed you in any way, terrible things would happen to me,' he shook his head, trembling. 'But I did not harm you,' he

347

asserted, his jaw jutting out in defiance. 'Yes, you lived a hard life, but never once did I raise my hand to you.'

'No, you left that to your bull of a slavemaster,' Pavo spat, jabbing the spatha point into Tarquitius' neck. 'Now, what of my father?'

Tarquitius glanced to the phalera. 'The answer is in your hands, Pavo.' He glanced to the eastern horizon. 'She said that the razing of Bezabde was not a mindless slaughter. Yes, the walls were toppled and blood was spilled until the streets were stained red. But she said that in the sands of the east . . . ' the senator's words trailed off, a frown forming on his brow as he peered past Pavo's shoulder, over the northern palisade. Then his jaw dropped.

'Senator?' Pavo frowned.

A hissing cut through the night air, followed by a sickening thud. At once, Pavo's face was showered with hot blood. He staggered back, blinking, as Tarquitius' eyes bulged, an arrow jutting from his mouth, the shaft still quivering. For a heartbeat, Tarquitius gazed at Pavo in terror. Then the senator's eyes rolled in his head and he slumped to the ground, limbs twitching.

'No!' Pavo gasped, dropping his sword, slumping to his knees, rolling the senator onto his back. But the life was gone from him.

Pavo leapt to standing and swept his gaze along the northern palisade. All seemed empty.

But then, in the darkness, the shadows rippled. Pavo saw a figure, crouching like a bird of prey on the edge of the palisade. Then the figure dropped from its perch.

Pavo rushed to the wall and leapt up. Outside, the figure had leapt onto the saddle of a Gothic mount, bow in hand. Pavo glared at the dark green cloak and hood and the shadows where the face should have been. His whole body shook as a sliver of moonlight revealed Draga's chilling half-smile, before the Viper turned to gallop back into the night.

Cries of alarm broke out as the sentries noticed the fleeing rider.

A swarm of thoughts buzzed through Pavo's mind, growing louder until he thought his skull would burst. Then one thought barged to the fore.

Kill him!

Pavo's blood boiled as he leapt onto the gelding and yelled. 'Ya!'

The sentries on the gate relented at last and opened the gates when Pavo revealed that a senator had been slain and that the killer was outside the walls. Optio Avitus' face had greyed as he heard Pavo announce this. But Pavo had no time for explanations. He had galloped from the fort and out into the gloom of the night, lowered in his saddle, teeth gritted. He had followed the Viper for miles as the green-cloak fled over the rise, across the wide plain, past the willows and to the first of the foothills.

He reached the foot of the nearest hill before he realised he was wearing only a tunic and carried no weapons. *Then I'll tear out his throat with my hands,* he swore, seeing the cloak disappear over the peak of the hill. He heeled his gelding, praying it could keep the pace.

He crested the hill and then stopped. The foothills ahead were bare and devoid of movement, Draga nowhere to be seen. He slid from the saddle and slumped to his knees, thumping a fist into the earth, biting back the urge to weep as the phalera dangled from his neck like a lead weight.

'You should know by now that I will always be one step ahead of you, Roman,' a voice spoke. 'I lurk in every shadow; I hear your every thought.'

Pavo's blood froze as he looked up. Draga had emerged from the darkness into the moonlight.

Rage washed through his veins and he launched himself forward with a roar. But, with a series of thuds, the ground before him was peppered with arrows and he froze. From the darkness, a band of chosen archers emerged, their next arrows nocked to their bows, trained this time on his chest. Ivo stood with them, the moonlight glinting in the milky matter of his ruined eye.

Draga cocked his head to one side, his expression sincere. 'You appear to be upset by Tarquitius' slaying? The senator had to die. It was just a matter of when.'

'He was about to tell me everything!' Pavo seethed, then his face fell as he saw Draga's self-congratulatory grin. 'You knew, didn't you? You knew he would be executed if he came back to the Roman camp. You knew I would try to save him. You wanted him to die when the truth was on his lips!'

Draga nodded. 'You're a sharp thinker, but you had to be taught a lesson. Just as your empire slew my father, I will slay every Roman in my path. And, just as you took your woman from my camp, I took the truth from your grasp. Learn your lesson well, legionary.'

With that, Draga's eyes sparkled and he lifted a hand, one finger extended. 'Now, it is time to seize my destiny.' With that, he dropped the finger.

At this, the twenty archers reloaded their bows with pitch-soaked arrows, and one appeared carrying a torch, igniting the missiles. They aimed skywards and loosed, and Pavo watched the missiles streak up across the navy sky. The earth under his feet rumbled, and dancing firelight lit up the nearest hillsides to the north.

Pavo knew what was coming over those hills; the Gothic horde was on the march and they would reach the Roman camp at dawn. Despite this, he buried his fear. He spoke steadily, fixing his gaze on Draga. 'In these past weeks I have wondered; is your heart entirely black? You taught me many things; good-hearted advice that served me well. But the biggest lesson is one I fear you have not learned yourself.' Pavo stabbed a finger to the ground. 'Many of *your* people will die tomorrow so you can have your revenge,' Pavo spoke steadily, 'yet you can't see that their blood will be on your hands, can you?'

The hills flickered to life as the first waves of the Gothic army crested them; a wall of torchlight and glinting helms, speartips, arrowtips and armour. Then the hills either side were awash with cavalry. Far more numerous than the Roman force. Draga's face curled into a cool grin as the archers nocked their next arrows and took aim at Pavo. 'The blood-letting was begun by your empire long, long ago, legionary. Ever since they slew my father and sunk a blade into my shoulder. Now, your kind will reap what they sowed that day, and the Viper's destiny will be realised. The tribes are united. The conquest of the empire is about to begin!'

Pavo braced himself, glancing around the archers, waiting on the order to be given. Twenty arrowheads would tear into his unarmoured body. Then, perhaps, he might meet Father in the afterlife.

But Draga extended a finger to Pavo's chestnut gelding, like a master dismissing a dog. 'Ride, legionary, go back to your legions. I give you this as our parting gift; one last dawn to make peace with your gods.'

Pavo stumbled backwards, then hauled himself onto the saddle. He heeled the mount round, but his gaze was fixed on Draga, who clenched a fist and sneered;

'By dusk tomorrow, your army will be carrion and we will tread through your corpses, Traianus' head mounted on our banner as we march to the south. To Constantinople!'

At this, Ivo lifted his longsword and beat it against his shield, then cried out. As one, the Gothic army roared out in unison.

Pavo's heart hammered. He heeled his mount into a turn and then a breakneck gallop back to the Roman camp, Draga's cold laughter ringing in the air behind him.

Atop the camp watchtower, Avitus swigged his soured and watered wine, eyeing the northern horizon carefully. Then he gazed through the mouth of the skin again.

'Found anything in there yet, sir?' The young legionary, Noster, chirped.

Avitus shot him a foul glare. 'What is it with you? Keep your eyes to the north, and your tongue still.'

At this, Noster dropped his smile and fell into a nervous silence.

Avitus screwed up his eyes and sighed; the time for bitterness was past. He had hoped that perhaps the lad Pavo might not slay the senator tonight. But then the lad had been seen fleeing the camp, leaving a commotion in his wake as the senator's body was discovered. It seemed any man was capable of dark deeds. 'Here, have a drink,' he handed the skin to the youngster. 'I didn't mean to bite your head off.'

'Thanks,' Noster nodded, then cautiously took a swig. 'Are you worried about the Goths – that they will come for us tonight?'

Avitus shook his head with a wry grin, his mind once again flitting with images of his past, each one eroding his soul. 'In these last days, I've been more worried that they would not come for us, lad.' Avitus glanced to the youngster.

Noster's face wrinkled in confusion.

'Ach, ignore me and my maudlin talk.' Avitus accepted the wineskin again. He made to take a swig when something caught his eye, on the ridge to the north. A rider was approaching at speed.

Avitus leaned forward. It was Pavo. Good lad, he thought, you're doing the right thing. Don't run from your problems.

But then Avitus noticed an orange glow on the northern horizon, behind Pavo. 'Dawn comes from the east, does it not?' he said to Noster, whose gaze was also fixed on the glow.

'Last time I checked, aye.' Noster replied, gulping.

Then Avitus heard Pavo's distant cries, saw his eyes wide with urgency, his brow furrowed, his arms waving. He threw down the wineskin and craned his neck from the watchtower. Now he could hear it, from the north; a distant din of rippling iron and thundering hooves.

Then, as Pavo raced to the north gate, his cries became clear. 'The Goths are coming!'

Noster fumbled for the buccina and Avitus' jaw fell open. 'Pavo! What in Hades did you do out there?'

Buccinas sang urgent notes and at once, the camp was awash with activity as dawn breached the land. Legionaries spilled from their tents, dousing fires, snatching up helmets, armour and weapons. Archers scuttled to the practice range, taking up quivers. Stablehands dropped brushes and buckets and began frantically tying saddles to horses. Mounted officers steered their beasts through the organised chaos, barking orders, rousing their men with words of encouragement.

At the heart of the square of XI Claudia tents, Pavo fumbled to pull on his mail vest over his linen tunic, then wrapped his swordbelt around his waist and pulled on his intercisa helmet. No time for polishing, no time for checking. The Goths were on the march.

'Pray to Mithras we can intercept them on the plain,' Sura muttered as he hefted up his shield and spear, rolling his head on his shoulders to loosen the tension in his neck.

Pavo looked to his friend, still bleary-eyed from sleep. 'Their numbers have swollen since they have been in the mountains,' he said in a hushed voice, keen not to panic the sea of recruits who readied themselves nearby.

'Good, I've got a bone to pick with these bastards,' Sura said with a shrug, barely disguising a nervous twitch in his cheek. 'The more, the better!'

At this, the nearest of the recruits broke out in a nervous chuckle.

Centurion Quadratus strode past, picking up on the mood, Optio Avitus by his side, as always. 'That's it, you mutts!' Quadratus roared. 'Let's get every blade ready, every dart in place. I've only had you in my ranks for what, weeks? And you're easily the best bunch of runts I've ever led!'

At this, the recruits fell silent, until the belly of one gurgled like a clearing drain.

Quadratus pulled a look of mock indignation. 'Mithras' sake, soldier! You'll get your chance to eat your fill of hardtack when we're on the march!' Then he clenched a fist, his bottom lip curling. 'Then, when we've shown the whoresons out there the way to Hades, we'll be feasting on pheasant and garum dates!'

The recruits erupted in a cheer at this.

Pavo grinned at his centurion as the big Gaul came closer. 'Glad to be marching with you today, sir.'

Quadratus smoothed his moustache. 'Aye, I'd be glad to have you with me too. But you're with Centurion Zosimus today.'

'Sir?' Pavo frowned.

'He asked for you and,' Quadratus turned to nod at Sura with a hint of a wicked grin, '*that mental bastard.*'

'Why?' Sura asked when his scowl had faded.

'Same as always, we need to seed the centuries with veterans.'

Sura and Pavo looked back blankly.

Quadratus glared at them. 'That means you two!'

Pavo looked to Sura and Sura gawped back.

Then Pavo hefted his ruby and gold shield and spear in one hand and saluted with the other. 'May Mithras be with you, sir, out there.'

Then he turned his salute to Avitus as well. For an instant, the pair's eyes met. He remembered Felicia's last words. *Find the truth, Pavo, I beg of you.*

He moved in close to the veteran, readying to ask the question.

But Avitus spoke first. 'I knew you didn't have it in you to kill the senator, Pavo. You're a good lad.' His words were solemn, almost sorrowful.

'And that's why I must ask you this, sir.' Pavo steeled himself, leaning in to the optio's ear. 'I have heard grim rumour that you are . . . were a speculatore. Is it true?'

Avitus' face fell and his gaze grew distant. Finally, he replied. 'I've waited a long time to speak with someone, Pavo. But first, let today bring what it must. Then we can talk.'

Pavo clasped his forearm to Avitus', the pair exchanging a firm nod.

With that, they parted, then Pavo followed Sura in a jog through the assembling centuries. All around them, the readied centuries streamed from the north gate of the camp. Outside, they formed up before the rise that led to the plain and Ad Salices, The Town by the Willows. Traianus cantered around them as they spilled from the camp, urging the men to keep a hundred feet between cohorts and to present a wide front.

Then Pavo and Sura heard Zosimus' gruff commands echo over the clattering of iron and drumming of boots. Just ahead, the big Thracian was barking his century into line, readying to join the exodus.

'Sir!' Pavo barked. 'Reporting for duty.'

Zosimus turned to him, his anvil jaw swelling as he grinned like a torturer receiving new subjects. 'Ah, about bloody time!'

'Which rank, sir?' Sura asked, glancing to the century as it gradually formed into an iron square, walled with ruby and gold shields and roofed with fin-topped intercisa helmets and speartips. But all of the men in the square bore the raw, fearful expressions of recruits.

'First rank, you're heading up the first file.'

Sura raised his eyebrows. 'But that's where the *tesserarius* stands?'

'Aye, it is – second only to the optio,' Zosimus replied with a sardonic smile. 'You're a clever bugger, aren't you?'

Sura cast a disbelieving glance to Pavo as he took his place at the front-right of the square. Then he wasted no time in barking his file into a tighter line.

Pavo looked to Zosimus. 'And me?'

Zosimus' face was sincere, and he held Pavo's gaze. 'Right where you are, Optio. I've never replaced Paulus since those whoresons slit his throat in Dardor.'

Pavo's heart swelled and his skin rippled with pride, disbelief and . . . that old trickle of icy fear. Could he lead these men as Zosimus' second in command? These men were raw, young, and so much depended on this battle.

'You're sure I'm ready, sir?' He spoke in a whisper, frowning.

Zosimus' top lip curled in distaste, and he leaned in to Pavo's ear. 'Knock that rubbish out of your skull, lad. Do you think I was ready? I nearly soiled my tunic when I was made centurion. Gallus promoted me with one line of advice: *lead as you wish to be led*. And Gallus has backed your promotion.'

Pavo glanced past the centurion, to the centre of the XI Claudia area, where Gallus stood. The tribunus' expression was ice cold as he surveyed the readying legion. Then he turned his gaze on Pavo, and gave him the faintest of nods. Pavo's thoughts swirled. Then he looked into the Zosimus' eyes. 'But, sir, when Lupicinus put me at the head of a vexillatio, I struggled . . . '

Zosimus cut him off, gripping him by the shoulders. 'Do you know what clinched it – for me and for Gallus?'

Pavo frowned, shaking his head.

'Crito; when we were in the dell, not long after you had taken down the bridge over the Beli Lom. He went to Gallus and recommended you. Said you were one of the finest men he had ever marched with.' Zosimus held his stunned gaze for a few heartbeats, then stepped away and roared to the century. 'Ready to move out!'

Pavo's skin rippled as he stared into the space Zosimus had stood. Crito; the veteran who had regarded him like an unwashed latrine for so long; the embodiment of his own self-doubt. Something had changed in the man in those last few weeks before he was slain. Perhaps it was the loss of his family at Marcianople; perhaps it was the realisation that they were all in it together at that desperate skirmish at the bridge. Whatever the reason was, this revelation felt like honey in Pavo's veins. Like sand trickling from a timer, his self-doubt drained away, leaving only pride. The phalera juddered on his chest as his heart hammered.

He turned to the century and filled his lungs, drew his spatha then rapped it on his shield boss.

'You heard the centurion. Pull together, stand tall, and . . . move out!'

Chapter 24

The early morning heat prickled on Pavo's skin and the scent of spring honeysuckle and wild rapeseed danced on the warm air. He looked east, across the verdant plain, his gaze hanging on the willow thicket shimmering in the heat haze over there. The town of Ad Salices lay nestled in the lacy shade offered by the trees. For a heartbeat, he could hear only the chirruping cicada song and it felt like an ordinary day, his armour momentarily weightless. Until he saw the trail of discarded belongings scattered outside the deserted village. Until he heard the barking officers and the rippling of iron beside him and all along the Roman lines that hemmed the southern edge of the plain. Until he turned his head forwards again, and beheld the massive Gothic horde that stained the northern end of the plain, their jagged cries and chanting now drowning the cicada song. Until the screech of a vulture split the air, and the sky began to darken with seemingly prescient carrion birds.

Swatting at a persistent mayfly, he eyed the army they were to face. Fritigern's ranks had swollen to over twenty thousand warriors. To a man, they were hungry for imperial blood, readied under a collection of Chi-Rho standards and the old pagan banners of the sapphire hawk and the emerald boar. *And all of them march unwittingly under the banner of the Viper,* he grimaced.

Over twelve thousand spearmen formed the tightly-packed Gothic centre. These warriors were tall and broad, blonde locks braided and knotted, weapons readied, eyeing the central party of their leaders eagerly; Fritigern and Ivo, with Draga lurking behind. Absurdly, while most of the Goths wore their red leather armour and conical helmets, many now wore Roman mail and scale vests and intercisa helmets, having plundered the legionary fabricae workhouses across Moesia.

Behind their deep and wide ranks of spearmen, a mass of some three thousand chosen archers lined the rise of the first of the foothills. Their quivers were packed, their fingers flexing in impatience to take advantage of this excellent elevation over the plain. Behind the archers, a thick ring of Gothic wagons plugged the entrance into the foothills and the path into the towering Haemus Mountains. The wagons formed a rudimentary barricade, sheltering the Gothic women, children and elderly, and doubtless a large supply of fresh weapons and armour. Bookending the Gothic ranks were two wings of cavalry, each numbering some two thousand. The front ranks of each wing wore full-face helmets like iron wolves, eyeing their prey across the plain.

'More's the better!' Centurion Zosimus grumbled by his side.

Pavo pulled a wry grin at this, then glanced over his shoulder at his century and then across the Roman lines that stretched out to his right.

The rear of the Roman army was finally settling into formation. Now, five legions – nearly eight thousand men – were readied; the limitanei wore iron-finned intercisa helms and mail shirts over white tunics, and they grappled spears and the ever-trusty spathas. Each of them gripped painted oval shields with three plumbatae clipped onto the inside. The comitatenses were even more finely armoured, wearing glistening scale vests, and additionally equipped with *lancea* javelins. Each man's skin was bathed in sweat, fingers flexing on weapons. Some glared at their enemy, chests heaving in fear and battle-lust. Others stood, silent, eyes closed in prayer, trying to block out the incessant Gothic chanting and rapping of weapons on shields.

The legions' flanks were protected by the Roman cavalry; two compact wedges of cataphractii and two cobbled-together alae of equites and equites sagitarii. Barely two thousand all-told. At the head of the Roman line was a thin screen of skirmishers: a cohort of sagittarii foot archers who wore ruby cloaks, mail shirts over their tunics and helmets with slim iron nose-guards; a few hundred *funditores* who were already strapping up their wrists and stretching their limbs and their slings; and a cohort of auxilliaries, clutching light javelins, swords and daggers, but unarmoured bar the few who clutched battered shields or helmets. Some eleven thousand men all told were to stand in opposition to the wall of Goths across the plain.

Two comitatenses legions – the IV Italica and the II Armeniaca – formed the Roman centre, while the II Isauria formed the prestigious right wing. Meanwhile, the limitanei of the I Adiutrix formed the inner left. And so it was left to the XI Claudia – each of the three cohorts less than half-strength, patched together with recruits and the tattered remains of the other limitanei legions that had strayed into the Roman camp – to form the far left of the Roman line. This was a position long-held as unlucky and doomed to break if the line was to come under too much pressure. Their job was to refuse the flank and prevent this eventuality at all costs.

And what a soldier to see that job through, Pavo affirmed, glancing a handful of paces to his right. There, Tribunus Gallus stood tall at the head of the XI Claudia. The legion aquilifer stood next to him in nervous silence, clutching the silver eagle standard, the ruby bull banner hanging motionless in the muggy, still air.

Pavo shuffled, rolling his head to double-check his intercisa helmet was firmly secured. Then he readjusted his mail vest, reaffirmed his grip on his shield and spear, then corrected his posture. His linen tunic was slick with sweat and still he couldn't brush away the nagging of his full bladder. He cursed under his breath.

'Every bloody time, eh?' Sura grumbled, just behind him, biting his lower lip and jostling on the balls of his feet.

'Reminds me I'm alive,' Pavo replied over his shoulder, gruffly. 'Long may it continue.'

'Not too long though,' Sura replied, squinting up at the sun, 'or we might cook out here.'

'The Goths need to move first if we are to have any chance,' Pavo replied, nodding to the far end of the Roman line. 'He's biding his time.'

There, heading up the Roman right, Traianus was dressed in full battle armour, crested with a purple plume, mounted on an equally well-armoured stallion. He was engaged in frantic discussion with Tribunus Profuturus and the other comitatenses tribuni. Traianus seemed to be insisting that they wait, despite the growing heat and despite some of the tribuni calling for the legions to make the first strike.

Pavo heard the nervous grumblings all along the ranks behind him. Standing in full armour in the searing sun was doing little to aid morale, especially when the Goths were in full song, their ululations and guttural chanting echoing across the plain. But he also saw the Gothic advantage in numbers, and that their archers held the high ground. There would be no victory by an early attack or by brute force today. Strategy would be the key. They would have to wait. Pavo noticed the magister militum gazed to the western horizon as his tribuni appealed to him for action. His brow furrowed. *Mithras tell me he has a plan!*

Then, young Noster spoke out from behind him, his voice hoarse. 'Sir, permission to down helmets and weapons and take on water?'

Centurion Zosimus twisted round at this, his incredulous expression glistening with sweat. 'You just keep your hand on your sword hilt and your shield on your arm!' The big Thracian shouted over the Gothic song.

But then, suddenly, the Gothic chorus stopped dead. All Roman eyes snapped forward. There, beside Fritigern, Ivo held his arms aloft, like a bird readying to soar. All Gothic heads were turned to him. Then, after revelling in the silence for a few heartbeats, the giant warrior took to rallying the Gothic army with a booming anti-Roman tirade. His every exclamation was met with a sharp, raucous cheer that shook the land, amplified by the foothills cupping their ranks and the Haemus mountains behind them. Then the grizzled warrior drew his sword and levelled it across the plain, tip pointing directly at the Roman centre. As one, the Gothic army took to battering their spears and swords on their shields, and threw forth a baritone roar that seemed neverending.

Pavo clutched the phalera through his mail vest and tried to block out the doubt that raced through his heart. But it was no use, morale was already disintegrating. The silence across the Roman lines was painful. He looked across the plain; at the centre of the Gothic line, Fritigern and Ivo were mounted at the fore. 'Fools!' He cried over the cacophony of the Gothic chorus, seeing the mounted Draga lurking behind the pair. 'They don't even know they've been led here, like cattle, to fight the Viper's war.'

At this, Zosimus scowled at him. More, Gallus also turned, glaring at him. Then a sparkle appeared in the tribunus' eyes.

With that, Gallus turned to the legion. 'Aye, as have we,' he boomed in response. 'You've all heard the rumours about the Viper, the one man who will bring all Gutthiuda crashing down upon the empire? A master of strategy, a shade, a *demon* . . . I've heard it all.'

The men of the front ranks frowned at this.

'Well that very whoreson stands just over a plumbata's throw across the grass.' Gallus' chest grew as he sucked in a breath and clutched the eagle standard from the aquilifer. 'He'll bleed like any man, and if we fight like the lions we are, then he'll bleed his last today! So are we here today to lie down before his mighty army? Are we?' Gallus shook his head briskly, a manic sparkle in his eyes. 'I am not!'

Pavo sensed the mood change at that moment.

Gallus ripped the spatha from his scabbard and held it aloft, the standard held high in the other hand. 'I have fought these whoresons on the plains, in the forests, in the mire and on the waves for longer than I care to remember. For what? Just to have them devour my corpse on this day, on this land, *our* land? I don't think so!' His words seemed to be piercing the Gothic chant, and the adjacent I Adiutrix and nearby IV Italica had all picked up on the rousing homily. Pavo could see heads being turned in the ranks of the II Armeniaca and II Isauria as well, with expressions of bemusement touched with hope.

Then, Gallus stabbed his spatha into the ground, and pumped the standard towards the sky.

'Remember we are the XI Claudia *Pia Fidelis*, men. The name was bestowed upon us for our loyalty and determination to stand firm when all seemed lost. Fight for your brothers by your side, men; fight for your people; *fight for your empire!*'

At once, the XI Claudia erupted in a roar that swept across the Roman ranks like wildfire, and then out across the plain like the first wave of intent. The Gothic chant notably hushed at this, albeit briefly. Pavo saw Traianus look up in astonishment, then cock an eyebrow in thanks to Gallus. Then his heart bristled with pride as Gallus in turn looked to him, eyes narrowed, and gave him that ice-cold look and a hint of a nod.

But within moments, the Gothic chant grew again to match the Roman resurgence. At this, Traianus lifted his huge, silver eagle banner, and the front-line comitatenses with him roused the Roman lines into an even louder chorus. Then all the roaring was drowned out by the low wailing of Gothic war horns.

Fritigern and Ivo waved the Gothic centre forward.

In response, the Roman buccinators raised their instruments to their lips, and replied with a near-deafening chorus of higher pitched notes, the age-old song of the empire going to war.

The standards across the Roman line were raised. Zosimus braced, ready to move, then hissed to Pavo. 'This is it! Let's keep the lads in formation at all costs.'

Pavo nodded, gritting his teeth. Then he turned to Sura. 'Ready?' He roared.

'Ready!' Sura grimaced.

As one, the Roman legions marched forward. The sagittarii, funditores and auxiliaries ran out ahead in loose formation. They loosed stones, arrows and javelins first to test range, then to make the first kills of the day as the foremost Goths were punched back from their charge by the hail. Hundreds of the blonde warriors toppled, stones embedded in skulls, arrows tearing out throats and javelins bursting through chests. But within a few heartbeats, the Gothic chosen archers packing the banking of the foothills had found their range with which to retaliate. Arrows darkened the sky and the Roman skirmishers up ahead fell in swathes, screaming, crimson blood jetting from their arrow wounds. Only the armoured sagittarii stood firm, the bulk of the arrows dancing from their mail shirts and glancing from their helmets.

The plain before Pavo jostled as he kept pace with Zosimus, seeing one of the last of the slingers, only a few strides ahead, spin on the spot, an arrow through his eye. Then an auxilliary crumpled beside the slain slinger, three flights quivering in his chest.

'They're getting mauled!' Sura cried, beside him.

'They need to be pulled back or it'll be a slaughter!' Pavo yelled, darting a glance along to the standards and the buccinators.

Mercifully, a buccina cried out. The surviving skirmishers heard the series of notes and gratefully slipped back through the narrow gaps between the legionary cohorts to form up once more, out of range of the chosen archers.

It was now time for the legions to go to work.

'We're drawing into archer range!' Gallus cried back over his shoulder. 'Front ranks, ready *testudo*. Rear ranks - ready your bows, aim for the archers on the banking!'

As one, the XI Claudia entered the arrow storm at a slow, steady march, shields raised overhead and around the edges of each cohort. The three rearmost ranks crouched behind the cover afforded by the ranks before them and readied their bows.

Inside the testudo, the din of the missile hail drumming down on them was deafening. One arrowhead split the wooden layers of Pavo's shield, coming to rest inches from his nose. All around him, legionaries clutched at arrows that had slipped inside the shield roof, piercing throats or tearing thighs. One young legionary screamed in frustration as he tried in vain to hold up his shield, but the arrow in his bicep forced him to drop it, then one arrow knocked his helmet from his head and a second hammered through his skull. But the testudo held and at last the hail slowed just a fraction.

Gallus pounced on this hiatus. 'Rear ranks . . . loose!' He roared.

Pavo and the front ranks bunched closer together, seeing that the Gothic spearmen were less than a hundred strides away. At the same time, the rear three ranks of each of the limitanei cohorts stood tall and rippled to present a canopy of taut bows, arrows straining at strings. Snatching glances to either side of his shield, Pavo saw the faces of the onrushing Goths drop.

Legionaries did not carry bows. Until now.

With a twang and then a hiss, the Roman arrow hail sailed overhead and hammered down into the chosen archers, stood high on the banking. This presented a window of opportunity for the funditores, sagitarrii and auxiliaries to push up once more. They rushed forward and loosed their missiles from behind the Roman lines, felling swathes of the nearer Gothic spearmen. Pavo issued a silent prayer of thanks to Emperor Valens for his insistence on training the border legions in archery.

As the Roman hail slowed, Gallus seized on the moment. 'Now, ready plumbatae!'

Zosimus, Quadratus and Felix echoed the order along the cohorts of the XI Claudia, as did the tribuni and centurions of the other legions. As one, the five legionary blocks slowed to a halt within a handful of paces. Pavo unclipped one of his darts from behind his shield, then raised it in unison with those around him. He trained his sights on the snarling wall of Goths, racing for the Roman lines, now barely fifty paces away.

'Loose!'

The dart hail streaked up from the Roman lines and then plummeted into the densely packed Gothic spearmen, smashing faces, shattering limbs, tearing through red leather cuirasses and splitting ribcages. Like a wave breaking on a craggy beach, the Gothic charge was ripped asunder; men were punched back into those following them, blood and strips of flesh thrown up like a spray.

'And again, *again!*' Gallus roared, glancing to the Gothic chosen archers who were taking aim in retaliation.

Pavo unclipped his second dart from behind his shield and launched it. It shattered the cranium of one helmetless Goth, showering the men behind him in a grey wash. But the enemy charge faltered less this time; the second dart hail had been staggered, less accurate and lacking the punch of the first.

Only a few paces separated the two masses of infantry now. There would be no time for a third volley. He grappled his spear and dipped his brow, waiting on the order.

From the corner of his eye he could see Centurion Zosimus' face curl into a snarl.

The big Thracian filled his lungs; 'Brace!'

'Pull together!' Pavo cried out. He heard Sura echo the order, seeing his friend pull some of the raw recruits closer. 'Stay alongside your brothers and they will fight for you!' He roared, his voice cracking. Snarling, foaming, wild-eyed Goths returned the roar with added venom as they bounded the last few strides separating the two armies. Then he pushed his shoulders into Zosimus on his right and Sura on his left, the three locking shields in a tacit bond of brotherhood. Memories of battles past echoed through his mind as the crimson veil tinged his vision.

'For the empire!' Gallus bawled.

'For the empire!' The XI Claudia echoed in unison.

The two armies collided, and the plain reverberated with the smash of iron and the guttural cries of men. Blood sprayed up across the collision. Limbs and heads spun through the air. The first rank of Goths leapt into and over the shield wall in bloodlust and due to the sheer momentum of their charge, some landing within the first few ranks of Romans. There they wreaked havoc, spinning, scything their spears and swords around the packed legionaries before being hacked down in a spray of blood. The second rank of Goths smashed against the Roman shieldwall; some hacked down those legionaries before them, others ran straight onto legionary spears, then their bodies were raised and ripped asunder, spilling a crimson fog over the front lines before the cadavers were hurled back into the Gothic swell. But the Gothic numbers were telling, and their charge had been deadly. Legionaries all along the front ranks of the XI Claudia had simply vanished under the impact, their bodies trampled into a paste of crimson speckled with white bone.

Yet the centre of the XI Claudia held good. Pavo butted his shield out at the next Goth who came at him, winding the man and then jabbing his spear down and into the man's larynx. The Goth's eyes had not even dimmed before he was trampled by his own kin and the next Gothic warrior barged into the fray. Pavo grimaced as another arrow smacked from his helmet and punched into the eye of the legionary behind him. He ignored the warm eye-matter that soaked his neck and targeted the Gothic warrior to his right who was swinging his longsword down on Zosimus. Pavo dipped his shield momentarily and speared the Goth through the jaw. The Goth's arms fell limp, the longsword toppling to the ground. Pavo wrenched at his spear, and it finally came loose with a meaty clunk, complete with the Goth's jaw and tongue. Pavo shook the spear to rid it of the gory mass, but it was stuck fast.

Then Sura's voice pierced the air by his left side. 'Pavo, watch your flank!'

Pavo spun to his right; Centurion Zosimus had stumbled and exposed Pavo's right side. A Goth leapt at the fracture in the shieldwall, hacking down for Pavo's neck. He raised his spatha, roaring in defiance, knowing he was too late, waiting on the death blow. Instead, he was showered with blood and offal, as a young legionary lunged forward to fill the gap and rip open the oncoming Goth's belly with a spatha swipe. Pavo didn't even have time to nod his gratitude, when a spear punched through the lad's chest, throwing him back and pinning him to the earth.

Pavo roared and smashed his shield forward, hurling his spear at one Goth then ripping his spatha from his scabbard to stab another in the gut. He glanced around for his next foe, then realised he was standing forward of the line. He stepped back, once, twice, three times, but still the left flank was retracting. This felt wrong, Pavo realised; the XI Claudia and the I Adiutrix were being pressed back too fast – beyond the point of refusing a flank. Then a buccina wailed three times, and he heard a Roman voice call out over the tumult.

'Hold your ground! Refuse the flanks!'

Pavo's eyes widened; if they were pushed round past a right-angle with the Roman centre, then they were doomed. In between parries and shield butts, he snatched glances up and over the Gothic swell to understand what was happening. Then he saw it: the two Gothic cavalry wings had cantered around the flanks of the battle, readying for a charge on the Roman rear. Readying to dash the legionary line against the anvil of Gothic spearmen.

Mithras, save us! He cursed inwardly and ducked back down under the swipe of a Gothic axe. He glanced to Zosimus. 'Sir? We're collapsing in on ourselves.'

All around them, the men of the Claudia and the I Adiutrix stumbled back, lamenting the sight of the Gothic horsemen. In return, the riders grinned like demons as they moved at ease, eyeing their prey.

'Where is our bloody cavalry?' The big Thracian growled, snatching glances over his shoulder in between beheading one Goth then braining another. The cataphractii were stationary, some two hundred paces back. And now the Gothic cavalry had rounded on the rear left and rear right of the legions unopposed. They were readying to charge.

'All is not lost.' Gallus gasped over the din of battle, hacking at the speartip of one Goth and then ducking from the sword swipe of another, 'I persuaded the magister militum to prepare for this eventuality.'

'Sir?' Pavo panted.

Then a buccina cry split the air. Four clean notes. Pavo looked to Gallus; the tribunus seemed to be whispering some prayer of thanks. From across the plain, a cry of joy broke out from the Roman right flank. At once, the push of Gothic spearmen abated in uncertainty. Pavo looked to Sura, who mirrored his frown. The pair looked across the sea of bloodied and hugely depleted intercisa helmets, broken spears and fluttering eagle standards to see that the flimsy timber fence surrounding Ad Salices had been pushed to the ground. Behind the fence, twelve ballistae and another twelve onagers were aligned, loaded with bolts and boulders and manned by eager crews. More, the ballista at one end of the lineup was the hulking four-pronged device. The Gothic cavalry wing closing on the Roman right suddenly halted. They turned in their saddles, eyes bulging as they saw the weapons trained on them, realising their flank was exposed to the artillery.

An absurd silence hung over the field for but a heartbeat. Then, Traianus' cry from the distant right flank ended it.

'Loose! Tear them apart!'

With the groaning of timber and thick ropes snapping free of tension, a storm of bolts and rocks hurtled through the air and smashed into the Gothic cavalry by the Roman right. The impact was lethal; horses and riders were crushed like ants under the rocks, their bodies tossed across the plain, and those who avoided the rocks were punched from their mounts by the rapier-like bolts, some skewering three or more riders and knocking many more to the ground.

From the Gothic centre, war horns wailed to rally the riders. But, as some of the shattered wing scrambled back onto their mounts, those still mounted heeled their beasts in panic, trampling over their kin, stumbling over the slain.

'Again!' Traianus roared. The crews scurried around the devices, loading them and then twisting the winches to stretch and ready them once more.

Pavo felt a mix of joy and terror wash through his limbs; the right was secure, but the left was moments from being shattered. The Gothic charge on that side had only faltered temporarily on seeing their other wing smashed by the Roman artillery barrage. Now they had resumed their charge and were only a hundred strides away at most. The ground shook with their approach and a chorus of terrified moans broke out across the Roman ranks.

Then the buccinas sang out a series of notes that saw the Roman cavalry alae on the secure right flank burst into life. They hared to the left to join the alae there, doubling their strength. As one, the Roman cavalry then swept across the rear of the legionary lines and then smashed the charging Gothic cavalry wing in the midriff.

The cataphractii led the way, punching into the Gothic formation as a wedge and then driving deep into their midst. Their lances wreaked havoc as they sliced through to burst clear on the opposite side, then turned back to carve another path of destruction. All the while, the equites sagitarii wheeled in circles to the rear of the Gothic wing, showering the riders with arrows and covering the charge of the cataphractii.

The Gothic charge had been broken at the last.

Pinned down and enraged, the Gothic riders lost all formation and were forced to skirmish against the swooping cataphractii, but without any momentum of a charge, their mastery of mounted combat was blunted. The Gothic cavalry were feared by Roman citizens as expert cavalrymen, but these ironclad demons from the east were shredding them. And then a clutch of Roman equites, several hundred strong, galloped round to the rear of the Gothic infantry lines. There, they swept across the banking, scattering the chosen archers.

'God is with us!' One voice from the eastern comitatenses cried above the chaos.

'Mithras is with us!' Zosimus barked back with gusto.

At this, the Roman line roared in a joyous release, spared from slaughter by a tactical masterstroke. Pavo felt the press of the Gothic spearmen lift completely as they backed off, wary of the equites at their backs and conscious of the sudden cessation of archer support. He panted, limbs trembling. He wondered why the thundering in his heart was not abating. Then he saw that Draga was in discussion with Ivo, the pair mounted high above the jostling Gothic spearline. Ivo nodded, then turned and relayed Draga's suggestions to Fritigern as if they were his own. Fritigern nodded hurriedly then called for the war horns. The horns moaned across the plain, and the Gothic cavalry were rallied by this, breaking free of the cataphractii death trap on the Roman left and the artillery bombardment on the Roman right. Then, from behind the wagons by the foothills, a fresh wave of some two thousand Gothic cavalry poured from the valleys. They raced around to the Roman right to flank the artillery, and in moments they were upon the crews of the ballistae and onagers, hacking them down without mercy. With that, the artillery fell silent.

Pavo looked to Gallus, who looked back with the same wide-eyed look of realisation. The Gothic cavalry had pulled free of the Roman snares and now they were reforming on either flank of their spearmen. The artillery and Roman cavalry charge had merely wounded the Goths. Now they were enraged.

Only one option remained.

At the Roman centre, Traianus held his sword aloft, the tip pointing to the Gothic lines. 'Forward!' Traianus roared.

The buccinas sang out and the battered Roman army charged into the fray.

The late-afternoon sun baked the carpet of dead and tortured the living who fought on in the clouds of flies and flocks of carrion birds.

Pavo's body was numb as he stumbled from foe to foe. He did not hear the screaming now, seeing only the red wetness at the back of each opponent's throat. That and the pure whites of their eyes, stark against the ubiquitous crimson masks worn by all on the field. The formations had disintegrated and the battlefield was speckled randomly with pockets of Romans and Goths, fighting to the last.

Pavo slashed out at one Goth who ran at him, cutting the man from neck to belly. Then, gasping for breath, he stumbled over the tangle of bodies, sliding on a slick of blood to fall by the staring eyes of a dead cataphractus; the blood had dried on the gaping wound on the man's throat and his mount was cleaved to its core. The eastern riders and the artillery had been the difference that morning, but that seemed so long ago. Both forces

371

had been shattered since then, and now only a few riders remained, fighting on foot. And the skirmishers had all been felled bar the tight pocket of sagittarii who fought on with their swords and daggers near the wrecked remnants of the Roman artillery.

He staggered to his feet again, hearing only a faint hiss, the tumult of battle sounding dull and far away. Then, from the corner of his eye, he saw Quadratus, locked in combat with a pair of Goths. Beside the big centurion was Avitus. The little optio was mouthing something to him, growing more and more agitated. Pavo squinted at Avitus, his thoughts dreamlike. Then, a searing pain ripped across his neck and, at once, feeling and hearing returned to him like a wave crashing onto a shore.

'Pavo! *Pavo!*' Avitus cried.

Pavo spun, roaring, clutching at the deep gash on the side of his neck. He only had a heartbeat to check it was not an arterial cut before the two Goths who had rushed him lunged forward again, jabbing and slashing their longswords. Pavo staggered back; out of formation like this, a Roman spatha was at a disadvantage against these lengthy Gothic swords. He butted and parried, but the Goths were relentless. His arms were trembling with fatigue and he held his sword lower and lower. Then Avitus rushed to his aid, sliding his spatha into one Goth's gut. But, before the optio could rip his blade free, the other Goth smashed his longsword across Avitus' forearm, and the little Roman fell back with a cry. Pavo roared out in fury at this, as did Quadratus, still locked in battle only paces away.

Avitus slumped to his knees, clutching the wound. The Goth who had struck Avitus lined up for the death blow, but Pavo tore a dagger from the eye socket of a dead legionary and hurled it. The blade punched into the forehead of the Goth, who dropped like a sack of rubble. Then he ran to Avitus.

'It's over for me,' Avitus panted, shrugging him away.

'No it's bloody not!' Quadratus roared over his shoulder from only paces away, still locked in a swordfight with two Goths.

'You heard your centurion,' Pavo cried, pushing his own sword hilt into Avitus' good hand, 'now get u . . . ' his words trailed off as he saw the black blood pumping from the optio's arm. The bone was smashed and his sword hand hung at an absurd angle

'Leave me!' Avitus barked, slumping back down.

Then the air echoed with the cry of a buccina. It was a series of shrill notes Pavo recognised, and it sent a shiver down his spine.

'Listen!' Avitus pushed him away. 'Traianus is calling for a last stand. Get back to the main body of the legions and protect the eagles!'

Pavo's eyes widened as he saw the optio's face greying, breaths coming in rasps. Avitus was dying. Then he heard Felicia's pained words in his mind, distant and pleading. *Find the truth, Pavo, I beg of you.*

Another wave of Goths rushed for the pair, followed by a trio of cavalry. He had moments.

He stared into Avitus' eyes. 'Sir, I have to ask you again . . . '

'Pavo!' Quadratus yelled, slaying one of his three opponents and glancing at the onrushing Goths. 'Watch my flank!'

Pavo glanced up, then back to Avitus. 'Were you a speculatore?'

Avitus' face slackened at this, and he gazed into Pavo's eyes, his pupils dilating. 'I was, just as her brother was. They sent him to finish the mission that I could not.'

'Pavo!' Quadratus roared, eyes widening as the Goths rushed closer.

Pavo frowned. 'What mission?'

'To kill Gallus,' Avitus choked on the words, shaking his head.

'Gallus?' Pavo gasped. 'Why?'

'We all have a past, Pavo. All of us,' he rasped, then looked Pavo in the eye. 'Tell her . . . I'm sorry.'

Pavo's eyes widened and his lips flapped uselessly, then he looked up to see that the Goths had their spears hoisted, ready to hurl them at

373

Quadratus' flank. He leapt up, throwing himself in front of Quadratus just as the Goths loosed their spears. But then, as the missiles hurtled for his unshielded midriff, Avitus jolted into a last spasm of life, up from his knees to lurch forward and into the path of the speartips.

Pavo froze. Quadratus spun round with a cry.

But the spears smashed into Avitus' chest. In a spray of blood, the optio crashed to the ground, his body shattered, his blood adding to the mire underfoot.

Avitus of the XI Claudia was gone.

'*Whoresons!*' Quadratus cried, his face twisted in pain. The big Gaul swiped the head from one of his foes and kicked another back into the mire, then rushed at the rest.

Pavo grabbed his wrist. 'Sir, it's too late,' he pointed all around, where the Gothic numbers seemed to be telling, the many clusters of them having formed into massed ranks again. But Quadratus wrenched his arm free. Then Pavo barked at him. 'He died to save you, sir. Now come on, we need to form up with what's left of the legions.'

Quadratus issued a pained growl and hurled his sword at the Goths, then turned and followed Pavo.

Pavo called back over his shoulder. 'We'll honour his memory with Gothic blood, sir, once we gather with the rest of the legions.' Then he looked up to see the cluster of only a few hundred legionaries some fifty paces ahead, bristling in defiance with broken spearshafts and bent spathas in a ragged square. There were barely a cohort's worth of them.

In their midst were the five silver eagles of the Roman army.

Amongst this cluster of bloodied men he saw Traianus, Gallus, Zosimus and Felix. Then he saw Sura on the front line, crying out, urging them on.

Pavo tumbled into the Roman cluster and shot glances all around; every direction presented Goths in dense packs; at least a third of their original number still lived. A full morning and afternoon of butchery and still the enemy had a massive numerical advantage. And now they encircled the Roman remnant, readying for the kill.

Then his eyes froze on Draga and Ivo who headed one wing of Gothic riders. He felt Draga's burning glare on his skin as it swept over the tatters of the Roman army.

The Viper had sighted its prey.

'Stand firm, stay together!' Gallus rallied those around him as he grappled the handle of a round Gothic shield, salvaged from a dead warrior. The battered legionaries pushed up next to him, shoulder to shoulder. Then the Goths smashed home and the compact Roman square was shattered.

Gallus was thrown back as the Gothic cavalry broke the Roman front rank, tearing the square apart, driving for the eagles and Traianus at the centre. His helmet fell into the gore and the passing hooves threw a spray of mud and blood over his face.

Beside him, Tribunus Profuturus scrambled through the crimson mush in an attempt to reach Traianus. 'Protect your leader!' He bellowed. 'Protect yo-' his cry was cut short as a sword sliced off his head in one swipe.

Gallus scrabbled back from the head as it bounced to rest before him, mouth and eyes still gawping mid-cry. Then he looked up to see the rider who had felled Profuturus, and his heart steeled. The silver topknotted locks and beard, the glinting bronze hoops, the arrowhead nose and the angry scar welt over one eye.

'Your part in history will be forgotten Roman,' Ivo trotted around Gallus as the rest of the Goths piled into the disintegrating Roman square, washing round the pair like a river round rocks. 'And your empire's time is short.'

Gallus stared at the warrior, then stood, grappling his spatha hilt. 'Your men may slay my army today, Ivo, but *by Mithras*, you will die with them.'

Ivo slipped from his saddle, and clasped the hilt of his longsword with both hands. 'Do you know how many legionaries I have slain? Do you know how many great men of the north coveted my status as Fritigern's champion, only to die on the edge of my blade?' He flicked the longsword around in his hands as if it was a light stabbing blade.

Gallus raised his spatha. 'It matters not. You have slain your last.'

Ivo roared in laughter at this, as all around him, legionaries were put to the sword, their screams cut short and their blood soaking the field. Then the big warrior's face fell into a glare, and he rushed forward with a battle cry.

Gallus whispered a prayer to Mithras and a sweet word to Olivia, then roared and leapt to parry the Goth's blade. A screaming of iron upon iron sent sparks across both of them. The force of the big man's strike was ferocious, and Gallus was thrown back, his spatha cleaved, the hilt and a shard of blade left in his hand.

'An ominous portent, is it not, Roman?' Ivo grinned.

Gallus backed off as Ivo stalked forward, then jinked to avoid a swipe of the giant's sword. The blade scythed through his mail vest, drawing a spray of blood from his chest, the vest falling loose, dangling from one shoulder. He felt something inside, something long buried. A cold realisation, creeping from his core, spidering across his skin. *Was it fear?*

Ivo roared in delight. 'Now, weapons gone, fear begins to consume you, does it not? You have moments to live, Roman; see my face, remember my words, and take them with you to *Hades!*'

Ivo raised his sword over his head and brought it crashing for Gallus' skull with a guttural roar. Gallus stared through the huge warrior, seeing the faces of all those who had fought by his side over the years, now merely memories. Then he saw Olivia, reaching out to him, smiling, tears staining her cheeks. At once, all fear was gone and his soul reverted to ice. He thrust the shard of his spatha up. His whole arm shuddered and the bones in his hand cracked as the sliver of blade punched into the edge of Ivo's longsword, halting the strike. The pair hovered, eye to eye. *To Hades with fear!*

'You mistake me for someone who fears death,' Gallus spoke in an even tone, then pulled the spatha shard away, pirouetted round and plunged the makeshift blade into Ivo's neck. He tore the blade along Ivo's throat and the artery was rent.

Gallus was showered in the giant's blood. He bored his icy, wolf-like glare into Ivo as the Gothic champion slid to the ground, confusion dancing across his good eye.

'Hold the line!' Traianus bawled, his voice cracking and rasping as he barged forward. As he reached the front of the huddle of surviving Romans, he hefted his sword overhead to strike at the Gothic mass. But a hand grappled his wrist. It was the tribunus of the IV Italica legion.

'Stay back, sir. Stand tall with the eagles. The men need to know you live,' he growled. 'If you are slai-' the tribunus' words were cut short as a Gothic spear hammered into his chest, showering Traianus with blood.

Traianus twisted to see the clutch of Gothic riders who had thrown the spear; Draga was mounted at their head. His gore-spattered hood was plastered to his face, covering all but one manic, sparkling eye and his teeth, clenched in a frenzied half-grin. The look bored through Traianus' armour to his soul, just like the look the boy Draga had given him on the wharf all those years ago.

Then the Viper raised his sword and cried out to his riders. As one, they charged for the heart of the Roman square.

Traianus' mouth fell agape.

Pavo leapt up to hack his spatha into a Gothic spearman's shoulder. The limb slid clear of the body and the man fell, howling, to be butchered by Sura, Zosimus and Felix.

'That one was for Avitus,' Pavo cried to Quadratus.

'Every one of these whoresons is for Avitus!' The big centurion bawled, then headbutted a Goth before plunging his sword through the felled warrior's chest.

The Gothic press was relentless. Pavo felt his limbs quivering, growing heavier with every parry and strike. Every breath felt like fire, rasping in his parched throat. Never had battle drawn so much out of him. But when he glanced up, the sight before him fired his blood like never before; Draga and his riders were charging for the legionary huddle, ready to leap over the crumbling shieldwall and into its heart.

He followed the Viper's manic glare and saw that it was fixed on Traianus – the magister militum was stumbling back to the centre of the Roman cluster.

'Sir,' he barked to Zosimus, 'take my place!'

Zosimus squinted at him through a crimson mask and then flicked his gaze to the Viper's charge. At this, the centurion's eyes narrowed and he nodded, barging into Pavo's spot, locking his shield with the legionaries either side. 'Go! Take that bastard's heart out!' The big Thracian cried.

But Pavo was already on his way, pushing through the crush of legionaries, focused on the Viper. His brow dipped and he flexed his hand on his spatha hilt.

A clutch of the Viper's riders raced ahead of their master and heeled their mounts into a jump into the Roman centre, hooves dashing out brains and longswords sweeping through necks like scythes. But Pavo ignored the screaming and readied himself, like a cat, as the Viper made to follow his riders.

378

Draga heeled his mount into a jump. Then, when man and beast were mid-leap, Pavo launched himself with a roar.

His shoulder smashed into Draga's midriff, barging the Viper from his saddle and away from the legionary last stand. The pair tumbled through the gory filth, rolling under Gothic boots and hooves as they grappled and wrestled. Then, finally, the chaos subsided.

They were alone. The Gothic swell had pressed on past them, driving into the Roman huddle.

Draga was first to his feet, longsword raised. Then Pavo scrambled back to level his sword with the man. The one he had once known as the warm and wise ambassador Salvian was a demonic shade of red under his hood, the wet blood bubbling under his nostrils as he snorted in indignation.

'You fool! You think you can stop me?' Draga spoke through a twisted half-grin as the pair circled one another. 'Look around you, your army will all be carrion long before dusk arrives. But rest easy as you go to your death, for you have played your part in bringing my vision into being.'

Pavo shook his head. 'You still don't see it, do you? You have dedicated your whole life to avenging your father's death.' He cast his free hand around the jumble of ruined corpses they walked upon. 'Yet to have your revenge, you bring thousands upon thousands of your own kin to their deaths. The empire wanted peace, Draga, and you must have seen this, in your position as an ambassador. You knew the emperor sought nothing but an alliance.'

Draga's twisted half-grin faded. 'Do not presume to know what I have seen, legionary. Some of the darkest deeds I have ever witnessed have taken place in the fine climes of the senate building in Constantinople, in the cool and luxurious upper tiers of the Hippodrome,' he leant forward and hissed, 'in the Imperial Palace itself!'

'And has that not swayed you from perpetrating such acts?'

Draga burst into a chilling laughter. 'It has not swayed me, legionary, it has inspired me.' The man's eyes sparkled like a roaring fire under the shadows of his hood.

Pavo flinched at this, then squared his shoulders once more, all the while conscious of the shrinking band of legionaries amidst the Gothic noose, only paces away. Then one eagle was plucked from the crowd, a Goth holding aloft the standard and the severed head of a legionary. Pavo glanced at this spectacle for just a moment, then realised what a grave mistake he had made.

Like a viper uncoiling to strike its victim, Draga leapt for him with a flurry of sword hacks.

Pavo fell back, troubled by the man's deft handling of the weapon. He could find time only to parry. Then his heel caught in a discarded conical helmet, and he crashed onto his back. In a flash, Draga had his swordpoint at Pavo's jugular.

Draga let a serrated laugh escape his lips as he pressed the blade, the edge pricking Pavo's skin. 'Now send a prayer to Mithras, legionary, and perhaps you will meet your father in Hades!'

Pavo felt the phalera burning on his chest. Something in his heart roared, and he clawed at the blood-soaked earth by his sides as he waited on the death blow. Then words of advice echoed in his thoughts. But not those of the lost ambassador, Salvian. Instead, they were the words of Brutus – that grim-faced bull of a centurion who had welcomed him into legionary life with a regime of sadistic training torture. Now long dead, like so many others.

Don't be a hero . . . be a dirty bugger!

As the longsword split through the skin of his neck, Pavo cupped a handful of earth and gore and hurled it at Draga's eyes. Draga staggered, blinded momentarily, the longsword retracting at the last.

Pavo pounced on the moment of respite, rising and hoisting his sword. He hacked forward, smashing at every one of Draga's parries with a newfound vigour. 'You call me legionary,' he cried, 'but you should know that I am Pavo of the XI Claudia *Pia Fidelis!*'

Draga, startled, parried. Their swords smashed together again and again until the Viper ducked left and jabbed his longsword towards Pavo's gut. Pavo jinked and swiped at the thrust, cleaving Draga's sword hand clean off with a dull clunk of shearing bone.

With a roar, the Viper fell to his knees, biting into his bottom lip until blood spilled down his chin. Then he bowed his head and his chest shuddered, the green cloak rippling in a sudden breeze.

Pavo held his swordpoint to Draga's chest, panting.

'You can finish me, legionary,' Draga rasped, squinting up at Pavo, 'but my vision is already a reality.'

Pavo glanced over to the dying embers of the Roman last stand. Another two eagles were being passed back over the Gothic heads, along with the bloodied corpse of one of the comitatenses tribuni.

'And know that with my death,' Draga continued, 'the truth about your father will evaporate also!'

Pavo's stare shot back to Draga. His eyes bulged, his heart thundered. 'You know Tarquitius' secret?'

Draga nodded with a weak half-grin. His hood had fallen to his shoulders and he wore that open and earnest expression; for all the world he once again looked like the man Pavo had known as Salvian. 'He talked incessantly when I held him prisoner in my tent. Serve yourself, Pavo. Drop your weapon and I will tell you everything in return.'

Pavo's thoughts swirled in conflict. To live and learn the truth, or to die here with his brothers, honour intact. He clutched the phalera as a nauseous panic swam over him. Then, like a splash of ice-cold streamwater over his heart, Pavo realised what he had to do.

He dropped his spatha.

'Good . . . good. You have made a wise choice, lad,' Draga purred, rising from his knees.

Pavo stared past Draga's shoulder, his eyes fixed on a point in the distance.

381

Then, in the blink of an eye, Draga's face contorted into a demonic grimace; he whipped a dagger from his boot with his good hand, then sprung up, thrusting the blade for Pavo's throat.

At once, Pavo's eyes snapped round to fix on Draga's. He swerved the cut and wrapped one arm around Draga's neck. With the other hand he grappled at his assailant's wrist, prising the blade from his grip and then turning it to rest the point upon Draga's breastbone.

'I knew in my soul that your blood ran black,' Pavo panted, 'but I had to let you prove it once more, to banish the doubts. Your army may be on the cusp of victory today, but your black heart will no longer lead them.' Pavo's expression grew cold, and he pushed the dagger into Draga's chest. The man stared at him, those sharp green eyes sparkling, the manic half-grin defiant as the blade pierced his breastbone.

Then Pavo rammed the blade in to the hilt.

Hot blood washed over his knuckles as he watched Draga's eyes dimming at last. With that, the body slumped to the ground.

The Viper was dead.

Pavo turned to see one eagle left in the middle of the Gothic swell. The ruby-red bull of the XI Claudia. Pride and sorrow rippled across his skin as he readied to rush for the fray, to die with his brothers.

He picked up a spear and a spatha and ran, screaming the last from his lungs, tears staining his cheeks.

Then he stopped.

They all stopped.

The air was filled with the cry of buccinas. Not just a few. Hundreds.

Pavo stared to the west. There, the foothills and the great mountain range behind shimmered in the dusky orange. Then, from the tips of the hills, twelve silver eagles soared into view, part-silhouetted by the setting sun. Under them fluttered twelve legionary banners. Pavo stood, eyes fixed on the unfamiliar emblems; dragons, wolves and bears. 'It cannot be,' he whispered, 'the western legions?'

But again, the buccinas cried out. And now an iron wall appeared below the eagles; some fifteen thousand legionaries, and two ala of one thousand equites on fine and fresh mounts.

At this, the Gothic swell was instantly dwarfed. Their victorious battle cries of moments ago turned to wails of despair, and even Fritigern seemed stunned into silence. But as the western legions marched forward, the Gothic Iudex was sparked into action, roaring at his men to retreat, urging them to break northwards for the hills.

As the last light of day faded, the Goths fled, leaving behind a bloodied, battered, gasping group of men. Some would call them legionaries. Pavo knew them as brothers. Sura returned his knowing stare, and beside him were Gallus, Zosimus, Quadratus and Felix. The five, together with a handful of legionaries, spathas shaking in their grips, formed a tight circle around the XI Claudia standard and Traianus.

Pavo glanced down to see Draga's empty eyes fixed in a dead stare at the sight.

Then he turned to the setting sun and felt its warmth on his skin.

'Column, halt!' Traianus bellowed as the noon sun baked the countryside of central Thracia. Then he nodded to the nearby stream. 'Fall out, slake your thirst!'

Traianus watched as Comes Richomeres and his unruffled western legions calmly took to their rations. Not for the first time since waking this morning, he whispered a word of thanks into the ether for his foresight in summoning the western legions. Despite the cynicism of the officials in the capital, it was the first thing he had done upon reaching Constantinople from Antioch; *they'll never come,* some said, *they care more for the Frankish foederati than for their eastern brothers,* others had sneered. *Easy words for overfed togas who did not have to venture outside the fine walls of the capital*, he mused wryly.

Then he turned to the stream; in contrast to Richomeres' men, the beleagured survivors of the Battle of the Willows had downed their burdens and now lined the sides of the brook. Almost to a man, they had dropped to their knees, cupping the cool liquid in their hands to drink and soak cracked and bleeding lips. Then they filled skins and emptied them over sun-blistered scalps, before wading in to submerge their burning and scarred bodies completely.

Traianus could not suppress a smile at this. Then his face fell when he glanced to the north, his eyes hanging on the ethereal heat haze over the Haemus Mountains. As the bathing legionaries' cries of relief rang out, he could see only the field of bones they had left behind yesterday; a portent of what was to come.

For the Gothic Wars had begun.

Then, once again, he saw the staring, dead eyes of the demon who had brought all this into being. Draga.

The man was black-hearted to the core, he insisted again.

But once more, doubt wriggled into his mind as he remembered that warm summer day on the wharf, all those years ago. The brutal slaying of the young Draga's father. The boy's deathly cold stare. Then, Traianus closed his eyes, biting his lip as he remembered the tear slipping from the orphaned Gothic boy's cheek.

Did we make him what he became?

He mulled over the things he had seen in his years; as much as he loved the empire, he was all too often ashamed of the deeds of those who acted in her name. His gaze dropped to the ground; indeed, he had many reasons to be ashamed of himself.

Then, something caught his eye; a few paces away, a tiny pocket of the survivors of the battle had stepped back from the stream. Tribunus Gallus was addressing them. He recognised the faces of those who listened to

Gallus' every word; the big Thracian centurion and the equally hulking Gaulish one bookending the little fork-bearded primus pilus of the XI Claudia. Then there were the two lads; younger, but scarred and bearing the telltale grimaces of veterans now. Then one of the lads - the one with the cropped, dark hair and the beaky nose – stepped away from his colleagues, lifting some bronze trinket from his tunic, examining it.

This lad had done his legion proud yesterday, slaying the Viper and saving Traianus from the creature's charge. At that moment, Traianus realised he had not thanked the lad, nor any of the others who had put their lives before his. *Perhaps it is time I made amends?*

He walked over to the legionary, squinting as the sunlight danced off the bronze medallion. Then he saw the markings on it as he approached. His eyes widened.

'What's your name, soldier?' Traianus asked, stepping towards him.

Pavo looked up, standing to attention, staring into the distance past Traianus' shoulder. 'Legionary . . . ' he paused, blinking, before correcting himself, ' . . . Optio Numerius Vitellius Pavo, sir!'

'At ease, soldier. You have proved your worth to me a thousand times over with your actions yesterday.'

Thankfully the lad complied, relaxing his shoulders just a little and looking Traianus in the eye.

'That's a legionary phalera,' Traianus noted, 'Legio II Parthica?'

'Yes,' Pavo replied, his brow wrinkling, a spark of interest in his eyes, 'my father died fighting for them, at the seige and sack of Bezabde.'

Traianus frowned, unsure how to approach this. 'Bezabde? Are you sure?'

Pavo's expression remained resigned. 'I'm certain of it,' he nodded. 'He perished like the rest of the legion in that clash.'

Traianus shook his head, fixing his gaze on Pavo's. 'I don't want to trouble your mind, lad, but not all of the Parthica were lost in Bezabde's fall.'

Pavo's eyes widened.

'In the east, in the desert salt mines, many live on to this day . . . '

Epilogue

High on the walls of Constantinople, Gallus closed his eyes, rested his palms on the baked battlements and let the brief, cooling breeze bathe his aching body. His wounds had been dressed and he had soaked in the tepidarium and caldarium for almost all of yesterday. This had helped to soothe the physical scars. Inside, though, the horrific death toll of the Battle of the Willows plagued his thoughts.

Gallus blinked open his eyes and looked across the shimmering domes, columns and acqueducts of the city. The streets were bustling as always, the populace eager to go about their daily duties; those who had lived their lives entirely within these walls were seemingly unaware of how close the Gothic horde had come to marching upon this great city. A hedonistic roar erupted from the Hippodrome at that moment, as if to underline his thoughts. One day, he thought, and one day soon, bigger walls would be needed to protect this place.

The Danubian borders were gone. The limitanei that remained – barely six legions, totalling less than ten thousand men – were now all stationed in the key strongholds south of the Haemus Mountains; the cities, towns and the raft of new forts that studded the southerly passes into those mountains. There they waited, their confidence shattered, on the next wave of Gothic attacks. And then there was the matter of the Huns. He shook his head, pinching the top of his nose.

'Time will heal the gravest of wounds, Tribunus,' Traianus spoke, emerging from the nearby gate tower.

'I wish that were true,' Gallus looked up as the magister militum approached. Then he closed his eyes again as the image of battle barged into

387

his mind uninvited; the verdant plain in the morning, then the crimson plain in the evening, speckled with chunks of white bone, cleaved meat and staring, severed heads.

'Even the greatest victories are stained with the blood of many good men, Tribunus,' Traianus spoke solemnly, turning to face out of the city and across the countryside, along the throbbing *Via Egnatia*.

Gallus followed the magister militum's gaze. Usually the great road that led all the way to Illyricum would be packed with wagons and migrants, flooding both to and from the capital to flog their wares and seek their fortunes. But today they came in one direction only; from the western horizon towards the Golden Gate, seeking shelter in the imperial capital. For while many inside the city dismissed the rumours of a Gothic invasion, those who lived outside knew differently. They had witnessed the great smoke plumes to the north, and then watched the bloodied survivors of the Battle of the Willows trudge south to be shepherded back to the capital. Panic would soon spread around this city, he realised.

Gallus shook his head. 'We did not defeat the Goths, sir. Yes we broke them, halted their march to the south, and the Viper is dead. But his ambitions have been realised; Fritigern is still out there, in Moesia, roaming freely at the head of the largest Gothic army we have ever encountered. And the Huns will press south again when they have grazed the plains of Gutthiuda dry. The borders have fallen. I have failed. My mind cannot rest until I have righted things.'

Traianus smiled wryly at this. 'And that is exactly the attitude I need from all of my soldiers.'

Gallus shared a moment of silence as they looked west, then he closed his eyes with a sigh.

'Don't let your spirits drop, Tribunus, for it is not over yet.'

Gallus turned to him. 'Sir?'

Traianus scoured the north-western horizon. 'Comes Richomeres will leave three legions with us before he returns to the west. Then, the remnants of the Danubian limitanei will be reformed to man the new frontiers. New soldiers will be levied from all corners of the empire. New armour and weapons will be forged by every smith in every city. We will fight this war with all we have.'

'But can the empire fund such an initiative?' Gallus gripped the battlements.

Traianus cocked an eyebrow. 'Can it afford not to? In times past, emperors would baulk at stripping the empire of its dignity and its rich heritage in the face of neccesity. Even Emperor Valens hesitated before giving me this order.' He turned to look Gallus in the eye, 'But the order *has* been given. Churches and palaces are being stripped of gold as we speak.'

Gallus' eyes widened, and he turned to squint back over the shimmering city; sure enough, workmen spidered across the domes and rooftops, and the tink-tink of chisels and hammers rang out. Even the churches were being stripped of their gold and silver Chi-Rho crests. *So the Christian God truly does aid our cause*, he thought, wryly, thumbing the idol of Mithras in his purse. He twisted back to look to the north, now the realm of the Goths. Then, memories of the wail of their war horns echoed through his mind. His train of thought ended with an icy shiver.

'But you should ease your mind of the troubles of this land,' Traianus continued, 'for a short time at least. Emperor Valens asked me to take note of the better men in your legion. He has a job for you elsewhere. A place where trouble is just as rife.'

'Sir?' Gallus frowned.

A roar of drunken joy erupted across the sun-baked courtyard attached to the inn, rivalling the cry from the nearby Hippodrome. The crowds bustling through the market stalls of the Augusteum twisted for a moment, peering over the ivy-clad half-wall to see the source of the joviality; a circle of bandaged men in legionary tunics, crowded around one table. Then, with a decisive thud, cups, ale and wine fountained up into the air from the midst of the circle.

'Whoreson!' Zosimus spat, wrenching his hand from the arm wrestling contest.

Laughter broke out as Quadratus grinned back at him, a hundred hands slapping the big Gaulish centurion's back.

'Easy!' Quadratus winced as one well-wisher slapped a little too hard on his stitched shoulder blade.

'Rematch!' Zosimus demanded, stabbing a finger into the table as Felix started handing out winnings from the gambling pot.

'Leave it out,' the primus pilus called back, 'even I could beat you.'

At this, Zosimus roared. 'Right, get over here!'

A roar of laughter erupted once more at this, and a perplexed-looking Felix could not fend off the other legionaries as they swept him back to the table to make good on his assertion.

Sitting at a table in the corner, Pavo looked on. A smile touched just one side of his lips as he watched them. Then it dissolved as he realised who he had picked up this habit from. He swirled his cup and took another swig of the bittersweet ale, then turned back to Felicia, nestled beside him. Her blue eyes sparkled as she looked up to him, and she had applied a striking ochre to her lips, stark against her milky skin.

'You're beautiful,' he stroked her hair, pleated into two tails, 'even more so now that you're smiling again. It seems like a long time since I've seen you so happy.'

She placed a hand on his knee. 'It's been harder than anything to let go of it, Pavo, harder even than losing Curtius in the first place. But I have let it go, and it feels like a dark cloud has been blown from my heart.' She looked around to check no others could hear her, then glanced to the twenty five brimming cups of ale at an unoccupied table. This was the legionaries' tribute to optio Avitus. A solitary cup of fruity wine had also been placed there by his good friend Quadratus. 'I don't take any comfort from Avitus' death. Had he survived, I can only hope that I would still have been true to my new convictions.'

Pavo nodded. The drinking had begun with a solemn toast to the little Roman. And beforehand, he and Felicia had decided that Avitus' past as a speculatore was to remain a secret. More, Pavo had kept Avitus' final revelation to himself; to tell Felicia that Curtius had been killed en route to assasinating Gallus would only stain her memories of her brother. No, what was done was done, and Avitus was gone. The little Roman had fought like a lion as a legionary since those days – perhaps, Pavo mused, to repent for some of the sins he had commited at the order of his shadowy superiors?

'He wanted you to know how sorry he was,' Pavo said, his mind drifting to that moment in the heat of battle when Avitus had bled his last. 'Neither your father nor Curtius, nor Avitus for that matter, would have wanted you to live in bitterness.'

She did not reply, instead closing her eyes and nodding with a gentle smile. A single tear escaped her closed eyelids. 'I'll never forget them,' she spoke softly, 'but now I have you, Pavo.'

Then she rested her head against his chest. He nuzzled into her amber locks and wrapped an arm around her, breathing in her sweet scent. He closed his eyes. This was it, he thought. Felicia was his woman and the rugged veterans of the XI Claudia were his brothers. Neither were his blood, but all were his family.

But they're not Father, a voice whispered in his mind again.

He blinked open his eyes and realised he was unwittingly thumbing the bronze phalera through his tunic. He frowned; every legionary from Illyricum to Constantinople would be vital in the war against the Goths, it seemed. His future lay in these lands. But Traianus' words burned in his thoughts.

In the east, in the desert salt mines, many live on to this day . . .

His mind flitted to the dunes from his dream. *What if . . . ?*

'We have our home here now,' Felicia spoke, her voice half-muffled as she pushed against his chest, 'and perhaps one day we could open an inn, just like *The Boar* in Durostorum?'

He kissed the top of her head and rubbed her shoulders, the idea soothing his thoughts.

But what of Father? The voice came again.

He pinched at the top of his nose, screwing up his eyes to clear his mind.

Then, a cry erupted from the cluster of legionaries and Zosimus stood, arms in the air, roaring in victory, his face beetroot-red. 'Yes!' He cried.

The winnings were handed out. Then a rather merry Sura bounded over and sat, causing the table to shudder. Pavo caught his cup just as it was about to spill, then shot his friend a grin, which Sura returned with interest.

'Made a killing,' Sura said with a hint of a slur to his voice, extending his hand to reveal a pile of folles. 'Next round is on me! Pavo, you need some more ale by the looks of it.'

Pavo shrugged, eyebrows raised, feeling the sweet giddiness of the first cup swirling behind his eyes. 'Aye, make it a large one,' he grinned.

'Felicia?' Sura asked.

'I'll stick to water, thank you,' she replied, a hint of disapproval in her voice as she glanced up to Pavo and then back to Sura.

Pavo smiled as Sura swaggered back to the bar and pushed through to get served. Then he noticed from the corner of his eye that a tall, lean figure had entered the courtyard.

Tribunus Gallus swept his wolven glare around the scene of his drunken legionaries. Instinctively, Pavo sat straighter, squaring his shoulders. He moved his ale cup out of view, hoping the Tribunus might not see him, tucked in here at the corner of the courtyard.

'XI Claudia!' Gallus barked.

At once, the crowd turned to Gallus and stiffened to attention. The Tribunus' nose wrinkled as he eyed the spilled ale cups and then glared at the isolated figure of Sura, halfway back from the bar, standing in his best legionary rigidity with a foaming cup of ale in each hand.

'Come dawn the day after tomorrow, I want you to muster at the northern city barracks.'

Pavo and the legionaries of the XI Claudia shared nervous glances. Was the next stage of the Gothic War upon them already?

'A vexillatio is to be identified and despatched to Antioch . . . ' Gallus turned to the corner of the courtyard to look Pavo in the eye. For just a heartbeat, the Tribunus' lips were touched with that elusive hint of a smile. 'We're going east!'

Pavo's heart thundered. He glanced to Sura, then to Felicia.

The phalera burned on his chest.

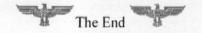

The End

GORDON DOHERTY

Author's Note

Dear Reader,

Firstly, I'd like to thank you warmly for reading my novel – support from readers like you means everything to me as an author. Next, I'd like to share with you my approach to blending the story of *Legionary: Viper of the North* into a very real and pivotal point in late antiquity;

In the 1st century AD, far to the east of the Roman world, somewhere near modern-day Mongolia, something happened that would tilt the course of history irreversibly. Aggression and overpopulation on those windswept and craggy steppes saw a horde of hardy, nomadic horsemen known as the Huns begin an inexorable migration westwards. They seemed set on chasing the setting sun, sending entire peoples into flight as they moved west. This triggered what historians now describe as 'The Great Migration', a momentous gravitation of population from the east towards Europe. The Huns' mastery of archery and mounted warfare saw them subjugate almost every tribe they came across in the steppes and then Scythia. The Roman historian, Ammianus Marcellinus, tells how peoples such as the Alani, the Agathyrsi, the Anthropophagi, the Budini, the Geloni, the Melanchaenae and the Neuri all fell under the Hunnic yoke over the next few centuries. These tribes were then pressed into service for the Hunnic advance on the next westerly target: Gutthiuda, land of the Goths and the last buffer between the Huns and the Roman Empire.

In late 376 AD, the Gothic armies were fractured, with many rival 'Judges' competing for ultimate power. But when the Huns appeared en-masse on their northern borders, they at last set aside their differences. After countless years of squabbling, the many disparate factions were at once forged together in the fires of adversity, with Fritigern emerging as their leader. But, caught unawares by such a ferocious army of invaders, the unified Goths quickly realised that they could not stand their ground and fight. So, like every other people who had found themselves in the Huns' path, the Goths fled for their lives, to the south, to the Danube and to the Eastern Empire.

The limitanei legions garrisoning the forts along the River Danube were understrength, underequipped and ill-prepared for any major border activity. Added to that, they found themselves as the guardians of Thracia and Moesia after Emperor Valens had summoned the bulk of the field armies of those provinces to the Persian frontier. So when Fritigern and a sea of Gothic warriors and families appeared on the northern banks of the Danube appealing for sanctuary, the legions had no option but to allow them entry. The exact number of Goths that arrived that day varies from source to source; some suggest up to one million, others estimate more conservatively at around one hundred thousand. Even at the lower end of the scale, this represented an unprecedented unification and mobilisation of the previously disparate Gothic tribes and posed a massive problem for the Roman province of Moesia Inferior. Ammianus, writing some years after the event, describes the Gothic crossing of the Danube as fervent and troubled;

'The crowd was such that, though the river is the most dangerous in the world . . . a large number tried to swim and were drowned in their struggle against the force of the stream.'

Emperor Valens is thought to have applied some retrospective spin to this tumultuous event, lauding the Goths as ready-made reinforcements for the patchy border legions. In reality, however, it was the first of many dark days for the empire. Famine soon gripped the overpopulated refugee camp and the surrounding Roman settlements. But it was the deeds of certain Romans that cast the darkest shadow; in the absence of the imperial field armies, it was left to a certain Comes Lupicinus to receive Fritigern and his people on the day of the crossings. Ammianus describes Lupicinus as; *'a loathsome general . . . the source of all our troubles.'* Indeed, it is thought that Lupicinus' actions and those of the men under his command triggered the subsequent Gothic revolt. Their ill-treatment of the Goths at the initial refugee camp near the Danubius – including the barter of rotten dog meat for Gothic slaves – is well documented, and is thought to have sparked Fritigern's march upon Marcianople in search of food. Then, at the city, Lupicinus' botched assassination attempt on Fritigern (the historical texts suggest the assassination attempt took place at a banquet within Marcianople, so I admit employing a poetic licence in my alternative presentation of this event) destroyed the last vestige of allegiance, prompting the enraged iudex to rally his armies and declare war upon the empire. Thus, the Gothic War had begun.

As Fritigern and his hordes rampaged around the Moesian countryside, many more Goths flooded over the Danube to seek refuge from the Huns and to swell the iudex's army. Added to this, many Gothic soldiers serving in the imperial ranks deserted their legions to fight alongside their kinsmen. Indeed, Suerdias and Colias of the garrison of Adrianople are cited in historical texts as noble centurions who initially had no intention of betraying the empire until the governor of the city forced their hand, demanding they leave;

'At first they remained loyal to Rome but the situation changed when they were ordered to move east . . . out of fear that they would join Fritigern.'

It is thought that the governor's order was part-borne of misguided resentment, as his villa had recently been ransacked by Goths. But it was a costly misjudgement. A baying mob of citizens under the governor's employ tried to expedite the departure of the Gothic garrison. Cornered by this armed rabble, the Goths had no option but to fight back, so Suerdias and Colias led their legionaries in slaying many of the hostile citizens. Enraged and disenfranchised, the pair and their men then raided the city's imperial warehouses of arms and supplies then left with haste, proceeding immediately to join Fritigern's ranks.

The Battle of Ad Salices, otherwise known as The Battle of the Willows, took place in the spring of 377 AD and was the first major field battle of the Gothic War. The site of the battle is unknown, but it is thought to be within twenty kilometres of Marcianople, near the edge of the Haemus Mountains on a plain with a small willow grove. Ammianus describes how the Goths lined up with their rear ranks taking advantage of the nearby high ground, and had a circle of wagons serving as a form of barrier or bunker. He explains how the hostilities began with a lengthy exchange of missiles before the infantry of the two sides clashed. Then he writes of how the Roman left wing faltered before being reinforced at a critical moment. The encounter is thought to have been particularly bloody, with Ammianus writing that;

' . . . the whole place was filled with corpses . . . some lay among them still half alive, vainly cherishing a hope of life, some of them having been pierced with bullets hurled from slings, others with arrows barbed with iron. Some again had their heads cloven in half with blows of swords.'

He goes on to say that the battle only ended when; *'At last the day yielded to the evening and put an end to the deadly contest.'* The battle was deemed to be a draw, and served as a bloody precursor of the many clashes that were to come.

While my depiction of Traianus' early military career is fictional, it is accepted that he led the army despatched from the east to fight at The Battle of the Willows. It is recorded that he held the position of 'Magister Peditum' at this point in his career, but it appears that this post and that of 'Magister Militum' became interchangeable in the later 4th century. Thus, I have decorated him with the latter title to achieve consistency and reduce confusion as to his rank. Put simply, he answered only to Emperor Valens. Also, Count Richomeres was almost certainly involved in the battle from the start, so for my take on his minimal part in the clash I again acknowledge a dose of artistic licence.

Regarding locations; Athanaric's citadel of Dardarus is fictional, but most probably such a fortified settlement existed after he and his people moved into the heart of the Carpathians seeking more defensible land. Likewise, the grim landmark of Wodinscomba (translating roughly as 'Wodin's Hollow') was invented to illustrate the climate of tension between Fritigern and Athanaric. Apart from these two places, all other features on the map pages give a realistic overview of the lay of the land at the outbreak of the Gothic War – a war that lasted for years and saw the fate of the Eastern Empire hang in the balance.

So the story has only just begun and Pavo and the legionaries of the XI Claudia will most certainly be back for more. I hope you anticipate reading the next volume as much as I look forward to writing it! Until then, please feel free to visit my website where you can find out more about me and my work.

Yours faithfully,

Gordon Doherty

www.gordondoherty.co.uk

Glossary

Ala; A unit of Roman cavalry, numbering anywhere between a few hundred and a thousand.

Aquilifer; Senior eagle standard bearer of a Roman legion.

Ballista; Roman bolt-throwing artillery that was primarily employed as an anti-personnel weapon on the battlefield.

Buccina; The ancestor of the trumpet and the trombone, this instrument was used for the announcement of night watches and various other purposes in the legionary camp.

Candidatus; The *candidati* were the hand-chosen, personal bodyguard of the Roman Emperor and successors to the old Praetorian Guard.

Capsarius; A legionary medic. His main function on the battlefield would be to tend to the wounded and to recover arms and equipment from the fallen.

Castrum; A defensive Roman military structure. Could be used to describe a permanent fort, a marching camp, a palisade on a natural choke point of terrain or a fortified bridgehead.

Caldarium; The room in a Roman bath complex containing a hot plunge pool.

Cataphractus; Roman heavy cavalry who would employ shock tactics, charging into enemy lines and flanks. The riders and horses would wear iron

401

scale and mail armour, leaving little vulnerability to attack, and their primary weapon was a lengthy lancing spear. In the fourth century, many *cataphractii* in the Roman army were of eastern origin.

Chi-Rho; The Chi Rho is one of the earliest forms of Christogram, and was used by the early Christian Roman Empire. It is formed by superimposing the first two letters in the Greek spelling of the word Christ, chi = ch and rho = r, in such a way to produce the following monogram;

Classis Moesica; The imperial fleet that controlled the waters from the Lower Danube to the northwestern *Pontus Euxinus* as far as the Bosporus (modern-day Crimea) peninsula.

Classis Pontica; The imperial fleet that controlled the mid and eastern *Pontus Euxinus*.

Comes; Commander of a field army of *comitatenses* legions.

Comitatenses; The Roman field armies. A 'floating' central reserve of legions, ready to move swiftly to tackle border breaches. These legions were considered the cream of the late Roman army.

Contubernium; A grouping of eight legionaries within a century (ten *contubernia* per century). These soldiers would share a tent and would receive disciplinary action or reward as a unit.

Cursus Publicus; The imperial courier system facilitated by state-funded roads, waystations, stables and dedicated riders. The riders were tasked with carrying messages all over the empire.

Decurion; Leader of a *turma* of Roman cavalry.

Dux; Regional commander of *limitanei* legions.

Equites; Roman light cavalry, used for scouting ahead and covering the flanks of a marching legionary column.

Equites Sagittarii; Roman horse archers.

Fabrica; The workshop of a Roman legion located within the legionary fort or camp. Skilled artisans and craftsmen such as engineers, carpenters, masons, wagon-makers, blacksmiths, painters and other artificers worked in the *fabrica*, using devices such as smelting furnaces and water cisterns to produce arms and equipment for the legionaries.

Foederati; Broad term for the variety of 'barbarian' tribes subsidised from imperial coffers to fight for the Roman Empire.

Follis; A large bronze coin introduced in about 294 AD with the coinage reform of Diocletian.

Funditores; Roman slingers who would wear little or no armour and be involved in the initial skirmishing before a battle.

Hasta; The Roman legionary spear, over six feet in length and used primarily for thrusting as opposed to throwing.

Horreum; The Roman granary and storehouse for other consumables such as wine and olive oil.

Hunnoi; The nomadic horsemen known as the Huns, who migrated west from the eastern steppes in the 4th century.

Intercisa; Iron helmet constructed of two halves with a distinctive fin-like ridge joining them together and large cheek guards offering good protection to the face.

Iudex; The fourth century Goths did not have kings as such. Instead, each tribe would elect a 'judge' or 'iudex' who would steer them through a period of migration or conflict.

Lancea; Short throwing javelin and successor to the *pilum* of the principate but with a far inferior range than the *plumbata*. Late legionaries sometimes carried a pair of these.

Limes; The Roman frontiers. These borderlands would be manned by the *limitanei* legions.

Limitanei; Literally, meaning 'frontier soldiers', the *limitanei* were light infantry spearmen who would serve in the legions posted along the empire's borders.

Magister Militum; Literally, 'Master of Soldiers'. The man in this role would report directly to the emperor and command each regional *dux* and floating *comes* situated within the broad geographical grouping of provinces he presided over.

Mithras; Mithras was the Persian god of light and wisdom and many Romans worshipped this deity, particularly soldiers. Followers of Mithras believed that he was born with a sword in his hand.

Onager; Roman catapult that could throw rocks or clay balls filled with an incendiary fluid.

Optio; Second-in-command in a Roman century. Hand-chosen by the centurion.

Phalera; A gold, silver or bronze sculpted disk worn on the breastplate during parades by Roman soldiers who had been awarded it as a kind of medal.

Plumbata; Lead weighted throwing dart carried by Roman legionaries, approximately half a metre in length. Each legionary would carry three of these and would launch them, overhand or underhand, at their enemy prior to sword or spear engagement. They required some skill to throw accurately, but had a tremendous range of nearly ninety feet.

Pontus Euxinus; The modern Black Sea.

Primus Pilus; The chief centurion of a legion. So called, as his own century would line up in the first file (*pilus*) of the first cohort (*primus*).

Propontus; The modern Sea of Marmara.

Principia; Situated in the centre a Roman fort or marching camp, the principia served as the headquarters. In a standing fort, the principia would be laid out as a square, with three wings enclosing a parade area. The legionary standards, wage chest and religious shrines were housed inside the wings along with various administrative offices.

Sagittarius; Roman foot archer.

Spatha; A straight sword up to one metre long, favoured by the Roman infantry and cavalry.

Speculatores; A shadowy secret police employed throughout the Roman Republic and Empire. They tended to focus on internal affairs and domestic threats, carrying coded messages, spying, and assassinating on command.

Strategos; Greek word meaning military general or 'master of strategy'.

Tepidarium; The warm room in a Roman bathhouse, heated by an underfloor hypocaust.

Tesserarius; Each legionary century had a tesserarius. They would be answerable to the *optio* and their chief responsibilities were organising night watch and protecting watchwords.

Testudo; Roman infantry formation where the legionaries in a cohort place their shields around all sides and overhead of their unit, thus providing thorough protection from missile hail.

Tribunus; Senior legionary officer. In the late 4th century AD, a *tribunus* was usually in charge of one or more legions of *limitanei* or *comitatenses*.

Turma; The smallest unit of Roman cavalry, numbering thirty riders.

Vexillatio; A detachment of a Roman legion formed as a temporary task force.

Via Egnatia; The highway constructed in the 2nd century BC running from Dyrrachium on the Adriatic Sea, all the way through Thrace to Constantinople.

Wodin; The chief god of the Norse pantheon. Analogous to the Roman Jupiter or the Greek Zeus.

Lightning Source UK Ltd.
Milton Keynes UK
UKOW05f0634170114

224795UK00001B/99/P